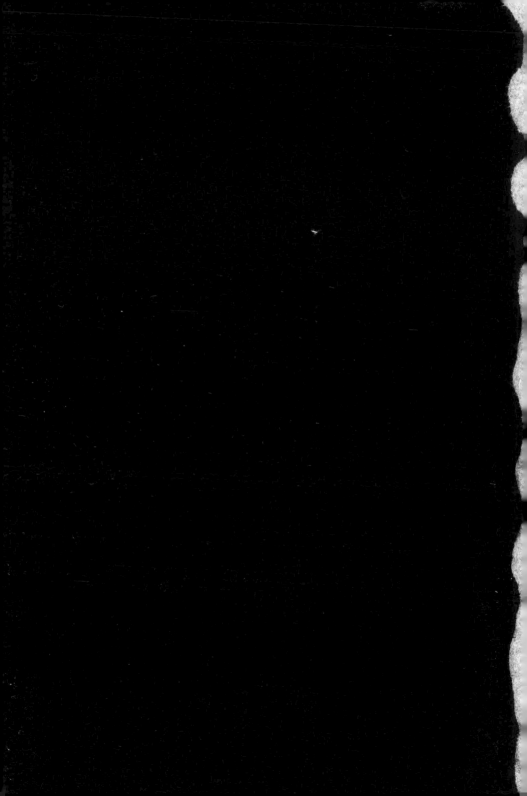

THE FIRST BOOK OF

ORE

To my D. G. Jeanette, who followed the kite
—CB

For Tali, forever my Papagena, who never doubted me
—BZ

Copyright © 2014 by Cameron Baity and Benny Zelkowicz

All rights reserved. Published by Disney•Hyperion Books, an imprint of Disney Book Group. No part of this book may be reproduced or transmitted in any form or by any means, electronic or mechanical, including photocopying, recording, or by any information storage and retrieval system, without written permission from the publisher. For information address Disney•Hyperion Books, 125 West End Avenue, New York, New York 10023-6387.

Printed in the United States of America
First edition
1 3 5 7 9 10 8 6 4 2
G475-5664-5-14015
Library of Congress Cataloging-in-Publication Data
Baity, Cameron.
   The Foundry's edge / Cameron Baity & Benny Zelkowicz.
      pages cm.—(First book of ore)
   Summary: When twelve-year-old Phoebe Plumm and her father are abducted by his employer, The Foundry, a corporation holding a monopoly on metal production and technology, and taken to a savage world of living metal that is rising up against its oppressors, Phoebe and her irksome servant Micah fight back.
   ISBN 978-1-4231-6227-8 (hardback)
   [1. Science fiction. 2. Adventure and adventurers—Fiction. 3. Metals—Fiction. 4. Fathers and daughters—Fiction. 5. Kidnapping—Fiction.] I. Zelkowicz, Benny. II. Title.
   PZ7.B1677Fou 2014
   [Fic]—dc23   2013029134

Visit www.DisneyBooks.com

CAM BAITY & BENNY ZELKOWICZ

THE FIRST BOOK OF

ORE

THE FOUNDRY'S EDGE

DISNEY · HYPERION BOOKS
New York

Cam & Benny would like to thank: Julie Kane-Ritsch and Eddie Gamarra at Gotham Group for their tireless work and inspiring support. Allison Binder for her sparkling wisdom and counsel. Kevin Lewis for taking a chance on our dream. Marci Senders for her impeccable eye. Maggie Begley for her insight and tenacity in promoting our passion. Jamie Baker, Andrew Sansone, and the entire publicity crew who helped this book set sail. All of our friends and family, who encouraged us every step of the way, devoting their time and resources through the marathon of years that went into this book.

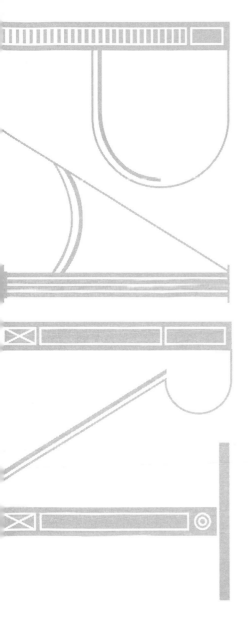

1

GOTCHA

he man in the fog was watching her. He was across the street, just outside a pool of street light, standing as still as the ghostly birch trees that surrounded him. At first Phoebe dismissed it as an odd combination of shadows, perhaps created by rays of porch light streaming through the bronze gates of Plumm Estate. But the longer she stared, the more the stranger seemed to peel out of the gloom.

Phoebe parted the shimmering drapes and pressed her nose against the window to get a better look. From her third-story bedroom, she could just barely make him out: a sharp black suit and bowler hat, a pale face with a thick curving mustache, and round black spectacles like two holes punched in his face.

What could he be doing at his hour? Bird-watching? Star-gazing? Maybe he was planning a heist. If so, he wouldn't get past the top-of-the-line security system her father had installed. It would certainly be a hoot to watch him get caught and see all the servants running around in a frenzy.

Still, the stranger was unsettling. Who wears dark glasses at night anyway?

Nobody, Phoebe Plumm realized with a sigh. There was no intruder. No stranger down there at all, just her imagination swirling in the mist. The most exciting thing she usually saw on her nightly watches was a tomcat scuffle or a sudden whirlwind of leaves, so she was left to invent things huddling in the dark for her own entertainment.

Phoebe didn't sleep well anymore, so she often gazed down from her twelve-foot-high picture window in the murky hours before morning. She watched with the hollow hope that a flare of headlights might sweep up the hammered-steel driveway. The last time her father had returned from one of his business trips, he arrived at four in the morning, and Phoebe was downstairs and in his arms before he could get his bags out of the trunk.

This was his longest trip yet—three months, nearly four. So Phoebe maintained her vigil, waiting every night for him to return.

She rubbed her bleary eyes and glanced out the window again. Just as she expected, the stranger was nowhere to be seen. He'd probably never been there at all.

Phoebe ran a finger across the greasy smear her nose had left on the window, just the sort of thing that got Mrs. Tanner's apron in a bunch. She placed a dozen handprints on the glass for good measure. *Hopefully the old cow will take her frustrations out on Micah,* she thought.

She yanked the silver curtains closed and padded across her enormous bedroom. Platinum sconces crafted to look like palm fronds glowed with a cozy light, illuminating when Phoebe passed. As she approached a shiny door, she heard the pleasant hum-click of precision machinery, and the shutters automatically withdrew like graceful fingers to reveal her Carousel.

It was a cavernous chrome closet with concentric, mechanized rings that bore hundreds of outfits. Phoebe tapped an oval pedal neatly inlaid into the floor, and the Carousel began to rotate in a swooshing parade, showcasing each garment beneath a soft spotlight. Phoebe watched vaguely as her clothes whizzed past, metal filigreed fabrics sparkling like fireworks. It took five whole minutes to cycle through them all. Finally Phoebe made up her mind, released her foot from the pedal, and the Carousel eased to a stop. A slender hydraulic arm unfolded and presented the chosen outfit to Phoebe—a cream-colored silk shirt decorated in darts of copper mesh.

Selecting a skirt was easier, since she wore the same one pretty much every day. The gray diamond-patterned fabric was fraying at the hem, and it was so big on her she had to cinch it in place with a belt of interlocking metal triangles. Phoebe knew the girls at the Academy whispered about her ratty old garment, but she couldn't care less.

Within its pleats, Phoebe had sewn secret compartments that contained her arsenal: a little coil of wire, a tube of Speed-E-Tak cement, a needle and thread, a small vial of machine oil, a bent nail, and a handful of other odds and ends. This was her sniping skirt.

It felt like home, a relic from so many of her memories, worn so often that it was velvety soft to the touch. Phoebe's cheek had caressed this skirt a thousand times when she was a kid. It had belonged to her mom, whose familiar scent used to linger in the fibers. But that was long gone.

She slipped into her clothes and took a look at herself in the full-length, oval mirror. Phoebe had inherited her father's long, almond-shaped face as well as his lanky build. Her wispy limbs and slender hands were okay, but she loathed her big awkward feet more than anything. And she was too tall for a twelve-year-old, teetering over most of her classmates, so she always slouched a bit to compensate.

Phoebe slapped some pink into her pale cheeks. Though her pinched mouth and needle-straight eyebrows made her look stern, her eyes were a luminous honey brown that exuded tenderness, a weakness she hid behind choppy dark bangs.

Her haircut was pretty much a disaster, with the left side trimmed in a clean line that grazed her shoulder, and the right side bobbed short and jagged. Mrs. Tanner had insisted on styling it the other day, and Phoebe had hated the result. So she had taken a pair of scissors to it herself, roughed one of the sides, and removed all the drab symmetry. It didn't look good, exactly, but at least now it was *her* haircut.

Phoebe swept her ragged locks behind her ears and pushed the button on her octagonal jewelry box, which bloomed open like a mechanical rose. Inside, a dozen different Trinkas dangled from hooks, each sparkling with tinted precious metals and lacey ornamental carvings. Ever since the Foundry had introduced these little mechanical pets, Trinkas were fashion necessities. Phoebe chose a plump one covered in soft gold bristles with a big happy mouth, emerald eyes, and bouncy appendages. When she held the Trinka at her throat and turned the key, the device extended two of its limbs and gathered them loosely around her neck. Giggling adorably, the Trinka swung back and forth like a necklace with a mind of its own.

Phoebe wrinkled her nose. She had worn this model for the last few days, delighting in its joyful swings, but today she found it dull. She rifled through the top drawer of her dresser, already crammed with unopened gadgets and gizmos, and stuffed the fuzzy Trinka among them. Its muffled giggles faded as the mechanism wound down.

She selected another Trinka from her jewelry box and ripped off the tag. This one reminded Phoebe of a tiny octopus. It had teddy bear eyes and four paddle-shaped tentacles beneath a bulbous silver head. When she pushed a hidden button, ruby light glowed from within the Trinka, making the paper-thin metal shell appear translucent. The light exposed infinitesimal clockwork innards, pumping and tittering, pulsing like a heartbeat.

The Trinka sprang into the air, somersaulted in place using its spinning tentacles to stay aloft, and then landed in Phoebe's hand with a soft chime of bells. It clung to her wrist like a bracelet as its light faded, leaving the surface opaque and reflective again. Phoebe approved.

She grabbed a strawberry-flavored Honeygum for later and slipped it into her skirt pocket. The sparkly beehive container was small and easy to hide, and she liked the challenge of pouring the syrup into her mouth without getting caught by her teachers. Better yet, chewing the candy goo once it thickened helped pass the time during the dull day.

Phoebe put on a pair of low-heeled black shoes with silver straps and snatched her gray, bell-shaped hat. She unlocked the embossed platinum doors and slipped into the dark corridor. A distant clatter of activity rang down the hallway, the sound dampened by the brocaded carpet.

She gazed up at the triangular skylights set into the vaulted copper ceiling. Even though dawn was barely starting to blush the sky, the servants were already bustling about downstairs. The smell of fresh muffins filled her nostrils as she descended a marble and gold staircase, each step carved to look like a feather, and entered the lavish dining room.

As always, Phoebe's breakfast was waiting on the burnished brass table that was as long as a shipping freighter. Today's selection included mini Parmesan quiches, blackberry pancakes, pork hash, and cinnamon toast. Mrs. Tanner always griped that Phoebe was malnourished, but really she was just never hungry. And she hated sitting at the monstrous table all alone, staring at the repeating patterns of shells and parallel lines in the metallic wallpaper until her eyes crossed.

Phoebe filled a cup with black coffee, popped a piece of cinnamon toast on a saucer, and headed for the veranda. Today was sure to be a scorcher, and she wanted to breathe some fresh air before it got unbearable outside. She slunk past the open door of the kitchen, which rang with clanging pots and pans, the hiss of an automatic Dish Wand, and the chatter of a Televiewer.

A shriek of laughter made Phoebe flinch. The cackle belonged to the chef, Mr. Macaroy, and she peeked in to see the commotion. Mrs. Tanner was scolding a maid, who had evidently done something that tickled the fancy of the hyena-like chef. Mrs. Tanner's sausagey arms were jiggling with every gesture, but Phoebe couldn't hear her sputtering because the Televiewer in the corner was playing the news at full blast.

". . . and the nation of Trelaine, prominent member of the growing so-called Quorum, has made its threats very clear. In his recent address to the Council of Nations, Premier Lavaraud said his patience was at an end. 'Should Meridian continue to hinder trade and withhold critical exports, she will find herself looking down the barrel of a gun.'"

The tall nickel-framed screen showed a severe man with a slick helmet of hair and a long scowling face. It cut to footage of some recent protest overseas, uniformed soldiers on horseback confronting angry citizens. Trelaine's capital city was in the background, a clot of hulking buildings beneath a miserable sooty sky.

Ignoring the dull drone of the news, Phoebe made for the filigreed door that led outside. She braced herself for a snap of cold morning air but was met instead by tepid mush. The city was in the grips of a heat wave, and summer was creeping up. Phoebe loathed the heat, but she would endure the perpetual sun of the Azsuri Crescent if it meant a few months of freedom from the Academy.

Birds sang cheerfully as she sat at a silver table draped with a silk tablecloth and laid her breakfast down. Phoebe sipped coffee and nibbled at her toast, gazing out upon the vast courtyard of herringbone-patterned hedges and titanium fountains.

Plumm Estate sat atop a huge terraced hill, situated perfectly to take in the wonder of Albright City, capital of all Meridian. It signaled to Phoebe like a grand beacon, a horseshoe of gleaming skyscrapers that wrapped around the semicircular bay. A suspension bridge extended from the center of the horseshoe to a solitary island teeming with high-tech smokestacks, warehouses, gargantuan factories, offices, and shipping docks. They were so densely packed that from afar it looked like the circuit board of an enormous Computator.

This was the Foundry—the apex of technology, the epi-center of innovation.

And soaring above the bridge, brighter than everything else, was the Crest of Dawn. It stole Phoebe's breath every time she saw it. The Foundry's magnificent logo was the pin-nacle of this famous skyline, towering higher than the tallest building in Albright City and marking the only entrance to the island. Held aloft by two titanic columns on either side of the bridge, the Crest of Dawn was a sculpted sunburst thousands of feet high, an explosion of glittering beams erupting in glori-ous metal fire.

Phoebe had visited her father's office at Foundry Central lots of times, and driving on the bridge beneath the Crest was always a thrill. No matter what time of day it was or where you were in the city, it was always the most brilliant point on the horizon. It was said that the sunburst could be seen from twelve hundred miles away, causing many to wonder what kind of metal it could possibly be made from.

The Crest of Dawn was perfection.

Phoebe didn't register the icy jet of water until it smacked her face. It blasted the cup from her hands, dousing her with hot coffee. She staggered back and looked down, mouth agape. Her burning eyes scanned the courtyard for her assailant.

There he was, in the mud beside the irrigation pipes, wheezing for breath. The filthy little twerp tossed aside the tools he had used to crank up the water pressure and clutched his belly in hysterics while the garden hose thrashed like a gut-ted snake. He was laughing so hard that his stupid, freckled face turned a grotesque, blotchy shade of purple. He pointed one muddy finger at Phoebe before collapsing backward in a snorting spasm of laughter.

"Gotcha!" he managed to squeak between choking guffaws.

It was Micah, Mrs. Tanner's ten-year-old son and the grease monkey of Plumm Estate. Phoebe wanted to scream curses in his ear until he was deaf, then strangle him with that stupid hose.

Mr. Kashiri, the Plumms' doughy gardener, ran up and grabbed Micah by the collar to reprimand him, but the lunatic hose sprayed him as well, which sent Micah flailing into another fit of giggles. At last, Mr. Kashiri snatched Micah and dragged him away through the hedges.

Phoebe knew what would come next, because it had happened too many times to count. Whenever Micah antagonized Phoebe, he had to answer to his mother, who used a heavy hand in her discipline. The next time Phoebe saw him, he'd have a fresh bruise or some awful new chore. Normally, she felt a twinge of guilt when Mrs. Tanner punished Micah.

Not this time, she thought as she looked at the coffee stain on her shirt. *This time he's gone too far.*

Now, any dimwit could play a joke, as Micah had proven time and time again. But Phoebe didn't do *jokes.* Her attention to detail elevated her above the average prankster, which was why she referred to her careful art as "sniping." She always made her attacks appear accidental, like a dose of rotten luck. For example, she might separate the supports in a recliner so the person sitting in it would slip between the cushions, or maybe she would file notches in the keys on someone's key ring to render them useless.

But Phoebe was righteous with her snipes, using them only on people who truly deserved it—like Micah. He was obnoxious and clumsy, and he had absolutely no respect for anyone. She had hated the little jerk ever since his first day on the job, when she had caught him trying to pop birds around the feeder with his slingshot. He was the ideal target.

At first, Micah had thought the snipes were his older brother Randall's doing, but eventually he caught on to Phoebe. He tried to expose her as the culprit behind things like the hot pepper in Tennyson's cereal and the earwigs in Mr. Macaroy's pillow. When that didn't work, he resorted to pestering her any chance he got. Unfortunately for him, it won him a whupping every time.

As she used the tablecloth to wipe herself off, her mind raced through all sorts of vengeful scenarios, and the minute Micah's laughter faded, she leaped into action. Phoebe rushed off the veranda, leaving the mess behind for the staff to sort out, and flew down the steps to the manicured courtyard. She glanced around to make sure no one was watching, and then marched through the silver arbor that led to the lane of servants' quarters.

Phoebe's golden brown eyes sparkled as she headed for Micah's work shed.

Gotcha, she thought.

THE
STRANGER

The scents of rich, oily brass polish and old smoke from the fireplace put Phoebe at ease the instant she entered her father's study. Dr. Plumm was not an orderly man, and the floor of his office was piled with stacks of books and ledgers that seemed to defy gravity. The dark iron shelves were precariously overloaded, and the narrow Computator tower on his desk sat atop a nest of scattered papers and files. Blue shards of light streamed through stained glass windows and raked across the bronze wall panels, illuminating drifting motes of ash and dust.

This was Phoebe's favorite place in the whole house. It felt like her father was lingering just out of sight, hard at work on some inscrutable project. She settled into his pillowed reading chair upholstered in luxurious Durall, a premium material made from velvety-soft metal fibers. Phoebe tousled her hair, which was still damp, and pushed a button on the armrest to start the chair's rocking function.

Her eyes drifted across the walls crowded with certificates, commendations, awards, and accolades for the great Dr. Jules Plumm. She could never remember exactly what her father did for the Foundry, but it was something really important, she knew that much. Not just anyone could get their photograph taken with the president. Phoebe studied the picture, though she knew every nuance of it by heart. Her father was in the middle, a lean rake of a man with a wry grin, the sunlight glinting off one of the lenses of his glasses. He was shaking the hand of President Saltern, who was on the right, boasting that winning smile of his. But her father wasn't looking at the president—instead, he was gazing to the left. To Phoebe's mom.

She wore a sleeveless, ankle-length dress made of overlapping silver rectangles that looked like shimmering scales, and there was a splash of lemonade-colored diamonds in her black bobbed hair. Her eyelashes, thick with mascara, were pinched tight in laughter, and her head was slung back with her mouth wide. She was clutching her husband's arm with both hands. It looked like they were sharing an inside joke at the expense of the most powerful man in the world.

Out of the corner of her eye, Phoebe saw the dimpled copper door of the study swing open. It was Micah, wearing heavy-duty cleaning gloves and muttering to himself. He dragged a sloshing bucket with one hand and clutched a filthy toothbrush in the other, not noticing Phoebe as he trudged toward the private lavatory in the corner.

"Get out of here," Phoebe said coldly.

Micah startled and almost toppled his bucket, but he quickly regained his composure. He chuckled and took a few moseying steps toward her. The splatter of freckles on the twerp's round face stretched in a snide, lopsided grin that made her skin crawl.

"Costume change, eh, Plumm? What happened to your other shirt there?"

"Some stupid little garden gnome thought he was cute. He was wrong."

"Ha-ha! Testy, testy. Did I spoil your *pwetty widdle* outfit?"

"Don't you have a toilet to scrub or something?"

Micah glanced down at his toothbrush and bucket and shrugged with feigned indifference. "It was worth it. Anything's worth it to see Freaky scream," he said, doing his ugliest impression of Phoebe's reaction to the hose.

She rose to her full height and leered down at him. Not only was Phoebe two years older than Micah, but she was also a glorious six inches taller. "Enjoy it while it lasts," she muttered ominously.

"What's 'at supposed to mean?"

"I guess I'd have to explain it to an inbred hick like you, wouldn't I?" She stepped close enough to make Micah uncomfortable, but he didn't back down. He brushed his rusty blond hair away with a stubby hand and wrinkled his pug nose.

"You're a stuck-up snobby kook, you know that?"

"Better than a crap farmer like you. Is that why you love scrubbing the pot so much?"

"You think you're *so* smart," he said, starting to go red.

"Ooh! I have a new name for you. Toiletboy. Has a nice ring to it."

Micah scrambled for the words. "Shut up! You're a . . ."

She raised her eyebrows, waiting for a brilliant comeback.

". . . a stupid freakin' idiot!" Micah finished lamely.

"Wow," chuckled Phoebe sarcastically. "Such wit."

"FREAKY!" Micah shouted, his fat mouth bent into an angry scrawl.

A horn blared outside.

"Gotta go, Toiletboy," Phoebe said, casually breezing past him. She clicked the yellow brooch on the band of her hat, and a spray of fine golden tendrils swished out like a metal ostrich feather. "Oh, and if I were you, which I'm glad I'm not, I'd watch my back . . . and front, come to think of it."

"Bring it on. I ain't scared of your stupid tricks!"

She flashed him a smile and left the study.

Phoebe skipped across the foyer, feeling a surge of elation. She so wished she could be around to see Micah stumble upon her snipe. As she approached the copper-plated front doors, she checked the time on the grandfather clock, a family heirloom shaped like an ornately filigreed skyscraper. Seven thirteen a.m. She was late for school and couldn't care less.

The horn bleated again, and she rolled her eyes.

She hefted open the great front doors and hurried down the wide slab steps. On the hammered-steel driveway below, Tennyson the chauffeur was finishing up a quick polish of the long, smoke-gray Baronet with his chamois.

The Plumms had seven Auto-mobiles in all. Phoebe's favorite was the classic, electric-blue Flashback her dad had named Shameless. Tennyson, however, preferred the Baronet, which was the largest and most impressive of the collection. It was a silver arrow of aerodynamic design, with sweeping fenders whose curves reminded Phoebe of brushstrokes. Parallel grooves ran along the body, giving the impression that the Auto-mobile was speeding, even when it was at rest. The Baronet was quite a sight, but it was no match for Shameless.

Tennyson ignored Phoebe and headed for the driver's seat without opening the door for her—their relationship no longer included even that basic formality. She stretched out across the oiled black and silver leather, her foot knocking up against the book bag she had left under the seat.

The Baronet hushed quietly out of the driveway and onto Shimmering Crest, which made a steep series of zigzagging switchbacks all the way down the hill. Tennyson whistled as he drove, clinking his wedding ring on the aluminum steering wheel. Phoebe assumed he was doing that to annoy her.

Two can play at that game, she thought. So Phoebe activated the Trinka strapped to her wrist and let the toy's spinning tentacles clatter across the ceiling. She did it again and again and looked in the rearview mirror to see if she was getting a rise out of Tennyson, but the chauffeur just whistled and clicked his ring that much louder.

Phoebe lolled her head to the side and gazed out the window as they whizzed from the hills and approached downtown. They plunged in and out of long shadows thrown by the forest of skyscrapers, making it seem like someone was flicking the world's light switch off and on. Phoebe craned her neck to try and see the tops of the buildings they passed.

There was the bronze Lion's Mane Hotel, whose sharp spires seemed to jab at the sky like the prongs of a trident. Then there was the Uniton Tower, home to Phoebe's favorite Televiewer network, which boasted gold windows that slanted in overlapping ribs, reminding Phoebe of a titanic stalk of wheat. Then the Opal District, a plaza of art galleries made of copper covered in a lush green patina. And the Central Library, which resembled the prow of one of the Foundry's impressive ocean liners. And the five silver pillars of the National Museum.

Phoebe rolled down her window to absorb the commotion of morning—the symphony of horns, the clamor of traffic, and the bustle of sharply dressed pedestrians, some walking dogs that were just as elegantly attired. These steely streets were the veins of the city, flowing with thousands of polished Auto-mobiles and pulsing with hordes of hurried people. The Link-Way hubs were packed, as riders hooked their Cable Bikes on to the lines and zipped across the intricate web of aerial wires. Phoebe counted three new building projects, with Over-cranes and Earthshakers hoisting beams into position.

She imagined what wonders these new structures would add to the world-famous skyline. Every year the capital grew more and more magnificent.

"Keep it closed," grumbled Tennyson as he rolled up her window from his control panel. "Got the air on."

Phoebe glared at the back of Tennyson's square head and then mashed her button to lower the window again. She slung her arms out of the Auto to prevent the chauffeur from rolling it back up.

As they drove through Paragon Park, Phoebe admired the chrome statue of Creighton Albright at its heart. The legendary inventor of the modern age was holding the globe aloft and gazing upon it with fierce pride. Every Dudscrub and Microcounter, every Auto-mobile and Megatanker, from the tiniest pin to the mightiest skyscraper, every glorious new advancement served as testament to his genius.

She wondered if Albright could have imagined the impact he'd have on the future. That four centuries later, his greatest invention of all, the Foundry, would remain the unrivaled source of progress and innovation.

"Hey!" Phoebe yelped as the window started to close on her. She yanked her arms back into the Auto and pulled the golden tendrils of her hat inside as the glass was sealed tight. She kicked the back of Tennyson's seat.

"I said, keep it closed," the chauffeur grumbled. "And no kicking."

Phoebe pressed the button repeatedly, but he had locked her window.

"You can't tell me what to do," Phoebe huffed.

"That's not what your father said. He told you to be a good little girl and obey me, remember? Upsetting the driver is a hazard."

Phoebe kicked Tennyson's seat harder.

They emerged from the shelter of the park, and Tennyson turned onto the road that hugged the coastline. As she did every morning at this spot, Phoebe slid to the opposite side of the Auto and stared at her feet. The Baronet was blasted with an intense light, a reflection from the Crest of Dawn, which towered over the island of Foundry Central.

Phoebe squeezed her eyes shut, but not because of the glare.

They were driving on a high bluff above the dark churning bay. Though the Baronet was soundproof, Phoebe could feel the crash of the waves, malevolent and hungry. She trusted that the guardrails would prevent the Baronet from going over the edge, but she could not bear the sight of the water below. Her heart pounded, and she tasted bile at the back of her tongue. She closed her eyes and counted backward from ten, knowing that when she reached zero, the ocean would no longer be yawning, waiting right below her.

Ten. Nine. Eight.

She thought of her father. How when she was little, she couldn't wait to see what gift he had brought her when he returned from his business trips. Nowadays, she just wanted him. She pictured his open arms.

Seven. Six. Five.

She imagined Micah's stupid face turning bright red as he

discovered the snipe she had set up that morning. That made her smile.

Four. Three.

They were definitely past the worst part of it by now, but Phoebe didn't like to take any chances. She searched for other glimmers of happiness.

Two.

All at once, the strangest sensation overcame her. It was a prickling chill at the back of her neck that had nothing to do with the dreaded bay below. Phoebe had a powerful urge to look, but she resisted it.

Just one more second to go.

One.

She opened her eyes. Foundry Bay was gone from view as the busy street angled around a bend. But the weird feeling was still there. Phoebe looked out the back window.

Behind the Baronet was an unfamiliar model of Automobile. It was jet-black with a dark bronze stripe down the middle. A row of oval headlights wrapped around the front of the Auto below a narrow, tinted windshield. For an instant, she glimpsed a face behind the smoked glass.

Curving mustache. Bowler hat. Round black spectacles.

Phoebe gasped. With reflections dancing across the dark windshield, she couldn't be sure. Was she imagining things?

No. It was the stranger she had seen from her bedroom window.

Her mind scrambled for an explanation. Was it merely someone who looked like him? It was a fairly typical fashion, plain black suit with a white shirt and gloves. Maybe he was a new neighbor who coincidentally shared her commute.

That's when it hit her. This man had been sent by her father, hired to watch over her like a bodyguard. That's why he had been surveying the house that morning and why he was following her now. Did that mean she was in danger? Her father was a big deal at the Foundry, after all. Maybe this was a precaution, what with all the anti-Meridian stuff going on.

Surely that was it.

Phoebe gave the stranger a little wave to let him know she understood. On cue, the black Auto drifted back and disappeared into the sea of traffic. Not exactly the reaction she was expecting, but it was no matter. She was relieved to know that her father was watching over her from afar.

Still, why didn't he just tell her? Her father could have sent word from wherever he was. It would certainly scare her a lot less if she knew this stranger was a bodyguard and not some creepy stalker.

She pondered this until they arrived at Beatrice Albright Academy for Girls. The campus was a vast grassy commons enclosed by a row of stately elms, and the front of the school faced the distant bay, whose waters glittered through the leaves. Her instructors always boasted about the inspiring historical significance of their school. But to Phoebe, it looked like some sort of burned-out fortress, with a clunky iron block design corroded by centuries of ocean air.

Lately, the Academy had been undergoing renovations, and while half of the sprawling campus was caged in by scaffolding, the other half had received a shiny new veneer that gleamed with fiery reflections from the Crest of Dawn.

Tennyson parked the Baronet. Phoebe slouched so that no one could see her, and he didn't say a word, knowing her routine. Every day, she watched as the other girls milled about, playing with their Spinner Purses and ridiculous hair mobiles until they all finally bobbled indoors. Only then would she slink inside.

The chauffeur resumed his obnoxious whistling and tapping. He glanced at her in the rearview mirror and gave her a smug grin. She had considered letting him off the hook for his previous slight, but this sealed the deal.

Phoebe searched one of the secret pockets in her skirt.

At last the bell rang. She grabbed her bag and shuffled out of the Auto, immediately feeling weighed down by schoolwork and the salty humidity of the bay.

Phoebe paused for a second, pretending to adjust her shoe as she pulled the bent nail from her pocket and wedged it beneath the Baronet's back tire. She slammed the door, and as Tennyson sped away, she thrilled to the pop and hiss of the punctured wheel. Hopefully, he would be stuck in traffic by the time he discovered the flat. That was sure to stop his stupid whistling.

"Gotcha," Phoebe said.

As she trudged up the steps, Phoebe scanned the driveway and parking lot, looking for the stranger's black and bronze Auto. It was nowhere to be seen. She took a last deep breath of the free world, sour and salty though it was, and forced it out, resigned to another day's hard labor at Fort Beatrice.

HEAT RISING

he day was worse than Phoebe had anticipated. Normally, she could endure Miss Castella's annoying enthusiasm for punctuation, she could even stomach Mr. Pomeroy's wretched frog-puke breath. But not today. Every class was like being trapped in a sauna. The renovations on the building were causing the air-cooling units to fail, which meant long stretches of sweltering muck interspersed with rare bursts of heavenly breeze.

They wheeled a bunch of brand new Flurrys into every classroom, but even the Foundry's top-of-the line fans, chrome devices built to resemble spinning snowflakes, did little more than stir the air like a hot, boring soup.

As the end of the day oozed closer, Phoebe shuffled down one of the gleaming remodeled hallways toward Mrs. Vondell's dreaded history class. She saw a boisterous group of girls and locked her eyes on the ground. Two or more geese were called a gaggle, she knew, but what was the term for two or more shallow, stuck-up, catty know-it-alls? A squall? A shriek?

Yeah, that sounded about right.

She wove through the crowd and snuck past the shriek of snots, hoping to go unnoticed. No such luck.

"Seriously, that can't be for real."

"I would just shave my head if I were her."

"Was it cut by a drunk?"

"More like a blind man."

This last dig came from Candice, and it stung the worst.

Back when they were kids, Phoebe and Candice had been inseparable. But when Phoebe needed her best friend most of all, Candice had abandoned her as if she thought tragedy was contagious or something.

Phoebe's breath felt fiery in her nostrils, and her face tingled with humiliation and outrage. She raked a hand through her butchered hair and fussed with its ragged, uneven edge.

She strode into Mrs. Vondell's classroom and flopped into her chair by the window, more irritated than ever that she had to sit directly behind Candice. As the waddling hippo that was Mrs. Vondell began her history lesson, Phoebe envisioned all the terrible accidents that might befall her ex–best friend.

Perhaps the workers would hit a weak spot in the roof, and the ceiling would collapse on her. Or maybe Candice's necklace would get caught in the blades of a Flurry. But between the sweaty classroom and Mrs. Vondell's monotonous voice dripping in her ear like a drug, Phoebe's mind drifted.

"That's correct. By 1646, the Alloy War had been going for sixteen years, claiming over thirty million lives," Mrs. Vondell droned, her multiple chins wagging to and fro. "And on October twelfth of that year, Meridian brought about a cease-fire by introducing . . . the what?"

Nobody raised a hand, but Mrs. Vondell carried on as if she hadn't noticed the class's profound disinterest. She turned back to the enameled metal whiteboard, angling her ample rump to the class, and wrote the answer.

"The Ferro-nomic Treaty, which finally permitted international trade of Foundry goods. A free market emerged for the other nations of the world, who lacked our spirit of innovation."

Phoebe's eyelids were heavy. She knew Mrs. Vondell expected her students to regurgitate all this stuff word for word on the test, but the day was nearly at an end.

Candice's muffled snort of laughter snapped Phoebe awake. She stared at the nauseating waves of perfect blond hair that that cascaded down Candice's back. The girl tittered at some private joke and flung her locks with a showy toss of her head. A handful of her curls spilled across the frame of the open window.

And an immensely satisfying snipe sprang to her mind.

"The global distribution of Albright's countless advancements in technology, manufacturing, and transportation resulted in major cultural and economic shifts. Greinadoren, Moalao, and the other primitive nations saw substantial improvements to their quality of life. But most importantly, Meridian became the most powerful country in the world. Now, can anyone tell me . . ."

There were only a few minutes left until the bell would free her from Vondell torture. She had to act fast.

Soft as a whisper, Phoebe eased the window sash closed on Candice's golden hair. She withdrew a paper clip from one of her skirt pockets, wedged it in the window mechanism, and twisted the wire around the knob to jam it. Candice was too engrossed in gossip to notice.

Phoebe wouldn't be the only one with an uneven haircut.

Satisfied, she prepared to bolt at the sound of the bell and glanced out the window to see if Tennyson had arrived.

Her breath lodged in her throat.

Beyond the workers' scaffolding and construction tarps wafting in the sea breeze, she saw the stranger in the bowler hat. His tailored black suit hugged his broad barrel chest, and he wore crisp white gloves on large hands. Gleaming steel trim lined his lapels and the soles of his shoes. He stood eerily still, the waxy tint of his skin making him look like a statue that might melt in the sun. His stout, gently curled mustache looked like a joyless smile, which made his appearance all the more disturbing.

Even through his impenetrable black spectacles, she could feel his stare.

The sudden clang of the school bell propelled Phoebe from her seat. She snatched her book bag and was halfway down the hall before she heard Candice squawk behind her. Phoebe imagined Mrs. Vondell being forced to cut the girl loose with a pair of dull scissors.

Gotcha.

She slowed as a swarm of students poured out of classrooms and toward the front doors. Normally, she would have escaped Fort Beatrice at full speed to avoid the mob, but seeing the stranger out front made her hesitate. That morning, she had felt certain that he was a bodyguard hired to protect her. Now she was not so sure.

If he was an ally, why did his glare feel so invasive, like he was impaling her with a mere look?

Phoebe flattened up against the lockers to avoid students storming past and considered another route out of the building. She slipped down a stuffy side hall that was shrouded in drop cloths and loud with the screech of power tools. A custodian shuffled out of a classroom hauling a heavy trash bag to the incinerator. The moment his back was to her, she dashed through the door he had left open.

A humid breeze drifted in from an open window that overlooked the athletic fields behind the Academy—away from the waiting stranger. She heard the shouts of kids playing outside and scanned the grounds to make sure no one was watching. Content that the coast was clear, she hopped up on the windowsill, swung her legs over, and dropped into the bushes below.

It was farther than Phoebe anticipated, but the hedge cushioned her fall. The mellow hush of ocean breeze tempered the brutal heat of the afternoon. It was such a relief to escape that stuffy old building.

From the bushes, Phoebe watched her classmates frolic, their lively Trinkas dancing in a colorful stir. Boys from the nearby prep school had gathered as well, pretending to ignore the girls but showing off nonetheless. Six of them were playing a frantic game of Springchuck, bouncing the coconut-sized copper gyroscope. You were supposed to catch the thing, perform some feat of agility, and then hurl it back into the circle of players. The gadget shot out at random, so it was impossible to predict where it would go, which was supposed to be half of the fun.

The older boys raced their Cable Bikes across the lawn toward a nearby hub. At the umbrella-shaped brass booth, they latched their Bikes on to the ascension line and zipped off overhead. The boys chased each other along the crisscrossed Link-Way high above, doing dangerous stunts as they switched their Bikes from wire to wire, to the giggling delight of the girls below.

Phoebe crept through the shrubs and made her way around the side of Fort Beatrice. A long line of Auto-mobiles parked in the driveway came into view, and she could make out Tennyson leaning against the Baronet, his arms folded disapprovingly.

And there was the stranger.

He had positioned himself between the chauffeur and the front doors of the Academy, as dark and unmoving as an inkblot. She considered trying to signal to Tennyson, but it was no use. He would not understand the need for discretion, and there was no way to get his attention without the stranger seeing as well.

The chauffeur mopped his brow and scowled at his watch. She knew exactly what he was thinking. Phoebe had a habit of ditching her driver in order to take the Zip Trolley home. How long would Tennyson wait before giving up on her?

She couldn't stick around to find out.

Phoebe broke into a jog and cut across the athletic fields. The wind brushed against her damp skin as she ran, waking her body after the long, dreary day. She made her way to the edge of the grounds and passed under the row of elms that bordered the Academy.

Sweet freedom!

She found herself on a residential street lined by brand-new tin-plated town houses with tall trapezoid windows. The symmetrical buildings were so alike that Phoebe wondered how the residents ever managed to find their way home. She crossed an intersection and headed up a street bustling with fashionable pedestrians. Phoebe dug into her book bag, withdrew her hat, and popped it on, activating its metal feather ornament with a flagrant swish. She was headed to the Zip Trolley stop on Illacci Hill, one of the classier shopping districts in Albright City, so she had to look the part.

The afternoon sun lit up the glass storefronts like a kaleidoscope. The bluster of Auto traffic filled the air, and the glittering gold sidewalks looked like fashion runways. Waves of city folk towered over Phoebe and broke around her like the tide, their shopping bags sizzling with brand-new purchases.

She didn't like crowds but found it easy to get lost in the shuffle. No one even noticed the scrawny twelve-year-old girl in the ratty skirt.

The window displays drew her eye. A glamorous hat store showed a lively beach scene populated by bronze mannequins in the latest summer fashions. There were sweeping striated sun hats that could retract to the size of a pillbox and adorable silver bathing caps with goggles that popped out when they got wet. At another store, she admired a pair of Scopers, sandals with heels that could extend to make you look taller. Not that Phoebe needed any help in that department.

She wove between the throngs of refined pedestrians and made her way to the gadgetariums farther up the hill. One novelty shop advertised the FroYoYo, a peach-colored yo-yo made of tin that (for some reason unclear to Phoebe) doubled as a frozen yogurt dispenser. The next store sold household luxury items, including Sleeksweeps and the Kinetik Komforts series, scalp and body massagers that resembled gyrating chrome spiders.

A Foundry truck with tank treads covering its back wheels was parked in the street. The cargo bed was segmented with overlapping steel plates, and its gate was open like an invitation.

She approached, dying to know what was inside. Probably the premiere of a brand-new product, something unbelievable that would be—

She froze.

Phoebe couldn't believe her eyes. She stared at the reflection in the truck's polished chrome bumper.

The stranger was behind her.

He was running at top speed, his long strides unwavering as if climbing the hill required no more effort than breathing. There was no longer any question. He was after her.

A shock of adrenaline rippled through her limbs. She ran with no destination, past pedestrians and across streets, heedless of the honking Auto-mobiles. She wanted to look back but didn't dare.

Halfway up the block she skidded right, and then dashed into the alley between a department store and a hotel. Her footfalls echoed and multiplied in the narrow passage.

Click-clack-click-clack.

Or were those *his* steps pounding closer and closer?

The skyscrapers rose around her like the bars of a silver cage. She burst onto Fourth Street in the center of the Financial District. The shadows were growing long and the buildings shone with the fierce amber glow of sunset. The sidewalks were even more crowded here, and she weaved between the masses, hoping they would conceal her.

The city had lost its comforting hum. Now everything was amplified and aggressive—horns shrieked, jackhammers roared. Phoebe thought she heard her name murmured in snatches of passing conversations, and her heartbeat thundered in her throat.

She shot down an alley and slammed against a wall to catch her breath, her lungs wheezing and straining for air. Her eyes couldn't focus, she was dripping with sweat, and her legs burned. Feeling light-headed, she peeled off her hat, savoring the chill that swept over her drenched hair.

Phoebe was not at all accustomed to this kind of exertion. Walking was okay—she loved to explore the city. But running? Long ago, she had talked her father into getting a doctor's note to permanently excuse her from gym, some fabrication about weak knees or something. Ever since then, she had avoided anything that might cause her to break a sweat.

What was she supposed to do now?

The chirp of the Zip Trolley sang out. It was like the call of a long-lost friend. This was her chance. She closed her eyes and tried to visualize where she was in relation to it.

Click-clack-click-clack-click-clack.

The sound of metal-soled shoes.

Click-clack-click-clack.

Phoebe peeked around the corner.

He was coming.

Her hat slipped from her fingers.

The sunset careening off the Crest of Dawn nearly blinded her when she spilled out of the alley. Disoriented, rushing down a street she didn't recognize, all she could do was chase the sound of the trolley whistle. She crashed into a vendor selling limeade Fizzies as she bolted onto a narrow walkway between towering black buildings.

Phoebe burst out onto Illacci Hill again, and there it was. The sight of the Zip Trolley with its bulbous facade and round, sparkling windows filled her with elation. It was just starting to roll away. She pumped her legs like a locomotive to catch up. Her heart felt like it was going to explode.

She reached out and snatched the back railing, feeling the deep vibration of the electric engine through her palm. Phoebe hauled herself aboard just in time to see the stranger rushing at her from the *opposite* side of the street.

Impossible. He had been behind her only moments ago. How could he have gotten over to the other side? It was as if he were everywhere at once.

The stranger jogged for a bit before giving up the chase, his eyes never leaving her. She heaved a rattling sigh of relief as the Zip Trolley whizzed away, her body trembling from exhaustion. No matter how fast he was, there was no way he would be able to catch up on foot.

Yet as the trolley sped over the hill and his black-hole stare vanished from sight, she had a feeling the stranger would not give up so easily.

OPERATION
SEEK THE FREAK

oiletboy!? Ha-ha!"

Jacko and Rory doubled over in laughter. Micah knew he should have stopped his story at the hose part.

They were hanging out in Micah's work shed, a little storage hut at the back of the estate where all the old busted equipment got dumped. Doc Plumm let him use it as a machine shop, and Micah had turned it into a wicked hideout. The place was a total sty, of course—just how he liked it.

"Whatever," Micah grumbled as he tied the lace on one of his work boots. He checked the grime-spattered pockets of his overalls and dug a thumbnail into his fingertips, an ongoing effort to build up some halfway-decent calluses. "You guys seen my wrench anywhere?"

"And you let her get away with that?" Rory snorted.

"'Course he did. The little slave's gotta obey his master," Jacko sneered.

Micah threw a lug nut at his friend, who dodged easily.

"Bet you love wipin' the queen's butt!" jeered Rory.

"Oh, Toiletboy!" Jacko called in a mocking, singsong voice. "Come hither this instant. My rump needs a scrub and you're the perfect height. Chop-chop!"

"Cram it!" Micah shouted as he hurled another nut, this time harder. It hit Jacko in the chest with a dull thud. Irritated, Jacko grabbed the first thing he could find, a toy pistol, and aimed at Micah.

"Wait, wait!" protested Micah, gesturing in panic to a tarp-covered shape. "Not around the—"

When Jacko pulled the trigger, the toy fired with a surprising buck. The shot ricocheted off the rear wall, whizzed inches from Rory's ear, and smashed a hole in a can of oil. Black sludge sputtered out and pooled on the floor.

"Sweet," gasped Jacko.

"Whoa! Is that the new Snakebite?" asked Rory.

"Naw, just a modifed S-80," Micah said as he snatched the gun out of Jacko's hand. It wasn't much to look at, with lumps of ugly solder holding it together and banged-up rivets pounded in at odd angles. "Replaced the chamber with the slide from an old crane-neck drill press. Swapped the mini-springs for some point-twos, and made a new clip that holds washers instead of BBs."

"This puppy shoots washers?" Rory asked, a gleam in his eye.

Micah nodded and slid the gun into a loop on his overalls.

"Nice work," Jacko said. "Midget." Rory laughed.

Midget, runt, dwarf—Micah had heard them all. His friends knew it set him off, and they loved to see him spaz. Sure, he was a little short for his age, but Micah more than made up for his size with guts.

"Say that again, Jerko, and I swear . . ." he threatened.

"Yeah, yeah. So you gonna show it to us this year or what?" Jacko asked, gesturing to the tarp.

Micah jutted his chin and made a show of thinking about it, poking through a heap of odds and ends on the bench and savoring their anticipation. "Seriously, guys, what'd you do with all my tools?"

"Get on with it!" groaned Rory.

Micah approached the draped form and paused for dramatic effect. "No touching. No breathing. Don't even look at it too hard."

Jacko and Rory rolled their eyes.

With a flourish, Micah whipped off the cover.

The vehicle's serpentine frame wound around two gleaming wheels made of overlapping platinum plates, and the chrome on the saber-shaped handlebars was polished to a mirror finish. Vents patterned its front hull like devilish eyebrows above the triangular headlight. Its body was deep red flaked with silver, like a sprinkle of snow on fresh cherries.

It was a brand new Cable Bike. They were struck dumb.

Micah reached into an exposed panel in the Bike's frame. With a mechanical whisper, a pair of hydraulic arms unfolded and swung overhead, creating the signature swoop. At the top of the mount was a torpedo-shaped winch head, which clung to the Link-Way cables and allowed the vehicle to race through the air. Micah got chills just thinking about it.

"No way," Rory whispered.

"They know you're takin' it apart like that?" Jacko asked, motioning to the pile of parts Micah had removed.

"I'm gonna put it all back," Micah said defensively. "Just wanted to see how it works, is all." He gave the fingerprint-smeared Bike manual a nudge.

Jacko grabbed one of the handlebars. "I'm ridin' first."

"What are you, stupid?" Micah slapped his friend's hand away. "It's a birthday present for Queen Stringbean. They'd kill me if they found out I—"

"*When* they find out," rasped a snide voice.

Micah's older brother Randy lingered in the doorway, a smug look on his acne-splattered face. Even though the school day was over, he was still wearing his navy blue and gold cadet uniform. Ever since he'd been accepted into the Military Institute of Meridian, Randy was so full of himself that his head barely fit through the door.

Micah wanted one of those uniforms. If it could make a jug-eared, zit-faced goon like Randy look good, it'd turn Micah into a genuine badass.

"No one invited you," he grumbled.

"I don't need an invitation, short stack." Randy grinned.

"Heh, short stack," repeated Rory.

"Shut up," Randy snapped. He shoved past Rory and Jacko and peered into the opened hatch of the Cable Bike. "You're dead when the Doc sees this."

"Well, he won't, 'cause I'm gonna put it together before he gets back."

"Too late, buttercup. The Doc's here." Randy cracked his long goose neck with a quick jerk. "And he's askin' for you."

"Yeah, right," snorted Micah. "Like I'd fall for that."

"Fine." Randy shrugged. "I'll tell him you're too busy tearing apart his little girl's birthday present to be bothered." He spun on his heels as if he had just received marching orders.

Micah couldn't take the chance.

"Okay, okay," he relented. "Just gimme a sec." He grabbed one of the parts he had removed from the motor and fit it back into place. He looked around again for his wrench.

"Did you borrow my tools, Randy?"

"Pffft. I don't touch your stupid crap."

"Why can't I find anything, then?"

"I dunno—'cause you're a retarded pygmy?"

Jacko and Rory chuckled. Micah sifted through the junk pile. Nothing. Must have packed everything away in his tool chest and forgotten about it. He whipped the lid open.

Twang. SPLAT!

A blast of white paint exploded into Micah's face.

The work shed rang with screams of laughter. Randy collapsed against the door frame while Rory and Jacko rolled on the grimy floor. Micah coughed up heaps of paint and tasted the bitter stuff trickling down his sinuses. His eyes stung as he tried to wipe them clean.

Beneath the splatters of white, his face burned red hot.

Micah stomped into the foyer of the manor, still fuming. He had tried to clean himself up, but paint still filled the folds of his ears and clung to his reddish hair. He was a total mess, but he couldn't keep the Doc waiting.

Worried servants were gathered near the closed study door.

"Make way. Comin' through," Micah said, elbowing to the front. He heard voices coming from inside. One was Tennyson, but it took Micah a second to place the other—he had never heard the Doc sound angry before.

"Where is she?" roared Dr. Plumm.

"I—I went to pick her up at school," Tennyson answered. "But sometimes she avoids me, like it's some sort of game. She always finds her way home, sir."

Micah nervously dug a thumbnail into his budding calluses. He cracked the door open and poked his head inside. Tennyson and Micah's burly sow of a mom faced the Doc, who stood silhouetted before the fireplace. Micah wondered why he had a fire going on such a hot day.

"Take an Auto. Find her," Dr. Plumm commanded.

"But sir, how am I supposed to—"

"I don't care how. Just go find her!"

As Tennyson took his leave, they spotted Micah lingering in the doorway.

"What in the burning hells?" his ma shrieked as she rushed up and snatched his forearm with one meaty hand. She yanked him so hard he thought his shoulder might pop out of its socket, and then scoured his paint-smeared face with her apron as if he were a dirty dish.

"Just look at yourself. And how dare you make Dr. Plumm wait around for your sorry carcass!"

She drew back her hand. Micah pinched his eyes, bracing for the impact.

"Deirdre!" the Doc interrupted. "I need you to pack a suitcase for Phoebe. Enough for a week."

She paused. "Of course, Dr. Plumm. Anything else?"

"Leave Micah with me."

With a huff of indignation, Micah ripped his arm free from her grasp and rubbed his shoulder. She fixed him with a threatening stare and grumbled as she departed.

Dr. Plumm had always been a lean man, but now he was a scarecrow. His long, sharp face was sunken and his glasses framed desperate eyes. It was as if he had aged a decade since Micah had last seen him.

"Do you know where she is?" Dr. Plumm asked, his voice hoarse and weary.

"You mean Phoebe? No, sir, I don't."

"Please." The Doc bent down to look Micah dead in the eye. "Think. How else would she get home from school?"

"Prob'ly Zip Trolley."

"Then go with Tennyson. Check all the stops." He crossed to his desk and snatched up a stack of documents.

"'Scuse me, sir. But I'd be faster on foot."

Dr. Plumm tossed the papers into the fireplace and turned back to Micah.

"There's only one stop nearby," Micah explained, "and I got the perfect shortcut to the park. Plus, Tennyson drives like a granny, sir."

"Go," the Doc said. Micah whipped his hand up in a military salute, then bolted through the door and down the hall.

A legitimate excuse to leave Plumm Estate was not to be taken lightly. And it was all the more important since it was a chance to help the Doc out.

Micah burst onto the front porch, and the humid dusk wrapped around him like a blanket. He raced down the steps toward the Baronet, which was just pulling out of the drive-way. Micah dove onto the hood and slid across it in a jumble. Tennyson screeched the Auto to a stop and rolled down the window to scream at him, but Micah was already halfway across the lawn. He bounded over the hedges, ducked into a somersault, and drew his modified Snakebite in one motion.

Almost perfect. He had been practicing that move.

As Micah hurried out the front gates, the manor glowed to life. Light danced across the hexagonal towers topped with bronze turtle-shell domes, and it blasted out through tall triangular windows to reflect on shining metal walls. There wasn't another place quite like it. Micah remembered the first time he saw Plumm Estate as if it were yesterday.

Three years before, the Tanners had come to Albright City from Oleander, a farming town in the Mid-Meridian state of Sodowa. When their father up and ditched them, Ma had been forced to support the family. Barefoot and broke, they hit the road in their beat-up old Auto and trekked to Albright City— he, Ma, Randy, and Margie.

It was right around then that Mrs. Plumm kicked the bucket.

None of the servants knew what had happened to her, or if they did, they weren't allowed to talk about it. And whenever Micah asked, he got his ears boxed. Whatever it was, it must have been bad.

But it was a good thing for the Tanners, 'cause the Doc was in sore need of help. Ma answered his ad, and the next day they were pulling up at Plumm Estate. Holy moly, were their jaws on the floor! At the time, Micah thought this place was the best. He didn't realize that working as a servant meant always getting treated like one.

And of course he didn't know about Li'l Miss Freaky and her stupid bag of tricks.

The Baronet pulled out of the driveway, and Micah slammed himself up against the gate to hide. He wasn't gonna let that creep Tennyson beat him to his target.

Commence Operation Seek the Freak.

Shimmering Crest was the main boulevard that zigzagged

down the steep hillside to the park at the base. That's where the Zip Trolley stop was. Instead of taking the winding road, he was going straight down the hill, a gnarly drop that cut through all the switchbacks.

Micah thought about Maddox, hero of the absolute best Televiewer show ever. He was a hard-boiled Special Ops soldier who didn't take crap from nobody. Right about now, the Greinadoren Kommandei would be everywhere, leagues of deadly shadows shifting in the trees. Maddox wouldn't even sweat. He'd just smirk and say:

"No guts, no glory." Micah growled it in his best Maddox voice and cocked his gun.

He leaped into position among the birch trees, pressing against the trunks. Nodding a command to his imaginary strike force, he hurtled out and fired his gun wildly. One washer missed, but two hit their mark, thudding into a tree.

Direct hit. Go, go, go!

Micah dodged imaginary fire and ran deeper into the clump of birches. He slid down a steep embankment, clung to exposed roots, and scrabbled down to the road below, tumbling the last few feet awkwardly.

The enemy's right on our tail! Watch your six!

Margie was the one who had turned him on to *Maddox*. His older sister was a hard act to follow with her perfect grades, a scholarship to MIM, and immediate recruitment into a special engineering corps. She was pretty much the only one who gave two spits about Micah.

He wondered where she was nowadays. They hadn't heard

from her in more than a year. Apparently, she was on some sort of top-secret mission. With all the threats of war and stuff on the news, he bet it was super important.

Micah raced across the street, crawled through the underbrush, and jumped onto the roof of a garage below. He clung to the rain gutter and shimmied to the ground.

The homes on this lane were nice, but nothing like Plumm Estate and the other mansions at the top of the hill. These houses were packed close together and made from cheaper alloys.

The sky was growing darker. He had to hurry.

They're closing in. It's now or never.

Micah made a break for it. He let loose a flurry of rounds as he sprinted down the block, plugging imaginary Greinder Kommies left and right.

CLANG!

He froze. One of his shots had nailed a nearby mailbox mobile. It was a pointless doodad, a few dinky brass propellers and dangling baubles. As Micah hurried over to inspect the damage, he noticed that the center pinwheel was held on by a platinum hex grommet, a size eight.

Just the kind he had been looking for.

With a quick glance around, Micah spit on his hands and used his newly developed calluses to unscrew the grommet. He crammed it in his pocket and continued on his way.

It was the Doc who had first encouraged Micah to build stuff, noticing that he had a gift for the gears. "When a *worker* finds a spare part, he thinks it's the missing piece of an old machine," Dr. Plumm once told him. "But when an *inventor* finds a spare part, he imagines it's the perfect addition to something new. Which one do you want to be?"

He didn't have to think too hard on it: neither. Being a worker was as lame as being a servant, and being an inventor sounded like doing math with a bunch of losers. No, he was destined for bigger things. And as soon as he was old enough to get into the Military Institute of Meridian next year, he'd prove it.

Micah hurdled over a steel picket fence, dashed across the yard, and scrambled down into the undergrowth, scaring a couple squirrels out of hiding. It was a sheer slope packed with thorny shrubs and thistles, but he muscled his way through it, feeling the brambles poke through his pant legs.

After a few steep drops, the heavy brush opened up to reveal the park. Gold and silver lampposts sculpted to look like metal dandelions illuminated the walking trail. The fireflies were out as well, flickering like copper pennies in the dark. A few folks hung around the silver fountain, while others jogged along the path.

None of them noticed the filthy soldier watching them from the shadows.

Hugging the outskirts of the park, he snuck from tree to tree and approached the Zip Trolley stop. He figured that Tennyson was at least five minutes behind, the way he drove. Micah huddled near some boulders so that he would have Freaky in his sights as soon as she arrived.

Unless he had already missed her. Or did she take a different route home? That would be annoying—just like her, come to think of it.

Minutes ticked past. Micah picked clumps of white paint out of his hair and waited. If he didn't find her, at least he had managed to get a whiff of freedom. And he got the size-eight hex grommet, so it wasn't a total loss.

He was just thinking about the long trek back up the hill when a familiar lanky shadow came loping down the trail.

Target sighted!

Seeing her again brought his anger back to a rolling boil. She had made him look like a moron in front of his brother and friends. Plus, she'd gotten paint all over his stuff. He whipped his gun out and closed in on his prey.

She looked nutty, hugging herself and throwing glances over her shoulder. Good, she was already nervous, here all alone.

Micah lunged out from his hiding place and ran at her pell-mell.

"BLAHHHH!" he screamed. Phoebe screamed louder. She got about four feet of air. Her reaction was even better than he had hoped. Micah took aim with his Snakebite and fired—*click, click.*

Dang! Outta ammo.

He squealed with laughter anyway, stomping and running around in little circles. She was white as a stinkin' ghost, and her eyes were big as eggs, though they narrowed to mean little gashes when she saw who it was.

Mission accomplished.

"I hate you! I hate you!" she hissed, and punched him all over his back and arms. Her weak little blows made him laugh louder, even though her bone-sharp knuckles kinda stung.

Oh man, this was too good. Micah had never seen her so raw. Maybe he could even get her to cry. That would be a first.

"Gotcha!" Micah cackled. "That's for the paint!"

Her nasty little mouth puckered, and she stubbornly jutted out her pointy chin. She tossed back her stringy mop of hair and marched away from Micah like a peacock on stilts.

"You little maggot," Phoebe snapped. "Next time I'll load it with bleach."

"Aw, come on!" Micah said, bouncing along behind her. "Don't be a sore loser. Hey! Wait up, Freaky!"

"That's Miss Plumm to you, Toiletboy."

"Pffft!" Micah scoffed. "Fine, be that way. I was gonna show you my secret shortcut back home so you could go cry to your daddy, but . . ."

"Oh, go unclog something, you—" She stopped abruptly. Her mouth hung open as his words registered. A firefly drifted past her face, lighting her eyes.

Then she broke into a full-tilt run up the hill.

"Hey, you can't go back alone!" Micah shouted after her. "He's gonna think I didn't do my job!"

KASPAR

Phoebe rocketed up the front steps of the manor and flung open the doors. The foyer was still and thick with shadows. Where was all the brightness and activity? Where was everybody? The hairs on her arms rose and she hugged her body tight, wishing she had something warmer to wear than just this short-sleeved blouse and loose skirt. She crept across the slices of moonlight splayed across the copper plank floor. The silence was heavy, save for the hollow heartbeat tick of the grandfather clock.

"Daddy?" Her voice cracked with uncertainty.

Phoebe's thin oval suitcase of crosshatched aluminum sat beside the front door.

Footsteps approached from the study. She tensed. The sound grew loud, pounding across the metal floor and reverberating through the massive hall.

Her father rushed forward, arms wide.

She leaped into his embrace. Her confusion over the last few months, the terror of the stranger with the bowler hat, all dissolved so fast that they might as well have never existed. He grasped her tight, lifting her until her feet dangled off the ground. She buried her face in his collar. He smelled like a machinist—the scent of sweat, grit, and smoky iron. It was always stronger when he returned from one of his trips, though he usually tried to cover it up with lemon-lavender aftershave. He seemed to have forgotten it this time, but she could not have cared less.

Phoebe felt a swell in her throat but fought it down. She hadn't cried in nearly three years and was not about to start. Not in front of him.

"Cricket," her father whispered.

Normally, she hated when he called her that—it made her feel like a five-year-old. Not now. She savored the word.

"You're here," she said. "But why are you all alone? Where is everyone?"

"I sent them to their quarters. It's just you and me." He looked over her shoulder at Micah, who was standing in the doorway and watching the reunion with nosey insistence. "That'll be all, son."

She hadn't heard Micah enter, and she didn't bother to look. Her world started and stopped within her dad's embrace, and not even the Tanner twerp could ruin it. The boy lingered as if he wanted to say something, but her father's stare made it clear he had been dismissed. He wandered out the front door, scuffing his feet in that lazy way that normally drove Phoebe up the wall.

But at this moment, she couldn't care less about Micah.

When Phoebe's dad lowered her to the ground, she saw that he was filthy, his features now haunted and severe. But then he smiled. His tired eyes crinkled gently, the worry seemed to fade, and he was her father again.

"I—I thought you weren't coming back this time," Phoebe confessed.

His smile vanished, and he placed his hand on her shoulder.

"We have to go," he insisted. "We have to get away from here. We're leaving everything behind. Do you understand?"

Phoebe shook her head no—she did not understand.

"Of course you don't. How could you?"

His grip tightened on her shoulder, and she looked down at it. His right hand was covered in a mottled green bruise and wrapped in a filthy bandage. Her dad pulled it away and gestured to Phoebe's suitcase.

"I had Mrs. Tanner pack our bags. We have to go," he said.

"But she's not permitted to touch my things. I need to check it to see if—"

A muted rustle of bushes outside. Her father looked up sharply and put a finger to his lips. A long silence choked the room. Phoebe fidgeted.

"Now," he said at last. "Through the sitting room. They're probably watching the front door."

"Who?" Phoebe whispered. "The man in black?"

"What man?"

"With the dark glasses. A hat and curly mustache."

His eyes widened. "It couldn't be. Not here in the city."

"He's been following me. He chased me."

"If they are here . . . Come, Phoebe. Now!"

Her father dragged her across the threshold and through the adjacent sitting room, suitcase in hand. He swept open the curtained glass doors that led to the side yard.

The stranger in the bowler hat stood blocking their way.

He looked like a corpse in the twilight.

Phoebe screamed, and her dad slammed the doors. The panes shattered, sending the intruder backward in a shower of glass. Her father grabbed her and ran. Their pounding steps thundered through the house as they dashed for the front door. But it swung open before they could reach it.

"Hello, doctor."

The words pierced the shadows with ice-pick precision. Phoebe felt her dad's hand slacken. They both took a trembling step back, and her father dropped the suitcase.

The dark figure that entered was uncommonly tall, like he had been painfully stretched. As the man stepped into a shaft of moonlight, Phoebe shuddered at the sickly sight of him. He was broad-shouldered with a sinewy neck, wound as tight as a rope, and his dark eyes were buried deep in shadowed sockets.

Every move he made was sharp and deliberate. Beneath his unbuttoned overcoat he wore a flak jacket of finely woven bronze fibers and olive-colored military fatigues, and his gloves and high boots were black leather. His splotchy complexion was the color of disease, and the skin was pulled so tight across his angular cheekbones and hairless skull that it gleamed.

But it was his mouth that held Phoebe's gaze. His chapped lips pulled back in a malevolent sneer to reveal tiny grayish teeth spaced too far apart in his gums, like a sparse graveyard of weathered tombstones.

"Kaspar." Her father's voice faltered.

Another figure appeared in the doorway behind the menacing soldier. It was the stranger in the bowler hat. He should have been sprawled out unconscious in the side yard. How had he gotten around the house so quickly? Phoebe backpedaled but bumped up against something.

No. It was impossible. The stranger stood behind her as well, glass shards dusting his black suit. She looked from one to the other—the two men were identical in every way, from their cadaverous color to the symmetrical curl of their smiling mustaches. They ignored Phoebe, their impenetrable black spectacles focused on her dad.

"Your files," Kaspar rumbled.

"What do you think you're doing?" Strength had returned to her dad's voice. "Breaking into my home, threatening my family. This is low even for you. Does Goodwin know his little lapdog has released Watchmen into Albright City?"

There was no longer any trace of fear in her father. Had

he looked frail before? Now he seemed to rise before her very eyes, emanating resolve.

Kaspar nodded to the Watchmen. One grabbed Phoebe by the collar, and the other seized her dad's arm, twisting it hard behind his back. She stamped on her captor's feet and swung her bony elbows wildly, but the Watchman didn't budge.

"Don't you touch a hair on her head," her father warned.

"Your files," Kaspar repeated.

"Explain yourself. Or so help me—"

Kaspar nodded to the Watchman holding Phoebe. A cold, white-gloved hand clamped her mouth as another wrapped around her throat, squeezing her windpipe. She thrashed and tore at his hands, but his grip was unbreakable. Her dad broke away from the Watchman restraining him but was yanked back viciously.

She couldn't breathe. The world swam before her eyes.

"Stop!" her dad shouted, pointing to the dimpled copper door at the end of the foyer. "Through there." The pressure on her throat released, and she sucked in a blessed lungful of air. She looked to her father for some kind of answer.

"Everything's going to be okay, Cricket."

Phoebe nodded, wanting desperately to believe him, but the glimmer in Kaspar's eyes made her think otherwise. As he strode past, she could smell the oiled leather of his gloves and boots, masking a bitter scent of decay. He kicked open the door to the study and marched inside as the Watchmen dragged Phoebe and her father along.

Moonbeams poked feebly through the stained glass

window but did little to penetrate the shadows.

"I warned Goodwin that you were nothing more than a common thug," her father snapped. "Do you really think you can get away with this?"

Kaspar looked at the flames and curled ashes in the fireplace. "What did you destroy?"

"My documents are classified, and you have no authority. When I inform Goodwin what you have—"

"Who do you think sent me, doctor?"

Her dad drew back. Then he clenched his jaw and composed himself. "Release her. Then we can talk."

The Watchman holding her father kicked the back of his legs, dropping him to his knees. Kaspar grabbed his hair and wrenched his head back painfully. Phoebe wanted to scream, but the sound died in her throat.

Another two identical men in bowler hats appeared at the study door.

Was she going crazy? It seemed like the world had been replaced by a hall of mirrors. Phoebe was beginning to wonder if she could trust her senses.

The Watchmen ripped open cabinets and seized files, gathering them into bundles. They carefully collected the ashes and burned fragments of paper from the fireplace, then unplugged the Computator and hauled it all away.

"I'll ask once more," Kaspar said, with a yank of her dad's hair.

Phoebe clenched her jaw.

Think.

No one was going to come to their rescue. She had to find a way to help them escape.

Phoebe looked around the room, searching for a weapon or a distraction of any kind. Perhaps she could throw one of those burning logs in Kaspar's rotten face or light the rug on fire with it or something. No, they would grab her before she even got close. Maybe there was something in her sniping pockets that could help. She tried to focus. What did she have? Firecrackers? No, she used the last one a week ago. There was a packet of itching powder. It would keep her captor busy for a little while, but she didn't have enough to use on all of them.

"Where is the rest?" Kaspar asked, his voice unwavering. "Tell me, or I will break her fingers."

The Watchman holding Phoebe snatched her hand in one white-gloved fist and spread her fingers wide.

She couldn't think straight. Her father turned to her, his darkened eyes suddenly drained of hope. His expression seared her heart.

Everything was *not* going to be okay.

Her dad croaked, "Behind the mirror."

The Watchman held her fast while another crossed to the six-foot mirror framed with etched iron and lifted it. She flinched as he hurled it to the ground. A cascade of shards splashed across the floor, and a wave of mirrored glass slid to her feet. She caught a glimpse of her broken reflection in the twinkling daggers, the image of her own shocked face broken into a thousand shattered pieces.

Embedded in the wall was a black iron safe.

"The combination is—" began her father, but Kaspar wasn't listening. He seized the handle, and with slow and deliberate effort, he peeled the front of the safe off of its hinges. The metal twisted in his gloved hands like wet paper. There was a series of loud pops as the steel bolts of the lock snapped.

This isn't happening.

Kaspar took his time, enjoying the horrific screech of the shearing metal. He hefted the door, which was several inches thick, then tossed it aside to grab the documents within.

"Now we go," said Kaspar in a maddeningly calm voice. "Mr. Goodwin awaits." A sick gray grin cut across his face as he leaned in close. "And he knows *everything*."

The Watchmen dragged them through the dark manor and out the front door. She kicked and writhed, but her captor's grip didn't yield in the slightest.

"Phoebe!" her dad called back to her.

Two stretched Auto-mobiles were parked in front of the house, their engines softly purring. They were identical to the one she had seen that morning, glossy black with a stripe of bronze. Watchmen sat placidly in each driver's seat. Dr. Plumm was hurled into one vehicle, Phoebe into the other. Two Watchmen climbed into the backseat on either side of her, and Kaspar leaned his head through the window.

"Take her to the pen," he said. "Wait for further instruction."

Her flickering fear congealed into something more definitive—a cold and sickening dread. Her throat constricted, and she couldn't breathe. It was as if the Watchman were choking her all over again. Reality finally sank in.

There was no escape.

The two Autos rolled down the driveway, leaving Plumm Estate shrouded in silence behind them.

Then the bushes rustled.

Micah stumbled out from the shrubs, scratching furiously after sitting still for so long. He had been wandering out front, trying to dodge his chores, when the Autos pulled up. As soon as those creeps in the hats appeared, Micah hid.

But he hadn't been expecting this.

What should he do? Going to the cops was a waste of time. And sure, it would take a while for those two Autos to wind down the switchbacks of Shimmering Crest, but not that long. The Doc needed help *now*.

Micah raced around to the servants' quarters at the back of the estate and peered through the window of the Tanner cottage. There was Ma, passed out on the couch with a half-drained bottle of cherry wine in her hand, snoring like a wildebeest. Fat lotta good she'd be.

Should he go find Randy? By the time his brother got through popping his zits, slicking back his hair, and putting his stupid cadet uniform on, the Doc would be long gone.

Micah ran to his work shed and flung open the doors.

A lopsided smile spread across his face.

He snatched his jacket off the hook and slipped it on. It was a souvenir replica of a real-life MIM pilot's jacket. When this was all over, and the Televiewer news crews came to talk to him about his daring rescue of Dr. Jules Plumm, Micah wanted to look the part.

A thrill rippled through him, and his mind started to race. He was going to be famous. He was going to be a hero. They'd probably let him into cadet school early just for the publicity!

Of course, what he was about to do would put him in a whole new category of trouble, earning him a kind of punishment that hadn't even been invented yet. It was stupider than anything he had ever done in his entire life.

Micah tore away the tarp.

For safety reasons, the drive motors on Cable Bikes came installed with a limiter bolt that capped their speed. No good if he wanted to catch those Autos. Micah ripped off the bolt with a wrench and slid the tool into his back pocket.

This bad boy was the Doc's only hope.

Just like Maddox. No guts, no glory.

CRASH
COURSE

Micah jogged alongside the Bike, leading it out of Plumm Estate. The hair on his arms rose as he listened to the muted whir of its segmented platinum wheels. The kidnappers were probably still zigzagging down the hill. If Micah could just get to the Link-Way hub around the corner, he'd be able spot them from the air. Piece of cake.

He tried to mount the Cable Bike, but his leg wasn't long enough to swing over. It took him a few tries, and he repeatedly cursed his size. Finally, he had to lean the Bike against a tree to climb aboard.

Once he was settled, Micah cranked the starter gear on the handgrip, and the Bike growled to life. He gunned the throttle, thrilling to every rumbling vibration. It was like having an electric panther on a chain. Micah had practically memorized the entire manual for the Bike, but in his excitement it still took him a minute to figure out how to pop the clutch and put it in gear.

The machine blasted forward like a rocket. He flailed for the handlebars and clung tight. This thing was way too fast. Way too dangerous. Way too perfect.

Micah squealed as the Bike shot down Shimmering Crest. He had to stand to reach both the handlebars and the footholds, and the wheels wobbled as he struggled to keep control. The Link-Way hub around the corner was lit up with a bright blue spotlight, and it was vacant. He pulled into the mounting niche, then he hit the release button and pushed the handlebars into their upright "flight" position.

With a hiss of perfectly balanced hydraulics, the back runner boards slid out, swung overhead, and snapped together to form the swoop of the cable arm. The two halves of the torpedo-shaped winch head joined around the ascension line that led to the Link-Way high above. The street wheels retracted into the frame with a soft purr, and the Cable Bike hung there, suspended just off the ground.

Micah strapped himself into the harness. His finger quivered above the silver switch that would engage the Bike.

Then he hit it.

With a jolt, the ground dropped away, and the Bike

screamed up the ascension line and onto one of the many parallel cable lanes. Before he knew it, Micah was whipping past caution signs sixty feet above the ground.

It was like being strapped to a missile. The air felt sharp and wild as it whistled through his nose and mouth. He looked down at the winking night-lights of the city and the sparkling bay on the horizon. It was everything he had dreamed it would be. He had never felt anything like it.

Micah whooped in exhilaration.

There was a cluster of Bikers ahead of him, puttering along on the right. Micah waited for the next crossover, the links between cables that allowed riders to switch lanes. He leaned his weight to steer left, his Bike slid over, and he whizzed past the slowpokes. No sweat!

Micah glanced down to see if he could locate the bronze-striped Auto-mobiles, but he was going too fast to see anything. Just as he squeezed the brake, they came into focus. The Autos were in close formation, about to merge into downtown traffic.

He pumped his fist in a victory salute but quickly grabbed the handlebars when the Bike began to wobble.

The Link-Way junction leading to downtown was dead ahead. He hit the turn too fast, and the winch head let out a grinding squeal. The Bike fishtailed violently under the taut, twanging cable. The world around him spun and shuddered, and for an instant, Micah was sure he was going to fall.

But when he released his sweaty hand from the shifter, the Bike steadied, and the blinding smear that was Albright City sprang back to normal. He noticed that the winch head was climbing in pitch, like a violin string being tightened.

Maybe yanking off that limiter bolt wasn't such a swell idea after all.

He risked a glance back at the road—the Autos were gone!

The steel canyon maze of Albright City closed in. Bikers raced above and below him, a chaotic horde speeding in every direction. Their headlamps tore streaks across his eyes. No way he could search the streets below for the Autos and keep an eye on the crazy cable traffic at the same time. He blasted past skyscrapers, his reflection flashing back at him from lofty office windows. Micah was eye level with massive statues of golden eagles and dancing maidens mounted atop the mirror-polished buildings. It would have been wicked if he weren't dead numb with panic.

He released the brake, and his Cable Bike accelerated like it had a mind of its own—a psycho mind that clearly wanted to kill him. Apparently, that limiter bolt he had removed also kept the Bike from constantly speeding up on its own. Must have skipped that page in the manual. This meant that he had to keep one hand squeezing the brake. Which was bad.

Micah spotted them, the two Autos dodging in and out of traffic below. He felt a charge and released his grip on the brake. The Bike roared. Not gonna lose them again.

He had already worked out what was going on with the kidnappers. These were spies from Greinadoren (or another one of those sneaky little countries), and they were going to hold Dr. Plumm ransom until he gave up some kind of vital Foundry secret. Now Micah would swoop down, free the Doc, and pound a few spy noggins in the process.

The Cable Bike was accelerating so fiercely that every turn of the handlebars threatened to throw him off balance. He squeezed the brake again and was met with a shriek and a hot blast of acrid smoke. Must have burned through half the brake pad by now.

Glancing down, he watched as the Autos turned onto the suspension bridge that led to Foundry Central. That was weird. Why would those spies drive up to the Foundry's front gates? It didn't make a lick of sense. Unless . . .

Micah's insides churned. What was supposed to be the best night of his life was starting to look an awful lot like a suicide mission.

Had the Doc been kidnapped by the Foundry?

He searched desperately for the junction across the bridge, but hundreds of Bikers were merging and breaking away, darting this way and that, following patterns he couldn't decipher. A big sign pointing toward the Foundry loomed out of the darkness. Micah cranked the handlebars, but there were too many riders cutting him off from the exit.

He was going to miss the stupid bridge!

Wedged between two Watchmen, Phoebe wriggled forward to get a glimpse of where they were taking her, but it was hard to see anything out of the Auto's narrow window slits. With her initial terror receding, she felt anger rising up in its place. It was time for a new tactic.

Phoebe hitched her breath, working up a convincing sob.

"P-please," she whimpered, "I'm scared. I want my daddy."
They didn't so much as glance at her.

"I—I feel sick. And I have to go to the potty."

Nothing. Their faces remained fixed straight ahead, eyes hidden behind those irritating black spectacles.

The Auto-mobile slowed. Traffic. Phoebe perked up—this was her chance.

When it stopped, she leaped across the Watchman to her right and forced the door open. For an instant, she could taste the pungent air of Foundry Bay and hear the bleat of horns. The choppy shudder of Aero-copter blades thundered overhead. She was swinging her leg outside when the Watchman yanked her back in and slammed the door. Phoebe glared at her captors, huffing and heaving.

A curious alarm went off in her mind. At first she thought it must be a trick of the stifling silence in the Auto, but staring at the Watchmen, she became convinced. Phoebe was the only one breathing.

Their broad chests were as unmoving as their expressions. She felt ill. None of this made sense.

A tiny movement grabbed her attention, a flicker deep within the ear canal of the Watchman on her right. She leaned toward him, and a sickly chill ran down her spine.

Something was writhing inside the Watchman's ear.

No time to think. Micah growled and gunned the throttle, rocketing past the other Bikes. He jetted across six lanes toward the exit, only to find his path blocked by construction barricades. Micah slammed the handlebars to the right and whipped around a corkscrew turn. His dinner climbed up his throat, and he wrestled it back down.

Another barrier popped up, and he flung himself to the left, evading a collision by inches. His head was spinning. He wiped the sweat from his eyes just in time to see an approaching junction. The Bike swerved onto an adjoining lane, and the winch head chattered in a spray of sparks. Ahead, the cable he was on dropped at a steep angle and disappeared.

Micah clamped his eyes closed in terror.

Then, with a sudden jolt, he was level again. He braved a look. Six empty cable lanes lay before him. Misty wind snapped at his face. The gargantuan rays of the Crest of Dawn shone ahead. He was above the bridge. The Foundry was in front of him, and the kidnappers' striped Autos were below.

He had done it!

Searchlights swept over the dark bay to his right. A dozen Aero-copters swarmed a black ship. Military boats were converging upon it, lighting the tide with huge lamps.

Micah squinted at lights in his eyes. More Aero-copters up ahead.

Wait, those ain't spotlights.

His heart stopped. Somehow, he had gotten on the wrong lane and was heading directly into oncoming traffic!

He howled a bloodcurdling scream and crushed the brake. Sparks exploded from the winch head like fireworks, followed by a flash and a deafening pop. The brake went limp. The engine lurched forward, out of control. Now there was no way to stop accelerating.

Horns blared. A blinding white wall of death raced at Micah, and he hurled his Bike to the left as the first oncoming rider blurred past. Then to the right, then back again. He shrieked, but the wailing engine and his ever-increasing speed whipped the sound away.

Micah lunged left to avoid the next, but the rider went left as well. He went right, and so did the oncoming Bike. Wildly, he feinted left, then zoomed right, barely steering clear.

One wrong move and he was dead meat.

He spotted a new lane, a red maintenance cable off to the right. Regaining some control of his swerving Bike, he dodged back quickly to avoid another head-on crash and snaked around two more riders. He made a mad dash for the red cable, forcing the handlebars with every last ounce of strength.

Micah rushed onto the maintenance line, and a shower of sparks burst overhead. His Cable Bike convulsed violently, then dropped a few inches as a new whine mingled with the screech of the gears. Something hot spun off and whistled past his ear. He looked up—the winch head was on fire.

This was not at all like his plan. Micah regretted the whole thing: spying in the bushes, stealing the Bike, all of it.

But it was too late now.

The sunbeams of the Crest of Dawn towered above like a glinting guillotine, and the island of Foundry Central yawned before him, waiting to swallow him whole. A quick look down to the street, and he saw one of the striped Autos pull into a security zone. The other one headed for a maintenance area, near where his red cable angled down to an abrupt stop.

End of the line.

He was dropping like a firebomb. Micah looked for a way off the Bike that wouldn't end with his funeral. The maintenance area sat in the shadow of one of the Crest's massive columns. There were empty service vehicles parked beside a row of flowering oak trees. Not a very good option, but what choice was there? Micah fixed his eye on a tree close to the end of the red cable and unclipped his harness. It was now or never.

The ground was an undifferentiated blur below him, and the flames of the ruined winch head licked at his ears. He swung his leg over the seat and prepared to pounce. The cable sang overhead, ripping through the disintegrating mechanism. The universe was filled with a thunderous roar. The earth rushed up to meet him.

Micah leaped.

He seemed to hang in the air forever, suspended. He could even hear how quiet and pleasant the night was, now that the flaming Bike was falling away.

Then he smashed into the treetop.

He fell like a pinball, ricocheting from limb to limb, reaching for anything to slow his fall. Branches raked his chest. Leaves filled his mouth. The world turned over and over, but he managed to wrap his arms around a limb and tumble the last eight feet to land in a heap.

A breathtaking explosion.

An angry fireball lit up the maintenance area. He felt a rushing blast of heat. Through the delirium, Micah chuckled and sang in his head.

Happy birthday, dear Phoebe . . .

In the smoke, Micah saw that two service vehicles were blazing as well. Not bad for a blind shot with a flaming Bike.

Armed security guards raced toward the explosion, shouldering their weapons and shouting orders while Foundry workers gathered in confusion. A hundred yards away, the bronze-striped Auto began to descend into the ground as if on an elevator.

Micah had to act fast.

He was bruised, scraped, and struggling to breathe, but as far as he could tell, he wasn't dead. So he picked himself up and staggered through the trees, around the back of the enormous column. From the rear of the massive structure, he spied the Auto and made a break for it.

The imposing fortress of Foundry Central loomed. He prayed the guards would be too preoccupied to notice him. If not, he wondered which would come first, the sound of gunfire or the punch of the bullet?

Lining the ground beside a towering security wall were several dozen black iron disks, like giant manholes. The Auto was parked on one, and as it sank below the surface, the petals of an iron iris contracted to seal up the hole.

Micah spurred himself on, faster and faster.

The opening was only a few feet across.
He was almost there.
Now three. Now two.
He dove.

YOU ARE BEING
WATCHED

Her father was gone.

Phoebe was alone, a prisoner in the Foundry.

Sodium lamps blared overhead as the bronze-striped Auto drove through a dull concrete parking structure. She could see hundreds of identical Autos lined up in neat rows or stacked atop one another like the shoes in her Carousel. The driver pulled into a narrow berth, and three of the Watchmen climbed out. They hauled her father's files from the trunk, then vanished down a long, shadowy corridor. The last Watchman grabbed Phoebe's wrist and half-dragged her through the concrete lot, passing pillar after massive pillar until she was nauseous from the monotony.

She wanted to collapse, to give in and surrender to despair, but she knew the Watchman would just pick her up and carry her. The thought of him, or *it*, grabbing her, holding her close, was the only thing that kept Phoebe going.

Ahead, she could see a steep stairwell descending into darkness. This must be "the pen" that Kaspar had mentioned. What was waiting for her down there? Were they going to lock her up? Or kill her?

Enough moping.

Phoebe could handle a single Watchman—she had already managed to escape one that day, after all. But what was her strategy? She slowed her pace and looked around. If only she could slip away, she could hide in any number of shadowy niches, and then . . . what?

She needed a distraction. Shoelaces. A primitive trick, but she had sniped Charlie Towers last summer by tying his laces to an Insta-mow. He didn't notice a thing until the automated grass trimmer turned on and hauled him across the athletic fields, kicking and screaming.

They were almost at the stairs. Phoebe could see a low ceiling and a dense nest of pipes. A boiler room. Not a place she wanted to experience.

"Ouch!" she yelped and stumbled. The Watchman tried to catch her, but she tore away from his grasp and sprawled on the ground, whimpering as if she had hurt herself. Phoebe angled her body to block the Watchman's view while she reached for his shoes.

They were gleaming, seamless black metal. No laces.

Her hope drained away.

"Hey, Whiskers!"

Her captor drew up sharply and turned toward the voice.

Something smashed the Watchman and sent him reeling over Phoebe, who was still on her hands and knees. The Watchman toppled over her back, turning a full rotation in the air before crashing down the stairwell with a sound like a trash bin being overturned. She sprang to her feet.

Disheveled and peppered by oak leaves, clumps of white paint still gumming up his hair, Micah flashed a cockeyed grin. He was so out of place here that it took her a second to recognize him.

"Run!" he shouted, and bolted away.

Phoebe stood rooted to the spot. Then she saw a white-gloved hand reaching from the darkness, clawing up the stairs. Her senses cleared in a snap. She chased after Micah.

They darted and dodged through rows of Autos, clambering over waxed hoods and leaving smears on windshields.

Click-clack-click-clack. She glanced back.

The Watchman was gaining on them, weaving through obstacles in single-minded pursuit. His bowler hat had fallen off, and his right cheek was smashed, so half of his curled mustache dangled limply. Instead of blood, dents puckered his face, revealing the glint of metal. There were no eyes behind his shattered spectacles, only black optical sensors.

The kids dashed down the nearest passageway, through a thick steel door, and slammed it shut. Micah barely had time to lock the bolt before their pursuer collided against the other side. There was a flurry of jarring blows as the Watchman pounded on the heavy door, which rattled against its hinges. Micah flattened himself against it as if his meager weight could hold it in place.

And then, abruptly, the assault stopped. There was a long moment of silence followed by the sound of the Watchman's metal shoes clacking away.

Phoebe huffed for breath and looked around, trying to figure out her next move. They were at the bottom of an unmarked stairwell lit by buzzing fluorescent tubes. Nowhere to go but up.

"Didja see that?" Micah yammered. "That was a freakin' robot!" He thought about it for a moment, rubbing the shoulder he had used to ram the Watchman. His eyes lit up "Wicked!"

"You . . . I—I can't believe . . . that you—" Phoebe gasped.

"Yup, I know. I'm pretty amazin'. You never seen anything so incredible in your life, and you don't know how to thank me."

"Just what do you think you're doing here?"

He blinked. Not exactly the reaction he had hoped for. "Uh, savin' your hide, what's it look like?"

"I don't need you," she scoffed.

"Y-you did two minutes ago! You were all on the ground, cryin' and groveling and—"

"I wasn't crying, you pest. I was in the middle of something."

"Ri-i-i-i-i-ight. Beggin' for your life, maybe!"

"I don't have time for this," Phoebe snapped. She bounded up the stairs, two at a time, and left him standing there.

Unbelievable, Micah thought. He had come all this way—risked his neck and—he almost died, like, a thousand times!

"Hey!" he hollered, chasing after her. "I don't give two crusty donkey craps about you, you prep-school priss. I came for the Doc. Just my luck I get Li'l Miss Freaky instead."

"Quiet!" she hissed from the landing above.

"So just point me to where your pa is, and I'll go rescue him and say I couldn't find you."

Her ear was pressed to a black door marked AREA-2B.

"Outta the way," he grumbled, and shoved her back. He threw the door open and strutted through it.

It opened on a hallway with brushed metal walls and elongated triangles of light embedded in the floor and ceiling. A man with a clipboard was walking down the corridor, his back to Micah.

The worker began to turn as he registered the sound of the door, and Phoebe yanked Micah back into the stairwell, clamping her hand over his mouth. She crammed her toe in the door to muffle the sound of it shutting. Micah tried to tear free, but she was stronger than she looked, burying her bony fingers into his fleshy face.

They heard the Foundry worker continue down the hall.

"Whaddya do that for?" he whined, rubbing his raw cheeks.

"Go home, Toiletboy. You're going to get me caught."

"The heckles I am! I didn't risk my life on that Cable Bike for nothin'."

"You don't have a Cable Bike."

"No, but you do." He thought about it. "I mean, *did*."

She narrowed her eyes. "What are you talking about?"

"Oh, right. Surprise! Your pa had one stashed for your birthday," he chuckled. "It was wicked. You shoulda seen it— brand new, top of the line. Totally hot. 'Specially when I blew it into tiny flaming bits."

"You wh—?" Phoebe lowered her voice to a hiss. "You evil little midget turd! No, you did not."

"Oh yeah, it was something. What an explosion! Really wish you coulda been there." He stood as tall as he could and puffed his chest, but she towered over him.

"How dare you! When I tell Daddy, he—"

"Speakin' of him, can we get goin'? I'm on a mission here."

Micah breezed past her and cautiously peered into the hall. Satisfied the coast was clear, he slipped through. Phoebe was speechless. She was outraged, yet had no choice but to follow.

Unlike the shadowy parking structure, this bright corridor offered no place to hide. A dozen shiny steel doors lined both sides of the hall, each with an illuminated keypad and hand scanner. As they turned a corner, Phoebe noticed a placard bolted to the wall: HIGH SECURITY ZONE—YOU ARE BEING WATCHED. She glanced up.

Mounted directly above her head was a whirring brass

Omnicam. The surveillance camera looked like a dandelion, its watchful eye fanned by an array of hinged rods holding dozens of interchangeable lenses and diopters.

She smacked the back of Micah's head, and when he spun to snap at her, she pointed up. His eyes popped open wide. They were in the camera's blind spot, directly beneath its electronic mount. But it was scanning back and forth like a metronome. If they moved either way, it would spot them.

They would have to go back down the stairs and find another route. But what about that Watchman? Surely he had notified the others by now.

Twenty feet away, a door slid open with a hydraulic hiss. Phoebe and Micah heard the muted clatter of machinery from within—the screeching of a metal grinder, the heavy thud of a rivet driver. The kids plastered themselves against the wall and held their breath as two workers in dingy blue uniforms emerged, carrying a thick metal beam between them. They crossed the corridor, and one of the men slid a security pass through an electronic reader. Another door opened, and the men went through.

Phoebe glanced up. The Omnicam was panned away.

She grabbed Micah's collar and ran after the two workers, sneaking in behind them just as the door slid shut.

Now they were in a wide passage made of whitewashed cinder block and lit with caged bulbs. Thick metal columns lined both sides of the hall, and layer upon layer of black footprints coated the floor. Phoebe waited until the workers with the beam disappeared inside another door, and then she slipped past them to hurry down the passage. But curiosity got the better of Micah, and he stood on his tiptoes to peer after the workers through a glass porthole.

"What are you doing?" she snapped.

"Just wanna see what they're makin'," he muttered.

She grabbed his sleeve and yanked him aside.

"Is your brain as stunted as your legs?" she spat. She watched with some satisfaction as his face flared bright red. "If you get caught, you're dead. Which works for me, actually. So on second thought, have at it."

Phoebe trotted down the hall and didn't look back as Micah caught up with her.

"You're really pushin' it, you know that?" he warned. "Don't you touch me again."

She just rolled her eyes and kept moving, ducking under the bright portholes. The thrum of machinery vibrated from behind every door, regular and percussive. The Foundry never slept. Its generators and assembly lines churned day and night. A couple of times, the kids had to hide behind the columns to wait for workers to pass. She tried not to think about how many thousands more were on the other side of these doors.

Phoebe leaned against the wall, gasping uncontrollably.

"You gotta be kiddin' me," Micah chided. "You wanna take a nap or somethin'?"

She was too winded to talk back. He gave her a dismissive wave and moseyed over to a water dispenser to take a drink.

"Come on, ya li'l baby. Get the lead out!" Micah said, and ran ahead with a new, obnoxious spring in his step. Phoebe nervously looked for signs of Foundry workers, then chugged some water and splashed a bit on her face.

Down the seemingly endless passageway, the sounds of activity grew muted. The doors became less frequent, most of their windows dark. There was also a salty dampness in the air that grew heavier the farther they went. The bay was close—she could feel it.

"Hey, Freaky, where we goin' anyway?" Micah asked as they approached an intersecting corridor.

"How should I know?" she heaved.

"Do ya even know where we are?"

"Gee, I dunno, Toiletboy. Guess I left my map at home."

"Then how you know we ain't supposed to go that way?"

"You want to go that way, be my guest."

"And here I thought you knew somethin' about this pl—"

"Hey! STOP!"

Phoebe and Micah nearly jumped out of their skins.

Around the corner of the intersection, three workers had just emerged from a factory door. One of them slapped a red button on the wall.

An earsplitting alarm shrieked. The kids ran.

There was nowhere to go and nothing to go on but adrenaline. They turned a corner and raced down another hallway. It had to lead somewhere. But there were no signs, and everything looked the same.

And then she heard it.

Click-clack-click-clack-click-clack. Metal shoes on concrete. Watchmen.

The sound was close, up ahead. Phoebe and Micah stopped dead in their tracks. The pace of the metal shoes quickened. It was hard to gauge how many, since the clatter sounded like a swarm of metal wasps. She turned back, preferring her odds against the human workers.

But the sound of metal soles approached from that way, too.

There was a door ten feet ahead. It was their only chance. Together they yanked it open and stumbled into a cavernous black chamber. They slammed the door and tried to lock it, but there was no bolt. Their eyes hadn't adjusted, yet judging by the echo of the alarm, they could tell it was a massive space. Daggers of moonlight shone through skylights hundreds of feet overhead, carving out the edges of machinery and nests of dangling chains. The floor of this vast hangar was lined with countless tall, indistinct shapes.

The kids scuttled behind one of the shadowy forms just as the door crashed open behind them. Watchmen stood silhouetted in the doorway. Slowly they entered, the click-clack of their shoes like the countdown on a time bomb. The door slammed shut.

Click-clack. Click-clack. The footsteps were spreading out.

Phoebe tugged at Micah's sleeve and pointed to a grate set high in the wall. In the pale moonlight that spilled through, they could barely make out the shape of an emergency ladder.

He started to scurry toward it, but she hesitated and strained her eyes against the gloom, trying to make sense of the murky shapes all around them.

And then the terrible truth struck her.

They were hiding in a sea of Watchmen.

BELLY OF
THE BEAST

The squadron of Watchmen stood in military formation, surrounding Phoebe and Micah on all sides. They were sleek chrome skeletons in various states of assembly, streamlined forms of contoured plate and precision circuitry. Every joint and angle was a marvel, a menacing promise of power and speed. Even though some were missing limbs or had open panels in their chilling, expressionless faces, the Watchmen seemed hungry to deploy.

This was an army.

Micah stammered and started to back away, but Phoebe stopped him. The Watchman were as motionless as statues.

But through the shrieking alarm, the metal shoes of their pursuers circled. The kids crawled through the inanimate battalion, doing their best to remain hidden. Hundreds of Watchmen stared down, as if at any second a mechanical hand might shoot out and grab them.

The overhead lights blared to life.

Phoebe and Micah stumbled back, exposed, and the gang of bowler-hatted Watchmen rushed at them. The pair made a mad dash for the emergency ladder bolted against the wall.

The Foundry agents closed in fast.

Micah scrambled up first, with Phoebe just behind. A gloved hand snatched her ankle and yanked hard. She almost lost her grip but got free with a sharp kick. The Watchmen climbed after them, moving in perfect sync.

At the top of the ladder, a narrow ledge led to the window. Micah reached it first, and with all his strength he yanked off the metal grate.

"Heads up!" he shouted.

Phoebe instinctively twisted out of the way, but the Watchman below her didn't. The grate bashed his shoulder and sent him spiraling off. The others continued to climb after the intruders, unfazed.

She whipped the tube of machine oil from her hidden skirt pocket, wrenched its cap off with her teeth, and squeezed the grease onto the ladder below. A Watchman grabbed the oily rung, and for a second it looked like her ploy had failed. But his hand slipped. He tumbled down, knocking four other Watchmen off, and they all crashed to the ground in a jumble.

As Phoebe hauled herself up the ladder, she could hear the sound of rushing water and taste the bitter, salty sea. The sensation made her tremble, and she fought to gain control. Just a few rungs to go.

"This way!" Micah urged from the top, framed by the night sky with the brisk wind whipping at his hair. He ducked through the open porthole and disappeared outside. Her stomach churned as she inched to the opening.

It was a sheer drop cloaked by dense, rippling fog. A fat drainage pipe connected to the next building, like an angled bridge, and Micah was grappling his way up it. He looked back.

"Come on!" he cried.

But Phoebe was a shivering, white ghost. A gap had opened in the mist, like the parting eyelid of some ancient leviathan, to reveal the roiling waters of Foundry Bay. The world faded, leaving her in mental blackness.

"What are you waitin' for, Freaky?" she heard him shout, but his words were as foggy as the air.

She clung to the porthole to keep from tumbling through it, only half aware of searchlights slashing through the mist. Her eyes were locked on the violent deluge below. The crash of the raging ocean mixed with the nearly human scream of the alarm siren.

Phoebe retreated inside.

"Are you crazy!?" Micah shrieked. He slid down the pipe and reached through the open window toward her. "C'mon!"

"I—I can't."

"Don't be an idiot. They're gonna get us if you—"

Something hit the corrugated wall beside his head with a clang. Embedded in the metal were two prongs attached to thin coiling wires that crackled with arcs of electricity. The lines extended down the ladder to a Watchman, who retracted the prongs into his fingers with a snap.

The Foundry agents had begun to hook their elbows and knees through the greased rungs of the ladder, one on top of the other, creating scaffolding for the others to climb. Another Watchman aimed his fingers at them, and they ducked as the shock prongs sizzled past their heads.

The Watchmen were almost here. They were done for.

Then Micah did something she would have never expected.

It seemed to happen in slow motion. She felt the whoosh of him rushing past and saw him plummet into the hangar below. But he didn't fall. Instead, he grabbed a hoisting chain in mid-air and swung over to an elevated conveyor belt, legs flailing. He hurled the chain back to Phoebe, who was so stunned she almost didn't grab it. She clung tight and swung after him, trying not to think about the painful strain in her arms.

Micah grabbed the chain to steady it while she shimmied down, and then he tied it off so the Watchmen couldn't follow.

"You're welcome," he jabbed at her.

There was a brilliant spray of sparks as a flurry of crackling shock prongs studded the pipe by their heads.

They raced up the zigzagging network of conveyor belts crammed with disembodied mechanical limbs and heads. Forty feet below, the Watchmen scurried around, some trying to find a way up while others jockeyed for a clear line of fire.

The kids kicked metal arms and legs off the assembly line, hoping to disrupt their pursuers with a rain of debris.

Then, without warning, the conveyor belt jolted, tossing Phoebe and Micah flat on their faces. Before they could stand, the speeding runway dumped them down a chute and to the level below. The Watchmen had started the assembly line to whisk the intruders back down to the ground.

They charged against the belt like hamsters in a wheel, but it was too fast. Despite their best efforts, they were creeping backward. Micah jumped up to grab the lip of an air duct that ran alongside the platform and hung on for dear life.

"Get in!" he ordered.

She crawled up his back, pushed the vent open, and wriggled inside the narrow metal tube.

"Owww!" he cried as Phoebe planted a shoe in his face for leverage. Once inside, she reached down and grasped his arm. It was a struggle—he was heavy, and his hands were sweaty and gross. But Micah got enough purchase to pull himself in.

"There," she said, wiping his sweat off her hands. "Now we're even."

"Even, my butt! You almost got us killed."

She ignored him and shuffled quickly through the air duct. It was barely wide enough for them to fit on their hands and knees, and she hoped it was too narrow for the Watchmen.

"You coulda told me you're scared of heights," he said.

"I'm not."

"So what was *that* all about, then? We coulda gotten out on that pipe."

"I didn't want to go that way."

"Look, if you got any other nutty hang-ups, I gotta know," he said. "I can't be savin' you from every little thing."

Phoebe clenched her jaw and focused on navigating the maze of air ducts for some kind of way out. Feeling keenly aware of Micah's judgment, she chose a new direction without hesitation whenever it branched off.

After a while, she heard a faint voice, and though she couldn't make out the words, Phoebe recognized it all the same. It reminded her of a cello, warm and resonant. There was unquestioned power in it—the voice of a man who was used to being obeyed. She crawled faster, homing in on the sound. Light shone through a vent ahead, and she approached cautiously to peek down.

There was a long chamber of burnished white gold hung with dark purple drapery. It glowed with fragmented light cast by enormous pyramid chandeliers. Her eyes rested on a heavy-set man with owl tufts of white hair. He was clad in a topcoat made of extravagant platinum-threaded Durall with billowing tails that made him look like a big shimmery locust.

Mr. Goodwin. Her father's boss.

An entourage of Watchmen flanked Goodwin as he talked to a nervous man in a pin-striped suit decorated with medals and golden epaulets.

"Yes sir, a Code Orange lockdown," the officer stammered. "But I need your authorization."

"All sectors?" Goodwin asked, inspecting his nails.

"Yes, sir. We have seized the unauthorized vessel in the

bay. Just another group of immigrant defectors seeking refuge. No indication of sabotage, but of course we—"

"And the explosion?"

"A Cable Bike accident, sir."

Goodwin looked up and stared at the officer.

"The Foundry does not have *accidents*, Strauss."

"Th-the security breach is being resolved as we speak. Our attention was focused primarily on the ship and—"

"You will proceed with the lockdown," Goodwin commanded, "and seal the tunnel once I am through."

There was a chime, as one of a series of hidden elevator doors slid open. Goodwin and his corps of Watchmen entered.

"Find the intruders. No excuses."

The door slid shut before Strauss could respond. He bustled away, and then the room was quiet.

Phoebe poked her head out to look around. Satisfied it was safe, she eased out of the duct and lowered herself to the ground using one of the purple draperies. Micah flopped down beside her, and they rushed to the elevators. She hit the button to call a second car while they watched the glowing display to see where Goodwin was going.

"Who was that fatso?" Micah whispered, glancing over his shoulder.

"That's Goodwin. He's the one. They were taking my dad right to him," she replied, an anxious thrill in her voice. "We have to follow him."

There was a rumble from the air duct. Something moving fast, growing louder. Could the Watchmen fit in that tiny space after all? She bit her lip as the elevator lights counted down past zero and started to display letters and symbols.

"We have to get out of here!" he said.

They were closing in.

"Not until we know where Goodwin's going," she insisted.

The duct was bowing with the weight of whatever was inside. They could see it warp and bulge. It was almost here. The second elevator chimed, and in a flash, Micah pulled her up against the wall and out of sight.

He was right, she admitted. They had no idea who might be in the elevator. She was getting too excited, too careless.

The doors slid apart, and thankfully, it was vacant. She took a last look at Goodwin's elevator—it had stopped at "M." They dashed into the empty car, caught their breath, and hit the same button.

They heard a nearby door crash open.

The kids flattened themselves against the inside of the elevator, out of sight. As the doors closed, ever so slowly, she watched the reflection in the foggy gold elevator wall. A dozen soldiers flooded in and surrounded the rumbling ducts, readying the spinning turrets of their rifles.

The elevator descended, and they both exhaled.

"Close one. Who is this Goodwin anyway?" Micah asked.

"Head of the Foundry."

He stared blankly. "You mean, like, he's—"

"The head. Of the Foundry."

Phoebe was exhausted, and by the looks of it, the twerp was as well. Or maybe that was fear sucking the blood out of his chubby face. So far, they had gotten away by the skin of their teeth. But their luck wouldn't last forever.

After a few moments, the elevator changed direction and sped up. Phoebe and Micah took an unconscious step closer to each other as they rocketed sideways. When it slowed to a stop, the kids plastered themselves against the inside panel walls and waited. The doors opened.

She didn't know what she was expecting—another hallway, maybe a different kind of warehouse or some sort of basement. But not this.

A sprawling underground train yard bustled beneath the Foundry.

The pair gazed up at an epic locomotive that was at least four stories tall and mighty enough to haul the Uniton Tower off its foundation. This titan of a train was sleek and sharp, a silver spear mounted on massive rails that ran into a black tunnel a thousand yards away. Three figures ascended a carpeted gangplank and boarded the train. Goodwin was in the lead, followed by Kaspar dragging a limp figure. Her father.

Phoebe's mind detonated.

She and Micah darted from the elevator to hide behind a giant crate. This depot was unfathomable, so enormous that it seemed impossible they were still inside the Foundry. The ceiling towered far overhead and was filled with a latticework of catwalks and suspended equipment. Hundreds of laborers and Watchmen were at work, sparks flying from rows of war machines being assembled in an earsplitting cacophony.

Micah was like a kid in a candy store.

"No WAY!" Micah jabbered, his eyes goggling. "Those are F-20 Bloodtalons! Wha—?! That's a Gyrojet modded with subterranean Blackout rounds and—custom new Lightforce 7200 rapid repeater guns! Those puppies can fire six thousand rounds a minute. Oh man, Randy's gonna be so jealous!"

"Don't you get it?" Phoebe hissed in his ear.

"Yeah," he said with a blissed-out grin. "I died and gone to heaven."

"No. We shouldn't be here."

Suddenly, the angry howl of the locomotive's horn erupted. It shattered what was left of her nerves. She waited for three Mini-lifts hauling chemical tanks to pass by, and when the coast was clear, she ran. Phoebe wove between rows of crates and pallets, using the shipping barriers to remain concealed. Micah was by her side as she crawled over the edge of the platform and dropped down behind the train.

With an electric zap and a tremulous thunk, the train's engine engaged, its wheels locking on the tracks. She scampered beneath the nearest freight car and scanned the network of machinery for some sort of perch. Micah caught on to what she was doing and pointed to an open spot in the chassis. Together, they climbed into the gap and out of sight.

Another blast from the horn, and then the train started to move. The oversized wheels squealed and rotated sluggishly. The gears and shafts churned inches from their heads. A railroad tie crept past below them, then another, and another. She shifted her hold on the struts. This wasn't a good spot, but maybe she could adjust once they were at a safe distance.

They gained momentum. The clack of wheels on rails was starting to accelerate. Gravel and ties began to blur. They were on their way, headed for the looming black tunnel.

The vibrations of the locomotive made it hard to hang on. Phoebe wished she was stronger, wished she hadn't skipped all those years of gym. The faster they went, the more her arms trembled from the strain, but she couldn't get a better grip without falling. There was nowhere safe to climb. The twirling shafts and pinions pressed in, so close she could feel their hot wind hit her face. One wrong move, and they would crush her for sure.

Micah wasn't faring any better. His teeth were gritted and every muscle was tensed. He shook his head and shouted something, but the screaming gears stole his words.

Blackness swallowed the world as the train plunged into the tunnel.

Phoebe fell.

The wind was crushed from her lungs. She hit the ground so hard that she bounced and rolled, turning over and over, she didn't know how many times—ground to ceiling, ground to ceiling before settling to a stop. Up ahead, Micah lost his grip as well and collapsed to the gravel.

The howl of the train faded to a phantom echo, and then was gone.

She lay on the tracks, her body charged with pain. It didn't feel like anything was broken, but she wasn't sure. She had never broken a bone before. Phoebe could feel a gathering tidal wave of despair, an angry ocean swell ready to break. Her mind was a seething void. After all she had been through to get here, after all this . . .

She had failed.

Her life felt meaningless.

She was never going to see her father again.

The ground beneath them trembled with a new sound. It was the harsh and grating squeal of metal on metal. The petals of an iron iris gate were emerging from the edges of the tunnel behind them.

Micah was on his feet in a flash.

Follow.

Did Micah say that?

"I said come on! Now!" he shouted as he yanked her to her feet and ran.

Follow.

There it was again. A voice—distant, but not at all far away. It was as if something in the darkness was summoning her, daring her to carry on.

"Freaky!" Micah hollered from the tunnel entrance. She could get out of the tunnel if she ran—the rotating blades of the iris door were still wide enough. "D'you hit your head in that fall? We gotta go back, this way, before it shuts! We gotta leave, NOW!"

Follow.

Phoebe turned her back to Micah and stepped into the abyss. Instantly, her stormy thoughts parted, and her mind was clear. Without a word, she marched. There was no turning back. If the train was going a thousand miles, she would go a thousand miles. There was nothing important behind her. The only thing that mattered was straight ahead.

"You ARE insane!" he screamed. "I ain't goin' in there!"

But she just kept on walking, her footsteps echoing eerily in this gargantuan tunnel with the light dying a quick death behind her.

Then, a heart-stopping clang.

The tunnel was sealed.

THE COLD
DARK

s Phoebe marched into the oppressive blackness, the echoes of her footsteps seemed to ask unwelcome questions. How far did this tunnel go? Where did it lead? What if these tracks ran for miles and miles under the ocean, with nothing in between?

She had to keep moving. If she slowed down, she might start to think about what she was doing.

"I said *STOP!*" Micah's shout split the air like a rifle shot.

Of all the people in the entire world to be stuck with in this pitch-black tunnel, Micah Tanner would have been her absolute last choice.

"Nice goin', Freaky!" he snarled from behind. "We're gonna die down here because of you. If a train don't come along and splatter us, then we'll shrivel up from no water or starve to death. Or get eaten by a giant frickin' cave slug."

Phoebe hadn't considered that something nasty could be down here, but she refused to give him the reaction he wanted.

"You don't listen to nobody, do ya?" he continued. "Did it ever occur to you that gettin' us killed might not be the best way to help your pa? 'Course not, 'cause you're a stubborn, spoiled loony!"

She ignored his tirade, trying to focus instead on her feet. Each step was bringing her closer to her father. Micah raced around her in the dark to block her path. He was so close that she could feel the heat pouring off of him.

"You don't deserve a dad that cool. Ain't he had a hard enough time without you bein' all bat-crap crazy? It's bad enough that his wife up and croaked, but now you— "

She lashed out at the sound of his voice. *SLAP!* Her hand found his cheek and cracked it hard, sending him sprawling to the ground.

"Don't you *dare!*"

Her voice sizzled with rage. She couldn't make him out in the darkness, but her hand throbbed from the impact. Phoebe hungered to hit him again but fought back the urge.

"I don't want you here," she snapped. "So don't blame me for your idiot idea to come in the first place."

She heard him adjust in the gravel.

"But like it or not, you're here. So you're going to work."

"'Scuse me?"

She bridled her wild anger, and her voice became more measured. "My father needs help, and you work for him. I am his daughter, so until I find him, you work for me. You do what I say, when I say it."

"Or what?" Micah's voice was hard to read in the darkness. Was he baiting her, or had she actually managed to subdue the twerp?

She spoke calmly, letting every cold syllable sink like lead into that thick head of his. "Or I will have your family fired and tossed out on the street and see to it that none of you ever works in Albright City again. Got it, Toiletboy?"

He was quiet for a long time. Finally, he hauled himself to his feet and approached her slowly. "Try and hit me again, and I swear I won't hold back 'cause you're a Plumm. Or 'cause you're a girl."

Unlike most of what Micah said, Phoebe believed his words now.

"I'm going to find my father," she retorted. "So are you going to do your job or what?"

"Whatever, Freaky."

"That's Miss Plumm to you."

"Pffft! Right, that'll be the day."

She heard him shuffle ahead, deeper into the tunnel.

"Fine," she sighed, catching up with a few loping strides. "You don't have to call me Miss, but you're not allowed to call me 'Freaky' anymore. Or loony, insane, crazy, nutty, or anything like that. That's rule number one."

"What rule?"

"If I'm going to do this . . . with you, then I have to establish rules."

"Fine. Then no more 'Toiletboy' either. That's rule two."

"You don't make the rules. But I'll consider your request." Phoebe thought that sounded reasonable. If she was going to be in charge, she wanted to be at least *somewhat* reasonable. "Do you have any matches?"

"Why?"

"Why do you think?"

She considered the contents of her skirt pockets, but there was nothing that could give them light. Then she remembered her Trinka, still clasped around her wrist. She fumbled in the dark to find its tiny button. Her toy radiated a pulsing crimson glow, a feeble light to guide the way.

"Oh," Micah responded, looking at their newly illuminated surroundings. "That."

The Trinka's tentacles began to twirl, and the toy fluttered out of her hands. Phoebe lashed it back to her wrist and tied its little arms in a knot. The Trinka didn't provide much light, but it was enough to keep them from twisting their ankles on the gigantic railroad ties.

"Wait, you had that thing with you this whole time? You only just now—"

"Rule number two," she interrupted, marching past him. "You may speak only when you have something helpful to contribute. Otherwise, keep your mouth shut."

"I'll show you rules, you stuck-up little . . ." he muttered.

They marched in silence. Phoebe was just beginning to think that she might be able to tolerate this new obedient Micah, when he began to whistle. It was like he'd been born to irritate her. She was about to establish another rule when she recognized the tune. Soon, he was kicking the gravel in time, and he began to sing:

> *"Meridian cast off all her bonds*
> *When Creighton Albright forged the bronze.*
> *With ball of lead and sword of steel*
> *We'll crush our foes beneath our heel.*
> *So praise the gold, the brass, and chrome*
> *Of Meridian, our mighty home!"*

It was "Our Shining Hearts," a song they taught every kid in grade school. Phoebe remembered singing it in the annual Alloy Day parade with her second-grade class. As Micah repeated the chorus, she recalled her parents' beaming faces in the crowd as she marched past, singing the praises of Meridian. How proud they had been of her.

He sang it again and again, and despite him being totally off-key, she didn't get sick of it. Soon, they were hiking in rhythm, which made the walk a little less tiresome. His singing eventually faded away, and they marched in silent sync.

"Why did you come here, really?" Phoebe asked.

"Oh, to serve you, Madame," Micah said with a bow.

"I'm serious."

"Duh. I wanna save the Doc, just like you."

"But why?"

He looked down at the fake badges on his MIM jacket and imagined his face plastered on every Televiewer across Meridian. The fame, the glory, maybe a little reward money— that's why he had come. He had never heard of a national hero being forced to polish banisters or scrub bathroom tiles.

"I just wanted to, is all," Micah replied.

Phoebe shivered as the tunnel grew cold. She tried to rub the chill out of her exposed arms, to no avail.

"Can I borrow your jacket, please?"

"Say what?" he asked in disbelief.

"Your jacket. I'm cold."

"You gotta be kiddin'!"

"I'm trying to ask nicely. All I have is a skirt and short sleeves. Can't you just be a gentleman for once in your life?"

"I'll pass," he chuckled.

"I can make this rule number three."

Micah stopped in his tracks to confront Phoebe, who had her hands planted on her hips. He shook his head in disbelief.

"You're somethin' else, I swear," he protested as he ripped off his prized MIM jacket and threw it at her. "Happy now?"

"Yes. Thank you," she said distinctly, as if trying to teach manners to a child. She slipped her slender arms into the leather sleeves and zipped it up. The jacket smelled like dirty boy, but it was better than freezing.

They resumed their march, Phoebe leading with her

glowing Trinka and Micah stomping hard, pouting. How long had they been walking—one hour, maybe two? Her feet were killing her, and she could barely feel her legs. All she wanted to do was curl up and go to sleep. What time was it anyway? Her stomach rumbled. She hadn't eaten since lunch, and her throat was parched. Phoebe thought about telling him to stop so they could take a break, but she knew he would just make fun of her again for being such a weakling.

As she listened to their footsteps, a strange realization struck her.

"That's weird," she said. "I think we're going down."

The slope started so gradually that she hadn't noticed it at first. But now every stone they kicked scuttled away and rolled downhill in a miniature landslide.

"Great," Micah huffed. "A bottomless pit."

Then, in the weak crimson haze of her Trinka, Phoebe thought she saw something in the shadows ahead. Her heart skipped a beat. The light began to fade, so she quickly hit the button again to keep her toy going. There was a faint shape in the gloom. Something with two spindly arms. Or antennae?

"Get down!" Micah whispered. The panic in his voice was unnerving. They lowered to a crouch.

"What is it?"

"Don't . . . make . . . a sound."

Phoebe's skin had gone clammy. His warning about killer cave slugs oozed back into her mind. They huddled there in silence for a long time, ears peeled for any movement.

Then she felt something crawling up her arm.

"BLAHH!" Micah shouted as he snatched her wrist and throttled it, the red Trinka light flashing like a fire alarm.

She screamed.

"Gotcha!" he said with snide laugh. "That's for hittin' me."

Phoebe growled and reared back to smack him again, but before she could, Micah trotted boldly up to the mysterious shape. Among the wreckage and scattered debris was what she had mistaken for a cave slug. It was a toppled machine, abandoned beside the tracks, like a ramshackle seesaw on wheels.

"Ha-ha, you're such a scaredy-cat! It's just an old pump cart," he said. "Railroaders use it to get around on the tracks. Too bad this one's junk."

She crossed her arms over her chest. "Fix it."

"Just like that, huh? You think it's that easy?"

"You tell me. You're the grease monkey."

"I'm tellin' you it ain't! You think they'd dump it here if it was any good?"

"Well, we have no idea how far we still have to go, right?"

"Yeah, but—"

"And this thing has wheels, right?"

"Duh! But—"

"Then quit being such a whiner." She untied the Trinka from her wrist and forced it into his hands. "And fix it."

Micah was trying to bubble up a nasty insult—she could see it in his eyes. Instead, he bit his tongue, snatched the light, and hunched over to inspect the pump cart. The machine was tipped on its side, a platform mounted on a row of metal wheels. Set in the middle was a seesaw with a red handle on either end. When he pumped the handle, it jangled free from its housing. He studied the contraption and sucked his teeth.

"So?" Phoebe asked.

Micah shot her an annoyed look, then hawked up some phlegm and spit into his hands. She wrinkled her nose. He slipped the wrench out of his back pocket and ducked out of sight. Phoebe could hear the cart squeak and rattle as he tampered with the broken mechanism.

It took a few minutes before he reappeared, covered in a new layer of grease. He gave his wrench a showy twirl.

"A couple of slipped joining rods, is all."

"That wasn't so hard, was it?" she needled. "So, it works?"

"It might, if you shut up and gimme a hand." He got behind the device and leaned against it, pushing with his feet. She grabbed hold and helped shimmy the thing toward the track. Once it was in place, he jumped up and hung from the edge of the cart, using his weight to pull it down. There was a groan of metal, and then a loud crack as the cart settled onto one of the massive rails.

"Good work," Phoebe said with a halfway smile. She climbed onto the pump cart. "Now turn it on."

Micah clambered aboard and shoved down hard on the red handle. The cart lurched forward a few feet, nearly throwing her overboard. She clung to the handle for balance.

"When I push down, you pull up," he chuckled. "Then you push, and I pull. Got it?"

She arched an eyebrow. "You want me . . . to what?"

"Oh, so sorry, Your Majesty," twittered Micah with a flamboyant air. "You're gonna have to lift a finger for the first time in your spoiled little life. I do hope you don't scuff a nail!" He strapped the Trinka to the front of the cart for a headlight.

Phoebe knew he was right and hated him for it. She pushed hard on the handle to prove to him that she could do it, but the resistance was so stiff that her lanky legs flailed in the air as she tried to force the thing down. He just laughed at her again, and they were off.

Within minutes, beads of sweat dotted her brow. She was glad to give her legs a rest, but now her arms ached. Micah, of course, was doing his best to make it look easy. But as their momentum built, she found it took less effort to work the pump. The handle rose and fell of its own accord and only needed a little extra pressure to keep it going.

She stared ahead, trying to find any indication that they were nearing the end. There was none. Phoebe hadn't the faintest idea how long it had been since they chased the train into the darkness. What if the other end of the tunnel was sealed as well? Would they be trapped here forever? What if Micah was right and this really was a bottomless pit?

Her arms were buzzing with the effort and there was a fierce ache in her back. They didn't speak. The only sound was the clatter of the wheels and the squeak of the handle.

On they rode. For hour . . .

     . . . after hour . . .

        . . . after hour.

And then, without warning, the light went out. The Trinka's glow didn't fade away like it normally did—it just snuffed out like a candle.

"Hit the button again," she insisted.

"I'm hittin' it," he called over the clatter of the tracks. "It's on, I feel it tickin', but there's no light."

Phoebe was about to tell Micah to stop messing around when she felt the strangest sensation. A sudden wave of cold overtook her, but it wasn't just some gust of air or an absence of heat. It had a presence, a weight. And it was alive. The air was dense with it, thicker and harder to pass through. She tried to breathe, but it felt as if an iron band was constricting her chest. Even the cart seemed to slow down.

Then it was gone. The Trinka light flared to life, and they gasped for air.

"What was that?" she said frantically.

"I dunno," he sputtered as he worked the handle. "And I don't care. I just wanna get as far away from it as possible."

Phoebe couldn't agree more. They urged their cart on, hefting and heaving the red handle. The burning sensation seeped back into their muscles, melting away the chill, and for once she welcomed it.

"*Meridian cast off all her bonds,*" she sang eagerly, and Micah joined her in the tune. Their voices reverberated like a talisman warding off the cold dark. She wasn't sure how much longer she could hold out. Pretty soon, Phoebe was going to have to rest, and she loathed the thought of confessing it.

She stopped the song mid-note.

"Look!" squealed Phoebe, her eyes opening wide.

"Keep pumping, Plumm! I ain't gonna do all the work!"

"No, behind you! *Light!*"

10

METAL

veryone that met Olivia Plumm instantly fell in love. She was as ravishing as she was silly, and so magnetic that she drew people in wherever she went. Phoebe's mother was also brilliant, with more degrees to her name than her father, which was a source of playful competition between them. She taught

Phoebe that the universe had begun as a single speck, and that everything we know, everything that is or will ever be, was contained in that one tiny, insignificant pinprick.

Much later, Phoebe would imagine the glimmer of light at the end of the tunnel like that, exactly as her mother said. It was a spark that would soon grow to a blaze. It was the beginning of everything.

They abandoned their pump cart. The kids had no idea what awaited them up ahead, but the squeak and rattle of the contraption was certain to draw attention. Phoebe removed her Trinka from the head of the cart and fastened it around her wrist as they continued on foot.

First came the sound—the thrum of machines, the growl of heavy equipment, and the chatter of countless metal-soled shoes. Then, the smell overtook them. It was subtle at first, but soon the scent developed into a peculiar rusty tang, a pungent mixture of smoky spice and iron.

It was her father's scent, Phoebe realized with a start. Or rather, what he smelled like without his aftershave.

The tunnel's end was just ahead, and after so many hours of darkness, the light was blinding. They shielded their eyes and scuttled into a narrow niche near the exit.

Outside the tunnel was another train yard, so vast it made the one beneath the Foundry look like a mere pit stop in comparison. It had the turmoil of rush hour in Albright City, with cranes reaching as high as skyscrapers and leagues of workers and Watchmen bustling everywhere. Train tracks extended through a dense plaza, then split into dozens of parallel lines. Transloaders hauled shipping containers onto behemoth locomotives, their electric engines breathing like giants. Powerful floodlights illuminated a grid of buildings that sprawled as far as the eye could see, forming avenues and intersections of bustling productivity. There were even several Aero-copter pads and a runway for Galejets.

Far in the distance, a massive security wall enclosed the perimeter. It was protected by watchtowers and turrets armed with what Micah eagerly identified as Frag-cannons. Lining the top of the wall was a row of mysterious coils that pulsed with an intense purple glow. Phoebe studied them for a moment, wondering what they could possibly be.

Without a word of warning, Micah sprang from their hiding spot. She could do nothing but stare as he zigzagged between trucks and cargo containers like a soldier under fire. He ducked underneath a tarp that was stretched over some shipping crates about twenty yards away. The fabric fluttered once, then was still, concealing him completely.

Her fists clenched so tight that her hands cramped. What did he think he was doing? He was going to ruin everything.

She sidled closer to the tunnel entrance and tensed her legs, preparing to spring into action. But there were too many workers. Every time she was about to go for it, another one came around the corner, hauling a dolly of steel crates or driving a Multi-chain conveyor.

Phoebe went for it anyway.

But she slipped. A strap loosened, and her right shoe fell off. She regained her balance and turned around to grab it, but the shadow of an approaching worker snaked across her path.

She dove for cover beneath the tarp and slammed up next to Micah, ignoring his look of outrage. Through a slit, they could just make out the figure—a Watchman worker in a blue Foundry jumpsuit and hard hat, his death mask of a face placid. He set down the steel box he was carrying and picked up the shoe.

Phoebe closed her eyes. She wanted to cry, but that was not an option. Micah nudged her, and she looked back as the Watchman departed, her shoe in his hand.

"Nice goin'!" he spat. "Might as well scream out your name and address and do a big ol' cartwheel while you're at it."

"This is all your fault!"

"Me? Am I the one who can't keep my stinkin' shoes on?"

"No, you're the one running out like an imbecile."

"Hey, I'm lookin' for the Doc. What are *you* doin'?"

"Quiet!" she urged. "I'm trying to think of a plan."

"Maybe first you should *try* to not get caught, and maybe—"

"Okay, rule number three. No more idiotic leaping into danger. You follow me from now on. Got it?"

"You wanna know what I think of your . . ." The words died in his mouth.

They heard footsteps right beside them and could make out the shapes of two human workers through the tarp.

"Look, I'm already pushing six K here," one of them said. "I can't handle any more."

"Just following orders," replied the other. "I need you to take this unit."

"But it's headed all the way out to Station four eighty-six. Can't you just wait for the next train?"

"I told you, Mr. Goodwin took my last Cargoliner to the Citadel. You got an issue, take it up with him."

Phoebe and Micah exchanged a look. The Citadel? If that's where Goodwin was headed, it was a good bet her father was there, too. They watched through the fabric as one of the figures grumbled to himself and entered something into a bleeping device.

"Guess we're taking this one, too!" he called out as he stomped off.

Before the kids could figure out their next move, the pallet jostled and rose off the ground. The kids clung to the crates to keep from spilling out. There was a series of hard lurches, and the buzz of hydraulics.

Then they plunged, once again, into total darkness.

A familiar chugging sound ratcheted, followed by a pronounced thunk, and the deep vibration of an engine. Phoebe and Micah had been loaded onto the back of a cargo truck.

The vehicle crunched into gear and rolled forward.

"Oh no, no, no," she whispered.

The truck was picking up speed. The muffled murmur of the train station was punctuated by a harsh rattle every time they hit a bump. There were a couple of sharp turns that sent the kids knocking into each other, and then the vehicle slowed to a stop.

"Prob'ly security," Micah mumbled, his ear pressed up to the wall. The truck began to move, then stopped once more. They sat longer this time. Phoebe felt sick with anxiety, certain that the cargo door would slide up at any moment, and they would be discovered.

She closed her eyes and tried to think. Nothing made sense. Ever since she had spied that Watchman from her bedroom window, she had nothing but questions. Obviously they were machines, but not like any invention she had ever heard of. They took verbal commands. They could respond to unexpected events, plan, and strategize. And like the one that took her shoe, she could swear they were actually thinking.

Why did the Foundry keep them hidden? They would sell like crazy. Who wouldn't want a robot servant of their own? Yet the Watchmen were so secret that her father was shocked to find out they were in the city at all.

At last, the truck started to drive again, rattling as it moved along. So far, so good. Phoebe glanced at Micah—she wanted to talk to him, but he was only ten, too little and too dense for real conversation. But maybe not entirely without his uses.

"Sounds like we're in the clear," he said, pulling his ear away from the truck wall. "Gimme that light."

"No," she replied. "It'll draw too much attention."

"We're in the back of a truck, Freaky. The driver—"

"What did I tell you about the name calling?"

"Whatever! Plumm then, okay? The driver can't see nothin', no one can. And I wanna know where we're goin'."

He was right. Again. She activated the Trinka on her wrist, and its little light guided her as she slipped out from under the tarp. Sure enough, they were in a big Foundry truck, one with a segmented cargo hold like the ones she used to thrill to see parked in front of her favorite shops. They squeezed between the crates and made their way to the rear.

The ridged metal floor was cold on Phoebe's shoeless foot.

"Shine it here," he said, pointing to a round hub in the floor at the base of the gate. She provided light while he crammed his fingers in the panel and manually unhooked the latch. With a tug of the hoisting chain, they raised the back gate a couple of feet and got on their bellies to look outside.

It was night, the hazy bright lights and glowing purple coils of the train yard fading on the horizon. All around them, the ground was hard and dead, pocked with clumps of ragged trees. In the distance, she saw a range of craggy mounds dominated by an enormous mesa with an odd, slanted top. There was a shimmering streak of silver running toward it.

The train tracks. And the truck was veering away.

"Wait, no!" Phoebe cried. Those rails were all she had to go on. "We have to jump."

Spindly trees grew dense around them as the truck drove up a steep grade. The road was bumpy, causing some of the hefty crates to shift and forcing the driver to slow down.

"After you," Micah said with a sneer. "Rule number three, remember?"

There was no time to argue. She crawled under the back gate and immediately felt a warm breeze waft through her hair. Phoebe lowered herself to the back bumper and clung there, unsure of how best to drop. Reluctantly she let go, falling hip and shoulder first. She hit the unyielding ground with a shock of pain, tumbled several times, and then came to a stop.

Better than the fall from the train, but it still added a few nasty bruises to her growing collection.

She heard Micah roll to a stop next to her, and they lay there unmoving, staring up at angular treetops that swayed beneath the night sky. The rough sound of the Foundry truck faded, drowned out by the forest. There were unfamiliar animal calls and a symphonic chorus of ghostly, tinkling chimes. A rich scent clung to their nostrils, acrid but not harsh, more moist and earthy.

They were exhausted. The kids had been on the run for hours, and yet judging by the host of twinkling stars above, it was still the dead of night.

"Do you know the constellations?" Phoebe croaked, her throat parched.

"Why?"

"To figure out where we are, genius."

"Don't they teach you that stuff in that snooty school of yours?"

"Would I ask you if they did?" she shot back. "You're the

hick boy. Don't you know all about outdoorsy stuff?"

"I know you're s'posed to bring a compass and a Celestron with you wherever you go, but I didn't exactly pack for a camping trip." Micah got up to dust himself off and mused aloud. "Let's see here, I know the tail of the Big Dipper points north. Or was that the Li'l Dipper?"

"Micah?" she breathed faintly, staring up.

The sky was all wrong.

The stars didn't twinkle—they vibrated, as if attached to a plucked piano wire. And some of them were moving. Not in arrow-straight streaks, but up and sideways, tracing intricate shapes across the night. There was no moon, but when the kids rubbed their eyes, they noticed fine silvery strands stretching between the stars, all connected like shining beads woven into a web by some unfathomable celestial spider.

This was not their sky.

If there had been anything in Phoebe's growling stomach, she would have thrown up.

"What is this place?"

Her question hung heavily in the air. Micah was speechless. With shaking hands, she held out her Trinka.

They were next to a rugged road at the sparse edge of a forest. The trees here were thin with odd angular branches and shiny bark that reminded her of birch covered in a sleeve of ice. Deeper in the forest, a low and nearly imperceptible tone rumbled their innards like the moan of an ill-tuned pipe organ. A breeze hushed through the woods, causing the fine leaves to flutter. Then came that tinkling sonata again.

Wind chimes. But there were none in sight.

A strange notion was rising to a boil in Phoebe's mind. She approached a stand of ferns, wincing as the sharp ground poked at her right foot through her bare sock. She reached out and touched a leaf.

Weakness washed over her. She was going to pass out.

"It can't be," she breathed, tracing the veins of the leaf with her finger. "It's impossible."

"This ain't real. This ain't really happening," Micah consoled himself.

"The plant . . ." she said, but words wouldn't come.

"What about it? It's just a —"

She flicked the leaf. It rang out like a cymbal.

Metal.

Micah's brow furrowed. But she was already moving to another plant, touching it in disbelief. "All of them!" she said with a mix of fear and wonder. She knocked on a tree branch, and it rang with a resonant hollow sound. There were individual boughs, branches, and twigs of bark covered tube, all different sizes and thicknesses. It was like bamboo made out of flaking steel. They were jointed at severe angles, and as Phoebe followed them with her light, she realized that all of the trees were interconnected.

It was like this entire forest had been built by a mad plumber. No matter how much she tried to comprehend it, the truth dangled just beyond her grasp.

Micah had picked up a metal twig and was rapping it sharply on whatever he could find. Everything from pebble to branch, root to leaf, it all rang with a different metallic sound. He giggled to himself.

"Micah," she called. Had he lost his mind?

He got down on all fours and plucked something from a cluster of leaves.

"Ha-ha! Nuts!" he snickered, and held out his hand. In his palm were six or seven hexagonal nuts, the same kind used on machines, but these were clumpy and tarnished, nestled in a silver pod. "Someone made it look like they was growing on that bush," he said giddily. "This is wicked! Almost looks like a real forest."

"What do you mean?" Her voice was hushed.

"This is just some Foundry thing," he scoffed. "That tunnel, the weird sky, this metal forest. It's all fake. This is probably Goodwin's private island, or somethin'. You know, like that story about the king who wanted everything made of gold?"

"I don't think that . . ." she trailed off. There was movement in the dark. A shadow in the forest had come to life.

"Sure it is!" he said with forced confidence. "Means we must be close. Goodwin's prob'ly got the Doc stashed away in some sorta mansion near here. Yeah, that's it!" Micah tried to convince himself. "Why don't we—"

They didn't even get a chance to struggle.

Phoebe sucked in a lungful of air to scream, but cold cable wrapped around her tightly, binding her hands and feet.

Then, before they knew what was happening, their stomachs dropped. Wind gushed past, and the ground shrank below. It felt like she was falling up, tearing through the treetops at a dizzying speed.

BUSINESS
AS USUAL

The throne room was hacked from tarnished gold and streaked with rust-red veins. Barbed columns and gnarled buttresses wove together like gilded serpents and formed a twisted ceiling overhead. Hundreds of roosts protruded from the rough-hewn walls, where flying courtiers had perched long ago, each niche sculpted to look like the sun. In the middle of the chamber stood a headless statue eighty feet high, posed in fierce triumph, its luster dulled with age. Dozens of wings sprouted from the back of the monstrous effigy, layered in feathers splayed like saw-blade sunbeams.

This grim palace had lain dormant for epochs, a reminder

of a more brutal time. Which was why the Foundry now used it for their headquarters.

The murky golden throne room was the center of operations, pulsing with the urgent activity of nearly a hundred personnel. It was outfitted with humming electric generators that ran banks of Computators and surveillance equipment. Workers and coordinators bustled about while dozens of black-suited Watchmen stood silently, poised to execute orders at a moment's notice.

Mr. Goodwin stared at a map projecting up from an illuminated table, his fluffy white brows furrowed. Three military executives gathered around the Chairman, clad in steel-trimmed suits ornamented with shining badges, medals, and stripes that signified rank.

"Meridian needs us," insisted one of the executives, locking his arms across his chest. "We can't let that Lavaraud clown put our national security in jeopardy."

"This is much more than rhetoric," another added. "The Trels are itching for a fight."

"Especially if these reports of the Quorum's rearmament are true," said a third.

"So let's give President Saltern what he wants and show Trelaine we mean business," the first said, pointing to the map. "We can divert resources from here, our stations along the Inro Coast. If we give the order now, reinforcements will reach Meridian within thirty-six hours."

A warbling chime interrupted their conversation.

"Pardon me, gentlemen," Goodwin said as he stepped

away from his advisers to address a conical brass intercom on his desk. "Yes?"

"Mr. Goodwin, I have Captain Strauss reporting," answered a tinny voice.

"Yes," he sighed and leafed through a stack of papers. The intercom emitted a series of clicks, and another distorted voice came through.

"Strauss here, sir."

"You are calling to tell me that you have the Plumm girl in custody."

"Um, no, sir. We're close, though. We have been reviewing the security footage. I just patched it through to you. It appears that she and the boy entered the Depot at approximately—"

"You let them cross over?" Goodwin interrupted.

"I . . ." Strauss trailed off. "Yes, sir. I take full responsibility."

The Chairman was silent. His crystal blue eyes glowed with the reflection of a nearby Computator screen as he watched the grainy images of Phoebe running from the tunnel and losing her shoe.

"Sir? Sir, I am rectifying the situation as we speak," Strauss said hastily. "They escaped on cargo truck number CR-0228. We have located the vehicle, and triangulated their potential location to a thirty-mile radius. My team is—"

Goodwin hung up on Strauss. He clicked a button on the intercom and spoke into it once again. "Get me Associate Captain Elias."

The Chairman watched the footage again.

"Elias here," came a different voice.

"Congratulations. You are our new Security Captain, First Class."

"Thank you, sir."

"Take charge of Strauss's team. Blanket the area in question. Detain the trespassers."

"Yes, sir. It will be done."

Goodwin clicked the intercom off.

"Strauss is a fool," muttered a flat voice.

Goodwin glanced over to a fabric divider, a white hospital partition concealing the silhouette of a man. "Was," the Chairman said as he approached the screen. "No matter, his mistakes will soon be corrected."

"Were it me, there would be no mistakes."

"Of course." Goodwin smiled warmly. "But I have only one of you. The Dyad Project is still in its infancy." He watched a group of scientists evaluate readouts from a bay of chirping monitors and check the diodes and leads attached to their subject. "How is he doing?"

One of the researchers checked the display. "Stable." The man shrugged. "Perfect, really."

"Perfect." The Chairman nodded. "Did you hear that?"

The scientists unplugged their probes and retracted their cables. Goodwin watched the white divider as the man's silhouette rose to its full height. Attendants flocked around it, strapping on a flak jacket and carefully securing long gloves.

Kaspar emerged, flexing and curling his fingers.

"Perfect," the soldier agreed, devouring the praise and bowing low.

"So what of Jules?" Goodwin asked. "Anything to report?"

"Nothing yet."

"He is unlikely to cooperate, but I believe with time we can convince him to give us what we need."

"I can be very convincing," Kaspar assured him ominously.

"Remember," warned Goodwin, "Jules is a friend and a valuable asset, so this is still a hands-off directive."

"Yes, sir."

"Good man." Goodwin chuckled and clapped the soldier's rippling shoulder. Kaspar's face tightened into a sparse grin, and he bowed as the Chairman returned to his advisers at the control center.

"It's decided," one of the military executives proclaimed. "If we cut back on our exports by twelve percent for the next two weeks, we can meet Meridian's military needs."

"We are ready to make the adjustments."

"Call off the lockdown," Goodwin commanded. "Return our security status to Code Yellow and resume production."

The trio of military executives stared at him blankly.

"What about the intruders?"

"And the reallocation? Meridian is vulnerable so long as—"

"The Foundry will not remain off-line for a couple of children." The Chairman waved his hand. "They will be caught. As for the troops, we will not accommodate Meridian's request."

The advisers began to talk at once, their voices rising in an irritated crescendo that quieted the moment Goodwin spoke.

"I have heard your concerns, and of course, Meridian's security is always our top priority. But what you fail to consider is that an escalation of forces combined with a decrease in output will be interpreted as an act of war by the Quorum. Would you really provoke Trelaine when they are already seeking confrontation?"

The military executives were listening.

"Not unless you want blood, and I for one do not," he continued. "Every minute the Foundry remains on lockdown, we lose money. It has been nearly four hours now, and we must make up for these losses. I expect all sectors to double resource acquisition and distribution by the end of the week."

"That's preposterous!" one the advisers claimed.

"Mr. Goodwin, you're being unreasonable."

"On the contrary," Goodwin argued coolly. "It is pure reason. Our enemies are organizing, gentlemen. And we know their demands all too well. More Foundry products, more Foundry metal."

"So we're just going to buckle and give the enemy what they want?"

"We are going to compromise and meet their needs before we find ourselves at a hostile negotiating table," he corrected, "or engaged in another protracted war. And we will charge accordingly. Then, once Lavaraud calms down and Trelaine gets what they want? Once the Quorum is sated?"

The Chairman clasped his hands behind his back and

turned to look up at the massive golden statue with sunbeam wings that dominated the control room. The menacing figure would have returned his gaze, Goodwin mused, had he not so carelessly lost his head.

"Business as usual."

ON THE LINE

P hoebe was bound tightly and dangling beneath her captor as they hurtled through the black pipe-work forest. Whatever carried her was frightfully agile, effortlessly zipping this way and that. It swooped and swerved to avoid impaling her on the branches, but she was still bombarded by jangling twigs and foil leaves that left red welts on her skin.

Shiny haphazard vines grew more prevalent as they ascended, knotted in loose clumps like exploded balls of yarn. The interconnected treetops grew so dense that they blotted out the night sky, and the wind whipping through the hollow branches sounded like a haunted chorus.

She was whisked around a massive, knotted trunk, and little columns of flame flickered into view, torches illuminating a village in the trees. Dozens of bulbous woven huts hung from the pipe-work boughs like oversized wasps' nests, linked together by a chaotic network of silvery vines. The night was thick with noises, like a fleet of squeaky wheels in desperate need of grease. There were figures too, hundreds of lithe shapes swinging and tumbling toward her.

Whatever held Phoebe dropped her. Her stomach lurched as the world turned over, but she didn't fall far. She landed on a springy surface, and Micah thudded beside her. They struggled to roll over and sit up, but the gags in their mouths kept them from talking.

A dull clang rang out, and a perforated cylinder jutting from silvery petals began to smolder. It grew bright, then burst into flames. These were not torches—they were fiery blossoms attached to metal stalks.

The kids froze. In the light of the torch blooms, hundreds of oily, eager eyes leered back at them.

They were surrounded by a mob of strange deadly machines that were almost as tall as Phoebe. They had long limber arms, stout hind legs, and two small appendages tucked in at their midsections. Their bodies were a rippling complex of intersecting segments and plates, perfectly camouflaged in this pipe-work forest. Mounted in the center of their chests were cylindrical spools of fine cable.

Slick black eyes glowered deep beneath jutting brows. Long faces stretched into pointed snouts like the muzzles of baboons, and pleated vents flared out around their nostrils. Flat, saberlike appendages arched back from their heads, twitching and swiveling like the ears of a jackal.

She had never seen anything like them. Not in her wildest imagination. And yet, there was something familiar about them, though she was too racked with fear and wonder to pinpoint exactly what. The feeling haunted her, like a dream.

A series of clangs sounded out as their captors struck the torch blooms, and a dozen flaming lights flared to life. Phoebe and Micah could see that they were on a small, suspended platform made from metal branches that were woven together with cables. She peered down through its loose mesh and saw only darkness below. A wave of vertigo hit her as she realized they were up so high in these treetops that the light did not show a hint of ground.

The squealing sound, which now mixed with scraping and chittering, grew in intensity. It was coming from the surrounding machines. There was ferocity in their gaze, a vitality that the dead-eyed Watchmen lacked. They had no consistency to their size or shape—some appeared large and broad, some slight and frail. She saw tiny ones staring innocently and hanging from others like infants clutching their mothers.

Mothers? That made no sense. Why would the Foundry make machines that looked like babies?

She swallowed hard and looked at these things anew. They were all decorated differently, with bundles of metal fronds, headpieces made of braided cable, colorful strips that looked like feathers, and wires beaded with trinkets. Many had scars and dents, and there were even some with damaged or missing limbs. The vents around their nostrils exhaled jets of hot air that condensed to white mist in the brisk night.

Impossible.

They weren't machines. Or at least nothing made by the Foundry. Unlike the Watchmen, these things were *breathing*. And as their staccato squeaking and grinding filled the air, she realized something else.

They were speaking. Not a language she could understand, but Phoebe was sure she was right. It was a harsh, grating sound, like sand crunching through gears, but there was a definite pattern. The noises rose and fell with meaningful enunciation, sometimes marked by simultaneous tones at different pitches. She watched as a group of the metal creatures exchanged heated, emphatic bursts of dissonance—a conversation, or more like an argument.

One of them wrenched open its terrible maw and shattered the night with an earsplitting mechanical shriek. It then lunged at the kids, coming so close that they could smell its foul breath, a hot wave of rust and rot. Rows of interlocking teeth and six-inch jagged metal fangs flashed in the torchlight. Inside the creature's mouth were throbbing veins and flexing membranes that shone like metal but pulsed like living flesh. Pistons around its muzzle strained as its slathering jaws opened wide, preparing to crush flesh and bone.

Phoebe and Micah recoiled.

A deep, quaking *thoom* interrupted the confusion, and the snarling beast halted. The gathered creatures fell silent. Then the crowd parted to reveal one of their ranks, a huge loping thing pounding on a colossal hollow tree trunk. Silvery bark flaked off like confetti, and chime leaves clashed with each blow. The creature rose on its back legs, a full nine feet tall, and its ear appendages splayed out like a halo of scimitars. It emitted a series of forceful barks. Screeching and rumbling broke out, punctuated by snarls and snapping jaws.

Phoebe looked over at Micah. His eyes registered the terror she felt. Whatever fate was being decided for them, it didn't bode well.

At last, a unanimous agreement appeared to have been reached. The creatures yanked the kids into the air once more, carrying them deeper into the village, followed on all sides by the screeching mob. Phoebe watched with fascination as the long-limbed creatures leaped from cable to cable. Before, she had thought they were flying, but in fact these creatures slid effortlessly along zip lines as if they knew every strand by heart. Their strange clamp hands cinched seamlessly on to the cables, and they sped along with barely a whisper. Occasionally, one of the creatures would unspool a new cable from its chest and launch the line with its spring-loaded secondary limbs, forging a new path through the pipe-work treetops.

Torch blooms glowed throughout the canopy, lighting the way. She saw more bulbous nests and angry mechanical faces staring from oblong windows. A great number of the huts were little more than burned-out shells dangling askew from pockets of bent and splintered trees.

Phoebe and Micah were deposited onto a gnarled tree

limb. The rest of the horde gathered around, perching high in the foliage and leering down at their captives. The creatures snapped the cables that bound the kids, and immediately Micah was on his feet.

"That's it, Ugly! I'm done gettin' tossed around, ya hear? You need to back it off, or so help me, I'll—WAAH!"

A creature shoved him backward with a whip-fast jab. Micah teetered, pinwheeling his arms to keep from toppling into the dark abyss. Phoebe grabbed his overalls and pulled him back to safety.

The crooked limb the kids stood on was one of many massive splinters jutting from the largest pipe-work tree they had seen. A jagged crater had been blown through the rusted giant, and cables had been wound around the craggy wreath of fragments to patch the pulverized trunk. This woven funnel formed a walkway that led up to a hollow at the center. It was a gloomy and ominous den, decorated with grisly totems and dark, viscous splatters.

The growling mob pressed in and gestured toward the dark opening.

"I ain't goin' in there!" Micah fumed.

Phoebe looked at the creatures closing in, some of them baring their jagged, razor-sharp fangs.

"I don't think we have a choice," she said, taking his elbow.

They shuffled along the shattered limb and took a tentative step onto the woven walkway. It was like trying to balance on a wobbly net. A profoundly low tone moaned from below. As it traveled upward and became more pronounced, the kids could feel it buzz through their bodies. A gust of fetid, moist air huffed out of the hollow and blew a discordant note, dispersing a cloud of drifting particles.

Behind them, the mob was growing loud and impatient.

So they climbed. Phoebe went first, grappling up the shaky spiral walkway. Micah followed her, his feet slipping awkwardly through the cable mesh as they scrambled into the wretched hollow. As soon as he had stepped through the opening, he turned back to face the creatures.

"Fine! We'll go in your stupid hole. But I ain't gonna forget this! Micah Eugene Tanner, that's me. Remember that name. 'Cause when I come back—"

A woven steel flap slammed shut.

They were sealed in.

"That's what I thought!" he shouted and shoved at the unyielding door. "You better run, you little yellow-bellied tree turkeys! I OUGHTA—" His voice cracked, skipping up an octave. He cleared his throat and tried to play it cool. "Anyway, I'm pretty sure they know the score."

"Yeah, you totally scared them off," Phoebe said as she lit up her Trinka.

"For real?" he asked. "Or you just tryin' to be funny?"

"No, you pretty much saved the day . . . Eugene."

"Look here, Little Miss Perfect, I don't care what you—"

"Save it." She looked around the slimy passage strewn with cables and jutting scraps of tree. "We need to find a way out of here." But even a cursory glance told her that there was no way to go but onward, deeper down the rank and dreary hollow.

Micah gave the door a couple of swift kicks to blow off his remaining steam. "Well, at least I did somethin'," he grumbled. "I stood up to 'em, least you could do is gimme that much."

"Not like it did any good, but sure, I grant you that."

"Now that's more like it," he huffed, content with her consolation. Micah peered into the darkness and let out an exasperated sigh. "I tell you what, though. I've about had it up to here with creepy, dark tunnels."

"Tell me about it," she agreed.

"And dang, this place stinks!" he said, wafting the air.

She touched the seeping walls of the hollow and smelled the reddish brown goop that smeared on her fingers.

"Egh! It's like rotten sap," she said, wiping the stuff off her hands.

"So . . . about this place," Micah started, biting his lip as he tried to piece together the words. "Like, are we . . . I mean . . . this ain't some weird Foundry thing, is it?"

"I don't think so."

"Metal forest, flamin' flowers, crazy monkey machines that wanna kill us . . . What the heckles is goin' on here, Plumm?"

"I don't know," she said, looking him in the eye, "but we have to find out."

Micah nodded. "I bet your pa knows."

"He probably . . ." She trailed off as something burbled deep within the cave.

"What was—" he began, but the sound grew harsh, a buzzing and hacking like someone trying to saw through a metal beam. Then, all at once, they knew exactly what it was.

Laughter.

His mouth hung open. "That ain't good."

"We gotta move quick and quiet," she said. "Let's find a way down to the ground and get back to those train tracks. Just . . ." She licked her lips, but her mouth was tacky and dry. "Just stay alert."

"You too."

Trying to act bold, she marched ahead, but her shoeless foot sank into a mushy puddle of slop. She cringed, and a chill ran up the back of her neck.

Phoebe really didn't want to know what she had just stepped in.

SPLINTERS OF
THE CHOKARAI

The woven surface beneath their feet was unstable, forcing them to cling to the slimy walls for support. The feeble light from Phoebe's Trinka did little to keep her from stubbing her exposed toes, so she stepped carefully to avoid any jutting metal slivers.

They soon found their path blocked by a membranous curtain stitched together from tattered sheets of translucent foil that might have been some kind of hide. Bracing herself for something lurking behind it, Phoebe whisked the curtain aside. Beyond it was another drape of the same material, and past that another. As they crept through the tunnel of veils, the stench became overwhelming, like boiling blood and burning garbage.

At the end of the seeping passage, their legs turned to jelly.

The opening looked out upon the pipe-work tree's cavernous heart. Every creak and drip was amplified with a tremulous echo. They could feel a steady draft of warm, pungent air wafting up from the depths with a low ambient drone. A cable bridge was strung across the chasm, leading to a nest suspended like a spiderweb in a smokestack. It looked ancient and distressed, a cocoon constructed from fragments of shattered trunk, bound together by tangled cable. Bent branches and shards were lashed around the outside of it, curving to form a dome.

"Not good," Micah mumbled.

Phoebe gulped hard. "Come on," she whispered. "Let's find a way out." She searched around the opening of the hollow, but the inner walls of the tremendous tree were featureless and slick with sap. There was nowhere to climb, up or down. The only way was across.

She steeled herself and took a step onto the narrow bridge, clinging to cables along the sides. Phoebe kept her eyes locked dead ahead, willing herself to not look down into the perilous void, and though it only took her a dozen cautious steps to cross, it seemed to take forever.

The floor of the nest felt sturdier beneath their feet. A fine gray dust coated every surface and hovered in the air, choking the meager clusters of torch blooms. The kids crept along the perimeter, holding their noses to keep from gagging on the stink. Piles of refuse buzzed with clouds of metal insects that looked like tiny fluttering wing nuts. Skins and hides hung from spiny branches, and a collection of what looked to be mummified mechanical creatures were propped up in perverse poses like an audience waiting for the show to begin.

They heard a scuffling sound. Phoebe and Micah looked for the source, their hearts racing, but the echoes were confusing and the shadows impenetrable.

Standing in the center of the nest was a cracked table made from a slab of broken tree. Decorated with an elaborate assortment of decrepit talismans and bowls, it looked part altar and part . . . tea set? Fragile-looking metal cups sat on a frilly foil mat beside polished bric-a-brac as if arranged by a meticulous granny. A boiling pot steamed nearby, a vessel that might have been the petrified head of a mechanical beast.

Confused, Micah reached out to inspect the weird gathering of trinkets.

"NO, BLEEDER! NO TOUCH-UCH!"

The kids jumped. The screeching voice seemed to come from everywhere, but they looked around and saw no one. Then came that scuffling sound once again, this time from directly overhead. A skeletal figure skittered across the top of the nest like an emaciated metal lizard.

They screamed, and it screamed back at them.

"Stick-icky fingers *rahkazess*, NO! No touch-uch!"

The creature swung across zip lines, seizing the cables with knobby clamp hands as he emerged from the shadows.

His head was a grinning human skull, yellowed and cracked with age. A deep fissure ran across the cranium, stained with brown crust that must have been dried blood. A crest of broken rib bones sprouted from the top of the skull, flaring out in a crown.

"Talky *rha'khalor*, bleeder lies-eyes. Come to Mehk. Choking Chokarai, crushing Chokarai, bring all to RUST-UST!"

The creature let out a horrid screech. He pounced.

But instead of the agile landing they expected, he clattered to the ground in an awkward heap, flailing like an overturned tortoise and knocking his skull mask askew. The kids now saw that he was the same as the other tree dwellers that had captured them, only ancient and withered. His body was wrinkled and peeling like scorched foil, and his frail form was a constellation of tattoos and carvings.

"Gah! No-no looky!" he squawked. The creature tried to hide his face —filmy eyes veiled in cataracts, and a bent jaw bearing a few lonely teeth.

"Pfffew, he's just a geezer!" Micah breathed in relief. "Here I was thinkin' we was in serious trouble."

"What do we do?" Phoebe asked.

For a moment, they just watched the wizened thing struggle. He looked so pathetic that Phoebe stepped forward to help him up, but he shrieked and drove her back. He scrambled for his mask and tried to slip it on, but his clamp hands were too arthritic and clumsy, and he kept dropping it.

Phoebe saw wheels inset in his palms, like blackened

pulleys. Again, that familiar feeling needled her, though she could not put her finger on it.

"*Krazomakish nhar-ark*, Dollop. DOLLOP!" he snarled.

A nervous, lopsided creature shuffled out from a dark corner. Though he walked on all fours, the kids could tell right away that this "Dollop" was not like the others. He was about waist-high to Phoebe, hobbling on back legs that were too short, and front limbs far too long. Dollop's body looked cobbled together from different kinds of metal, like a toy model made from several kits. His head was triangular and maybe a bit oversized for his body, and his two huge eyes bulged out at either side, giving him the appearance of a hapless bug.

"H-h-halt, cruel and evil b-bleeders," Dollop stammered in a voice that was much more polite than commanding. "We'll be just one m-m-moment." He hurried over to the ancient one and helped him fasten on his skull mask.

"You speak our language?" Phoebe gasped in relief.

"Why y-y-yes! Your f-f-filthy Bloodword is quite e-easy. But, um, the Ascetic . . ." Dollop motioned to the withered old creature. "H-he pretty much only speaks Rattletrap. He's a little, er, slow in his advanced age."

The elderly creature scrambled back to his feet. "Bleeders," he growled, chattering the mandible of his skull mask. "Angry killing-ing, hacking Chokarai, bones to mash, bloods to eat. WHY kill-ill Chokarai?"

"We didn't kill no one!" Micah protested.

"We're sorry to offend you," Phoebe pleaded, "but who is Chokarai?"

"This!" the Ascetic snapped. "Chokarai *ahz vil'ott*. Chraida praise-aise to Chokarai."

"I don't understand," she said.

But the Ascetic was lost in his train of thought, his words becoming an indecipherable purr as he waved his arms in the air and began to sway and dance slowly in place.

"Sorry. He, um, h-he does that sometimes," Dollop explained as he cooed to the shriveled old creature in quiet, reassuring tones. But the Ascetic broke away from Dollop and leaped onto the altar. He turned his gaze upon the kids and pointed at them with a gnarled finger. His voice bristled with malevolence as he barked harshly.

Dollop cleared his throat with a tinny cough and raised his voice to speak over the Ascetic's guttural pronouncements. "The Ascetic c-condemns you and all bleeders," he translated. "His people, the chraida, c-curse you for killing the Chokarai. That's ummm, that's their name for the fo-fo-forest."

"But we haven't done anything wrong," Phoebe explained.

"Where's he get off, cursin' us?" Micah blustered. "Tell him that ain't fair!"

Dollop hastily relayed the message, and the Ascetic cack-led in response.

"He says F-Foundry doesn't know, um, fair," Dollop squeaked. "He s-says it isn't f-f-fair you bleeders slaughter mehkans and, er, k-kill chraida."

"Hold your horses there, Goggle Eyes!" Micah strode toward Dollop, who took an anxious step back. "We ain't got nothin' to do with the Foundry."

Phoebe held him back. "We didn't hurt anyone," she said.

In a spastic fit, the old chraida wrenched the kids by their collars and yanked them close. They struggled to break free, but he held them fast.

"Chokarai brings-ings bleeders," the Ascetic gurgled wickedly as Phoebe and Micah pulled back from his putrescent breath. "What to do-do-do? Read Splinters, shavings, and slag, Chokarai will choose-ooze your *gro'thsylah-ha-ha*!" The Ascetic burst into a convulsive fit of laughter and shoved them away.

"Uh, he says that the t-t-tree will decide your f-fate," Dollop translated.

"Gimme a break!" Micah said with a roll of his eyes.

"Dollop, please," Phoebe implored. "Please ask him to let us go. We haven't done anything to the Ascetic or his people. We shouldn't be here. We're lost, and we don't have much time. We need to find the Citadel and—"

The Ascetic's maniacal laughter choked into a high-pitched squeal. Dollop fell backward with a mortified gasp, trembling and hugging his body as if trying to hold it together.

"N-n-no," Dollop chattered. "Nuh-uh. N-never speak of it! It's a v-vile thing."

"You've heard of the Citadel?" Phoebe asked.

"H-how could we forget?" He ducked under a pile of rubble to hide. "It is an ancient ab-b-b-bomination. A sc-scar from which Mehk may never heal."

"Cool! So how do we get there?" Micah chimed in.

Without warning, the Ascetic burst into wailing, uncontrollable tears. The withered chraida crawled over to one of his grotesque mummified companions and laid his weeping head on its lap. He was inconsolable, his metal shoulder plates shuddering with every sob. The kids looked at each other, unsure what to do. Phoebe reached out to touch his wrinkled arm.

"TEAAAA!" the Ascetic hollered abruptly, followed by a flurry of shrill giggles that echoed throughout the nest. He bolted upright and blasted past the kids, galloping on all fours toward his altar and kicking up a cloud of gray dust in his wake. Micah twirled a finger around his temple.

"Please," Phoebe said, following the old chraida. "You have to tell us. We're looking for someone important and—"

"Shush-ush, no talky, bleeder," tutted the Ascetic. "Let spilling Splinters speak-eak." He whispered some grinding words and stirred his boiling pot. Dollop sprinted to his side and busied himself by adjusting the little knickknacks on the altar. But the Ascetic shooed him away and corrected the arrangement of the curios with great precision. He dipped two cups into the cauldron, gingerly wiped the rims clean, and offered them to Phoebe and Micah, an enthusiastic grin visible beneath his skull mask.

"Uh, thank you," she said, taking the hot cup in her hands. "Will you tell us where the Citadel is if we drink this?"

Dollop whimpered again, peering fearfully from behind the altar. The Ascetic nodded vaguely at the kids and pointed to the cups, the jaw of his skull mask clicking eagerly.

"So . . . what kinda tea is this exactly?" Micah asked.

"You go first," Phoebe instructed him.

"Pffft, in your dreams!"

"Don't be rude."

"I don't like tea. 'Specially not crazy spider monkey tea."

"Fine, we'll go at the same time, okay?"

"Whatever."

They raised their clinking cups in unison and looked at the contents. It was a translucent brown fluid with a hunk of something hard and dark at the bottom. It looked exactly like . . . well, tea. They eyed each other suspiciously and brought the steaming cups to their lips. The Ascetic leaned in anxiously.

The kids took a sip. Their eyes popped wide. This was the smell they detected when they first arrived—blood, chemicals, rot, garbage, all boiled down to one concentrated, obscene taste. Micah gagged and rubbed at his tongue to scrape away the foul residue. Phoebe covered her mouth so that she could spit more modestly.

The ancient chraida clapped giddily and snatched the cups from them, a vicious gleam twinkling in his rheumy eyes. He poured the scalding liquid into his bare hand, and out from the cups clinked a pair of jagged stones. Not stones, Phoebe noticed, but chunks of metal from the tree—just like the broken shards that cluttered the nest. The Ascetic pounded these pieces with a few vigorous blows, and then gathered the fragments into his shaking hands. He closed his eyes, chanting in Rattletrap as he listened to the deep drone that moaned up from the depths far below.

"The Splinters speak-eak," he croaked. "Spirit words, broken thoughts, and burning-ing froth."

With great ceremony, the Ascetic cast the pile of metal filings down on his altar, and they stood on end. So did the hair on the back of the kids' necks.

The Splinters began to shift, and Phoebe and Micah watched them in wonder. The little shards shuffled and swam, dancing as the Ascetic swept his hands over them. Images and arcane words appeared in the Splinters, but they were fleeting, swishing away into swirls and scattering, only to form again as he flicked his wrist.

The Ascetic's eyes rolled back in his head, lost in concentration. Phoebe and Micah, too, were so mesmerized that none of them noticed a rhythmic thrumming. The noise grew and grew until the tree shuddered all around them.

The old chraida snapped out of his trance. There was terror in his eyes.

That was when the sound finally registered.

Aero-copter blades.

THE FALL

The Splinters on the altar shook with the thunder of approaching engines. The Ascetic's nest trembled. A rib of broken tree shook loose from the roof and crashed down, scattering debris.

The old chraida dashed across the cable bridge and disappeared into the hollow. Left with no other escape, they scrabbled after him, fleeing back through the dank tunnel. In her haste, Phoebe stepped on something sharp and yelped as it cut into her shoeless foot. No time to see how badly she was injured—she could only hobble and try to keep her weight off it.

As she and Micah ran for the exit, they saw the heavy flap

peel open. Three chraida finished securing the feeble Ascetic onto a cable zip line, then sped him away through the treetops.

"Hey! What about us?" Micah cried.

The kids rushed to the mouth of the hollow and looked out upon the chraida village. Searchlights sliced down through the darkness, reflecting off metal leaves and casting a million fragments of wild light. A torrent of wind parted the tree-tops to reveal Aero-copters, their onyx bodies blotting out the stars. The twirling blades embedded within their frames chugged like a collective heartbeat. Their bases irised open, and hydraulic arms bearing shielded platforms emerged and maneuvered through the canopy like the heads of a hydra.

"We gotta split!" shouted Micah.

"How?"

"There!" He pointed to a wind-blown zip cable that ran down and out of sight. He pushed past her and tested the line with a few hard tugs. "Come on!"

There was commotion in the village as chraida tried to fend off the invaders, leaping at the aircraft, casting nets, and hurling crude weapons. The Aero-copters' articulated plat-forms hissed open to reveal cruel cannons. In a blinding flash, the guns whirred out a spiraling shower of white rounds.

Phoebe looked away, but she could not avoid the screams.

Then another desperate cry pealed out behind them.

"Help!"

She recognized the warbling voice. "Dollop?"

"Nothin' we can do for him now," Micah said. "We gotta—"

But she had already turned to limp back through the

tunnel despite his furious protests. Dollop had information about the Citadel. He was her best shot at finding out where Goodwin had taken her father.

As Phoebe rushed into the Ascetic's suspended nest, something smashed against the tree outside. The whole cocoon swung wildly, like a birdcage struck with a sledgehammer. She staggered, clinging to a beam for support. Debris fell around her. Cables snapped and sang.

"What are you doin'?" hollered Micah. "This thing's gonna fall!"

"H-here! Under here!" Dollop's desperate voice squeaked.

Beneath the crumpled altar they could see a slim metal arm. She pulled and shoved at the slab, but it was too heavy for her. Aero-copter blades boomed all around them, and Phoebe felt her blood thrumming.

"Help me!" she screamed.

Micah ran to her side. Together, they strained to lift the massive altar. It only raised a couple of inches, but that was enough. Dollop yanked himself free and skittered to the far end of the demolished den. He hesitated, staring back at the kids in wide-eyed terror, unsure of what to do.

"F-f-follow," he stuttered at last, and then vanished.

The word struck Phoebe. It was the same one that had beckoned her into the train tunnel. She felt a surge of exhilaration. No time to linger.

They booked after Dollop with Phoebe hobbling as fast as she could. The little creature wormed his way through a gap in the woven floor and into a crawl space so tight they had to wriggle along on their bellies.

It wasn't long before Micah stopped, blocking the way.

"What is it?" she asked.

"Look." He squeezed over so that she could see. "Think you can make it?"

The crawl space ended in the base of the nest. A twanging cable stretched over to the inner wall of the tree five or six yards away. Dollop pulled himself across the line, grabbed on to rungs carved in the tree's surface, and then rapidly climbed down into the darkness below.

She and Micah had to catch up or lose their only guide.

"I'll go first," he said. "Wrap your arms and legs around it and hang underneath, then you can inch across and—"

"I get it. I did this a thousand times in gym class," she lied.

"All right. Don't get all snippy." He grabbed on to the cable and slung beneath it, scooting his way across like an inchworm. He made it look easy.

Now it was her turn. She held on and let gravity swing her below the line. Her legs were stronger than her arms, so she favored them, locking her ankles tight. Phoebe felt her arm muscles tremble with exertion, but she ignored it and focused on moving as fast as she could. Within a minute, she was at the wall and easing onto the notches cut into the rough tree.

That wasn't so bad, she thought.

Then her foot slipped. Micah shouted. Adrenaline flooded her body. She clung to the cable, flailing and kicking her legs wildly as she tried to regain her foothold, but the rungs were slick with sap. Phoebe wedged her shoe into a crevice in the wall and, using that as leverage, she pulled herself close enough to find a solid grip. She let go of the cable and clutched the rough carved handholds for dear life.

"You okay?" Micah called up.

She realized with a pinch of embarrassment that her skirt was whipping all over the place, and Micah was right underneath her. Nothing to be done about that now.

Slowly, one notch at a time, they climbed down the wall. She tried desperately to not think about falling, and instead concentrated on maintaining her grip. The adrenaline was wearing off, and now she was feeling spent and shaky. Every time she forced her uncovered right foot into the grooves of the wall, a flaming dart of pain shot up her leg.

Micah, on the other hand, was climbing down at a steady clip. He was used to running and scaling trees, twisting ankles, and getting beaten up. The kid was tough for his age—she could see that now. But not Phoebe. Had she ever felt exhaustion like this in her entire life? Did she ever have to strain for any reason at all? Of course not. She had servants like Micah to do everything for her. She gritted her teeth and bore down into the slick handholds.

Micah is right, she admitted hopelessly. *I'm just a stuck-up, pampered little brat.*

A crash overhead tore Phoebe from her self-pity. Great sheets of falling metal bark sheared through the Ascetic's nest, smashing it apart and severing cables with a tumultuous twang. The mummified bodies, the dainty teacups, the shattered altar—it all came spiraling down. The tree shuddered as debris ricocheted off the walls and cascaded in a cloud of shrapnel. It plunged into the darkness and hit the bottom with a violent clang.

Her breath was coming in short rasps now. She kept climbing, rung by rung, each step a new agony. Phoebe needed ground beneath her again.

"Come on!" Micah shouted. She saw him disappear into a hole in the wall. An exit. Almost there, just another few rungs.

A sudden stillness settled around them, and she felt a change in the air pressure. A few motes of that gray powder drifted around her as she took a step down. Then an unfathomably low tone rolled out of the darkness below, an elemental note groaning from deep within the ground. Another rung down. It was the primal song of the forest, that strange, organ-like harmony they had heard blowing out of the hollow trees.

Last step.

She reached for the foothold, but her toes did not find it. An explosion of wind surged up and lifted her like a feather. Phoebe was weightless, floating. She clung to the rung and tried desperately to pull herself toward the wall. Within the roaring wind was a deluge of gray dust, rippling past her, trying to drag her away. She buried her nails in the wall and fought against the flood with all her might, flapping upside down like a sail in a hurricane.

Phoebe had a flash of her inevitable fate—she would be sucked up into the tree and ejected out the towering top. And then, the fatal, crushing fall.

She closed her eyes and prepared for the end.

Hands grabbed her wrists. She was pulled against the tide. Micah hauled her into the safety of the tunnel, and they collapsed. The wall of gray dust rushed past as they lay there, shaken. Phoebe was seized with panic, gasping for air. She stared at Micah, not quite seeing him, not quite believing.

"You're okay," he said. This time it wasn't a question, more like he was reassuring himself.

As the howl of wind died, they heard Dollop's distant footsteps and snapped alert. In seconds, the kids were back on their feet and stumbling after the little creature. She activated her Trinka to light the way.

They followed through hollow branches that led from the main trunk like a network of sewer tunnels. Sap gummed up around their feet, making progress slippery and slow, but soon they found their guide scampering down a hole in the floor. She aimed her Trinka into the cavity and spied Dollop crawling straight down a vertical pipe. He was spread-eagled, lowering himself carefully with his extended arms and legs.

Phoebe tried to imagine herself doing the same thing, holding up her entire weight and inching down, down, down to who knew what. Something collapsed within her, as if her insides suddenly deflated and shrank away.

"I can't," she confessed. "I can't do it. I can't go on."

"You have to," Micah insisted. "You just gotta squeeze

against the side, with your back to the wall and feet out. Take it slow, ease down bit by bit."

She had nothing left. No strength to go on and yet no will to resist. All she could do was offer a weak nod and lower herself into the hole. With her legs crunched against her chest, she pressed hard against the side with her feet and reeled at the pain. She relaxed her muscles and slid down a few inches, sloshing down the slick tube like a clog in a shower drain.

It was misery, and her legs were killing her. But she had to. Micah said she had to.

He climbed in after her, and they scooted down inch by torturous inch with no sense of how far they had to go. A rumbling explosion shook the branch like a gong. Phoebe slipped down the tube and tensed her poor wobbly legs, barely managing to stop. She felt her grip weakening. There was only so much she could take. She started to let go.

Then there was a sloppy struggling in the pipe up above. Gobs of goo splatted down on her.

"Look out! I'm—" was all she heard.

Micah crashed on top of her. Phoebe tore loose and plummeted too. A thrashing knot of limbs and screams tumbled into Dollop.

They all fell.

The pipe opened up, and they were launched out into the forest. The trio crashed through foil leaves, snapping past metal branches. They plunged into a tangle of chraida cables, and Phoebe grabbed fistfuls in a desperate bid to slow her descent. She clung and fell, then held on tighter and dropped some more. Fully ensnared now, her momentum slowed. She flipped and turned and grappled in the mess of lines as the blurring ground spun into view.

The cables stretched and creaked, but held, and at last she eased to a stop ten feet above the forest floor.

Then Micah shot out of the darkness, swinging from a loose cable like a crazed orangutan. He zipped past her, let go of the line with a flourish, and landed hard, tumbling over and over in a chaotic somersault. He rammed into a silver sapling with a hollow thud.

Far above, through the maze of angular branches, search-lights still scanned the canopy. The rumble of the Aero-copters was like a distant storm.

She squirmed to untangle herself, then hung down from the lowest cable and collapsed roughly to the ground.

Micah was already up and dusting himself off. He caught sight of her and laughed. "You're a mess."

She got up on her elbows and brushed her tangled hair from her face. They were both coated in splatters of viscous sap and dusted in gray powder.

"Where's Dollop?" she croaked.

As Phoebe started to pull herself to her feet, she grazed something warm in the underbrush. She recoiled and used her Trinka to see what it was.

"Oh no!" she gasped.

There, among the fallen leaves and tire tracks, was a slender metal limb. Dollop's severed forearm. She covered her mouth. Micah came up beside her to see, and a grim expression settled on his blunt features.

"Poor Dollop," she whispered.

The forearm twitched. The kids recoiled as it slithered off, bumping into roots and foliage to find other wriggling pieces. They fused on contact to form an elbow and shoulder, then hopped away. Astounded, Phoebe and Micah followed the limb over to a slipshod Dollop, who was partially reconstructed and hobbling as fast as he could. The rest of his parts clumped and stuck to him until he was complete and running away at top speed.

"Dollop, wait!" she cried.

The terrified little creature skidded to a stop and looked back, his luminous eyes glinting and reflecting back at the kids in the dim light.

"Please, we need your help. The Citadel, we—"

An engine growled nearby. They looked through the trees—approaching headlights, lots of them. The Foundry was combing the forest.

When they looked back, Dollop was gone. Her heart fell.

"Come on, Plumm. Forget him. We gotta go!"

Micah pulled her sleeve down to cover the glowing Trinka, and they sprinted away from the lights slashing between the trees. The rumbling hum was growing louder, accompanied by the crunch of wheels on metal foliage. More searchlights up ahead. Micah looked around in a panic. A fallen log lay decomposing and rusted in the undergrowth nearby. He shoved Phoebe inside the decaying pipe and crawled in after her. Then he gathered up arms full of leaves and debris and used them to cover up the hole.

It was black inside, but flaring light sliced through cracks in the log, so the kids peered out through the slits. Heavily armed vehicles rolled past, their headlamps revealing a platoon marching among them. Wind blasted and shook their cover as an Aero-copter shuddered past.

Had they left any footprints? Would their tracks be easy to follow, or would they be lost among the fallen foil leaves?

Through the glare, Phoebe was able to make out one of the figures. He wore mottled gray-and-rust-colored army fatigues with bandoliers of magazines strapped across his armored chest. Beneath the helmet and gleaming face shield, she recognized that vacant, haunting expression.

These were Watchmen soldiers.

After what seemed an eternity, the lights and vehicles moved away, growing fainter and fainter until they were gone.

The forest returned to silence. The kids lay in the dark for a long time, their minds reeling and their bodies numb.

"Micah," Phoebe whispered.

"Yeah?"

"The chraida . . . We brought the Foundry right to them. They . . . they died because of us."

He yawned and she could smell his sour, hungry breath. Her eyelids were sticky with sweat and getting heavy.

"It's their own dumb fault. It ain't like we asked to be tied up and taken to their stupid village anyway."

"But all of those innocent people."

"What *people*? All I saw was a bunch of monkey machines that wanted to kill us."

"You know they're not machines. You saw them."

"They shoulda known better than to nab us," Micah said.

"That doesn't give the Foundry the right to murder them."

Did her father know what the Foundry was doing to the chraida? He couldn't even bear to squash a cricket—instead, her dad would catch it in a jar and set it free outside. He would never stand for this.

She couldn't fight off fatigue any longer. Sleep was taking her. Their hiding place was painfully uncomfortable, but her body demanded rest. The Chokarai forest all around them was quiet as Phoebe drifted off.

But her head echoed with the screams of dying chraida.

AWAKENING

When Phoebe roused after only a scant few hours of rest, she wondered if it might have all been some sort of insanely vivid fever dream. But between the dim slivers of dawn sifting into their shelter, and Micah's raucous snores, she knew it was all very real.

Outside, she could hear the Chokarai stirring. Metallic hoots and ratcheting cries percolated all around her, mingling with the melodious tinkling of leaves in the breeze. This forest was alien, yet its morning ambience was soothing, even rejuvenating. She savored the sensation, basking in its serenity.

At last, she shoved the foliage aside and crawled out of the hollow log. Fireworks of pain exploded across her body. Her back was knotted and sore, as were her arms and legs. Muscles she didn't even know she had screamed for attention. Her wounded foot throbbed, made all the worse by the fact that she was woozy with hunger.

Why, then, did she feel such a tingling sense of exhilaration?

Phoebe thought about everything that she and Micah had done. They had eluded a thousand Watchmen and infiltrated Foundry Central, the most powerful organization in the world. They had discovered a land made of living metal and narrowly escaped being killed by its savage creatures. And had any human throughout history ever met the Ascetic?

Maybe one, she mused darkly as she recalled his skull mask.

But Phoebe had survived all that. How many times had she told herself she couldn't do it? Yet here she was. Every time she hit the wall, every time she thought the pain was too much, Phoebe had overcome it and faced down everything thrown her way. That quitter, that spoiled brat who couldn't be bothered to lift a finger, was no more. Her father didn't need that coddled little girl right now—he needed a savior.

It was all up to her. Okay, her and Micah.

She pushed past the stiffness and pain, stretched her aching muscles, and inhaled the earthy iron scent of the Chokarai. The branches of the silvery forest were draped in a peach-colored mist that was starting to burn off. Everywhere she looked, tire tracks cut rutted trails, and boot prints meandered in all directions. There were big circular stamps the size of manholes made by some massive machine she couldn't recognize and hoped to never see.

Her foot was bothering her, so she leaned against the log to examine it. She peeled off a blood-crusted sock and saw a puncture wound on the ball of her right foot. It was sore and red, but she was relieved that it didn't look too serious. Still, it was only going to get worse the more she had to walk.

Phoebe limped around, scanning the forest floor for something she could use. She found a strip of metal bark and gathered up a bunch of fallen foil leaves. With the bark as the sole of her makeshift shoe, she wrapped her foot and ankle in layers of the crinkling foliage. She searched her sniping pockets for her coil of wire, but as she dug around, her fingers grazed something else. She gasped when she realized what it was.

Honeygum! She had hidden the snack in her pocket for class and completely forgotten about it. Her stomach howled at the thought of sustenance. She dug out her wire and used the strand to bind the leaves and bark securely around her foot. The ragged boot wasn't comfortable in the slightest, and it looked absolutely ridiculous, but it was better than nothing.

Once that was out of the way, Phoebe poured rich strawberry Honeygum syrup into her mouth, drop by sumptuous drop. It was the best thing she had ever tasted in her life. She was relishing the candy, delighting in the sensation as it gelled in her mouth, when Micah blasted out a husky snore.

It would be so easy. She could gobble up the rest of the candy and secretly spit out the gum once he woke up. She wanted to—more than anything she wanted to—but despite the growling protests of her empty stomach, she saved half of the Honeygum for him. He needed his strength as much as she did, and any little morsel would help.

Phoebe poked her head in the hollow log to find Micah passed out with his mouth hanging open, oozing drool. The opportunity was too good to pass up. She looked around for something that might do the trick. There, on the wall of the pipe log, she spied some sort of slithering critter. It was about the size and color of a plum and covered in nubby feelers like wavering fingers. It was clearly made of metal, but as she gently prodded it, she discovered to her astonishment that it was the consistency of congealed bacon fat.

Whoever heard of squishy metal? And yet it was undeniably true.

A long neck protruded from the critter's squelching mass, bulging out in a lumpy head. It had three antennae, two flat ones on top and a round one centered below, like an electrical plug made out of snot. It used these nodules to probe at the rust on the log. She scrunched up her nose as she plucked the thing up. It was heavier than she expected, and its wet feelers wiggled around to touch, maybe even taste, her skin.

It didn't seem dangerous, but it was thoroughly revolting. And perfect.

Quiet as a cat, she crept over to Micah and carefully peeled up his collar. She eased the rust slug off her hand and let it slink down the front of his shirt.

His snores stopped abruptly. He twitched and giggled and

flopped like a little child being tickled. Then he lay still again. Phoebe bit her lip as the bump continued to roam. With a shrill squeal, Micah jolted upright and clanged his head on the pipe. He tore out of the shelter and pawed at his body, contorting himself and dancing spastically until the rust slug came sloshing out a pant leg of his overalls.

Micah was just starting to calm down when he noticed Phoebe doubled over in a fit of hysterical laughter.

Now he got it. His face melted into red-hot, freckled fury.

"Gotcha!" she managed to squeak out in between snickers. "That's for the train tunnel. A cave slug for a cave slug."

He charged at her, but before he could say anything, she presented him with the half-eaten container of Honeygum.

"Breakfast is served," she said with a sweet smile.

The sight of candy disarmed him. He whipped it out of her hand, slurped it down in one gulp, and chewed voraciously. "Where'd you get this? You got any more?"

"Sorry, Charlie. That was it."

He eyed her suspiciously. "Why you bein' so nice?"

"I'm not." She shrugged. "I just don't want you to faint on me." Phoebe didn't know why she couldn't simply thank him for saving her life the night before. She wanted to, but something in her resisted fiercely.

"Guys don't faint," he said, chewing his gum with his mouth open.

"Yeah, well, guys don't do that dance you just did either. What do you call that move anyway?"

"Laugh it up. But watch your back, 'cause this ain't over."

"Not by a long shot," she agreed with a twinkle in her eye. "But unless you got something better to do, we should probably get going."

Though Micah was surely just as sore as she was, he worked the kinks out of his muscles with an ease that Phoebe envied. He stretched his arms over his head and cracked his neck with a quick jerk. With a few glances, he assessed their surroundings—pipe-work forest in every direction.

"Where to?" he asked.

"I was hoping you might have a clue."

"Well, looks like the Foundry headed off in that direction," he said, pointing down the most rugged and pronounced swath cut by the vehicles. "Question is whether it leads to the Citadel or not."

"N-n-not."

The kids jumped at the unexpected voice and ducked behind a stand of silvery trees. Foliage rustled nearby as an asymmetrical form poked out from behind the underbrush, bulging amber eyes fixed warily upon them.

"Dollop!" Phoebe came out of hiding and took a few steps toward him, but the little guy scampered farther away on four wobbly legs. "You came back."

"I—I did. That is, I was told to."

"By who?" Micah asked suspiciously.

"The Great Engineer. Everseer. The M-M-Mother of Ore." Dollop stroked something on his chest. "Makina."

The kids exchanged a look. "Say wha?" Micah asked.

"It-it is said in accord fourteen, edict two, m-mark twenty:

'Thy savior is thy m-master. Serve those who giveth themselves unto you, for um, only then shall you be served by-by Me in turn.' Or is it, um, edict two, mark twenty-two? I-i-it's definitely one of those," Dollop stuttered. "Th-the Ascetic saved me first, bu-but you bleeders saved me most recently. I think that c-c-cancels out the previous time, especially because the chr-chraida mock the Way . . . a-along with everyone else. Of course, we c-c-can't be certain without consulting an axial."

The kids didn't have a clue what he was talking about.

"I—I ran last cycle, err, because I was afraid. Of you. B-because you're horrible," Dollop explained matter-of-factly. "But I p-prayed for g-guidance, and She has placed me in your s-s-service. For wh-what purpose, I'm not quite sure yet. But the Way is quite clear on this matter."

"Well, whoever *She* is, thank her for us," Micah said, cracking his gum.

"Does that mean you'll take us to the Citadel?" asked Phoebe.

At the sound of the word, Dollop hid himself once again, and for a few tense seconds, they thought he had run off. But then he hesitantly reappeared just long enough to motion them to follow.

Dollop led them away from the Foundry tracks, keeping far ahead and safely out of reach. He vanished into shadows and shimmering shrubs but paused every now and then to make sure that they were close. As the kids walked, they marveled at the Chokarai. The forest teemed with unfamiliar calls, chirping and chattering and screeching in the canopy.

Rays of sun broke through the silvery treetops and dappled the ground, which shone with clumps of gritty, unrefined ore. Poking up through the underbrush were tiny tubes no bigger than straws. They were new growths, sparkling sprouts just starting to stretch toward the sky.

Phoebe chewed on her Honeygum and stared at the shoots in wonder. More of that gray powder, the same stuff that blasted up from the big tree, was drifting down and settling on the little tubes. Was the big tree feeding these little ones? Or was this maybe some kind of pollen or spore?

Dollop popped his head out from behind a shrub, startling the kids.

"Wh-why don't you cruel and evil bleeders know how to, um, get to the Ci-Ci-Ci-t-t . . ." He trailed off, unable to say the name of the place.

"We ain't exactly from around here," Micah noted.

"B-but Foundry is in the Ci-Ci-Ci-t-t . . . in there. Bleeders are F-Foundry, so why don't you—"

"We're not with the Foundry, I swear," said Phoebe

Dollop stared at them, his massive amber eyes blinking in befuddlement. Then they bugged out in sudden horror, and his limbs began to rattle.

"Th-then don't go there. No, n-never go. It's, um, a terrible place. Hor-r-rible things happen there, and that. Ancient, evil, uns-s-speakable things!"

"You don't understand. We have to get to the Citadel," she pleaded. "The Foundry, they took . . . someone. And we have to save him."

"They nabbed her pa," Micah chimed in.

She shot him a warning look, but he just shrugged in reply.

"Y-your people?" Dollop asked delicately. "Your clan?"

"My father," explained Phoebe.

"But why?" Dollop was confused. "Why d-does Foundry hunt bleeders?"

She winced. "We don't know. And actually, if it's not too much trouble, would you mind not calling us 'bleeders'? It's kind of gross."

"Oh-oh." Dollop rubbed a cavity in his forehead. The kids hadn't noticed it before, but now that he was closer they could make it out clearly. His body was oddly patterned with different kinds and colors of metal, but his head was like a badly assembled jigsaw puzzle. And right in the middle of it was a dent or a missing piece. "Wh-what do I name you, then?" he asked.

"Well, we're humans," she said. "But I'd rather you just call me Phoebe."

"And I'm Micah."

"Fuh-fee . . . bee. Mick . . . h-huh. Hoo . . . man." Dollop let out a tinny warble that must have been a laugh. "Your names are s-s-silly."

"Look who's talkin'!" huffed Micah.

"Anyway, we better get going. Lead the way, Mr. Guide," she said.

Dollop considered this, his bulbous eyes going wide. "Guide . . ." He mumbled the word to himself. "I'm a guide." He stroked something on his chest again—it was a brilliant golden symbol, a circle split down the middle by a crooked, vertical line like the teeth of two interlocking gears. "Of-of course. That's what I am. Um, th-that's my function. I'm a guide, I—I show you the path! I'll lead you to the Way!"

The kids nodded at him, uncertain smiles on their faces.

"Thank you, Makina. Praise the gears!" the little guy said, leaping off in sudden exuberant worship. As he darted in and out of the trees, they saw that he was popping off his detachable limbs and rearranging them. When he danced back into view, he was taller, now chest high to Phoebe, and he no longer loped on all fours like a chraida. Instead, he had reassembled himself to mimic human proportions and was off and running upright on two legs.

"Come, evil blee—er, um . . . C-come on, follow me!"

Dollop scampered off, but Phoebe held Micah back.

"Just be careful, okay?" she whispered.

"About what?"

"Don't tell him my dad works for the Foundry."

"I didn't," he said defensively.

"I know, I'm just saying keep it between you and me."

"Sure, whatever," he said. "Come on, we're losing him!"

Dollop was so swift and energetic now that the kids had to run to keep up with their newly transfigured guide. As the morning got brighter, the forest shone with vibrant life. Soon, the trees thinned out, and a wide rugged lane appeared.

"Wait," Phoebe whispered. Dollop skidded to a stop and came running back. "This road. Who uses it?"

"A-a-anyone. Everyone. Umm, there are a few check-points, bu-but we can go around those." He considered her question. "That's a good thing, r-r-right? A road to lead us to the Ci-Ci-t-t-ta—"

She motioned for him to be quiet, and the three of them peered through the trees. Far down the road, there were little glimmers of light—moving reflections on the silver leaves. She focused, trying to make out any sounds of danger. Phoebe couldn't be sure, and it might have been nothing, but she thought she could hear engines in the distance.

"Trucks. Must be Foundry," she said.

"Good," muttered Micah. He snatched up a fallen pipe branch from the forest floor and gave it a few hearty swings to test it out. "They'll never know what hit 'em."

He stalked toward the road, but she pulled him back.

"Don't be stupid!" she hissed. "We barely managed to escape last night, and now you want to pick a fight?"

He wrestled free from her grip. "Look, maybe half a Honeygum is enough for you, but I'm starving. And I ain't exactly in the mood to eat a buncha metal." Micah motioned to the forest all around them. "Where there's Foundry, there's people. And where there's people, there's food."

"No way," she insisted. "We have to lie low and stay out of sight."

"What about water, huh? It don't take long to drop dead from thirst, and I ain't about to go down like that."

"Dollop," she said to their little guide, "where's the nearest stream?"

"S-stream?"

"Yes. We need to find some water."

"Uh, no. No water in Mehk. Gives us r-r-rustgut."

Micah smirked and gestured to Dollop, as if that settled their dispute. She felt a twinge of panic. How long could they feasibly last before dehydration set in? Micah gave his club another test swing.

"Anyhoo, here's the plan. Both of you, grab a stick, and I'll take point. It'll be a quick raid, in and out. We got the element of surprise so—"

"I'm not going to let you do this."

"Try and stop me!" he blustered. "I ain't gonna pass this up just 'cause you're scared. No guts, no glory."

Phoebe scoffed. "Isn't that from some stupid show?"

His face turned bright red, and a vein throbbed in his forehead. Dollop hid behind a thicket, looking fearfully back and forth between the kids.

"I said no, and that's that," she insisted, crossing her arms firmly over her chest.

"And I said YES!"

"You're out of line. Don't forget that I'm in charge, and you're just a servant. Rule number three, Micah—you follow me."

He trembled with rage, fists clenched and jaw jutted.

"We don't stand a chance against the Foundry," she said. "We will have to find food and water somewhere else."

"Where?" he demanded through gritted teeth.

"I don't know. But we will."

"You're gonna get us killed," he snarled.

"No. I'm trying to stop YOU from getting us killed." She stared him down. "Dollop. We have to stay away from this road, from all roads, any place that might be crowded. Is there another way we can go where no one can find us?"

Their guide peered out at them from behind the bushes and pinched his eyes shut. It almost looked like he was in pain as he rubbed the missing gap on his head, like he was trying to massage out a lost memory.

"W-we could . . . maybe . . . probably . . . g-g-go through the brasslands?"

His hesitation worried Phoebe, but she didn't see that there was much choice. And she didn't want Micah to see her waver. She felt bad, pulling rank on him like that when he was clearly just trying to help, but it was a terrible idea. They couldn't afford to take such reckless risks.

"Good. Let's go," she ordered.

"Y-yes!" Dollop nodded enthusiastically. "I am a g-guide. I—I will guide you, and whatnot!"

Their little ally headed back into the forest, looking around for a moment to try and get his bearings. Phoebe followed, ignoring Micah as he threw down his stick and stood rooted in place. As Dollop finally found his way and skipped off, she heard the boy let loose a string of angry curses.

But after a moment, he stomped after them to catch up, and Phoebe breathed a sigh of relief.

EXPOSED

icah didn't so much as look at Phoebe while they chewed their Honeygum and crunched through the Chokarai. Mechanical screeches and calls faded as the path led through a sickly swath of the metal forest. The trees were limp with thinning leaves, their trunks brutally gouged and spray-painted with numbers, and piles of ore had been ripped from the ground, then dumped beside the open scars.

"A tr-tr-tragedy," Dollop muttered mournfully. "The Covenant will not, um, stand for this. No, n-n-not one bit."

"Covenant?" Phoebe asked.

"Wh-where?" Dollop said excitedly, stopping in his tracks to look around.

"No, I was just asking."

"Oh, r-r-right." He lowered his voice to a whisper. "The Covenant is a myst-sterious, uh, super-secret army of freedom f-f-fighters, sworn to defend Mehk. They s-strike in the night, s-swoop from the skies, and er, even burst up from underground!" Dollop said, leaping up dramatically like a toddler during storytime. "They can k-k-kill with a stare! Ex-explode things with their minds! Ka-bo-o-o-om!"

"Uh-huh," Micah said, not in the least bit convinced. Phoebe wasn't sure what to make of it. It sounded ridiculous, but then again, she had already seen so much that she never would have believed.

They arrived at the edge of the Chokarai. Beyond a border of scraggly trees lay a sprawling grove of symmetrical stumps. These were not ragged and splintered logs, but uniform and meticulously severed just above the ground. The clear-cut scar stretched for miles.

"The C-C-Covenant will fix this," Dollop vowed as he looked out upon the leveled forest. "They will m-make them all pay. Uh, you'll see."

"Wicked," Micah breathed in wonder.

But she didn't share his sentiment. This was horrible. These woods were the chraida's home. No wonder they had wanted to kill her and Micah. She was about to tell him as much when she noticed he was not looking at the stumps at all. He was shielding his eyes to stare up at the sky.

To her astonishment, it was not a flat expanse of color and clouds. Instead, she saw a spectacular writhing nebula of liquid blues and yellows, shimmering like reflections in a puddle of oil. Rather than a sun, there was a glowing ring suspended overhead, halfway between horizon and zenith. They squinted against the glare, trying to make sense of it. The ring must have been more than a hundred fiery celestial bodies, like a circle of smoldering coals.

"Oh good!" Dollop said cheerily, chomping on a handful of crusty gray seeds and spitting out their shells. He gestured to the suns. "O-only a couple more clicks until the fusion. We're making good time. Th-this-a-way!"

The sight of food made their empty stomachs grumble, a rude reminder of their predicament. Phoebe picked up one of the discarded shells and sniffed it hungrily. She would have tasted it if it didn't smell exactly like silver polish.

Dollop led them around the clear-cut grove to a spot where the forest gave way to rolling hills covered in tall golden grass that swayed in the breeze. The glaring solar halo reflected off the amber waves like flames. Jutting up at irregular intervals throughout the landscape were tall, curling spires. They reminded Phoebe of brown stalagmites, but it was hard to make out what they might actually be.

When Dollop led them to the first glinting hill, she realized at once that the sea of knee-high golden reeds were thin and sharp as a fencer's foil.

"Lemme guess," Micah said, flinching as one of the blades scratched him. "The brasslands?"

"Pr-pr-precisely!" Dollop said. "Now if my c-calculations are correct we—"

The blades of brass suddenly thrashed around him, and the air exploded into a fury of spinning black wings. Dollop screamed and dove, and the kids ducked as a flock of agitated creatures buzzed past. They soared off into the sky, carried aloft not by wings, but by a series of fringed propellers.

Micah's eyes bugged out, and he clutched his throat. He hocked and forced something down with a hard swallow.

"You okay?" she asked. It was the first thing she had said to him since their argument.

"What do you care?" he snapped. "Them stupid things made me swallow my gum, is all."

"C-close one," Dollop said as he picked up his arm, which had come loose. He pointed to the kids with the detached limb. "G-g-gotta look out for vetchels. They'll, um-um, eat your eyes right out of your head. V-very rude indeed." He shoved his arm back in place and continued on his way.

As they trotted through the brass, Phoebe was grateful that she had wrapped her foot in protective metal leaves. She had to walk carefully, folding the reeds down with each step and then leaping forward to avoid the whipping recoil. Even so, the sharp reeds often snapped across her calves, leaving crisscrossed scratches. It was slow going, but the brush eventually grew high above their heads, and she no longer had to worry about the razorlike tips.

Now that she was closer, Phoebe could see that the jagged brown spires scattered across the land were made from layers of dead, windblown brass reeds. They were hardened into sweeping shapes that wound up from wide bases to create ribbon-like structures reaching ten to fifteen feet overhead.

The fiery ring in the sky rose and contracted as the day progressed. It might have astounded Phoebe had she not been so uncomfortable. She peeled off Micah's jacket and used it to fan herself, but it did little to break the heat. She wanted to say something to Micah, but he didn't want anything to do with her. Any mention of food or water was likely to result in a nasty "I told you so."

Dollop must have read their body language. He looked back at them with sympathy pooling in his big eyes. "Poor Phoebe Micah. You are huh-hungry."

She nodded, but Micah just made a dismissive grunt.

"I-I'm sorry. I c-can't help you," he said, repressing a little shudder of revulsion. "I don't know w-w-where to find you any elderly humans."

The kids shared a baffled look.

"Y-you know, for you to . . . eat."

The kids burst into laughter. "We don't eat old people!" she corrected.

"I th-thought . . ." Dollop blinked rapidly, bewildered. "I thought that after you h-h-hatched from the head of your bir-birthing host, you ate—"

Micah chuckled. "Hatched from *what*?"

"I think you may have the wrong idea about us."

"Where'd you learn that crud anyway?"

"Ev-ev-everyone knows that. It's, um, common knowledge."

"Well, you oughta get your facts straight," Micah retorted.

"Hmm, I—I wish an axial were here. They'd s-straighten this out. I—I was raised in a housing of the W-Waybound, and they taught me everything I know . . . ev-everything I can remember, at least. They t-t-taught me all about you evil bleeders and your f-filthy language. Uh, n-no offense."

"None taken," said Phoebe. "I guess."

"Ar-are you certain you don't, umm, feed on your elderly?"

"Positive," she nodded.

"That's a relief. But strange . . . I—I must have it mixed up. I do that s-s-sometimes. B-because the axials are wise beyond measure and are n-n-never wrong. They're the ones who, uh, showed me the Way."

"What way is that?" Micah asked.

They crested the top of a hill, and a surge of warm wind blew over them, cooling the sweat on their bodies. The brasslands stretched as far as the eye could see, a golden ocean roiling in the breeze, crashing up against corkscrew spires. The solar ring had merged into a single blazing orb overhead, firing up the sky with swirling orange and crimson rivulets that reflected off the waving stalks in a dazzling inferno.

"The Way is h-harmony," Dollop trilled.

As the three of them took in the majestic view, a shape rolled in the distance. It was nearly the same color as the reeds, a tumbling and bucking mass that flowed over the hills and dove out of sight.

Dollop spoke in a soft, reverent tone.

"*O M-Makina, Divine Dynamo, Tender of the Forge. Thou art the*

Everseer, our Mother of Ore. We that seek to find our f-function in Thy infinite and infallible plan, shall through the Way become vital components in Your sacred machine."

The ground vibrated, and the whirling shape reappeared, racing across the land like wildfire. Phoebe could see that it was not a singular form but a herd, a field of swerving wheels caught up in a frantic race, some unfolding and springing ahead like salmon in a swarming school. One of the wheels rolled away from the pack and unfurled, pausing to nibble at a brass reed. The creature stood waist-high, its curved body a streak of shiny gold with white vertical stripes. It had a narrow beaked head that twitched, quick and wary, and only two nimble legs, one each in front and back.

"As Th-Thy faithful creations," Dollop continued, *"we praise Thee and bes-s-seech Thee to help us, um-um, build interlocking unity in Your name, O Great Engineer, to create peace on Mehk and in the Shroud hereafter."*

The grazing creature turned its head. For a split second, it looked right at Phoebe, its pale eyes finding hers. Then the metal animal leaped forward like a gazelle, flipped in midair, and folded in on itself to form a wheel once again. It was quickly lost within the twirling, migrating herd.

"Th-that is known as the Bond of the Way," Dollop said blissfully. "S-sounds even better in the original R-Rattletrap."

Phoebe hadn't breathed since her fleeting moment of eye contact with the creature. Chills rippled through her. A lump formed in her throat.

"It's beautiful," she whispered. Dollop nodded, content.

"No doubt," said Micah.

She looked over at him. Surprisingly, even he was transfixed.

"Are you still mad at me?" she asked with softness in her voice, a vulnerability that took Micah aback. For once, she did not hide it. And for once, he did not mock her in return.

"I . . ." he started. "I'll get over it."

"Thanks."

They watched the spinning herd race toward the horizon.

"I can't get over this place," he exclaimed, changing the subject. "Dollop, what'd you call it? Mehk? I can't wait to tell everyone when we get back home. This is gonna blow people's minds. Jacko's gonna lay a two-ton brick!"

"No one's going to believe us," she said.

"Shoot, what I wouldn't give for a FotoSnap. A couple pics is all it'd take to prove it. We'd be famous!"

Phoebe smiled. So did Dollop, a silly grin bending his face.

"The Way has made you hap-p-py again. You-you are interlocking."

"Huh?" she said, taking a step away from Micah.

"No, we ain't."

"M-Makina is the mother of all, not just mehkans. E-e-even humans are a part of Her sacred machine, don't you see? The gears of fate have engaged. W-we are like the fusion," Dollop said as he pointed to the sun. "Connected. Like the Chok-k-karai," he said, pointing toward the distant pipework forest. "Like the tr-trelligs." He pointed excitedly at the departing herd of twirling creatures. "All c-c-connected!"

Phoebe couldn't explain it, but somewhere deep inside she felt truth in his words. It seemed to make sense beyond any rational explanation. But the smirk on Micah's face said that he felt otherwise.

"I-I've been following the Way my entire span, s-s-seeking my function, but I never found it. Until now!" Dollop was jubilant, hopping up and down, his loose parts separating and reconnecting with every bounce. "Sh-She led you to me. And now I know. Now I have a function. I'm a . . . I am . . . a . . ."

"A guide?" Phoebe offered helpfully.

"Yes! A guide! I—I am a guide!" He spun with joy.

"Speaking of which," Micah said, "how much farther till the Citadel?"

"I have no idea!" Dollop sang.

Their eyes went wide as he twirled around and around.

"Wait. Dollop, what are you saying?"

"No clue where we are! We've been l-l-lost for clicks! Isn't it magnificent!?"

The three of them hunkered down in the shade beneath a copse of corkscrew spires. They didn't know what their next move was, but standing out in the unbearable heat was not an option. They were drained and drenched in sweat. The Honeygum in Phoebe's mouth had long since gone stale, but she kept chewing it to stave off hunger pangs. She felt weak and achy all over, as if she were getting sick. Dollop's ecstasy had been replaced by inconsolable sobs. He had been at it for minutes on end, maybe hours.

"I-I-I'm not a guide," he blubbered. "N-n-not a guide . . ."

That was all he kept saying, over and over, and they could think of nothing to say in response. Micah was lobster-red from the heat, sullen and silent. He channeled his rage into shooing away sizzle bugs. She didn't know what else to call them because Dollop was too unresponsive to share their real names. When the metal midges had first appeared, the kids tried to swat them. But instead of stinging, the mehkan pests seared them like tiny hot pokers. The sizzling sound they made on skin was foul, and the pain was even worse. All they could do was try and fan the torturous things away.

A guttural rumble shook them out of their stupor—a revving sound, an engine growling across the plains.

"Did you hear that?" she asked.

"Moto-bike," Micah declared with a start. "Sounds like an old model Torrent. Maybe a Fireball GT."

"Foundry. We gotta move."

"N-no," Dollop said, sniffling. "No Foundry. N-n-not out here. That's a-a-a reticulated ulkett. Nasty things, ulketts."

"No way," said Micah. "That's a Moto-bike. I'd know the sound anywhere. My old man used to fix 'em."

"I—I don't think so. It's an ulk-kett. Th-these are their hunting grounds."

Given their situation, Dollop's confidence did little to settle Phoebe's nerves. Surrounded by brass reeds that towered overhead, she couldn't tell where the sound had come from and did not want to risk walking into an ambush. She looked up at the twisting growth they were using for shelter. The spire, made of layers of hardened brass reeds, didn't look sturdy, but it would have to do. She shinnied up it, moving carefully to avoid slicing her skin on its many barbs. It screeched in complaint but held her weight as she climbed.

It was sweltering with the suns reflecting off the sea of brass. She shaded herself with Micah's jacket and scanned their surroundings. Gold and more gold as far as she could see. In the sky, there were soaring mehkans like kites with fluttering tails. At first, she worried they might be predators, but they wound in far-off lazy patterns and showed no interest in the kids at all.

No Foundry vehicles in sight.

She was about to climb down to share the news when something caught her eye. It was faded by distance and distorted by the heat, but— could it be?

The angular top of a slanted mesa. She had seen the landmark before, from the back of the cargo truck the previous night, before they were captured by the chraida. The train tracks ran that way. That was the direction Goodwin had taken her father—it had to be! She raced back down the spire, stumbling as she landed. Micah jumped to his feet, ready to run.

"What is it?" he asked, shooing away the sizzle bugs.

"I found it!" she cried. "The train tracks are this way!"

"Seriously?"

"Yeah, come on." She motioned.

"Two points for Plumm!" He held up his hand to her, and she slapped it, beaming with pride.

"Yes. W-well done," Dollop moaned. "Phoebe is, um, a much better guide than I ever was."

"Aw, come on. Buck up," Micah said.

Phoebe agreed, "Maybe directions aren't your thing. You did your best."

"Do you suppose, uh, perhaps, M-M-Makina might have a different function in mind for me?"

Micah shrugged. "Yeah, that!"

"M-maybe you're right," Dollop chimed. "Until I know what part I play in Makina's inf-f-finite and infallible plan, my work is never done. The Way is quite cl-clear on this matter." He hopped to his feet and wiped away his tears. "It-it's all for the best, really, Phoebe being our new g-guide. B-b-because I think the ulketts are circling. Y-you do not want to meet an ulkett, believe me."

The three companions set off in their new direction with Phoebe in the lead, their ears peeled for any sound of danger.

"Hey, maybe that's your thing." Micah nudged Dollop with a smirk. "You can teach us about all of the scary crud that wants to kill us."

Dollop's amber eyes lit up. "T-t-teacher," he intoned.

"I'm pretty sure he doesn't get sarcasm," she whispered.

"Te-e-e-eacher. I-I'm a teacher. I t-teach!"

Dollop's chatter took their minds off the trek. He was eager to tell them about the interconnected components of Makina's sacred machine, as he called it. The excitable mehkan rattled on about how a certain creature (though he couldn't recall its name) exuded an oozing varnish that preserved the flaking metal skin of others. And about the rhouth and the t'ulk—two species that were defenseless on their own, but together could create a powerful electric charge to ward off predators. Or was that their mating ritual? At one point, he had the kids tickle the scabby feelers of a roving plant, only to recall that it was an acidic ryzooze waiting for prey. When the thing nearly took off Phoebe's hand, they all agreed that Dollop was not much of a teacher either.

Since Micah was the better climber, he occasionally scaled the coiling brass growths to ensure that they were still heading toward the mesas. It was hard going, but when the clustered suns at last separated back into a ring and began their descent, the heat became less brutal. Of course, Phoebe's feet still felt like lead and her mouth like it was full of cotton balls, but she would take what relief she could get.

It was then that they saw the oasis.

The sunken glade stood out from the monotonous brass-lands, distinguished by lush, fanning fronds with a waxy reddish hue. And twinkling between the leaves was the unmistakable ripple of water. Micah was off and running for it, and Phoebe was hot on his heels, her parched throat crying for relief. They crashed through the copper leaves with green patina blossoms and raced for the pond. The air had an astringent aroma, stinging their nostrils like fermented citrus. They splashed in knee-deep, reveling in the refreshing chill, and scooped handfuls of the liquid into their desperate mouths.

As soon as the greasy orange stuff hit her tongue, Phoebe wanted to throw up. Micah refused to accept that it was undrinkable, but after three attempts that left him retching, he gave up. It was like trying to chug gasoline.

"Water," croaked Micah, nearly in tears. "I just want a drink of water!"

Dollop slurped a handful of the orange fluid. "N-n-no," he corrected politely. "Tastes pretty much like v-v-vesper to me." He dunked his head into the oasis and drank greedily.

But Phoebe wasn't thinking about water, or even about the foul taste that coated her mouth. She was transfixed by the shapes that danced beneath the vesper surface and around her legs. At first, she thought they might be a hallucination, but when she rubbed her eyes, they were still there. She stared into the depths, feeling like her heart was being squeezed in a vise.

Dollop was right—everything was connected. But not quite in the way he meant.

How could she not have seen it before? How could she have been so blind? That uncanny, fleeting sense of déjà vu she had felt before now hardened to a stone in her gut that grew heavier by the second. Micah saw them too. He forgot his dehydration and stood beside her in somber silence. Slowly, she unstrapped the Trinka from her wrist.

Now she understood why Mehk was a secret.

Phoebe laid the Trinka in the shallows of the pond and watched the gliding forms gather around it. They were bulbous silvery creatures with four paddle-shaped tentacles that spun like propellers. A little red organ fluttered within them, pulsing softly with a warm glow.

They were identical to her Trinka.

But alive.

The swimming mehkans inspected the Foundry trifle as it sank into the vesper like a ceremonial offering. They wrapped their appendages around it, nudging the corrupted carcass as if attempting to bring it back to life.

STRIKING A
BALANCE

oodwin waited atop his favorite tower in the Citadel, swirling a glass of arterial-red wine. His balcony was sheltered from the brutal suns by a cascading ceiling that looked like a melted candle, with hardened gobs and streams of dripping iron—a waterfall of molten metal frozen in time. High gnarled parapets blocked out the fierce gusts of wind, making this spot a strangely serene refuge within the otherwise ghastly fortress. Goodwin came here often to clear his mind and take in the glorious, panoramic view of Mehk.

It was a land brimming with promise.

The Citadel was surrounded by moors of harsh serrated ore, choked with barbed-wire brambles and drowning in foul lagoons of rusty sludge. It was an ideal strategic location because no one could approach from any direction without being spotted a great distance away. These dead lands were haunted with history, eons of misery that struck fear in the hearts of mehkans. Just to the west were the peaks of the Vo-Pykaron Mountain Range, stormy blue formations draped in an ominous leaden sky. And to the distant south lay the Mirroring Sea. He could stare at the silvery surge for hours, entranced by its hypnotic pulse—a vast, glittering expanse of liquid metal destined to shatter over and over against the midnight-black shore.

Approaching boot steps clicked on the floor behind him, but Goodwin did not turn. There was a scrape and a scuffle as someone was forced into a chair.

"Does that bottle look familiar?" Goodwin asked. He held up his glass to admire the wine's velvety, ruby hue. "It was given to me on my sixtieth birthday, a present from my dear friend Doctor Jules Plumm. An 1864 Chequoisie—a truly remarkable gift." He took a luxurious, unhurried sip. "Whatever happened to that man?"

The Chairman turned around. Jules was seated at a table adorned in white linen, topped with the extravagant bottle and a glass goblet. Behind him glowered Kaspar. Jules's features were drawn and taut, but a smile ghosted on his chapped lips, and his eyes twinkled bright behind his crooked glasses.

"I don't know," Jules said, "but I'll drink to his passing."

Goodwin chuckled softly and nodded. "I thought you might want a taste."

Kaspar plucked the bottle up and poured him a glass.

"It is almost a shame to enjoy it here," Goodwin said as Jules drank deeply. "I find the air here disrupts the fragile nose of a delicacy like this. Ah well. Are you hungry? I could have something else sent up, if you like."

"I seem to have lost my appetite," Jules muttered.

"Good, down to business then."

Jules emptied the rest of his glass in one gulp. "Thanks for sharing, James," he said as he wiped his cracked lips. "But your pet monster and I are late for another delightful interrogation session, so if you'll excuse us—"

He tried to rise, but Kaspar roughly shoved him back down.

"Please," sighed Goodwin. "Stop this charade. Seeing you like this pains me, it really does."

Jules spat out a hollow laugh.

"I have been patient with you," the Chairman said. "But no more. Talks are failing. I received notice just this morning that Trelaine is following the Kijyo Republic's lead and has begun to pull their ambassadors from Albright City. They are now the third nation of the Quorum to do so."

"They won't be the last," Jules warned.

"I will not allow another conflict."

"We've given them little choice."

"On the contrary, we have done everything in our power to accommodate them. We lifted key embargos, lowered tariffs, especially where the Trels are concerned. And yet still they are insatiable. The Quorum will not be content until they have what is rightfully ours. But there can only be one Meridian."

"Or no Meridian at all."

"And you wonder why you are under suspicion of treason? Don't be naïve. Meridian will never fall, not with the Foundry as her guardian. We ensure peace because war is bad for business." Goodwin savored another taste of wine and surveyed the landscape once more. "But how can I maintain it when you seek to undo all we have worked for? Sabotage, conspiracy, and provocation—those who work against the Foundry never succeed, Jules. You know this. We cannot tolerate defectors."

"Is that what you think I am?"

"No, you are much more."

Goodwin set his wineglass atop the dark gold parapet. It was balanced precariously, paper-thin crystal resting hundreds of feet above the dead lands.

"We live in a fragile time," Goodwin mused, tracing the edge of his glass. The wine shimmered within as he nudged it closer to the edge of the rampart. "Every one of us, every choice we make is a grain of sand on the scales. All it takes is one grain, one mistake to send us crashing into oblivion."

The glass wobbled, then tipped, but Goodwin stopped it before it fell. A few drops plummeted into the barbed-wire brambles far below.

"You have been working with Trelaine. What you have told them?"

"After twenty-seven years of devoted service, you believe

I would be so foolish as to compromise our security like that? You know me better."

"Kaspar," said Goodwin with a casual gesture. The grim soldier stepped forward and withdrew a Scrollbar. He slid the nickel-plated rods apart to reveal a handheld Computator screen that displayed a document. "You are one of my oldest friends and most trusted partners," Goodwin continued, his voice heavy with regret. "Do you deny this is you in these Dialset transcripts? We have not yet decrypted the other voices, but they are undoubtedly Trelainian accents."

Jules studied the glowing Scrollbar screen, the words reflecting in his spectacles. "I swear to you. This isn't what you think."

"Then explain. We do not have the luxury of time."

A long silence descended, punctured only by the cold creaking of Kaspar's leather gloves as he flexed his hands.

"The truth . . . The truth is, I've had enough," Jules said in a broken voice. "I can't do this anymore. Ever since Olivia . . ." He took a heavy breath and tried to compose himself. "I was seeking asylum in Trelaine for Phoebe and me, and these calls you intercepted are of me trying to arrange safe passage."

Goodwin assessed Jules with a calm and unyielding expression.

"I've been suffering, James. I was looking for a way out."

"I am sympathetic to your hardship, I always have been. I, too, am no stranger to suffering, but it is inevitable—an unfortunate fact of life. Sometimes even necessary, when it is in favor of the greater good."

Goodwin strolled behind Jules.

"Take Kaspar." He laid a hand on the soldier's armored back. "Think of what he has volunteered for, what he has willingly endured and suffered for the Dyad Project, for the benefit of the Foundry. And yet he doesn't go crawling into the eager arms of our enemies. His loyalty remains unbroken."

"I am not Kaspar. I am a husband. And a father."

"What did you offer them in exchange?"

"My life's savings."

The Chairman narrowed his eyes at Jules. "You expect me to believe they have no interest in your tenure at the Foundry?"

"I secured diplomatic immunity. My secrets are protected by Trelainian law," Jules said defiantly. "I knew my actions would make me a fugitive, but it was never my intent to become a traitor. I have been loyal every day of my life."

"To whom?" The kindness that had warmed Goodwin's words was gone. "What about last month? April the twelfth and twenty-third, were you loyal to us then?"

Jules did not answer.

"The work you did to cover your tracks was ingenious. It took a data team several days to decode the phony paperwork, but there is no account of your true whereabouts. Whom did you meet with, and what did you tell them?"

"I told you, I haven't said a word," Jules said defiantly.

Goodwin leaned in to study Jules's gaunt face. "You force me into an unfortunate position. What would you have me do?"

"Let us go to Olyrian Isle. Give me an early retirement. I

understand I've forfeited my civilian life, but in the protected isolation of a Foundry settlement you can rest assured that I'll have no contact with the outside world."

"The Isle is for those who have earned the privilege of enjoying their remaining years in peace after a lifetime of devoted service. Do you deserve such an honor?"

"Then at least send Phoebe there. All I care about is keeping her safe."

"Would that I could."

Jules opened his mouth to say something, but Goodwin took the Scrollbar from his hands and called up something else on the screen. It was a grainy surveillance video playing in a short loop. Jules stared at it, and his brow furrowed. It took him almost a full minute to comprehend what he was seeing.

That momentary hitch in his voice, those tears that were brimming in his eyes only moments ago, they had all been quite convincing. Yet as Goodwin read the man's face now, blanched and panic stricken at this unexpected horror, he knew for certain that it had all been a ruse.

"The children have been lost in Mehk for nearly a day," stated Goodwin.

"How . . . how could this be?"

"Like her father, Phoebe appears to be resilient—and foolhardy. There is no guarantee we will be able to locate them in time."

Jules could not tear his eyes from the monitor. His hands were shaking. Goodwin sat down beside him and pulled his chair close.

"If you truly care about your daughter, then cooperate. Tell us the truth about your exchanges with the Trels. Then you can lead the charge to find Phoebe. We will broadcast your voice across Mehk, blanket the territories, and the children will be sure to come to you. But we must act fast," Goodwin said, finishing his last drop of wine. "The scales are tipping."

Jules sank in on himself. He nodded almost imperceptibly.

"That will be all, Kaspar," the Chairman said.

The silent soldier offered a bow and tossed something onto the table in front of Jules, an object that had been balled up in his fist. Kaspar left the two men on the balcony, and Goodwin poured himself another glass of wine.

Jules was focused on the crumpled object as it unfolded before his eyes. It was a battered piece of black leather with a silver strap. Phoebe's shoe.

"I am listening," Goodwin said.

THE GHOSTS
OF FUSELAGE

When the train tracks finally came into view, shimmering beneath rust-red mesas on the horizon, Phoebe and Micah felt no victory. A ravenous hole had yawned open within them, a profound emptiness worse than hunger or thirst. They kept to the brass thickets that sprouted alongside the rails, remaining out of sight in case a train came rumbling past. The three of them had not exchanged a word since the oasis. As they walked in unison, their feet scuffing rhythmically in the brush, Phoebe grimly recalled their marching song.

"Meridian cast off all her bonds
When Creighton Albright forged the bronze
With ball of lead and sword of steel
We'll crush our foes beneath our heel . . ."

Their childhood rhyme was a cruel joke. Creighton Albright's face gazed down from lofty statues throughout Meridian and graced every single coin. He was idolized as the greatest inventor of all time, father of the modern age.

But the Trinka told the real truth.

Those nuts and seeds in the Chokarai didn't just look like hardware. It was no coincidence that the rust slug she had sniped Micah with resembled an electrical plug. And of course the chraida had been so eerily familiar. Their wheeled clamp hands and the lithe grace with which they swooped on their zip lines were the very essence of Cable Bikes.

Their dying screams still clawed at her memories.

The vetchels and the trelligs, every mehkan that Dollop had shown them and every one they had yet to meet, from the kite birds overhead to the brass reeds underfoot—these were Albright's true discovery. He was no inventor. Every gadget she had ever desired, every thrilling new convenience, the flashy vehicles and the magnificent buildings, they all belonged to Mehk.

Phoebe's city, her country, her very life stood on a metal foundation built from the bones of a murdered world.

Everything is a lie.

"It's not fair," muttered Phoebe.

They looked at her.

"It's not fair," she repeated.

"Yeah," Micah said to Dollop. "Why don't you guys try and stop them?"

"Th-they have CHAR," he whispered helplessly.

"Say what?" asked Micah.

"Un-undying d-d-death. It's a t-terrible weapon that dissolves metal forever. Where CHAR has been, th-there's no life, only bli-i-ights that no mehkan can ever, ever approach. Ever."

"But I mean, there's gotta be millions more of you than them," Micah argued. "Why is nobody fighting back?"

"W-w-we are. The Covenant is sworn to defend Mehk."

"Come on, Dollop. I'm bein' serious."

"I—I—I am too. Very serious. I never jest about th-the Children of Ore. Their sacred mission is to, um, return us to the W-W-Way."

"Then where are they?" Phoebe asked.

"Th-they are, it's just that . . . Well, they are a *secret* army, s-s-so they have to be . . . secret," he tried to explain. Micah just rolled his eyes.

"I don't understand," Phoebe said. "How did the Foundry take over like this?"

Dollop sighed wearily. "The axials t-teach that many phases ago, the Way united M-M-Mehk. W-we were at peace. Uh, but we strayed from Makina's p-plan. The Ona, may her golden ember blaze, tried to w-warn us. She—er, the Ona, that is—was the Great Engineer's most faithful m-m-messenger.

194

She told us not to, um, f-forsake the Way. But we did."

His voice quavered. "We t-t-turned our back on Makina. That is why the b-bleeders came. Why the CHAR came. The bleeders k-killed the Ona, and when w-we needed Makina most of all, She was gone."

He was on the verge of tears but maintained his composure.

"It-it-it's our fault. W-we broke the heart of our dearest M-M-Mother of Ore. If we hadn't shun-n-ned Her, She would have protected us. But Sh-She left, and the Great Decay began. The interlocking harmony She sh-showed to us rusted away. N-now mehkans fight mehkans. Hate an-and fear drive us apart. We have all, um, forgotten our f-f-function. Now Her s-sacred machine is being taken away from us piece by piece!"

Dollop ran off ahead, unable to take it anymore. Phoebe considered going after him, but she hadn't the faintest idea what she could say.

"I wanna know what really happened," Micah mused as soon as Dollop was out of earshot.

"What do you mean?"

"Well, Dollop's great and all, but does he really expect us to believe all that Way mumbo-jumbo? Makina and Oona? And the Covenant? Gimme a break! He's nuttier than an outhouse rat. Nuh-uh, I wanna know what the Doc's got to say about all this."

"My dad's not a part of it."

"You kiddin'? He's a big shot at the Foundry. They're all in it together!"

"But they kidnapped him. He did something to make Goodwin mad."

"So?"

"So that means that he's against them. I'm telling you, he's not a part of it. I know him better than anyone. He wouldn't do this. He wouldn't."

Her face hardened with certainty, and he backed down.

"Maybe," Micah said with a shrug.

Despite how sure Phoebe sounded, a sliver of doubt remained. All she could think of were her father's long absences. And every time he returned, the smell of smoky grit and iron—the breath of Mehk—clung to him like a shadow, no matter how hard he tried to hide it.

The expanding halo of suns sank toward the horizon as the end of the day neared, turning the liquid blue sky raw and enflamed. The amber hills of the brasslands grew piebald and sparse as the travelers neared the mesas. Clustered white formations like crystallized cauliflower forced their way up through the cracked, clay-red ore, dotting the landscape like a fungus.

Because they no longer had much cover, they had to hike on the other side of a ridge to remain out of sight. And that's when they saw it—a split in the train tracks up ahead. Two separate paths led off into sweltering haze.

"Ain't that perfect!" Micah huffed as they came to a halt.

Phoebe tried to shake the weariness from her head.

"And it ain't like the stinkin' sun's any help neither. If it would just rise in the east and set in the west like a *normal* sun,

196

we could at least figure out some kinda direction to head in. But no! In Mehk, it's gotta set everywhere!"

"B-beautiful, isn't it?" Dollop gushed. "Sunfall is my fav-v-vorite part of the cycle."

"Yeah, yippie! It's just dandy-rific!" Micah hollered.

"Come on," Phoebe rasped disapprovingly.

"WHAT?" His eyes flashed.

It sure doesn't take much to set him off, Phoebe thought. She swallowed the dryness choking her throat and struck an even tone.

"Look, I get it. I'm starving too. But we can't start losing it now. We just have to figure this out." She saw the heat in his eyes begin to cool. "Preferably soon, before night. I'd rather not be stuck out in the open once it gets dark."

Micah grumbled and exhaled sharply like a snorting bull.

"Deal?"

He nodded.

Together they assessed their surroundings, but there was nothing to suggest which way to go. Phoebe thought about asking Dollop's advice, but they couldn't afford to waste time on another wrong path.

Which left her with a simple choice: right or left.

"What's that?" Micah said, pointing off in the distance.

Smack-dab between the two sets of train tracks, perched on a far-off ridge, was some sort of structure. It stood alone, huddled in the multiple shadows of the setting suns.

"Whaddya think?" he asked.

She looked to see if there were any better options, but there were none.

"Let's move fast. There's nowhere to hide down there if a train comes."

Micah agreed. They made their way down the slope and glanced along the rails to make sure the coast was clear. The three of them hopped the first beam and crossed the twelve-foot span of track. Phoebe wondered how many had been killed to create this expanse of steel. What mehkan was butchered, its carcass used to construct those massive trains?

As they hurried across the open plain and toward the structure, a gaggle of little iron balls with shifting segments rolled across their path, squeaking like frightened field mice. They zipped around the kids' feet and vanished into tiny holes in the ground. Dollop slowed his gait and gazed at the bubbly white formations, which were growing in tall stands like piles of giant soapsuds. Many were broken and shattered on the hard, cracked ground.

"Oh, aren't they l-lovely!" Dollop sang. "They're called . . . uh . . . whatsit . . . er . . . Hold on, it'll c-c-come to me. . . ."

The companions mounted the ridge, their aching thighs screaming as they climbed. The thought of a place to rest drove Phoebe on, but she held out the fleeting hope for a drop of water or a bite to eat. She thought about her last meal back at home, that mountain of food she had barely even touched—Parmesan quiches, blackberry pancakes, pork hash, and cinnamon toast. She swallowed her tasteless, rubbery

Honeygum at long last, trying to convince herself that it was a bite of gooey pancake dripping with warm maple syrup.

They crested the rise, and the building came into view. It was in serious disrepair, layered with haphazard shingles.

"Weird place to build a house," Phoebe thought aloud.

"Chusk! Th-that's it," Dollop cried, poking at one of the white nodules on the ground. "It's, uh, called chusk. W-wonderful stuff, so many uses."

"Ain't a house," Micah said as they approached the structure. "It's a gambrel-roof barn. Dontcha know the difference?"

"You're such a hick," she said with a little grin.

Micah was about to shoot back, but Dollop interrupted with a chuckle. "Oh-oh! You know who, uh, loves to eat ch-chusk?"

The barn moved.

With a ponderous groan, the giant pile of grating metal sheets picked itself up and turned. A horrifying clutter of saw-toothed appendages emerged from a gap underneath, hacking away at a hunk of chusk while its slobbering mouth devoured the pieces that flew off. The monster's extremities splayed open to reveal black eyes glittering from the inside knuckles.

Phoebe was the first to scream. Micah was the first to run. Dollop nearly fell apart as he scampered away at top speed.

The mehkan charged after them, extending eyeball-laden legs and dragging along its sheet metal shell in an earsplitting screech. Every frantic step made Phoebe's injured foot blaze with pain. She could barely keep up as her friends raced around looming chusk growths. The rampaging creature smashed through the barriers like toothpicks, almost on top of them.

They hurled themselves down a slope, sliding and skidding to the bottom. The beast slowed at the crest, eyeing the decline cautiously, but it did not attempt to clamber down after them. Instead, it retracted its legs and began the laborious process of turning its massive body around. The trio wheezed and caught their breaths, watching the horrendous mehkan above them lift its rear end and let fly a splattering explosion of grayish feces. The rancid stench hit them full blast.

"Yeah, right back at ya, pal!" Micah burst into laughter.

"Ugh! Disgusting!" Phoebe said, covering her mouth. Between the overpowering smell and her throbbing wound, she felt close to collapsing.

"Y-y-yup, that's a grundrull all right," Dollop said as the giant mehkan finished its business and shambled away. "They're a little t-t-territorial."

"Ya think!?" Micah shouted.

"W-wait. This is g-great news! Grundrulls are tended by langyls, who—who harvest chusk from their stinky. L-l-langyls are a, um, lovely people." Dollop clasped his hands together in excitement. "I b-bet they'll be happy to help us!"

"Happy to help humans?" Phoebe asked skeptically.

"W-w-well . . ."

"Wait, are you tellin' me these langyls are crap farmers? You mean, like, picking up poop is their *duty*?" Micah snickered at his own pun.

"Sounds like your kind of people, Toiletboy."

"Th-this way," Dollop chimed. "L-looks like a lang town up ahead!"

"Hey!" Micah called after Phoebe, who giggled as she limped off. "You said you wouldn't call me that! What happened to rule number two?"

They followed Dollop toward a settlement nestled deep in the sunken basin. The setting suns lined the horizon like a row of fiery bullet wounds, bleeding out dusky swirls of maroon and magenta. As the lip of the valley rose around them, the vanishing light made it hard to see. At least none of the buildings looked like they might get up and attack, which was a start.

But with every approaching step, it became more and more clear that something was wrong. Chusk grew abundant and unmanaged, forming tumorous reefs that they had to clamber over. Signs of destruction began to mar the terrain. There were craters gouged into the ore and lumps of scorched shrapnel scattered like refuse. The streets ahead looked more like a pile of rubble than a settlement.

Dollop was trembling so violently that bits of him began to shake loose and clatter to the ground.

"Come on," said Micah. "Don't go all to pieces on us."

He shook his head. "N-n-n-n-no. H-h-h-h-haunted."

"Aw, gimme a break," Micah scoffed. "Are these more of your psychic brain blower-upper Covenant thingies?"

"What is it?" Phoebe asked.

"U-u-u-u-u-uaxtu. Em-em-em-em-ember-reapers. E-v-v-v-v-vil spirits dr-drawn to dead places, um, hungry to m-make more!" He gathered his parts and started to flee, but Phoebe held him back.

"We don't have a choice. We need shelter," she said.

"N-n-n-n-n-not here! An-n-n-n-nywhere but here!"

"Get it together. Ain't no ghosts gonna hurt you. Not with us here to protect ya. Right, Plumm?"

"That's right."

"So just stay behind me, and we'll hightail outta here at the first sign of any ghosts or ghoulies or whatever."

"P-p-p-p-promise?"

"You betcha," Micah assured him.

"And everybody keep an eye out," Phoebe added, looking at the ominous ruins. "For anything."

They made their careful way into the devastated town, Dollop's loose pieces chattering like frightened teeth. It was eerily quiet. The broken bones of a surrounding wall and mournful fragments of buildings rose around them like a mausoleum.

Something wide wobbled under their feet, and Phoebe kicked aside debris to inspect it. For a fleeting instant, she wished she hadn't given up her Trinka, whose light had been invaluable. But emerging stars crept across the sky, stretching their shimmering webs like cracking ice, and in the pallid glow, they could just make out a sign.

" 'Fuselage,' " Micah read aloud.

"Foundry," she whispered, as if the mere name might stir up the phantoms that filled Dollop with such fear.

"How do you know that?"

"If it was mehkan, we wouldn't be able to read it."

"Whoa! Check it!" Micah shouted as he ran down a ruined avenue. It was a graveyard—blasted hulls of Foundry machines locked in the grips of decomposing grundrull carcasses. The air was rancid, buzzing with clinking mehkan insects that hovered over corpses, their struggle immortalized in rust.

"We need to get out of sight," Phoebe said.

"Why?" Micah asked, kicking aside a blackened chunk of ore. "Ain't nothin' here. This place is a ghost town."

Dollop began to quiver fiercely at the sound of the word.

"Empty," Micah quickly corrected. "I mean, it's empty."

They proceeded down the dark narrow lane, wending around toppled smokestacks and the shattered frames of factory equipment. Bullet holes peppered every surface. Micah prodded one with a finger and discovered the perforations were filled with some kind of hardened white cement.

There was a sound like the warping of paper-thin metal. They spun around but only saw a couple of crumpled-up sheets of corrugated tin. Phoebe leaned forward. The metal wads were lined with wires that trembled as she neared. They unfolded in the blink of an eye, and she staggered back. Two more crinkled sheets opened up, then zipped off, transforming into a blur of shapes. They bent and folded to fit under low passes and flattened to slip through gaps, moving across the ground like newspaper scattered by the wind.

"L-langyls!" Dollop cried. "Wait, ex-ex-excuse me! We need your h-help! P-pardon me!" He took off running after them, calling out in Rattletrap.

Phoebe tried to follow him but stumbled over something,

knocking it away with a clatter. It was a Watchman head, severed and partially crushed. Micah plucked the mechanical skull from the ground, and they both stared into the empty shell. Though they couldn't see well in the dark, they could make out broken circuit boards and some sort of a fat bundle of cables that must have been its fried Computator brain.

He let go of the Watchman head and gave it a swift drop-kick. The skull bounced and tumbled into a nearby pile. Melted faces, severed limbs, and fractured torsos cluttered the ground, knee-deep in some places. There was even one skewered on a pole, its robotic entrails dangling in a nest of wires.

Phoebe knew the Watchmen were not alive, not like mehkans, but she was still unnerved. The sight of the mutilated humanlike figures was visceral, and it made her sick. Micah, on the other hand, was indifferent. He rooted through the mess of bodies, searching for something.

"What are you doing?" she asked anxiously.

"Figures," he huffed, picking up a melted hunk of metal and tossing it aside. "All these bots and not a single working Dervish rifle between 'em. Not even a freakin' hand-cannon. I mean, gimme a—Oh, hold on a sec. . . ."

He pulled something from the dead soldier's grasp.

"Guess you won't be needing *this* anymore," he muttered. It was a worn clublike weapon with a handgrip covered in unintelligible knobs and a business end that flared out into a ridged coil. He fiddled with the scorched gadget, trying to turn it on, but it appeared to be busted.

"Better than nothin'." He shrugged.

And then the looted corpse twitched.

It bucked as if seized by an external force.

The kids backed away. Something was emerging from the Watchman's torso.

It was the size of a warthog, with five stout piston limbs, dripping with grease from the Watchman's innards. Its entire front half was taken up by a horrifying mouth, a sparking crevice of circular grinders and rotating blades. Knotted along the outside of its whirling maw was a nauseating array of spiny protuberances and paddles. It began to pump up and down on its cylindrical legs, faster and faster, as a fiery light flared through vents in its side.

CRACK! It sounded like a gunshot. The abomination was gone in a blast of light. The kids spun in a panic, jolted from their momentary paralysis.

There was a thud as the creature landed behind them, its hydraulic legs recoiling from the leap. Micah brandished his new club as a pile of debris next to them shuddered and parted. Another creature appeared, its dreadful mouth gnashing. They leaped like monstrous fleas—*crack, crack!*

Dozens of them pressed in.

Hungry.

A RACE
OF SPARKS

Phoebe was running for her life all over again. It felt like she hadn't stopped since they entered Mehk. She was hollow, a mere shadow of herself, as disconnected as a puppet.

They raced through Fuselage, hurdling debris and whipping around corners to flee the sparking mehkans. Startling bangs blasted as the fiends leaped in pursuit. Micah seized a leaning stack of wreckage and toppled it behind them to block the way, but the predators scampered up walls, using their piston legs to punch holes and give them purchase.

CLANG. One of the sparking monstrosities landed in front of them. It was so close that they almost slid right into its whirring grinder mouth. Micah grabbed Phoebe and yanked her into another alley. Each time her feet hit the ground, she felt heavier and heavier. Her legs threatened to buckle, but she pushed harder and harder.

"There!" he cried.

At the end of the lane stood a building with shattered windows and a fractured roof. Emblazoned on its facade was the familiar sunburst logo. The gunshot crack of their pursuers drove them toward it. They sprinted past toppled security walls and into a vast courtyard where blackened shells of war machines were strewn about like toys. The kids slammed against a battered door, but their combined weight barely budged it. Something inside was blocking the way, leaving only a narrow opening. Phoebe went first, sucking in her breath as she squeezed inside. Halfway through, her skirt snagged.

"Hurry!" Micah shouted.

The blasts were getting close—no time to free herself. With all of the force she could muster, she threw herself forward. There was a loud tearing sound as her skirt ripped, and she fell face-first into a gloomy antechamber. She picked herself off the ground, and Micah wriggled in behind her. They shoved the door closed as rocking blows crashed against it. Hideous clattering mandibles scratched at the gap, spraying sparks and singeing the kids' arms. Panting, Phoebe and Micah rammed another desk against the makeshift barricade.

Piston legs thumped on the outer walls as the hunters searched for a way in. The kids glanced frantically around, trying to orient themselves. They were in a decimated foyer that reeked of the Foundry's opulence. Scorched rugs lay in tatters, jagged holes pocked the wood-paneled walls, and broken furniture blocked every passage. The only escape was a winding staircase, its fractured balustrade missing posts like a broken-toothed grin.

They raced up the cracked marble steps to a massive pair of ornate doors. The kids plunged through the entryway and into the ruins of a huge chamber. The wooden floor was splintered and peppered with broken glass, and the remains of a crystal chandelier dangled like a glittering severed head. The few fragments of wall that remained showed once-cheerful colors and details of geometric silver filigree. Slender doors that led to an elegant balcony were now just melted ribbons of iron sagging over amputated ledges.

No sooner had the kids gotten their bearings than flickering sparks appeared in the dark. The grinding sounded from all sides as monsters crawled through the open roof, perching on skeletal fingers of wreckage and scuttling through cracks in the ravaged walls.

There was nowhere left to run. Micah readied his club, trying to find a target. The weapon trembled in his hand—he barely had the strength to hold it.

Phoebe's heart boomed as the creatures advanced.

Then, out of the darkness, a shrill whistle pealed.

A pinpoint of light appeared on the ground, and the monsters hesitated. They focused their attention on the glowing spot. The nearest pawed at it as another few got low on their haunches to watch. Then one of them pounced at the light.

Twittering appendages folded in to seal off their grisly grinder mouths, and the paddles atop their heads perked up and swiveled. In an instant, the swarm of fearsome beasts turned into a litter of playful puppies.

Phoebe clung to the wall, trying desperately to remain on her feet, but Micah was still on guard, scanning the room for the source of this distraction.

Lingering in the darkness was a tall, well-dressed man with willowy limbs. He was projecting the light from a lantern mounted on his head.

She froze—was it a Watchman?

The man took a loping step out of the shadows. He appeared to be dressed for the opera in an exquisite Durall ensemble consisting of tailcoat, top hat, umbrella, and crisp white gloves on waggling fingers. But despite his attire, he was anything but human. His limbs were long, flexible hoses of tarnished metal, and instead of a lantern on his head, the lantern *was* his head. Sprouting out from his extendable neck was a complex periscope that projected light, fanned by an array of dewy lenses that slithered on vinelike stalks.

Even in her stupor, Phoebe recognized this unusual face. He was an Omnicam. Or rather, this mehkan's people were hunted for their heads, which were used to make high-tech security cameras like the ones in the Foundry.

The elegant figure whipped his head to the side, and his spotlight zipped out of a hole in the wall. Several of the frisky mongrels bounded after it in pursuit. Another shrill whistle sounded as a squat form emerged from behind a pile of rubble, a rusty pipe clutched in his thick mitt. The sight of the stranger's weapon made Micah grasp his own club tighter. But instead of threatening them, the stout figure hurled his pipe out a window, and the remaining mutts hopped after it with a joyful screech of gears.

The whistler was a fat little mehkan, shorter even than Micah, with knobby brown hide and a wild explosion of quills on his head, bunched into bushy muttonchops and eyebrows. He had a lumpy, potato-shaped face and beady eyes that moved independently, like a cast-iron chameleon. A disk with dozens of holes of various sizes sat where his nose should have been, and he wore a shaggy overcoat of overlapping metal fiber flaps, fronted by an outrageous green-striped necktie.

The tall mehkan's spotlight bloomed to a warm glow. He focused his luminous eye on Phoebe and Micah, blinking rows of horizontal shutters like a signal lamp. The squat one bowed low, a gear-toothed grin of tarnished gold twisting his wide mouth wider.

Phoebe felt herself fading. Her lips were moving, but she couldn't weave the words together in her muddled head.

"You all right?" Micah whispered nervously. "You don't look so hot."

She offered a vague nod.

"Jubilations and salutations," growled the fat mehkan. They were surprised to hear his gravelly baritone speak their language. "The pleasure be thoroughly ours, little acquaintances. We mean you not a modicum of harm."

"Who's 'we'?" Micah demanded. "Who you callin' little?"

"Oh, me most humblest apologies. How unforgivably boorish." The fat mehkan licked his hand with a black tongue and flattened down his bushel of spiny hair. "Mr. Pynch, at yer gentle service. And this be me esteemed associate, the Marquis." The debonair mehkan tipped his top hat and bowed.

"We coulda handled them monsters," Micah said.

"The sparkies?" Mr. Pynch let out a grating rasp of a laugh. "Rambunctious mayhaps, but not monsters. Mere scavengers, rapacious for ore long expired. Purely pusillanimous they be, I most suredly assure you."

Micah stared blankly, baffled by his jumble of big words.

The fat mehkan looked up sharply. His disc-shaped nose rotated, spinning like the cylinder of a revolver. It whirred and clicked into place, and he sniffed the air.

"Me nozzle tells me we got company," Mr. Pynch growled to the Marquis. His bizarre nose spun again, this time lingering at a larger nostril hole. "Anomalous . . . Can't identify it. Quick!" he barked at the kids. "On yer guard!"

Micah dropped into a defensive stance with his club.

Phoebe had no fight left in her.

They heard something plodding up the stairs.

Mr. Pynch held his breath and blew as hard as he could, ballooning up and popping out an arsenal of spines from under the flaps of his coat. The steps were getting closer. The Marquis snapped the shutters of his signal lamp head closed, while his lenses stood on end. He drew his umbrella like a rapier and took a few swipes like a fencer preparing for a duel.

Phoebe's breath was coming in short, ragged gasps. Blood pounded in her ears, and her vision was blurry. The world went dark around the edges. She felt like she was watching herself at the end of a tunnel.

The doors crashed open. A horde rushed in.

Sparkies.

They all had wiggling objects clenched in their stubborn jaws. Behind them staggered a familiar figure.

"Dollop!" Micah cried.

"Th-there you are!" he warbled, stumbling in and trying to wrestle his limbs away from the sparkies.

"You know this mehkie?" Mr. Pynch asked, confused.

"S-s-sorry, I g-g-got a little t-turned around. Gimme that b-back!" He swatted at a critter that refused to let go of his detachable arm. "I mean, I w-was trying to t-t-talk to the langyls when—Phoebe!"

She had held on as long as she could. The unrelenting terror, the agonizing hunger and thirst—it was all too much. Her body failed. That last burst of frantic energy had drained her dry. A dizzying wave of nausea took her, and she swooned. It felt like she was falling forever, falling into nothing.

If she hit the ground, she didn't feel a thing.

20
HARD TO SWALLOW

 cold splash.

Water!

She coughed and sputtered. The trickle of water was heavenly in her ash-dry throat, even if it did have a slight metallic tinge. Drop by drop, she came back from the brink, and the world re-formed around her.

Phoebe cracked her eyes to see Micah pressing a steel canister to her lips. Dollop stood nervously beside him, together with Mr. Pynch, the Marquis, and a pack of curious sparkies. She took the container from him with shaking hands and drank greedily.

"Welcome back," Micah said. His words were muffled by something in his mouth, but she couldn't make out what it was. She closed her eyes and drained the canister, shaking it even after she knew it was empty.

"Th-that was a close one," Dollop said, and scooted away from a sparky who was eyeing him hungrily.

"More," she rasped. "More."

Micah chuckled and refilled her cup from a dented metal jug. She emptied the container again.

"All be wholesomated! Miss Phoebe prevails," Mr. Pynch trumpeted. The Marquis extended his telescoping legs and rose above the crowd to offer a wave.

Phoebe looked warily at the two mehkans, unsure of how they had learned her name. She had been laid out on a pile of singed curtains in the corner. There was a jumble of toppled tables strewn with foul-smelling garbage. Gobs of food clung to shattered plates, black and crusted beyond recognition. The buffet counters were demolished, and a cracked punchbowl had left a dark red explosion all over the white silk. It was torture, staring at these rotten remnants of a feast. She turned to Micah and realized that he was chewing.

"Food!" She snatched the half-eaten ration bar from him.

"Hey! Watch it, Grabby."

She gobbled it ravenously. It was vaguely peanut butter flavored, dry and crumbly. A couple months ago it might have been considered stale, but to Phoebe it was divine.

"W-we thought you had, um, g-g-gone to rust!" Dollop stammered. "A-a-are you feeling better?"

Phoebe nodded and smiled her thanks.

"Now don't get all fainty again when I show you this," Micah teased. He gestured to a meager stack of beaten-up cans and a few packs of durable staples. Phoebe could barely believe her eyes. She snatched up the nearest can and ripped the lid off with shaking hands. Black beans—thankfully unspoiled. Taking in a huge gulp, she let the dark, salty juice saturate her mouth. The beans were creamy and soft, and though she tried to chew slowly and make them last, her body screamed for more. Micah joined her and opened a can.

"Switch," he said, scarfing down half a tin of yams. The kids traded and quickly devoured their long-awaited meal. Licking his lips, he reached down to open up another one.

"Wait," she said. "Is this all there is? The water, too?"

"Pretty much, yeah."

"We should go easy then, right? We need to make this last."

He froze, mouth agape and itching to open the can in his hands. But he knew she was right. Micah tossed it back into the pile and swiped his finger inside his empty tin of beans.

"Where did you find this?" she asked.

"Pantry over there." He motioned, sucking his finger clean. "Pynch pointed it out."

"An expiring human be an abominable thing me associate and I could not bear to witness," the fat mehkan piped as he inspected the tin lid that Phoebe tossed aside. He wiped the syrup off and popped the disc in his giant mouth. "Consider it a benevolent favor. A freebie, as it were."

Mr. Pynch flashed a wink from one of his wonky eyes.

She looked at him suspiciously. "How long was I out for?"

"I dunno. Maybe five minutes," Micah said. "Why?"

"Nothing." She dismissed the thought and took a moment to absorb her surroundings. A dark notion cast its shadow in her recuperating mind. "This place . . . Is this what I think it is?"

"You don't know?" Mr. Pynch said with surprise. "Why, it be a festivity hall. A venue for customary human carousals."

"Festivity? You mean, like, parties?" Micah asked.

She could almost hear the music and the merry laughter of revelers, almost see the twirling couples in their formal attire. Every bit of decadent joy had been paid for in mehkan blood. This was once a Foundry ballroom.

"It's disgusting," she said.

"Pardon?" Mr. Pynch queried.

"It makes me sick."

Mr. Pynch bent his huge mouth in a contemplative frown and shared a look with the Marquis, who shrugged. The dapper mehkan was more interested in the empty cans, as was Dollop. With the kids' approval, the three mehkans split the discarded tins and dined upon them, chatting casually in Rattletrap. Lacking a mouth, the Marquis tilted his periscope head back to reveal a gap in his neck. He tossed in the metal bits and chewed by pumping his entire torso up and down. The pack of whining sparkies gathered and begged for scraps.

"What're y'all talkin' about?" Micah asked.

"Ah," Mr. Pynch said, motioning to Dollop. "Our charming counterpart here was just commentating on the fact that he never has seen a lumilow and balvoor, such as meself, cavort together. Sworn nemesi, our peoples be!"

He had a good laugh at this with the Marquis, whose lamp shutters fluttered delightfully.

"It-it-it's true!" said Dollop. "Ever since the Great Decay, um, I heard balv-v-voors can't even set foot in Dyrunya."

"As you say," Mr. Pynch said, picking at his stained teeth with a protruding quill. "Indeed, times be tough. But whereas strife drives most toward prejudicial aspersions, me associate and I see it as a fertile opportunity for collaboration."

Dollop pondered this, nibbling on a chunk of can and shooing away sparkies.

A few of the critters jiggled vigorously, shaking off grease and rust like wet hounds. With some hesitation, Micah reached over to scratch one behind its paddle ears. The creature jerked away and looked askance, then reconsidered and leaned into his petting, throttling a piston leg in satisfied response. Micah looked at Phoebe, a grin lighting up his face.

"What about you, good Dollop?" Mr. Pynch asked. "Yer particular assemblage be unfamiliar, even to seasoned expeditionists such as ourselves. Where do you hail from?"

"S-s-sorry?"

"Yer haven, yer birthplace?"

"I . . ." He looked down at his hands. "I d-don't know."

"Well, what be yer heritage? Who be yer clan?"

Dollop glanced away, his amber eyes flickering with distress.

"I see," Mr. Pynch said, stroking his muttonchops thoughtfully, his nozzle ticking away. "A foundling? An orphan?"

"For real?" said Micah.

"You don't know where you're from?" Phoebe asked.

"I—I—I—I forgot," he said, methodically rubbing the crevice in his head.

"No matter," Mr. Pynch comforted. "It just so happens that the Marquis and meself be veteran gallivanters, and we confabulate with a great many mehkies. If you have the penchant, me lad, we would be honored to make some professional inquires into yer . . . particularities."

"Tr-tr-truly?" Dollop chimed. "You'd—you'd help me find . . . me? I mean, my cl-clan? You w-w-would do that?"

"Indeed we would," Mr. Pynch growled cordially. "So tell me, how comes it that you be traveling with this pair of delightful humans?"

"Th-they saved me!" Dollop chirped. *"Serve those who giveth themselves unto you.* The Way is quite c-c-clear on this matter." He stroked the emblem on his chest, the icon of two intersecting gears depicted with a jagged vertical line.

Mr. Pynch let out a guffaw. The Marquis covered his luminous eye, overcome by a peal of silent giggles. Dollop shrank back a little.

"Har-har, what a rollick! Be that a genuine, unalloyed dynamo?" Mr. Pynch chortled as he looked at the symbol on Dollop's chest. The Marquis flashed his signal lamp at Mr. Pynch, a flickering pattern that looked like some kind of visual language. The fat mehkan whispered back in Rattletrap.

That set Phoebe on her guard. She nudged Micah to see if he had noticed the covert exchange, but he was preoccupied with his battered club. He had slipped the wrench out of

218

his back pocket and was focused on taking the weapon apart, ignoring the sparky that nudged his legs for attention.

"Forgive us. It just be that, well, we haven't observated a genuine Waybound in quite a lengthy spell. It be so antiquated, so . . . provincial. You be the rarest of breeds nowadays."

"It-it-it's okay. I-I'm used to it," Dollop said, slumping over.

"And what of you, me brave young wanderer?" Mr. Pynch purred to Phoebe, his nozzle making a slow, repetitive click like a gun being loaded. "How do you come to be in Fuselage?"

"We walked," she said curtly. "What about you two?"

"Scouring for that which might perchance have some utility." He indicated a huge, lumpy sack in the corner that was bound with perforated steel straps. The bulbous bag was overflowing with picture frames, candlesticks, a wall clock, wooden utensils, and various other human goods.

"You're s-s-s-stealing?" Dollop gasped.

The Marquis flared his lamp and shook his head no.

"Scavenging, to be more precise-like," Mr. Pynch corrected. "Just as the sparkies and yer comrade here have clearly done."

Micah looked up and shrugged.

"Yeah, who gives? It's just stealin' from the Foundry anyway," he said, trying to rub the scorch marks off his pilfered weapon. He held it up to read something off the blackened grip. "Lodestar XC-8. Wicked!"

"It-it-it's still stealing though," Dollop explained. "And—and stealing is against the Way."

"That may be, me dear mehkie," Mr. Pynch rumbled

cheerfully as he lay a hand on Dollop's shoulder. "Yet wouldn't yer Engineer smile down upon our sin? It led to the salvation of yer comrades in the form of sustenance, after all."

Dollop stroked his dynamo and considered this.

"Why did you help us anyway?" Phoebe asked.

"What she means is," Micah said, shooting her a sideways glance, "*thanks* for the help."

"You be kindly welcome," Mr. Pynch said with a bow. "To elucidate, me associate and I be in the *business* of helping people. And helping people of the human persuasion be our speciality." The Marquis flickered his light warmly to the kids.

"You aren't scared of humans?" she asked.

"Do you intend us ill?" the fat mehkan inquired.

"No. But how do you know we're not with the Foundry?"

"Lost as you be? Sojourning with a Waybound? Endearing yerselves to the locals?" Mr. Pynch chuckled as he motioned to Micah, who was scratching the exposed belly of a contented sparky. "But even if you were Foundry, what of it? Why fear the inevitable? We might as well fear the fusion o'erhead, or the ore underfoot. Or the gauge in our pockets."

The Marquis blinked another message to his companion. Mr. Pynch nodded, then leaned his fat body back to roll forward onto his feet.

"Come with me," Mr. Pynch said, crunching through broken debris. "I be keen to show you something."

With great trepidation, Phoebe strode across the ballroom to join him, keeping a safe distance. Dollop and the Marquis followed, but Micah stayed put. He was far too engrossed in trying to repair that stupid club.

Mr. Pynch motioned out the balcony. Far off in the recesses of night was a scattering of settlements. Tall smokestacks churned out blankets of billowing smog, and lights glimmered through the haze. It reminded Phoebe of the nighttime view from her veranda back home—the view of Foundry Central.

"It be known as the Chusk Bowl," Mr. Pynch said. "An ancient farming kinship. You see, only grudrulls can eat chusk and break it down, so langyls share an intimate bond with them. When langs shed, they relinquishate their skin castings to grunds, who utilize them to fabricate their shells. In exchange, grunds permit langs to harvest chusk fibers from their excrement."

Micah, still working at his weapon, snickered at the word.

"Chusk weave be hearty, infinitely useful, and provides the langs with a spectaculous profit." Mr. Pynch held out one of the jagged flaps of his metal fiber overcoat for Phoebe to touch. She reached out with some reservation—it felt like a rough version of fabric she was accustomed to back home.

"And the langs be not alone with their interest," Mr. Pynch said.

"The Foundry. Chusk is Durall."

"Very perspicacious of you, Miss Phoebe," he rumbled. "The langyls negotiated a partnership with the humans, and now the Chusk Bowl be Foundry owned and operated. All was agreeable, and the gauge flowed freely. But some langyls were no longer acquiescent to the arrangement. The Foundry be intolerant of such betrayals, and responded by soundly obliterating them, thus leaving behind this potent lesson for all who might consider such impetuments in the future." He spread his arms wide to present the bleak ruins that lay around them.

A beam of light appeared on the horizon, one of those behemoth trains departing the langyl settlements, probably carrying a shipment of newly minted Durall. Phoebe thought about her father's stunning wardrobe, the upholstery on his reading chair, and the gleaming Durall carpets in their home. Was he involved in the Foundry's business with langyls?

She shivered against the night air. Mr. Pynch wandered back inside.

"Why are you telling us all this?" she asked, following him.

"To illustritate what happens when one opposes a human—when the nasty thought even crosses yer mind. That be a misjudgment me associate and I have never made."

"B-b-but all those poor langyls . . ." Dollop moaned.

Mr. Pynch stood side by side with the Marquis, the tall mehkan dusting himself off fastidiously and flattening the wrinkles in his pristine tuxedo.

"Aye, the poor langyls," Mr. Pynch agreed sadly. "Yet tragic victims though they be, the langs unwisely volunteered to a partnership they later chose to negate. You think the Foundry be disgusting, engaging in felicitatious activities in this salon while mehkans suffer under their dominion. That be undoubtedly true. But here be another truth—humans pay on time and their gauge never be counterfeit. And in such a troubled age, that be of great value to adventuring business-mehkies such as we."

Phoebe wanted to vomit up her beans and yams.

"As I afore-mentioned, we be in the business of helping people." Mr. Pynch smiled. "We have proffered the generous favor of nourishment—the first one always be on the house." He settled his hands on the lapels of his chusk-weave overcoat. "Now, how else may me associate and I be of assistance?"

"Actually," Micah chuckled, finally looking up from his toy, "there *is* somethin' we need pretty bad. Just so happens that we're on our way to the—"

"To bed," Phoebe interrupted. "We need sleep. Thank you for the food, and for your offer, but we have had a long day."

"Say no more," Mr. Pynch said. "We'll reconvene our negotiations on the rise." The Marquis bowed graciously, swiveled about on bendy legs, and then trotted across the ballroom to their stash of pilfered goods.

Micah gaped as Phoebe retreated to the opposite corner.

"Oh, and never you mind about security," Mr. Pynch called out. "We be the lightest of sleepers and honored to stand vigil." His stained smile glittered from across the ballroom.

Phoebe turned away and gathered discarded tablecloths to use for bedding as Micah and Dollop joined her.

"What's up?" said Micah. "What's the harm in asking?"

"They work for the Foundry," she replied.

"Aw, they'll work for anybody. They're in it for the money."

"You think that's a good thing? Any mehkan that would

even consider helping the Foundry can't be trusted."

"What do you say, chum?" Micah asked Dollop.

"Who, m-m-me? Uh, I dunno." He shrugged. "Th-they're . . . okay?"

"Well, I have a bad feeling about them," said Phoebe.

"So that's it, then?"

"Yes. We can't afford the risk."

Micah wanted to talk back, she could tell. He glanced down at his broken Lodestar, his lips pinched into a hard line. But when he looked back at Phoebe, his eyes were cool and his demeanor indifferent.

"Now let's just get some rest," she said softly. "In the morning, we can search this place and see if there's anything else we can use. Maybe there's a map or something to help us find the Citadel."

"Sure," Micah said as he plopped down. "You're the boss."

With Dollop's help, she finished arranging tablecloths into a makeshift bed and lay down. Her stomach growled, but she knew they would have to pace themselves with their limited supply of food. Micah continued repairing his Lodestar, disassembling it and fiddling with the pieces. The sparky that had been cuddling up to him earlier nuzzled at his side.

Phoebe yawned. "Since you're staying up, you should take first watch, okay? We can't let them out of our sight."

Micah didn't respond, intent on his project.

"Just wake me up when you're ready to switch," she said. "Did you hear me? I said wake me up, okay? Micah?"

"Yup," he said, scratching his head with the wrench.

Dollop crammed an empty trash bin full of linens and crawled into the impromptu cave. He pressed a hand to his dynamo and closed his eyes, murmuring prayers in Rattletrap. Phoebe looked away from him, feeling like she was intruding, and glanced to the other end of the ballroom. The Marquis strobed a message to Mr. Pynch, who grumbled a gruff chuckle in response.

As Phoebe drifted off, she wondered what was so funny.

THE MEND

Phoebe rocketed up the front steps of the manor and flung open the doors. The house was still and thick with shadows.

"Daddy?"

She blasted past the dimpled copper door to his study. He was standing before the fireplace with his back to her—a lean silhouette carved out by the low light of licking flames.

"Daddy!"

She ran toward her father to embrace him. He turned.

Her blood froze.

His skin was hard and fixed into an eerie grin that did not reach his dead, black eyes. His brittle smile cracked, and fissures snaked across his dented face, revealing the unmistakable shine of metal.

The fireplace roared. She screamed, but no sound came.

He began to grow, stretching, towering to fill the room.

"Cricket," came his voice, vague and very far away.

She looked down at herself—her flesh was gone, replaced by overlapping scales of metal skin. She could feel a searing gush of life in her ductlike veins and a whirring engine where her heart used to be.

Phoebe was a mehkan.

"Cricket." This time the word was a rusty peal.

In her father's white-gloved hand was an enormous glass jar. He leered down at her, sparks crackling in his fractured eyes. She tried to get away, but her legs were bent backward like an insect, snapping in ways she did not understand. Phoebe pounced and flailed, but she was not fast enough.

The jar slammed down around her. She leaped like mad but only clanged against the glass ceiling. His monstrous hand tightened. Cracks shivered across the dome overhead. The gritty crunch of splintering glass.

Her father's hand came crashing down.

WHOOMF.

The sound was like the ignition of a powerful gas jet. She threw back her tablecloth covers and scuttled away in a panic. Nearby, Micah laughed.

"Up and at 'em, Plumm!" The sparky he had befriended ran circles around him, bouncing on piston legs.

Her heart was pounding. She glanced around the room,

trying to shake the dream from her blurry mind. The ballroom was transformed, now awash in streaming light, refracting rainbows through the crystal chandelier. Dollop sat with Mr. Pynch and the Marquis on the far side the room, gobbling up handfuls of glop from a hexagonal shell. The mehkans were huddling around a carefully arranged stack of little curved rods knotted with symbols.

"H-h-happy rise!" Dollop called over to her. Mr. Pynch waved, and the Marquis flickered a cheery hello. "Th-they're teaching me how to play, um, Sliverytik. It's gr-great fun, and I lost all five games, but—"

Mr. Pynch played his hand by adding pieces to the stack, which re-formed to an intricate new shape with a little ticking sound. Dollop's shoulders sank.

"Uh, m-m-make that six games."

"Peaches?" Micah said out the side of his crammed mouth and offered her a can. She took it and quickly devoured the remnants, letting the succulent fruit chase away her grogginess.

"What happened last night?" she whispered, eyeing the mehkans across the room warily. "You were supposed to wake me up, remember?"

"Eh, you needed your beauty sleep. No worries. Dollop and I kept watch." He whipped the Lodestar up and twirled it around his hand in a practiced gesture. "'Sides, I had to get this puppy up and runnin', didn't I?"

The weapon was dented and held together with new scrap-metal additions, but she could tell Micah had spent all night repairing it. The coiled tip glowed with a purple light and emitted a steady hum. As she ate, he pointed the Lodestar at her and squeezed a trigger on the handgrip. The glow surged, and the can was whipped from her hand, drawn to the flaring coil with a clink.

"Fire in the hole!" Micah called out, aiming his club at the mehkans across the room. He fiddled with the knobs until he heard the cheery ping that announced that the Lodestar was ready. He squeezed the trigger again, and *WHOOMF!* A fuzzy bubble bloomed out of the purple coil, a pulse of wavering energy that launched the can like a missile. The sparky took off after it, squealing with delight, but the Marquis extended a telescoping arm and caught the can with the tip of his umbrella.

"Much obliged, Master Micah," called Mr. Pynch. He scooped up the Sliverytik rods and shuffled them expertly while addressing Dollop. "You be quite the expedient learner, me lad. How's about we toss a round for keeps?"

The Lodestar's hum rose in pitch, ending with that pleasant chime. Micah beamed as brightly as his new toy.

"Worked up a new pulse switcher out of bits and bobs I found lyin' around," he boasted. "It's the same as them big ol' coil dealies—the ones we saw lined up around the train yard. The Foundry must have all kinds of crazy magnet weapons here. Pretty freakin' sweet, right?"

"Yeah," Phoebe said, chuckling. There was something new about him, like the Lodestar had fed his growing confidence. "I'm impressed."

"I mean it's no gun, or nothin'," he mused, "but it's wicked strong. I'm still gettin' the hang of it."

"Hey, what's with the getup?" she asked, suddenly registering that he was decked out in a strange, oversized outfit that was bunched up and tied off at the arms and legs. His grin grew even wider as he hooked his thumbs under his collar, flipping it up. It was a singed, mismatched set of industrial coveralls, complete with gloves and protective pads. The jumble of yellow and gray was imprinted with a snazzy pattern of interlocking triangles. On the sleeve was a patch bearing the Foundry's sunburst logo.

"Hundred-percent Durall. Musta cost a freakin' fortune!" Micah squawked, his voice cracking awkwardly. He was too excited to be embarrassed. "Snatched 'em from a busted storage room downstairs. Now we don't have to get all sliced up anymore. Go ahead, try 'em on."

He gestured with his Lodestar to another set of gear that lay folded on the ground. She grabbed the pile and saw what was hidden underneath.

"Boots!" she gasped. Each scuffed shoe had come from a different pair, since the color and size didn't really match, but it was a miracle. She could have hugged him.

Micah just shrugged.

"Thank you," she said with a smile. Phoebe grabbed the metal jug and poured a little water into the empty canister. "Let me get changed. Can you gather up the food and—"

"Oh, you mean that?" he said, motioning to a heavy-duty Durall rucksack filled with their meager supplies. She laughed.

"You're the best," she said, lightly touching his shoulder. He looked down at her hand. "Give Dollop a heads-up we'll be leaving soon. I'll be right out."

"Not a problem." He grinned at Phoebe's back, watching her hurry out of the ballroom with her cup of water. "I got it all under control."

She wandered down a hall littered with debris, past a marred bust that might have once been Creighton Albright, and found a blackened washroom. The plaster walls were ripped to shreds, the stalls were leveled, and the silver sinks were crumpled, but it would do for a minute of privacy.

Phoebe slipped out of her skirt, tossed aside Micah's stinky jacket, and pulled on the coveralls. Although it was heavy, the jumpsuit was surprisingly comfortable. It was made for an adult, a smoker, she guessed by the smell of stale cigars, and it draped over her willowy frame like a woven metal bathrobe. She zipped it up, then rolled the sleeves and cuffs, securing the folded material with the attached straps. After snapping the protective elbow and knee pads into place, she discovered a hood hanging in the back with a transparent shield for the eyes. This connected to the face mask that unfolded from the collar and contained a breathing apparatus. She tested the mouthpiece and inhaled, then coughed—yup, the previous owner was definitely a smoker.

Phoebe sat on a pile of rubble and unwrapped the wire and metal fronds that bound her blood-caked foot. The sight unnerved her. She couldn't believe how far she had managed to walk on it. Her sock was crusty red and plastered to the wound. She bit her lip to keep from crying out as she gently removed it. The gash was nearly an inch long, swollen and tender, but thankfully it didn't appear to be infected.

She didn't know the first thing about dressing wounds, so all she could think to do was clean it with water. Phoebe found some tattered hand towels and tore them into strips. She wrapped the pieces around her feet and crammed the rest into her Durall boots, which were several sizes too large. The second she slipped her feet in and eased them down onto the soles, she let out a blissful sigh of relief.

Her eyes fixed on her sniping skirt, crumpled on the floor. There was a ragged tear from when she had squeezed through the barricaded door last night. After nearly two days in Mehk, the garment was covered in snagged seams and little punctures, but it was basically intact. She fished her needle and thread from one of the secret pockets that she had stitched into the pleats and set to work fixing the tear.

Phoebe's mother had taught her to sew. They used to sneak into her father's closet and steal clothes for her to practice on. Together, they would rip armpits and tear pant legs, giggling all the while. The challenge was for Phoebe to make the mend seamless so that her dad wouldn't notice. She suspected he had been playing along the entire time, pretending to be oblivious.

Her mother had also taught her that some tears could not be mended.

Luckily, this was not one of those tears. She made quick work of it and pulled the skirt on over the industrial coveralls.

The combination looked utterly absurd but she didn't care. She grabbed her Durall gloves, the cup, and Micah's jacket. As she turned to leave the washroom, Phoebe caught a glance of her reflection in a cracked mirror that remained on the wall.

Is that . . . me?

Her hair was a matted nest, her face sunburned and stained with sweat-streaked grease. She held her own gaze for a long moment, marveling at the hardened girl staring back at her.

She was doing this. She was going to find him.

Would her father know her? She barely knew herself anymore. He would recognize the skirt—all the more reason for her to keep wearing it. And what would her mother have said to him if she had learned the truth about Mehk? Would she forgive him, or was this a tear that could not be mended?

Phoebe looked down at the Foundry patch on the sleeve of her coveralls. She dug her bony fingers underneath the stitches, ripped it off like a scab, and tossed it aside before marching out of the washroom.

TOO DIM FOR
A LODESTAR

P hoebe returned to the ballroom to find everyone laughing—
all three mehkans were gathered around Micah, who was playing
fetch with the sparky by launching chunks of metal debris with
his Lodestar.

"Now that's a fashion statement, if ever I saw one," Micah
chuckled, pointing at her skirt and coverall combination.

"Ah, Miss Phoebe. A marvelicious ensemble, to be certain," complimented Mr. Pynch as he sealed and secured his
big bulky satchel. "Not only do Foundry accouterments protect yer delicate hide, but they look snappy, too."

The Marquis nodded his approval, meticulously dusting

his fancy Durall attire with a small collapsible pocket brush.

"L-l-look, Phoebe!" chirped Dollop. "I'm a bag boy. Th-that's my, um, my function!" He held up the Durall rucksack containing their limited supply of food. Unfortunately he held it upside down, and it all spilled out and clanged to the ground. "Whoops, s-sorry."

"No worries," Micah said. "You'll get the hang of it."

Mr. Pynch ratcheted a valve on his giant satchel, and it compressed, expelling all the air until it looked like lumpy leftovers wrapped in foil.

"Well, after much trepidation on the part of me associate and I," Mr. Pynch began with a frown of worry on his lumpy face, "we accept yer propoundment. It undoubtedly be a garrison of much unspeakable malfeasance, and we be operating contrary to gut-wise instincts, but gauge talks, as they say. So we shall perform as yer dedicated chaperones."

She looked at them, uncomprehending.

Mr. Pynch rattled on. "As a precautionary measure, I advise a strict avoidance of public thoroughfares. Best to travel a sequestered trajectory and remain unscrutinized—in-coggy-neato, if you will—and I have formulated the ideal route. So we all be prepared for embarkation then?"

"What are you talking about?"

The Marquis flickered at Mr. Pynch, whose nozzle spun. "Master Micah hasn't informed you?"

"Informed me . . . of what?" she growled, leveling her eyes.

"Gimme us a minute, fellas," Micah said. He launched a chunk of metal from his Lodestar, and the sparky pounced after it. The three mehkans, after a brief exchange in Rattletrap, nodded their agreement and wandered out of the ballroom, though Dollop cast a concerned look back at them as he departed.

"Let's have us a chat," he smirked, leaning the Lodestar on his shoulder.

"What did you do?" she hissed.

"Only what needed to be done. I hired 'em to take us to the Citadel."

"You WHAT?"

"I'm gonna find the Doc, and I'm gonna save him," he said as if it were obvious. "It's prob'ly best for everyone if I take the reins from here."

She studied his face for a moment, and then a smile played on her lips.

"Very funny. You almost had me going," she laughed. "Good one, we're even. Sorry about the rust slug, okay?"

But he shook his head, his grin never fading. The truth sank in. She began to tremble with rage. That smug sneer on his fat, freckled face made her want to scream.

"What did you tell them?"

"Everything," he replied. The sparky came bouncing back, and Micah sucked the hunk of metal from its clattering jaws with the Lodestar.

"You . . ." She tried to control herself. "You told them about my dad?"

"Not that. Just what we said to Dollop," he huffed. "I ain't gonna give away your dirty little secret. I'm not an idiot."

"You are if you trust those two!"

"What's trust got to do with it? I know how to handle jokers like that. You just gotta know how to work 'em. And if they step outta line?"

Micah cranked up the settings on his Lodestar so that it hummed more intensely. He fired it, and she flinched as the air pressure from the purple detonation blasted her face. The metal chunk smashed through a plaster wall at the opposite end of the room, leaving a gaping hole.

"Quit screwing around with that thing for one second," she snapped. "This isn't about you or me. This is about finding my father."

"Exactly. So quit bein' so stubborn about it, and step aside," he said, starting to get frustrated. "We're gettin' nowhere fast, followin' you. You got no plan and you keep passin' out all over the place." He rolled his eyes back into his head and pretended to swoon.

"I do have a plan. And those criminals aren't a part of it."

"Oh yeah, what's 'at? Wander along some more train tracks and hope we get lucky? Some plan!"

She didn't have a comeback for that.

He assumed a tone of forced calm that irritated her all the more. "Look, we both want the same thing. It just so happens that you don't have a clue how to go about it, and I do. No biggie, I'll take care of it. I'm lookin' out for you. I already put food in your belly and shoes on your feet, didn't I?"

"You just can't remember your place, can you?" Phoebe snarled. She took a menacing step toward Micah to loom over him, but he was unfazed. "You are still my servant. You do what I say, when I say it. Got it, Toiletboy?"

"Yeah, about that," Micah said, smiling as he retrieved the chunk of debris from the bouncing sparky's jaws. "I quit."

"Really? Just like that? You would sell out your entire family for . . . *this*?" She gestured to him and his stupid Lodestar. "So you can finally be in charge of one thing in your pathetic little life? When we get back, Micah Tanner, I swear I'm going to make sure that—"

"Yeah, yeah," he said, teasing the sparky with the bit of metal. "That we're all fired, that my entire family starves to death, that whole thing. Got it. Now if you're done bellyachin', it's time I establish my command. Rule number one . . ."

It took everything she had to keep from punching him out.

"Gimme back my jacket," he ordered.

Phoebe wadded up his coat and threw it at him as hard she could. It knocked him off balance, and although he pretended to laugh it off, his reddening face betrayed his anger. He turned up the knob on his Lodestar so that it buzzed like a hive of furious bees. She felt heat emanating from the flaring coil as its glow intensified and took a wary step back.

"You were planning this all along, weren't you, you little rat?" she spat.

"I gave you your chance, Freaky. Now it's my turn. I'm quicker, I'm stronger, and I got the skills. Face it—I'm the man for the job."

"You're not a man. You're a midget with a magnet."

That got him. In a fiery fit of rage, Micah cranked up

his Lodestar full blast. It vibrated so fiercely that it started to rattle, and Phoebe feared it might explode in his hands. He mashed the trigger and a giant bubble of force knocked them back, throwing off his aim. The metal chunk exploded into the enormous crystal chandelier. Icicles of glass careened down.

They watched it for a tense moment, hoping. Then the supports gave way, and the entire thing plummeted, ceiling and all. Phoebe, Micah, and the sparky dove away. The chandelier detonated on the floor, pulverizing wood in a splintering crash.

As the dust settled, Micah looked around at the damage.

"Whoops," he said.

Fuselage looked more desolate in the daytime—a wasteland of sun-bleached rubble. Not a single structure or an inch of ground was untouched by the conflict. The group made their way out of the abandoned Foundry building with the sparky hopping along beside them. As they navigated through the leveled town, Micah presented his jacket to Mr. Pynch.

"There y'are, just as promised," he announced. "A genu wine Military Institute of Meridian bomber jacket. I'll even throw in them medals of honor there for free, 'cause that's the kinda guy I am."

"A lavish vestment indeed, Master Micah," admired Mr. Pynch as he caressed the faux leather and chintzy little adornments. "And a wise expenditure. You won't be disappointed." The Marquis held it up to see if it might fit him, and then stuffed it into the giant foil sack strapped to his back.

"That's all he paid?" she scoffed. "To get us to the Citadel?" They looked at her strangely.

"I mean, it's just a cheap souvenir," she said. "It's not worth anything."

"Don't listen to her," Micah retorted. "She's full of it."

"Sorry he tried to scam you. Eugene can be like that."

"Eu-Eugene?" Dollop asked, adjusting the rucksack.

Phoebe acted surprised. "Yeah, that's his real name. He didn't tell you that either?"

"No, it ain't!" Micah said, getting angry. The sparky whined beside him.

"How about this?" she suggested. "Since it's such a measly payment, why don't you just lead us to the train tracks? Point us in the right direction, and we'll take it from there."

"Not this again!" Micah threw up his hands.

"Tracks, Miss Phoebe?" queried Mr. Pynch. "Not an advisable route."

"I'll take my chances."

The fat mehkan inhaled, expanding his massive belly. "As yer newly contracted retainer, I must advise you against such measures. It be a roundabout digression, adding a cycle or two to yer journey. And if I am to understandimate it, you require the punctual rescue of a person of interest?"

Mr. Pynch waited for her response, but when none came he continued. "Then there be the Holkhei land bridge. That alone would require half a cycle to ambulate, with nowhere to retreat should a locomotory engine traverse during yer crossing. You'd be most assuredly cast to rust down in the ravines or pulverized flat as a baby drebbling. Oh, and did I mention the silver steppes?"

"No," Phoebe grumbled.

"Just one further notation," Mr. Pynch continued merrily. "Trifle though his presented raiment may seem, it be an exceptional sort of rarity here in Mehk, and therefore quite profitable. Many thanks for yer concern, but it be more than adequate compensation for our services. So then, with yer permission, Master Eugene . . . Let us avaunt!"

Phoebe stared at Mr. Pynch silently, her eyes boring into him as he marched away, followed by the Marquis and a nervous-looking Dollop.

"Nice try, Stringbean," Micah snickered, twirling his Lodestar in a purple flash that got the sparky all excited again. He caught up with Mr. Pynch and muttered, "Forget the Eugene stuff, all right? Let's just stick with Master Micah."

She followed along behind them, fuming.

"So tell me, Master Micah," rumbled Mr. Pynch pleasantly, "what do you make of the grand mystery of Kallorax?" Dollop shuddered at the name, and the Marquis gave him a reassuring pat on the back.

"Well, I think—I mean, yeah, it's, uh . . ." Micah shrugged.

"Surely you have audibilated the infamous name."

"Refresh my memory."

"Kallorax was a megalarch thousands of phases ago during the Ixardian epoch. A demon was he, a sadistic ruler of genocidal proportions. The Citadel swirls with his enigma."

"Oh right, *that* Kallorax."

"Yet what ultimately became of him and his nefarious regime be lost to the vagaries of prehistory. Innumerable legends have attempted to ascertain the peculiarities of their disappearance. However, despite all those quandaries, the Citadel remains as the sole relic of their existence, a monument to the horrors of his heinous reign. Fascinating, no?"

"Th-they were smited," insisted Dollop.

"A *peculiar* theory," granted Mr. Pynch with a smile.

"They were bl-blasphemers. M-M-Makina punished them."

The Marquis chimed in with a flickering message.

"Me associate here claims that the Taviri chargers of old drove them out, others say they were obliterated by an untraceable pandemic. Or perhaps, as our charming companion here suggests, it was the hand of the Great Engineer Herself. But the fact of the matter be that no one truly knows."

Micah was enraptured by Mr. Pynch, who led the group through the labyrinthine streets. Phoebe dragged behind, not wanting to be any closer to Micah and his new best friends than necessary. She noticed that Dollop had slowed to a stop, a perplexed look scrunching up his face. He was staring at a ten-foot-wide pit that had been filled with small bits of wreckage and granulated ore. There was a distinctive pattern to the loose debris, a series of lines radiating out from the center like the spokes of a wheel.

"This sh-shape," he pondered. "It, uh, reminds me of s-something. Something imp-p-portant."

"What do you mean?" Phoebe asked.

He shook his head, frustrated. "I kn-know who m-makes

this sort of h-hole, but I just can't seem to, um, place it."

"Get the lead out!" Micah called back. "Time's a wastin'!"

"If he doesn't shut up, I swear . . ." Phoebe said under her breath. "Come on, Dollop. Better leave it alone."

"So str-strange," he said. Dollop gave the pit a last glance before hurrying to catch up, the rucksack jangling on his back.

Soon they emerged from the shadow of the crippled buildings into the arid landscape of the Chusk Bowl. The lip of the basin rose all around them, rust red and barren, sweeping up to the swaying reeds of the brasslands above. A handful of grundrulls meandered aimlessly in the distance.

The sparky trotted at Micah's heels until it realized they were leaving Fuselage, and then it began to whine and nuzzle against his leg. Micah gave the creature a final vigorous scratch behind its row of ears.

"All right boy, last one. Let's make it count," Micah said, sucking up a piece of debris with his Lodestar. The critter unfolded his chittering mouthparts to expose its grinders and sprayed out a jolly blast of sparks. Micah aimed his weapon up in the air like a mortar and fired. The blast knocked him back on his heels as he sent the scrap sailing away. With a squeaky squeal of joy, the sparky bounded after it in a fiery crack.

"Gonna miss that pup," Micah sighed.

They watched the sparky spring away like a crazed flea, and then turned to resume their journey. Only the Marquis's gaze remained fixed on Fuselage. Two diopters on stalks slithered in front of his signal lamp eye as he locked his stare intently on the sky above the ruins.

Suddenly, he spun and strobed a bright warning.

"Quick, obfuscate!" barked Mr. Pynch. "Down, down!"

The group huddled behind a growth of wild chusk.

"What is it?" Micah asked, but Mr. Pynch motioned for them to be quiet.

At first, it looked like a few mehkan birds in the distance, maybe more of those vetchel things. But they were flying unnaturally, hovering and tumbling, freezing in mid-air. Despite being miles away, the kids could make out three X-shaped aircraft. The black forms slung low to scan areas around Fuselage before reversing, spinning end over end, and returning to formation.

They were converging above the Foundry building.

"GBX-20 Shadowskimmers," Micah whispered. "Usually used for recon."

"Uh, what d-does that mean?" asked Dollop.

"Foundry spy drones," Micah responded grimly.

"What it means is that they heard a big crash," Phoebe said flatly, looking deadpan at Micah. "Like, say, I don't know, a chandelier falling, and figured they should check it out."

"No way!" Micah blustered.

"No matter," Mr. Pynch said as he dabbed sweat from his knobby brow with his garish green necktie. "The Marquis's exceptional opticle provided ample warning. They be too far-flung to spot us, so . . ."

He hesitated, watching as the drones dropped lines down, lowering dark oval shapes through the busted roof of the

Foundry building. He said something in Rattletrap to the Marquis, who changed diopters to get a better look.

A gust of wind blew past, and Mr. Pynch's nozzle went haywire, spinning this way and that. He gasped.

"V-Stalkers! Run!"

The fat mehkan took off like a spooked jackrabbit with the others racing behind him. The Marquis, slowed by his heavy load, extended his legs to keep up. Every stride tripled, quadrupled in length, and soon he was in the lead.

"What . . . are they?" panted Micah.

"Trackers . . . deadly . . ." wheezed Mr. Pynch, his rotund form jiggling with the furious pace. "High ground . . . lose 'em . . . in the brass!"

They scrambled up the ridge, clambering desperately for footholds. Phoebe was thankful for her gloves and boots as she scurried over the spiky crumbling ore, but the oversized coveralls made her feel clumsy. Looking back over her shoulder, she saw black shapes that must have been the V-Stalkers darting through Fuselage, scaring up dust trails in pursuit.

She barreled over the ridge and into the reeds. The tall blades of brass thrashed around her, scraping along her Durall coveralls as she caught up to Micah and Dollop. Mr. Pynch and the Marquis were nowhere to be found.

"Wh-where did they go?" Dollop whimpered.

"Pynch?" Micah called out, turning in a circle.

"See!" Phoebe snapped at him.

She knew it. This was exactly what she was afraid of.

What happened next came so fast they could barely react. Mr. Pynch and the Marquis burst out of the reeds and grabbed the kids roughly. The Marquis seized their wrists and whipped off their gloves. Mr. Pynch extended a quill and jabbed it into their palms. They cried out, but the mehkans didn't stop.

"H-h-hey. Wait!" Dollop cried, too scared to help.

Phoebe fought, but their grip was unbreakable. With the Marquis's help, Mr. Pynch rubbed their bloody hands on something in his stubby mitts—a pair of orbs the size of oranges. They looked to be made of intersecting gears and segments that emitted high-pitched whirs. It was two of those little critters they had seen the day before, the ones the kids had almost mistaken for field mice. The tiny mehkans unfurled, a mess of shifting plates and pinions, impossible to tell the head from any other end. They were smeared in blood.

"Clykkas, in the brush," Mr. Pynch hurried. "Fast as can be. Now they got your scent." He grabbed Micah's Lodestar and shook it. "Blast 'em."

Micah was confused at first, but a light sparkled in his eyes as the reality of the situation dawned on him. He tweaked his weapon and attracted one of the clykkas to his magnetic coil.

"Aim higher, back toward Fuselage," Mr. Pynch urged.

Micah squeezed the trigger. With a *WHOOMF,* he sent it squealing. He snatched up the second clykka and blasted it, too. The critter's panicked screech faded as it sped away.

The five of them peered through the brass reeds and down into the Chusk Bowl. The rushing black V-Stalkers were hesitating, as if recalibrating their path. Then they scattered, bolting this way and that, zigzagging through the maze of Fuselage to seek out the blood-soaked clykkas.

"Not a moment to tarry," said Mr. Pynch, crashing through the waving thicket like a bull. The Marquis struggled with the weight of his satchel and clung fast to his top hat as he sprinted off. Dollop was right on their tails.

Micah licked his wound. He raised his eyebrows at Phoebe in a haughty gesture that said "I told you so" before racing off.

She glanced at the gash on her hand, drops of her blood speckling the ore. Phoebe did not want to follow them, but there was no other way. Reluctantly, she crammed her glove back on and hurried to catch up.

23

AGAINST THE TIDE

aintaining Mr. Pynch's pace was no easy task.

"Huzzah!" the fat mehkan hollered. He fumbled through the flaps in his overcoat, withdrew a dingy silver cap, and slapped it over his nozzle. "Dis way!" He veered left and trampled a path through the chest-high brass, into a patch where the reeds looked blanched and flimsy. Instantly, Phoebe understood why Mr. Pynch had plugged his nose.

"Barf! Smells like Randy's armpit died," Micah moaned, covering his face.

No, it's worse, she thought. It was like month-old meat rotting in a public toilet. And it was getting more putrid with every step. They moved through a patch of growths that was like lengths of scraggly, exposed rebar. At first glance, Phoebe thought the sickly stems were covered in shimmering hairs, but a closer look filled her with revulsion—there were squiggling little maggot things growing out of the wretched metal plant, thousands of them.

"Worbweed. Guarandeed do bask our scend," Mr. Pynch said through his capped nozzle.

The ground was blanketed with the grubs, which spurted like blisters as the kids walked over them. She could taste bile in her throat and dreaded the thought of losing her breakfast. By the time she thought to use the breathing apparatus in her coveralls, they were out of the wormweed patch. With meticulous attention, the Marquis plucked the squirming things off his tuxedo. Then he extended his legs and slipped a lens over his opticle. After surveying the land, he shrank back down and offered a jaunty thumbs-up to Mr. Pynch.

"Be apologies for de exzessive pudrescenze," the fat mehkan said before popping off his nozzle cap. "But it be a judicious precaution. As you can plainly observate, the occasional cavorting of me associate and I with the Foundry has its benefits, as it familiarizes us with their technical apparati. And now that we be relieved of our pursuers, we can proceed apace."

The halo of suns was rising in the sky. Mr. Pynch shielded his eyes as he gazed up at it, oily perspiration beading his knotted brow.

"It be said that Kallorax fancied himself a god of the suns, incarnated here on Mehk to subjugate the weak."

"Th-that's terrible," Dollop gasped.

"Wicked!" said Micah.

"Indeed he was," growled Mr. Pynch, lowering his tone like a storyteller around a campfire. "Legends tell that he slaughtered millions of his own subjects, incinerating them by the scores. The Citadel be a chamber of nightmares where he burned his enemies in a raging fire, until their red-hot bodies softened and melted and oozed their liquefied entrails out upon—"

"St-top, stop, stop!" Dollop said, covering his ears.

The others laughed, all save for Phoebe.

Mr. Pynch reached for his necktie to dab away his sweat, but stopped in his tracks. It was gone. At first he was concerned, but a knowing grin split his face, and he waggled a finger at his partner. The Marquis touched his chest as if to say, "Who, me?" But then he produced the tie from his pocket with a flourish.

"Bah! How'd you manage that, ya slippery fingersneak?" Mr. Pynch chortled as he laced it around his neck.

Phoebe was shocked, but the others apparently thought it was hilarious. Dollop touched his chest, and upon noticing that his dynamo was missing, laughed even harder. The Marquis plucked off his hat and reached inside it, withdrawing the golden emblem with a delighted flutter of his fingers.

"Nice!" Micah commended as the dapper mehkan returned the dynamo to a giggling Dollop.

"Gotta watch yer personables around the Marquis," the fat mehkan chuckled. "His loosey-goosey arms can creep up on a body. Reminds me of the time we eluded Tchiock and his gang of ruthless brigands, back in our viscollia-running days down near Kholghit. T'was a good many phases ago when . . ."

Micah was enraptured by Mr. Pynch's blather, but Dollop was distracted as he reattached his dynamo. He muttered to himself and scratched the dent in his head, trying to work something out. Phoebe hung back to walk with him.

"Not rhyktors," he mumbled. "They d-don't burrow."

"Dollop," she whispered to get his attention.

"A clutch of oudh? No, that's not it. But I—I swear I know who made that pit." He startled as he noticed her stare. "S-s-sorry, did you say something?"

"I can't believe he robbed you like that," she said, glancing ahead nervously. "Those two are crooks." The Marquis looked back and beckoned, his lamp eye flashing brightly, but she and Dollop remained at a distance.

"Oh, n-no!" he giggled. "Th-that's just a little game he plays. He took my dyn-n-namo twice this rise, but he—he gives it back. I like him. He's n-nice."

"But isn't stealing against the Way?" she asked, baffled. "Don't you think they're up to something?"

"Up?" Dollop wondered. "Th-they taught me how to p-play Sliverytik, which was fun. And they offered to help me f-find my clan. For a s-small fee."

"A fee? See what I mean?"

"But—but they're business-mehkies. And n-now they work for us." He shrugged. "Th-they saved us from those St-Stalker things, so they can't be on the F-Foundry's side, right?"

"Maybe," she said.

"And—and if all they wanted to do was r-r-rob us or hurt us, couldn't they have done it last night?"

"Not with you and Micah keeping watch."

"Wait . . . W-w-watch who?"

"Last night. Didn't you stay up and stand guard with Micah?"

"We both recharged. Mr. P-Pynch did all the watching."

Something curdled inside her. She glared at Micah, yukking it up with his new pals. As they bantered, he grabbed odds and ends from the ground, tossed them up, and then tried to blast them out of the sky with ore chunks fired from his Lodestar—like this was all some kind of joyride.

Little liar, she smoldered.

But despite her suspicions, she had to admit Dollop had a point. They never would have escaped the V-Stalkers without Mr. Pynch and the Marquis.

"C-come on, let's catch up!" he chirped and scampered ahead. "I don't wan-n-na miss one of, um, Mr. Pynch's stories."

She took her time rejoining the group. The terrain began to change, with softer plants sprouting among the brass, reddish and waxy, swaying like kelp underwater. There were thickets of fat fanning fronds and creeping barbed-wire vines specked in iridescent bulbs. Small coppery critters that looked disturbingly like syringes poked their needle noses into the bulbs to fill up on turquoise nectar. The ore beneath their feet was becoming moist and gritty like wet coffee grounds, and the air was thick with the citrusy scent of vesper. The thought of it made her uneasy, and she slowed her pace.

". . . so I vamoose quicker than a ripple-billed qintriton

before they discover what I left in their trunk!" she overheard Mr. Pynch's gravelly baritone. "And that be how the Marquis acquired his most illustrious frontispiece, the first in his ever-expanding ensemble of extraordinary human attire."

The Marquis gave his metal-threaded top hat a twirl.

"Durall be a bit pretentious for me particular predilection. I prefer a nice cotton-poly blend, but to each mehkie their own," Mr. Pynch said, waggling his flashy necktie. The Marquis pooh-poohed him with a dismissive wave.

"I bet y'all seen a ton of action." Micah tossed an ore rock, took careful aim, and *CRACK*. It burst apart. "Booyah!"

"Exquisite marksmanship, Master Micah," praised Mr. Pynch. "And yes, me associate and I have persevered through many a prodigious endeavor."

"No guts, no glory, I always say," Micah proclaimed, puffing his chest out.

Phoebe wanted to crawl out of her skin.

"How eloquently phrased! I wholeheartedly concur. I meself have performed near twenty-seven valiant rescues of the Marquis here and—"

The Marquis's lenses stood on end, and he flared his opticle.

"Aye, aye," the fat mehkan grumbled. "Me pompestuous associate points out that *his* tally of rescues of *meself* currently counts at forty-four. Though I maintain that at least two of those be entirely attributed to dumb luck."

Flustered, the Marquis unslung the massive foil sack and dropped it on his partner. Mr. Pynch reluctantly shouldered the bag and spat out a stream of Rattletrap curses that made

Dollop gasp. Micah laughed, tossed up another ore rock, and blasted it out of the sky.

"Two for two!" he cried, pumping his fist in the air.

They applauded him, but Phoebe just rolled her eyes.

"Impressive! We be fortunate to have a patron of such fearless talent."

"Yeah, my pa was a sharpshooter, and so's my sister Margie," boasted Micah. "She's ranked Apex-Seven in the army, which ain't half bad."

"Aha! So it be an inherited trait?" Mr. Pynch inquired.

"Well, by the time I was old enough, Pa was too drunk to teach me. When he was around," Micah said. He kicked hard at the ground to loosen up an ore rock to blast. "But Margie showed me a thing or two. So yeah, you could say it was inherited. She taught me that you never hold your breath. You gotta shoot in that one . . . still . . . second, just before you breathe in."

He tossed up the chunk, took a big breath, and then let it out. *WHOOMF.* He missed the rock by a long shot.

"Guess you're a slow learner," Phoebe jabbed. Micah spun to face her.

"An invaluable lesson, irregardless," Mr. Pynch intercepted with a smile. "We be nearing Tendril Fen. Sally forth!"

"S-s-sally, s-sa . . . sal . . ." Dollop squeezed his eyes shut and pounded the dent in his head with a fist. "Sal-l-l . . . SALATHYL!" he screamed with joy.

They all looked at Dollop, not comprehending.

"Th-that's it! That's who made the pit back in F-Fuselage. A s-s-salathyl!"

Mr. Pynch chuckled. "There haven't been salathyls near the Lateral Provinces in hundreds of phases. They be a rarified breed, only thriving in scant pockets beneath the Ephrian plains."

"That's because the C-C-Covenant k-keeps them secret, um, so no one expects them to at t-tack from underground! They pop up and KA-BOOM!"

Dollop leaped into the air and flailed his arms. He looked at the others expectantly, but Mr. Pynch just wheezed out a laugh while the Marquis strobed his amusement. Micah saw this and joined in the laughter as well.

"Ah, what a refreshingly credulous young mehkie," the fat mehkan sighed. "Whatever will you come up with next?"

"So you guys don't buy that supersecret army junk either?" Micah asked.

"Not j-j-junk! They have the lof-f-ftiest of functions!"

"Oh, tales of this ilk be circulating since time immemorial," Mr. Pynch explained. "Although I must admit our friend Dollop here be the first I ever encountered to unabashedly advocate for their veracity."

"Yeah, I figured they was made up."

"Indeed, folk today believe all manners of balderdash, so long as it brings hope. They cling to any fantasy rather than face the rather disagreeable truth that the world be cruel. Especially in bleak days such as these."

"N-n-no, they are real!" chimed Dollop, determined. "The Children of Ore helped Fuselage. Th-they are coming to s-s-save us all."

"Aw, come on, chum. Get real," Micah said, digging into the rucksack on Dollop's back. He withdrew the water jug and took a big slurp. "Them langyls was wiped out. Ain't no kiddie stuff gonna make it better."

"Big words, Mr. Maddox," Phoebe burned.

"Was I talkin' to you?"

"You're the one running around quoting a Televiewer show," Phoebe scoffed. "Talk about kiddie stuff!"

"Quit testin' me, Plumm, or I swear I'll—"

"You'll what?"

The Lodestar quivered in his white-knuckled fist. Mr. Pynch cleared his throat and laid a hand on Micah's shoulder.

"I pray it not be overly presumptuous to interject, but I believe I ascertainate the nature of yer conflagration." The kids looked at him. "Miss Phoebe considers me associate and I to be unscrupulous sorts, unworthy of her confidence, and Master Micah contracted us against her own behest. Be that the approximate shape of things?"

"Bingo," Phoebe said.

"Would it resolve matters if we retracted our services, refunded yer payment, and took our leave?"

"NO!" Micah argued.

"Absolutely!" Phoebe replied.

"I see," Mr. Pynch said, his nozzle twirling. "I confess, Miss Phoebe, yer reservations be not unfounded. Aside from the measurable assistance we have already provided, you have limited reason to trust us. But professionals we be, and we take pride in the satisfaction of our clientele. It would shame us gravely to terminate the contract when we be so close to your objective."

"How close?" Phoebe asked.

"Less than a cycle. After we procure a vellikran in Tendril Fen, we'll have a jaunt down the Ettalye, and then a brief ascent will take us into the legendary Vo-Pykaron Mountains." Mr. Pynch gestured to the horizon, and through the coppery foliage Phoebe could see a distant army of jagged peaks.

"Th-that's right!" Dollop agreed. "The Ci-Ci-Cit . . . It-it-it's just beyond the m-m-mountains. I—I—I remember now."

"Precisely. A shortcut will wind us through the mighty metropolis of Sen Ta'rine, and from thence, a mere click to your destination."

"See?" Micah sneered.

"By fusion on the morrow, our collaboration be at an end."

She looked at Dollop's excited face and Micah's smirk.

"What say you, Miss Phoebe? A truce till then?"

She gave a reluctant nod.

"Excellent." Mr. Pynch beamed. "You won't be disappointed. Me associate and I be impassioned to demonstrate our merits to you, dear heart."

Mr. Pynch strolled off, and the Marquis tipped his top hat with the handle of his umbrella before following him. Micah slung his Lodestar into a loop at his hip and threw the water jug hard enough at Phoebe to knock her back a step. With a lingering scowl, she drank from the jug, stuffed it back in the rucksack, and took the bag from Dollop to relieve him.

"Th-thanks," he chimed. "I-I'm pretty sure my function

isn't b-b-bag boy. Come on, we're, um, almost to the river!"

The word hit her like a punch in the gut. The astringent sting of vesper was pungent. Her legs grew unsteady as she stepped through the reddish vegetation. She could hear rapids, and her strength begin to ebb. Phoebe pushed past a waxy copper thicket and joined them at the edge of an embankment.

"There she be," Mr. Pynch declared proudly. "The River Ettalye. Tireless, benevolent life stream of this region."

The river gouged a quarter-mile-wide swath through the landscape, extending as far as the eye could see. Phoebe quavered, feeling sweaty and ill. But she refused to let Micah see—she would not give him the satisfaction.

I can do this, she vowed.

"Tendril Fen be just below," Mr. Pynch said, scampering down the embankment beneath the weight of his sack. "Don't fret about getting spotted here. It be a backward little hamlet, but all the same, better to let me do the oratizing."

There was a village sprawling across the shallows of the Ettalye. Nestled among hulking trees with wide canopies of drooping foliage, Phoebe could see squat dome structures floating on separate islands. It was the worst thing she could imagine—a town built right on top of a river. She wanted to turn and run, but she had to keep up with the others.

They descended the embankment and strode beneath clinking, dangling branches as they entered Tendril Fen. Phoebe saw that the willowlike foliage was actually mossy chains of varied length and thickness, dappled green at the tips.

The huts were built from sun-hardened ore and floated

on islands of river reeds. They bore big, scooping gears that churned the vesper, and pungent smoke wisped from pointed chutes in their dome roofs. Thick viaducts made from woven chain branches connected the sloshing isles and anchored them to the trees. Buoys like stained yellow teeth bobbed in the vesper.

Mr. Pynch proceeded into town, merrily ambling across one of the bridges. Phoebe trembled as she watched the others cross. She clenched her jaw and took a tentative step onto the chains. They dipped under her weight, and foamy orange fingers grasped at her boot. She fixed her eyes straight ahead and made her way as fast as she dared across the walkway.

There was an unexpected splash, and Phoebe nearly toppled into the river. One of the buoys rose from the vesper—a dingy yellow-robed figure that was beanpole-thin and eerily tall. Identical creatures erupted nearby on stilt-like legs. They backed away, gawking with downturned mouths and frightened eyes. Mr. Pynch gritted a Rattletrap greeting, but they did not respond.

"Just ignore 'em." He laughed. "They be substantiating their stereotype. Most mehkans consider syllks more than a wee bit feebleminded. This-a-way!"

Phoebe stumbled across the bridge and tried to collect herself. This appeared to be some sort of market. There was a syllk fishmonger with a rack of squidgy critters like knots of Bike chains, and carvers crafting waterwheels from sections of metal tree trunk. As soon as their dark, glistening eyes fixed on the kids, they abandoned their wares. All around them, villagers scurried away, their clinking robes flapping. Mr. Pynch perused the catch of the day and snatched up a string of them. He drew out a handful of shiny red, oval-shaped rings and left them in a neat stack for the fishmonger.

"Fresh culps, anyone?" he rumbled. The other mehkans nodded eagerly.

She felt eyes boring into her back and turned to see an uneasy crowd forming on the islands, groups of huddled syllks staring from beneath chain canopies. More emerged from squat huts, waddling out on legs folded beneath their billowing gowns. She could feel their anxious terror and hear their low gurgling whispers.

Humans were not welcome here.

Phoebe wanted to cry out and explain that despite her appearance, she wasn't like the others. But it was useless. The syllks would never understand. She was the enemy, the same as any other bleeder invading their home.

"Come on, Plumm. Hurry it up," Micah chuckled back to her. "You're lookin' a little green, there."

Phoebe wanted to put him in his place, but she knew she couldn't speak without betraying her panic. The penetrating stares of the villagers shredded her with guilt, which melted miserably into her fear of the churning tide.

Mr. Pynch led them across another precarious bridge to a hut that bore a mess of waterwheel gears with chains running into the river like the threads of a loom. The vesper surrounding the island was sprouting with tufts of feathery, palmlike growths dappled in green corrosion. A squatting syllk began to retreat inside his hut, but Mr. Pynch hailed him in Rattletrap. The fat mehkan unstrapped the foil satchel, drew out a set of wicker doormats and a wooden salad bowl, and then offered his treasures to the syllk with a dirty golden smile.

Phoebe focused on her breathing and studied the syllk to distract herself from the roiling river. His yellowed robes weren't clothes at all, but a flowing membrane of chain-link skin that twitched and pulsed. Folded beneath this mesh curtain was a pair of arms covered in cinching, hook-like digits. His head was a jowly protuberance with a toothless frown, and his dark eyes squished and flickered behind layers of translucent lids. The syllk glanced at the humans and retreated farther into his hut. Mr. Pynch bombarded the nervous villager with florid Rattletrap, offering up more treasures from his sack.

Everything began to fit into place in her mind. She remembered his words: *a jaunt down the Ettalye*. Mr. Pynch was trying to charter a boat.

No sooner had this realization struck her than Mr. Pynch laughed. He thanked the villager profusely and resealed his bag with a twist of the valve.

"One vellikran coming up!" he announced.

"A velli-wha—" Micah began, but his voice was drowned out by a clattering mechanism. The syllk operated his waterwheel, manipulating chains by grabbing them with the clenching hooks along his arms. The vesper behind them bubbled and frothed, and one of the feathery green growths splayed open.

The fronds were attached to stems that spread out wide.

No, they were legs.

A long thorax breached the vesper, speckled with greenish corrosion and encrusted in copper barnacles. Bundled antenna slashed about at its front, surrounded by a ring of milk-bubble eyes. The fronds of its three spindly legs stretched across the surface to keep it gracefully afloat. The vellikran shook, sloughing orangey oil from its rear, which was a skirt of the same palm material. Then its tail began to spin, chugging and fluttering like a propeller. The creature buzzed faster, tugging at its tether, raring to race across the river.

"No . . . freakin' . . . way," Micah muttered.

Phoebe nearly collapsed. If there was anything in the world worse than a boat ride, this was it.

The syllk strode into the vesper to secure a chain bridle on the vellikran's body. He cranked a wheel on the harness, and four panels swung up from the steed's side, coming together to form a tall bucket for passengers on its back.

"All aboard!" trumpeted Mr. Pynch. He tottered across the jangling leash that led over the vesper and hopped into the bucket, tossing his big satchel in the back. The Marquis bounded up the chain next and settled near the front. He scrubbed at splatters on his pant legs with a handkerchief.

"D-d-does it bite?" Dollop asked, as he climbed up. "H-hi there, girl. You're a n-n-nice girl, aren't you?" he cooed. The vellikran responded with an abrupt shake of its flanks. Dollop scampered aboard as fast as he could.

"You look like crap," Micah needled Phoebe. "'Bout to pass out again?"

"Shut up and leave me alone."

"My pleasure," Micah chuckled. "Ladies first."

She closed her eyes, blocking him and all those staring syllks from her mind. She tried to force out the sound of the crashing river too. A few steps, that was it. Just had to look ahead, not at the orange surge beneath her feet.

Phoebe clenched her jaw and walked out onto the leash. The walkway wavered. Another step, then another.

The chain jostled. Her feet slipped.

The Ettalye grabbed her like a cold, oily hand. She thrashed and strained to keep her head up, but the vesper splashed in her mouth, driving her to greater panic. Immediately, the three mehkans were upon her, their faces full of concern as they hauled her, drenched, into the vellikran bucket.

But not Micah.

He was bent over in a fit of giggles. With another swift shake of the leash, he showed her what he had done. He then scrambled up the chain like a sewer rat, hopped into the bucket, and leered down at her.

"THAT was for the rust slug . . ."

His words faded as he saw her. Phoebe's heart convulsed in her chest. Fright warped her features. Tears pushed at the corners of her eyes, threatening to fall. But she refused. She had vowed a long time ago that she would never cry again, that no one else was worth her tears. Especially not Micah.

She crawled away from him and squeezed herself around Mr. Pynch's huge satchel, putting it between her and the others. Fumbling for her hood and face mask, she yanked it down over her head to seal herself off from the world.

There was an exchange of muted voices, the dull jangle of chains, and a whirring drone as the vellikran embarked. Phoebe hugged her knees and closed her eyes, focusing on the thing she wanted most of all.

To forget.

24

A SMALL PRICE
FOR PEACE

"I understand your concerns, but the terms are not negotiable," Goodwin explained coolly "My offer is exceedingly generous. Now, what is your decision?"

The Chairman stood with five representatives of the elusive Board, directors sent from Foundry Central to supervise this meeting. Each of them wore an identical, unassuming gray suit and a tiny silver earpiece. Kaspar lingered by the door, his long shadow hanging over the proceedings. The conference room was wood-paneled and dark, lit only with a few soft pyramid lamps and a giant Televiewer screen that took up one wall.

Projected on the screen was a man's glowering face. He was decked out in an embroidered uniform that clinked with military medals, and his slicked-back salt-and-pepper hair clung to his skull like a helmet. He leaned away to consult a league of solemn, black-wigged magisters beneath the giant yellow and indigo crosshatched flag of Trelaine.

Goodwin was immobile, betraying none of the tension of the moment. But he could feel it weighing down the room.

Premier Lavaraud turned to address him. "We accept."

The directors nodded in approval. Goodwin's demeanor suggested that he had never doubted this result.

"But know this," Lavaraud continued. "Trelaine will not tolerate another betrayal from Meridian."

"I do not play politics, Premier. The Foundry always delivers on its promises."

"You have one week to produce this *exceedingly generous* offer of yours. Should you fail," he said, planting his hands on his desk, "I will submit to the Quorum that we take immediate and drastic action."

"You have my word—I am committed to avoiding such measures."

"Let us hope so. And let us hope your word is better than that of your swine-suckling Saltern."

"The President's remarks were unfortunate," Goodwin admitted. "But I believe our agreement today represents movement toward a peaceful resolution. I am glad we could bypass the usual channels in order to address these urgent matters face-to-face."

"One week," Lavaraud reiterated. "I assume you are satisfied with our intelligence regarding Dr. Plumm?"

"I am. You have my thanks for the full disclosure."

The Premier gave a curt nod, and the image on the Televiewer flickered off. Kaspar faded up the light.

"A promising first step," Goodwin noted.

"Promising? We call it a blasted victory," laughed Director Malcolm, a leathery old gentleman with brilliantly white-capped teeth.

"Our work is not yet done," cautioned Goodwin. "But we are well on our way to assembling the first shipment. Once they receive the payment in full, we will see how the rest of the Quorum responds to Lavaraud's move."

"Who would have guessed the Trels could be bought?" remarked Director Layton, a blond middle aged woman with beady eyes and hawklike features.

"They are proud, but they are not fools," Goodwin mused. "In the end, everyone has a price."

"When they see the boon coming to Trelaine, the other mongrels will come begging for a similar deal." Director Malcolm smiled.

"Let us hope so," agreed the Chairman.

"Can we provide that?" asked Director Layton. "The Board has observed that harvesting in sectors seven and ten is on the decline. We are impressed by the boost in overall output these last few days, James, but can you sustain it?"

"I can and will," Goodwin reassured her. "The bridge across the Veltran Gap is near completion, and it will give us unfettered access to thousands of untapped acres to the west. And the new hatcheries are allowing us to harvest units nearly eleven percent faster than previous estimates."

"We've studied the recent numbers," said Director Obwilé, a handsome and contemplative young man with dark skin and glasses. "Impressive."

"Largely due to the new Durall plants coming on line," Goodwin explained. "Our response to Fuselage, regrettable as it was, sent a clear message. Now the rest of the Chusk Bowl is working around the clock."

Director Malcolm guffawed. "The Transit Coordinators must be pulling their hair out trying to move it all!"

"A welcome problem, to be sure," said Director Layton.

"Does that mean the Board approves?" Goodwin inquired.

She affixed him with her dark gaze and touched her ear-piece. "We are quite pleased, James. Although when news of our deal with Trelaine reaches President Saltern, he'll be furious that you went behind his back."

Goodwin sighed. "Saltern has been uncooperative of late. All of that swagger may get his constituents salivating, but it is counterproductive to our aims. I owe the President a visit. He needs to be reminded of his place."

Director Malcolm flashed his blinding smile and rose. "Well then," he trumpeted, "shall we make an announcement?"

The Chairman nodded. "An excellent idea. We should—"

"If I may," interjected Director Obwilé.

Goodwin raised an eyebrow. The Board members regarded him silently.

"This is wonderful news, of course," the young director said, "but we were hoping to hear an update on the trespassers."

"The children, you mean?"

"The security breach. The Board is rather surprised at your lack of concern."

"I am aware of their location and am frankly more intrigued by their progress than in capturing them."

"You would gamble with the Foundry's safety so brazenly?"

The smile left Goodwin's face.

"On a day with less momentous news, I might be inclined to take offense at your rather extraordinary insinuation."

"James, you would do well to—"

"I understand your concern, but soon they will be found, alive or otherwise. In either case, the Board can rest well knowing they are of no consequence. Shall we?"

Director Obwilé adjusted his glasses and looked to the other Board members, who scrutinized the Chairman emotionlessly.

Goodwin left the conference room flanked by the directors. They strode out onto the platinum and marble landing to look down at the central lounge, which swirled with Foundry elite. The atrium was a wonder of light and crystal, twinkling like the firmament, with four statues of winged women holding up the intricate chrome ceiling. With velvety Durall sofas, lilting music, and an ever-replenished bar and gourmet kitchen, this lounge was the pinnacle of luxury.

One would never guess it was in the heart of the Citadel. These resplendent walls, awash in silversilk draperies and priceless oil paintings, had witnessed unspeakable horrors.

Torture chambers had been converted into a decadent complex with living quarters, an entertainment theater, and a gymnasium complete with indoor pools. For the executives and supervisors stationed in Mehk for weeks at a time, it was like a grand hotel.

The hundred or so revelers hushed their conversations as they noticed Goodwin and the representatives from the Board. The music faded, and Director Malcolm pushed a tumbler of fine spirits into Goodwin's hand. The Chairman waited for silence before speaking—he savored their anticipation.

"Friends. For too long, we have lived under a growing threat of war. While we strive to improve the lives of every man, woman, and child, the Quorum rattles its sabers. They hunger for our innovations, try to lay claim to our metal, and left unchecked they would seek to achieve their ends by force. But we are unmoved. In the spirit of peace, we have extended our hand to Trelaine."

Murmurs spread, and Goodwin couldn't help but smile.

"I have spoken directly with Premier Lavaraud, and he has accepted the terms of our offer. Upon completion of the agreement . . ." He paused dramatically. "Trelaine will withdraw from the Quorum."

Gasps rippled throughout the assembly.

"This is not my achievement," Goodwin continued. "It is *our* achievement, that of the entire Foundry. And with this bold first step, so begins the end of the Quorum. Unhindered, we will build a better, brighter future."

The lounge erupted into applause.

"Thank you all," Goodwin called out over the din.

"To Meridian," Director Malcolm cheered.

"To Meridian!" Goodwin bellowed in approval and took a deep drink.

The lounge rang with cries of "To Meridian!"

Goodwin looked around the room to see eyes brimming with tears and people embracing. Enduring peace was on the horizon at long last.

Director Obwilé was the only one not drinking.

From the corner of his eye, Goodwin saw the towering shape of Kaspar duck away. The Chairman frowned and followed him down a high-ceilinged corridor lined with slim golden buttresses.

"Where do you think you're going?" Goodwin demanded.

"I don't like these affairs," Kaspar grumbled.

"I told you to wait until I had a moment to deal with you."

"I'm sorry, sir," he said, turning to face Goodwin's wrath.

"Not good enough. Do you know what you have done?"

"Only my job, Mr. Goodwin."

"Quite the opposite. I ordered you not to use excessive force. So what do you do? You send him to the medic, nearly dead from loss of blood. His condition is dire, and now there is risk of infection. Explain yourself."

"I . . ." Kaspar muttered, cowed, ". . . lost control."

"That is because Jules is smarter than you," Goodwin snapped and took another swallow of his drink. "He provoked you into incapacitating him to prevent me from getting what I need."

"But he is useless now," Kaspar argued. "We have his confession, and the Trels confirmed his story. Why are we still playing his games?"

"Did I seek your counsel on this matter?"

"No, sir."

"Then keep your simpleminded presumptions to yourself."

Kaspar flinched. Goodwin felt a twinge of guilt—it was the drink talking. He collected himself and settled his temper.

"Jules told the truth about his arrangements for asylum in Trelaine, yes, but he is holding something back. I suspect he has been selling information to the Quorum, although I cannot prove it. Yet. He is a conspirator, and I will not have you jeopardizing Meridian's safety by interfering with my acquisition of that information. Do you understand me?

"Yes, sir." Kaspar bowed even lower.

"You are certain you are still up to the task?"

"I will not fail you."

"Good. Now, be patient." Goodwin lifted Kaspar's chin with a finger to look him in the eyes. "It won't be long, dear boy. I will let you know when your gloves can come off."

A perverse grin cut across the soldier's cracked lips. The Chairman affectionately slapped Kaspar's hard, sallow cheek and downed his drink.

Then he turned to rejoin the celebration. He had earned it.

NO.

hoebe's first hint they were making progress was the needle-like chill that cut through her coveralls. She huddled on the floor of the passenger bucket, bundled up in her hood and face mask, but it didn't help. Gusts of wind moaned, making the ride more turbulent and further agitating her anxious stomach. She clutched her head in her hands, praying for land.

The buzz of the vellikran's tail and the rhythmic thrash of the river merged into a muddled drone. She let the noise lull her into a trance, neither awake nor asleep. Time felt like a snake shedding its skin, and the slithering seconds and hours slowly peeled away.

And then, at long last, they came to a shuddering stop.

There was some conversation, and the foil satchel rustled behind her. A hand gently touched her shoulder.

"Ph-Ph-Phoebe?" came Dollop's voice. "Um, we're here."

She didn't respond. There was a clink of chains, a crank of gears, and the panels of the passenger bucket dropped away. The biting wind forced her from her stupor like a cold pinch. She dropped from the bucket and hit the ground, her legs numb from being cooped up. Ignoring the others, she shouldered the rucksack and climbed the steep shore toward a gunmetal-blue mountain range that disappeared into brooding clouds.

Phoebe took a few deep breaths, letting the tension and nausea of the last several hours seep away. The thought of climbing into these mountains was daunting, but anything was better than the river. Behind her, she heard the others come ashore. The vellikran emitted a chirrup, and its fantail whizzed as it skidded along the river and headed home.

"What the heckles is that?" Micah's voice was awestruck.

Alarmed by his tone, she risked a glance across the Ettalye. A pall clung to the distant horizon, a black umbrella hanging over the land like a cloud of spilled ink. The terrain beneath it was a sunken crater, as if everything trapped in the shadow of this lingering blackness had been eaten away. Obliterated.

"CHAR," rumbled Mr. Pynch. "Devours any ore it touches. One of the Foundry's more ignominious practices. That particular blight be nearly four hundred phases old, and thrice as big as the day it was dropped."

"M-M-Makina help us," Dollop moaned, a hand placed over his dynamo.

"Would that She could. Interminable it be and ever expanding. The cycle will come when this one consumes the Ettalye herself. Best not to speak of it."

Mr. Pynch turned away with a shudder, and the others followed. But Phoebe couldn't tear her eyes from the blight. She felt a clutching in her chest. How many of these ravenous black cancers had the Foundry inflicted upon Mehk?

She hung back, hiding behind her hood and face mask, as they rounded the steep banded shore and took in the stormy peaks ahead.

"There they be," Mr. Pynch trumpeted, trying to lighten the mood. "Giants of fanciful legend, fabled in story and song. The final gamut of this cycle's sojourn—the Vo-Pykaron Mountain Range."

"B-b-b-beautiful . . ." Dollop said with wonder.

"Must be gettin' close," Micah said, glancing at Phoebe.

"To be certain, Master Micah. With any fortune, we'll outpace the rain and arrive at Sen Ta'rine in a click or two. Then, following a safe and secure recharge, we shall commence to the Citadel after rise."

"I wouldn't say no to a good night's sleep," he replied.

"You'll adore Sen Ta'rine! A plethora of trade. We can easily obtain whatever digestibles yer innards desire. As for meself," the fat mehkan buzzed, sliding a black tongue across his glinting chops, "there be a cracklin' slab of roasted flugul with me name on it."

Mr. Pynch marched ahead, followed by Dollop and the Marquis, who strapped on the oversized foil satchel and slid a lens in front of his opticle to inspect the sky. Micah lingered for Phoebe to walk past.

"What's up, Spaceman?" he said, pointing to her hood and face mask. "You just gonna pout the rest of the way?" She ignored him.

They hiked into the foothills, which were spotted with low growths the same blue-gray as the mountains. As they walked, the protrusions became taller and more frequent. They were monochromatic, though some were darker or more vibrant blue, and others speckled in silver or gold polyps. Phoebe observed their variety—there were swollen sausage shapes covered in tubelike spouts, clusters of rigid cones, and others like tangled, sinewy nets.

"Now where be that obstinate trail?" Mr. Pynch wondered as he bent over to sniff the ground. The Marquis made himself taller to scan the landscape.

"You don't know where it is?" Micah asked.

"Well, Master Micah, it can't exactly be pinpointed as such," replied Mr. Pynch patiently. "For it never quite resides in the same place twice."

"The trail . . . moves?"

As they proceeded, the vegetation fused and blanketed the ground, coalescing into bundled stalks that braided to form pillars a dozen feet wide. These joined in a vast network of columns and arches that rose up to create the mighty mountains. The Vo-Pykarons were alive, like pyramids of metallic coral reef.

But the image of CHAR lingered in Phoebe's eyes. She imagined it spreading, creeping across the river and devouring this lush landscape.

"Aha!" Mr. Pynch tugged at a tangle of pale blue tendrils. The growths recoiled to reveal a path that led up one of the giant stalks. "We be in business."

Bitter wind swirled around them as they began their ascent, and dark clouds cloaked the afternoon suns. Their progress was made even more difficult by the restless growths, whose shifting movements made it hard to get a foothold, sometimes clinging to them as they passed.

Phoebe strayed so far from the others that she looked up after a momentary reverie to find them gone. At first, she was alarmed, but instead of trying to catch up, she stopped in the middle of the path to absorb the silence and majesty of the mountains around her. It felt like she had been abandoned on a stormy blue moon, the sole visitor on an unforgiving world.

After the brief solitary moment, she trotted ahead until she found the group around a bend in the trail. They hadn't even noticed she was gone. The Marquis was jumpy, his lenses swapping methodically as he inspected the sky. She looked up and realized that these were not regular clouds of condensation, but opaque conglomerations of ore clinging to the sky like scabs. A low rumble rolled out, and the rugged clouds resonated like gargantuan metal cymbals. The Marquis flickered an urgent message and opened his Durall umbrella.

"I fear you be right," said Mr. Pynch. "I had aspired to

avoid any inclement weather, but it appears the Vo-Pykarons do not sympathize. Master Micah, I must advise that you muster up that hood of yers so—"

A piercing howl split the air.

They froze in their tracks. Mr. Pynch and the Marquis dropped to a crouch and crept through the azure brush for a look, and the others followed.

Phoebe saw a broad valley dipping between the peaks. Flares crackled in the shadowy recesses formed by the pillars of an adjacent mountain. Another monstrous shriek erupted as a truck surrounded by Watchmen backed out of the darkness. It was being driven toward a gathering of identical vehicles in the valley, about twenty of them parked around a black platform. The trucks were familiar, their cargo beds covered in overlapping steel plates.

No—these were not vehicles. They were mehkans. The twenty-ton beasts were armored in heavy, segmented carapaces like the plates of an armadillo, and they glided across the rugged ground on tank-tread feet.

Hard-hatted Watchmen workers were mounted on what looked like Cyclewynders. Popular back in Meridian, these vehicles were sleek and agile with a row of sharp wheels down the center and long flexible bodies that could negotiate hairpin turns. The Watchmen jabbed at the bellowing mehkan with crackling electric prods affixed to their bikes. The creature stomped and bucked, but the attacks were too numerous.

Phoebe wanted to scream. Wanted to vomit. Wanted to tear the Watchmen apart with her bare hands.

"P-p-poor liodim," warbled Dollop, covering his face.

Soon the battling mehkan quieted, and the Watchmen drew back. Slowly, it turned to join its brethren, as if the fight within it had been snuffed out.

"Why they just sittin' there?" Micah hissed. "What's wrong with 'em?"

"Mesmerizer," whispered Mr. Pynch. "They be enslaved by its sound."

At first, all Phoebe could hear was the burr of Cyclewynders. But beneath that was a drone coming from the platform in the middle of the pacified herd.

More cries rang out. A pair of small liodim tottered out from another recess. Howling, the cubs raced toward their herd. Watchmen closed in.

What are you doing? she thought fiercely. *Run. Please run!*

The Foundry workers lunged at them with crackling prods, but the little ones proved more agile than their parents and dodged the electric barbs. So the Watchmen raced across the cubs' path. The Cyclewynders confused the baby liodim, causing them to panic and stumble and roll onto their backs. They lay defenseless, kicking their stubby legs in the air.

The bikes bore down on the helpless young.

She didn't want to look. Yet she felt compelled by an invisible force. She stared, unflinching, at the Foundry's brutality.

The Watchmen ran them over. The choking shrieks of agony tore her apart. The cubs tried to run but only managed to drag their injured bodies a few feet before the Cyclewynders plowed into them a second time. Again and again, the Watchmen sliced the baby liodim, until their pitiful, gurgling cries faded and nothing was left. Their butchery complete, the Watchmen sped off into the open network of giant stalks beneath the next mountain.

As the cubs died, so too did something within Phoebe.

"Come," Mr. Pynch muttered to his stunned companions. "Nothing we can do." He got to his feet and began to follow the path once more. The others shuffled behind him, turning their backs on the scene.

No.

That voice again, the one she had heard in the tunnel. The same voice that had summoned her into Mehk. The cries of the baby liodim mingled with those of the murdered chraida. She thought of the ruins of Fuselage, the terror on the syllks' faces, the black plague of CHAR eating away at this world.

She thought of the Foundry. Of her father.

Was she the same as him?

No.

A fire ignited. It grew intense and focused, tempering her mind like metal in a forge. Phoebe knew what she had to do.

"No."

The others stopped in their tracks and turned. She pulled back the face mask of her coveralls and stared at them. Her expression was iron.

"Pardon?" asked Mr. Pynch.

"I'm going down there," she said. "I'm going to stop this."

The Marquis flickered a message to Mr. Pynch, whose nozzle spun so fast it made a little whistling sound.

"What? Are you nuts?" Micah goggled.

"No."

"This is just another one of her stunts." He rolled his eyes to the others.

"B-but they'll k-k-k-kill you," whimpered Dollop.

"Miss Phoebe. Please auscultate yer friends' wisdom." Mr. Pynch smiled, his hands clasped together. "An attempt to engage here be a fool's errand."

"Don't be stupid," added Micah. "What about the Citadel?"

"This is more important."

"Bullcrap! Not after everything we been through."

"This is *because* of everything we've been through."

Micah went quiet.

"I'm not asking you to come," she said. "But I'm going."

"B-b-but what about your, um, clan? Your f-f-father?"

"I . . ." She paused for a moment, a crack in her resolve. She ached for her father's embrace. His voice. She clenched her jaw. "I can save the liodim. I don't know about him."

Mr. Pynch's smile vanished. "Yer passions be rousinating, dear heart, truly they be. None has more compunction for the plight of the liodim than meself. But simply put, this fight cannot be won. Surely you comprehend. To oppose the Foundry be a grievous blunder."

"Especially for business-mehkies such as yourselves," she stated flatly.

"Precisely. Why jeopardize our livelihood and endanger future contracts with the Foundry?" Mr. Pynch asked.

"Because you know this is wrong."

"Wrong? The world be wrong. And it not be our obligation to fix it all."

"Of course not," she answered. "Because there's no money in it for you."

Dollop looked from Mr. Pynch to Phoebe, unsure.

Mr. Pynch growled. "Master Micah, resolve this. Or we will abscond with yer payment and abandon you here."

Phoebe had heard enough. She turned and marched away.

Mr. Pynch puffed up, and the Marquis narrowed the shutters of his opticle. They swept around Phoebe from either side and blocked her path.

"Me apologies, but we cannot allow it."

Every muscle in her body went taut.

"Outta the way, Tubby!"

A purple light flared as Micah cut in, wielding his Lodestar. The two mehkans took a wary step back. Phoebe looked at Micah, astonished.

"You're right," he said to her, shrugging. "Ain't gonna say it twice."

There was no time to thank him.

"Be reasonable," gritted Mr. Pynch, his wonky eyes fixing on the Lodestar. "Me associate and I be trying to prevent yer unwitting suicide and—"

"We're doin' this whether you like it or not," Micah said.

"Then our deal be terminated."

"Heard you the first time! Let's go, Plumm."

"Me too!" Dollop cried and scampered up beside them.

Her spirit soared.

"Good man!" Micah clapped Dollop on the back, making his already shaky joints rattle. He clutched his Lodestar tighter, staring hard at Mr. Pynch and the Marquis. They faced off for a long, tense moment.

Finally, the pair of angry mehkans stepped aside. As Phoebe and her two friends strode past, Mr. Pynch unleashed an accusatory streak of Rattletrap at the Marquis, who planted a hand on his hip and flashed back a bright, curt retort.

Phoebe left them to bicker among themselves.

There was work to do.

26

THE STORM
BREAKS

Climbing up the Vo-Pykarons had been far more difficult than falling down them. Phoebe, Micah, and Dollop tried to use the blue undergrowth as handholds, but the prickly mountain foliage seemed unwilling to help. Giant scalloped petals created an unstable surface, and sticky hoops snagged them as they descended to the valley floor.

The trio raced toward the herd. Thunder rattled so powerfully it felt like they were standing on a kettledrum.

"Time to knock some heads," Micah spouted gleefully.

"No," insisted Phoebe. "We're here to save the liodim."

"Oh, right," he said. "How?"

"The Mesmerizer. We have to stop it."

"Copy." He pointed at the rucksack. "Better lose that."

She slipped the bag off her shoulders and stashed it behind a stand of cobalt growths.

"You all right?" Micah asked Dollop.

"I—I—I—I—I—I . . . Bu-bu-bu-bu . . . Ma-ma-ma-ma-ma . . ." The mehkan was too petrified to speak.

"Just try and keep up," he encouraged.

They ran deeper into the valley, hiding among the vegetation that cluttered the lowlands. Vast, open mountain bases rose on either side, shadowy caverns with plenty of places for danger to lurk. As Phoebe and the others approached the liodim, the Mesmerizer's hum bored into their guts. They listened for Cyclewynders but could hear none.

The herd didn't even acknowledge their presence. The brawny mehkans were about twenty feet long, with segmented shells that extended and retracted ever so slightly with each breath. Clustered beneath their massive forms was an interlocking mess of gears that powered muscular tank-tread legs. Their armored heads were low and wide with drooping ears, and each of them had a silver-slatted jaw that looked like the baleen comb of a whale.

Their deep-set eyes were closed as they listened to the hypnotic drone.

The three rescuers pushed through the liodim to where the Mesmerizer sat on a low, circular platform with readouts and flashing indicators. A big drum was embedded in its center, rotating like the barrel of a music box.

"Keep a lookout," Phoebe instructed Dollop.

The mehkan nodded nervously and slipped out of the ringed herd to survey the valley ahead. Micah took out his wrench and searched for a panel or a power source, anything that might shut the Mesmerizer off.

"'Sibilance, timbre, frequency . . .'" Phoebe read, trying to decipher the displays.

"Nothin'," Micah said, scrunching up his face. "Must be controlled remotely."

"So what do we do?"

Micah bit his lip. He climbed on the platform and jammed his wrench into the drum. With a quick crunch, it ground his precious tool to a nub. He stared at the useless thing, fuming.

Every passing second multiplied her anxiety. Phoebe fumbled through her sniping supplies and found a tube of Speed-E-Tak cement. She tore the cap off and squeezed it onto the Mesmerizer. No effect at all. She started to sweat.

Frustrated, Micah cranked up his Lodestar and braced himself. The weapon flared as he shot out a magnetic wave. The barrel sped up for a moment, raising its pitch, and then returned to normal.

"That's it!" Phoebe cried. "But reverse it. Slow it down."

He gave the weapon a second to recharge, then switched the polarity and pulled the trigger again. This time the Mesmerizer slowed to a crawl, hampered by the magnetic tug. The liodim stirred.

"More!" she insisted.

They saw movement between the surrounding beasts. Dollop was squeezing through the herd, scrambling toward them in a panic. His face was frozen in a mask of fear, too terrified to say the words. But they understood.

The Watchmen were coming.

Dollop raced past, but Micah grabbed his arm to hold him back, and the limb popped off in his hands.

"Wait!" Phoebe hissed. "Over here!"

Micah returned Dollop's arm, and the two of them followed her as she squeezed between the shells to hide among the tranquilized liodim. The soft purr of Cyclewynders approached. Crouching to peer through the legs of the liodim, she saw glimpses of Watchmen speeding past. If any of them paused to look closely at their livestock, all would be lost.

They were trapped.

Thunder clanged. Peering up, Phoebe's knees went weak. The sky was a craggy metal asteroid threatening to crash down at any moment. Micah shot bug-eyed glances in her direction, no clue what to do. Dollop held on to his parts, trying to keep himself together. Phoebe looked around, her mind scrabbling for a solution. Her eyes fell upon her big lumpy boots.

It came to her in a flash. She tore at the shoelaces.

Micah and Dollop looked at her as if she had lost her mind. She ripped off her boot, dug inside, and pulled out the torn wads of hand towel.

"Get ready to run," she whispered as she yanked the boot back on.

"What are you—" Micah started to ask, but she was gone. Phoebe sidled up next to one of the liodim's wide, fishlike heads. With shaking hands, she balled up some of the rags and crammed them into the beast's ear. It twitched a bit but otherwise did not react. Realization flickered on Micah's face.

Staying low and looking out for Watchmen, she sneaked around the front of the passive creature and stuffed the remaining rags in its other ear.

Lids flashed open. Golden mehkan eyes met hers.

It roared. Not the sound of pain that had alerted them to the roundup—this was rage, and her ears rang with it.

Cyclewynders revved as Watchmen approached the disturbance. Phoebe and her friends slipped toward the back of the herd, twisting to weave between their shells. The crackle of prods rang out, so close they could smell the acrid smoke. The herd was growing tense, shifting and slamming together, and paths around the trio opened and closed.

Phoebe checked to make sure Dollop was keeping up. He was right beside them—or his legs were, at least.

"No!" Phoebe hissed.

Dollop's knock-kneed lower body quivered. His remaining pieces lay scattered among the agitated liodim behind them.

Micah rushed back, spied a scrabbling arm, and scooped it up. Phoebe saw another piece flopping between two lumbering beasts. She wedged between them and snatched it as one liodim collided with the next. The impact rippled through the herd, heading toward them like falling dominos. Micah yanked her free just as the massive shells slammed together.

The liodim with the plugged ears came into view, ignoring the shocks of the Watchmen as it rammed the Mesmerizer. The Foundry agents launched long, tethered harpoons into its hide and reversed their Cyclewynders to restrain it. The crazed beast reared up on its hind legs.

Dollop's head lay on the ground beneath the mehkan.

Throwing caution to the wind, Micah raced for the enraged creature and pointed his Lodestar. A purple bloom flashed. The berserk liodim came crashing down on the Mesmerizer, which crumpled in a detonation of sparks.

Dollop's head flew to the Lodestar.

The drone was gone. The liodim awakened.

The air was sundered with mad howls. Electric prods hissed. One of the beasts plowed into a Watchman, flinging him like a rag doll. Three others crunched together, roused and growling. Another Cyclewynder wove away from the uproar, only to get sideswiped and smeared beneath treads. The herd was out of control. Some liodim were rampaging, others were breaking away, charging for freedom. Phoebe felt a surge of exhilaration.

They turned to flee as a panicked Dollop finished reassembling himself.

A Watchman on a Cyclewynder darted forward, driving his crackling prod at Phoebe. In a purple flash, Micah fired the Lodestar and blasted him from the bike. But other Watchmen spotted the light and steered away from the herd.

They ran.

Phoebe heard a ricochet, felt a sharp blow on her shoulder. Something hot sizzled past her face. Were they being shot at?

She glanced back just as the Watchman that Micah had struck was pulverized by an escaping liodim. The three of them leaped out of the way, and when the beast rumbled past, she saw something whiz down and ping off its shell—a ball of gray metal. Phoebe looked up. The storm was breaking.

It was raining bullets.

"Hood!" Phoebe rasped, her voice lost in the thunder.

She yanked up his head cover as the downpour began. Bullets pounded with searing, bruising blows across their heads and shoulders. Dollop's mehkan hide protected him, but if it hadn't been for the Durall coveralls, the kids would have been shredded. They secured their masks as they ran.

Three, then four Cyclewynders zipped by. Micah watched them circle and readied his weapon. He aimed carefully but didn't get the chance to fire a shot. A mounted Watchman grabbed him from behind and whisked him off his feet. The Lodestar clattered away. Phoebe ran to help, but another Cyclewynder intercepted, snatching her up, kicking.

It's over, she thought.

Then there was an unexpected crunch, and the bike beneath her wavered. The driver's grip went slack, and Phoebe tumbled to the ground. She rolled over and caught a glimpse of a bloated brown ball of spikes. With a wrenching screech, it peeled off the disabled Watchman's back, and he collapsed with his vehicle in a heap.

The Cyclewynder carrying Micah raced on. Then, in a flash, he was airborne, tugged away by long snaky arms and deposited carefully on the ground. The Watchman spun back to retrieve his captive, only to be blinded by a brilliant beam of light. The bike swerved and capsized, tumbling end over end as it crashed across the ore.

Dollop, who had watched all of this in a state of shock, picked up the Lodestar and passed it to Micah. Phoebe staggered to her feet and joined them.

The three of them stood there, not believing their eyes.

"After much deliberation," Mr. Pynch hollered over the downpour, "me associate and I decided that deceased clients would mar our spotless reputation."

Two more Cyclewynders closed in.

"We can negotiate the rate of our emergency rescue clause later," the fat mehkan shouted. He inflated once more and rolled toward the approaching Watchmen, who swerved out of the way. The Marquis motioned for them to follow, and then raced for the vaulted recesses beneath the nearest mountain.

Searchlights cut through the storm, sweeping over peaks.

Aero-copters.

Phoebe, Micah, and Dollop plunged into the darkness. Though they were now sheltered from the falling rain, streams of bullets poured through pockets in the ceiling. They crashed down in waves, coating the ground with a carpet of ball bearings that made every step treacherous.

Mr. Pynch hightailed it to catch up, the pair of Cyclewynders hot on his heels. The fat mehkan dodged and wound between the giant stalks, but the serpentine bikes were far more maneuverable.

The Marquis dashed back to help his partner. One of the Watchmen accelerated to run him down, but just before impact, the Marquis shot upward, extending his legs and bowing them out. As the Cyclewynder raced through, the Marquis thrust his umbrella between his legs, hooked the Watchman's neck, and yanked him from his bike. Mr. Pynch leaped over the Marquis, inflated in midair, and bellyflopped on top of their attacker, perforating him. The fat mehkan rolled out of the way, leaving the Watchman spastic and short-circuiting. The Marquis flipped his umbrella around like a golf club and wound up. He swung with all his might, caught the Watchman squarely on the chin, and popped off his fizzing head like a champagne cork.

Meanwhile, the remaining Cyclewynder looped for another charge. Phoebe stumbled over to a tall, puffy funnel growing from one of the columns—it was overflowing with pellets of rain. She called to Dollop and Micah, who ran to her side, grabbed the lip of the fat formation, and helped topple it.

A gush of bullets flooded the Watchman's path. The Cyclewynder fishtailed. But just before the bike slid out from under him, the Watchman dove from the vehicle, rolled several times, and landed on his feet. He ran at the kids, wielding his hissing prod.

WHOOMF. Micah blasted him with a magnetic pulse, but the Foundry agent anticipated and braced himself against a column. As the Lodestar recharged, he lunged and bashed the weapon out of Micah's grip. But before the Watchman could strike, Phoebe and Dollop seized his arm and hung on, lifting their feet so that their full weight prevented him from attacking. The prod crackled, painting her vision with dazzling patterns.

Micah snatched up the Lodestar, reversed the polarity, and sucked up a spouting stream of bullets. He fired at the Watchman, and the purple shotgun blast folded his head like a tin can. Something moved inside the fractured remains of his skull, a thrashing and wriggling belt gone haywire.

The sparking Watchman collapsed, and Micah let out a whoop. But the victory was short-lived. Outside, lights flared as figures rappelled from above.

Mr. Pynch and the Marquis caught up, and the fat mehkan gritted to his partner in Rattletrap. The Marquis adjusted his opticle, changing its light to a deep purple color that made the growths fluoresce brightly.

"Here!" Mr. Pynch hurried toward a big blob of brilliant white on the side of the mottled wall. The others gathered around it, and the Marquis changed his opticle back to normal—the radiant blotch vanished.

Mr. Pynch touched the area where they had seen the white glow. The hard metal surface gave way to his touch, melting into a spongy gel.

The Aero-copters slung low, blasting a tide of bullet rain off their shuddering blades. The clacking boots of Watchmen soldiers raced into the shadows behind them.

"Inside, now!" Mr. Pynch ordered.

With no room to second guess, Phoebe pushed her arm into the mushy surface. The wall slurped around her, slowly sucking her in.

It felt like being consumed.

She held her breath and dove in.

REKINDLING

The gelatinous wall squeezed Phoebe on all sides, blotting out her vision and cutting off her air. Just before fear of suffocation set in, she spilled out on a ridged floor.

She pulled away her hood and mask to catch her breath as the others tumbled in after her. The Marquis's opticle dimmed and brightened in rapid succession as if he were panting. His light reflected off the glass-smooth cavern walls. She looked back at the jellylike barrier as it hardened, mimicking the texture of the wall until no trace remained.

They sat there for a long while, unmoving. The shudder of Aero-copters, the crash of bullet rain, and the stomp of soldiers were scarcely more than whispers. It was as if the chaos had already faded into distant memory.

The silence was broken at last—by Micah's laughter.

"That was . . . the best thing . . . EVER!" he wheezed.

"It was sheer insolence," Mr. Pynch grumbled, mopping his brow with his necktie. "Utterly temerarious. In fact, it be the most capricious, fatuous, suicidalizing behavior I ever did . . ." His tie flopped apart in his fingers—a rip up the middle had split it in half. He inflated and barked a barrage of Rattletrap curses, which made Micah laugh all the more. The Marquis shook with silent giggles and pointed to his partner's shredded tie. Even Phoebe broke into helpless laughter. It was like releasing a long-held breath.

Dollop, however, just watched in sullen silence.

"Ah yes. Kudos! Touché! It be one great big jocundity to you all," Mr. Pynch snipped, pointing at the Marquis. "I don't know what yer cachinnating at. You think the Foundry will do business with observated saboteurs?"

The Marquis shrugged and flickered out a rapid response.

Mr. Pynch scoffed. "I hardly see how that—"

The Marquis nodded insistently and pointed at the kids.

"Absolutely not," Mr. Pynch said, crossing his arms over his chest. "I won't be tellin' 'em that. It'll go straight to their cockamamie heads."

"Tell us what?" Micah asked.

The Marquis's light got brighter, forcing Mr. Pynch to shield his eyes.

"All right, all right! Shutter that pesky peeper of yours." Mr. Pynch angled his wonky eyes at the kids. "Me exceedingly indulgent associate congratulates you on yer victory and admires the demonstrable merit of yer characters."

"Hey thanks, chum!" Micah grinned.

Phoebe looked at the Marquis and felt a gush of pride. He was right—it *was* a victory. She beamed at him, and the light dimmed a little as the Marquis sheepishly hid his opticle.

"Meself, on the other hand," Mr. Pynch said, yanking off his shredded necktie and flinging it to the ground, "I believe you two be more trouble than yer worth." He stomped off, deflating flatulently with every step. As they all got up to follow, Phoebe paused to scoop up the discarded scraps of green silk.

The Marquis illuminated the cavern, revealing shining blue-gray walls that looked cauterized, as if something had melted right through the ore. The passages were ridged and irregular, some only a few feet across and others wide enough for a liodim. There were countless pathways branching off in every direction, so that it felt like wandering through an enormous ant farm.

"Say, where's your big bag of junk?" Micah asked.

"If you must know, we was forced to ensconce our precious valuables in one of me many hidey-holes." Mr. Pynch shot a disgruntled glance over his shoulder. "Including yer proffered payment, I might add."

"Oh no!" said Phoebe.

"Oh yes," retorted Mr. Pynch. "Which means me associate

and I be fulfilling our end of the contract speculatively, pre-
suming some vagrant doesn't absquatulate with me 'junk,' as
you so gracelessly put it."

"You're a man of your word, Pynch. And so am I," declared
Micah. "You saved our butts back there, and I'm gonna make
sure it's worth your while."

"I'm sure you will," he muttered. The Marquis turned back
and mockingly mimed a grumpy Mr. Pynch, which cracked
the kids up. "Not like me loot bag would fit in these accursed
plasm channels anyway."

"Plasm channel?" Phoebe asked.

The Marquis nodded excitedly and rotated the housing of
his opticle to flood the cavern with deep purple light. Scattered
throughout were dozens of the same luminous white-violet
shapes they had used to enter these tunnels.

"Yes, yes, plasm," Mr. Pynch grumbled, annoyed at the
distraction. "Lazy but harmless mehkans. They be blubbulous
globules that live for thousands of phases and do nothing but
eat mountains, albeit imperceptibly slow. Lucky for you, the
Vo-Pykarons be saturated with such digested capillaries." He
swatted at the Marquis. "Now put the light back on, and no
more interruptions. I need me full concentration so we don't
all rust in this blasted goo tube."

The Marquis switched the light back, and they quietly
continued on their way, trying not to bother Mr. Pynch, who
grumbled in irritable Rattletrap. She thought about asking
Dollop what he was saying, but their little friend was so far

behind he was just a pair of glinting amber eyes in the dark. All the talk about Mr. Pynch's bag made Phoebe long for their abandoned rucksack. The familiar ache of hunger pulled at her stomach, and her throat was dried up. It wouldn't be long before the need for sustenance dominated her thoughts again.

They marched in silence for hours, wandering through wide corridors and squeezing through steep passages. They wound around the plasm channels until Mr. Pynch stopped so abruptly that the Marquis collided with him. He sniffed at the air, and they heard the whir-click of his nozzle. The Marquis's opticle blinked rapidly as he pointed to a tunnel on his left. Mr. Pynch responded and motioned insistently to the right.

"Lost," whispered Micah to Phoebe.

"Don't worry," she said. "They'll get us out of here."

Micah gave her a surprised look.

After a brief spat, their guides turned around and started marching back the way they had come. Mr. Pynch wore a puckered scowl and didn't acknowledge them as he stomped past. The Marquis just shrugged apologetically. They backtracked through the channels and came across Dollop, huddled against the wall and hugging his knees.

"Dollop?" Phoebe said gently, "What's wrong?"

"M-m-m-me. I'm wrong."

Micah helped Dollop to his feet, and the three of them followed after the Marquis's light, which was vanishing down the glossy tunnel.

"Aren't you proud?" Phoebe asked. "Of what we did?"

"Wh-what *you* did, not m-m-me. I d-didn't do anything."

"'Course you did." Micah clapped a hand on Dollop's shoulder. "You were our lookout. Hey, come to think of it, maybe that's your function!"

"It-it's not, and you kn-know it," he whimpered. "I pr-pray every night for Makina to reveal my p-p-purpose in Her infinite and infallible plan, err, for s-s-some sort of sign. But n-nothing. I don't have a f-f-function."

"Come on, don't say that," said Micah.

"You were brave," Phoebe offered. "That's what matters."

"All I did was, um, fall apart and alm-m-most get you two k-k-killed. I'm ho-hopeless. Always w-w-was," the little mehkan moaned. "It's prob-b-bably why I was abandoned, why I don't have a cl-clan."

"No way," replied Micah. "You don't know that."

"We never would have gotten this far without you," she reminded him. "We need you."

"You w-won't once you find your f-f-father. Uh, m-m-my service will be done. Then, in a couple cycles, I'm so stupid I'll f-f-forget all about you."

"You ain't stupid, all right? Now cut it out," Micah argued.

"Even at the housing of the W-Waybound where I—I was raised, I always m-m-messed things up. I-I'd get the prayer of thanks mixed up with, you know, the prayer of m-m-mourning. I'd, um, fall apart in the middle of s-s-sacred rituals, and the axials would have to stop the ceremony to r-r-reassemble me."

"Everybody messes up sometimes," Phoebe reassured him.

"But n-nobody messes up *all* the time. Just me." Dollop

slowed his step and began to lag behind again. "Please, just . . . just let me be alone."

Phoebe went to comfort him, but Micah grabbed her arm and shook his head. She looked back until Dollop was once again shrouded in shadows, just a pair of reflective eyes lingering in the dark.

"Huzzah!" came Mr. Pynch's reverberating cry.

The kids followed his voice down the winding canals, feeling the air grow fresh as they approached. The passage opened up to a series of lofty chambers like interconnected ventricles in the heart of the mountain. The floor was littered with bullet rain, some of the pellets softening and splitting like beads of mercury as they were absorbed into the ore. The ceiling fifty feet overhead was dotted with irregular skylights, which cast glowing pools across the glassy surfaces.

Mr. Pynch and the Marquis observed the night sky.

"An auspicious development," Mr. Pynch grunted. "By our constellular calculations, we be closer to Sen Ta'rine than I suspected. As your reluctant employee, I advise you to respite here a spell while we arbitrate the most desirable route."

"I could use a rest," Phoebe agreed with a sigh.

"Sounds like a plan," said Micah.

Behind them, Dollop quietly slipped in and found himself a dark, secluded pocket. The Marquis fussed about, found a comfy little alcove, and drew his collapsible pocket brush. He fastidiously swept the bullet rain away and beckoned the kids to come over and sit.

"Thank you," Phoebe said politely as she settled herself.

"Aw, man," groaned Micah in relief as he plopped down nearby and began to peel off his boots. "Are my dogs barkin'! You're the best, Marq."

This took the Marquis aback, and his opticle light turned a warm and rosy color. Mr. Pynch ambled over and grabbed his partner by the collar, dragging him away. His voice and the Marquis's light faded, and the kids were left in silence, illuminated only by the dim, fluctuating glow of stars.

A wave of stink assaulted Phoebe's nose as Micah started cleaning out the gunk from between his toes. She held back her comments and glanced over to the darkness where their depressed little friend had disappeared.

"I'm worried about Dollop," she said.

"Yeah," agreed Micah. "Hopefully he'll just forget he's bummed out."

After a moment, he began to chuckle and shake his head.

"What?" she asked.

"Nothin'. It's just . . . That was pure wicked. You got guts."

It was probably the greatest compliment he could muster, even if it did sound suspiciously like a catchphrase from *Maddox*. Smiling, Phoebe avoided his gaze and noticed that her skirt had been torn by the bullet rain. She dug in her sniping pockets for the needle and thread and set about making her mends.

"Randy and his stupid cadet buddies never pulled off anything half as sweet," he said. "Nice to see you prank someone who deserves it for a change."

It took her a few seconds before his meaning sank in. All those bullies she had sniped throughout the years—Candice, Tennyson, even Micah—at one time, cutting them down to size had been the most important thing in the world. That was a different life. The Foundry was the only enemy that mattered now.

"Can I ask you something?" she said.

"Shoot," he said, cracking the knuckles of his toes.

"Why did you lie to me?"

"I didn't!" he said defensively. "About what?"

"In Fuselage. About you and Dollop keeping watch."

Shock registered on Micah's face. "Look . . . I just," he said, searching for an answer. "I mean, here's the thing. I didn't . . . I only—"

"I'm not mad," she said.

"Really?" he said, unsure. "Then why you askin'?"

Phoebe squinted at her stitching, holding it up to the dim light. "We're almost to the Citadel. We don't know what we're going to find when we get there." She looked up at him. "I—I need to know I can trust you."

"You can," he said, unflinching.

"No more leader stuff. No more servant. We're in this together, okay?"

"Deal." Micah held out his Lodestar to provide light.

"Thanks," she replied.

Micah fidgeted and leaned a hand back casually. The wall wobbled, then gave way as his arm sank into a viscous puddle.

"Stupid plasm!" he hollered, extracting his hand with a slurp. Phoebe's infectious laugh filled the chamber.

"I'm not laughing *at* you," she giggled. "I'm laughing *with*—"

"Yeah, yeah," he muttered. "So, can I ask you somethin'?"

She regained control and nodded.

"Before. When you said you don't think you can save your pa . . ."

"We'll find him," she said. "I just, I don't know who he is anymore."

"You think he's really one of them?"

"I don't know. I don't know what he's done. He let . . ." The image of the butchered liodim cubs flashed in her mind. "He let this happen. It feels like . . ." she whispered. "I feel like I've lost him, too."

"Huh? Whaddya mean?" he asked.

Phoebe laid the sewing in her lap and swallowed. For a long moment, she was silent, touching the clumsy stitches on her newly repaired skirt. She wanted to tell him, wanted to explain, but was unsure how to begin.

"This was my mom's," she said at last.

Micah went deathly still.

"Sometimes I hide in her Carousel. It still smells like her back there. I—"

She had to stop.

"Anyway, that's where I found it," Phoebe said softly. "This was her favorite skirt. I've always loved how it felt."

His eyes were intense, on her. She couldn't meet his stare.

"We were on vacation in Callendon. I was swimming on the beach. I went out as far as I could, even though she warned me."

Phoebe felt tears coming, but she was a master at suppressing them.

"I got caught in the undertow. She swam in after me, dragged me to a rock. The tide pulled her under."

Her voice wavered, but she kept it steady.

"I waited for her. I waited for her to come up."

It was several minutes before either of them spoke.

"The river," Micah said. "What I did to you . . ."

His mouth was dry as sand.

"I'm sorry. I didn't . . . Phoebe, I'm so sorry."

Finally, she dared to look at him. But now he couldn't meet her gaze.

"Praise the g-g-gears!" Dollop's voice cried out.

Grateful for the interruption, Phoebe and Micah raced across the chamber. They found Dollop beneath an oblong skylight, bouncing and pointing up with a look of childish delight on his face.

"What is it?" she asked.

"W-w-wait," he said. "It's c-coming."

For a minute, nothing happened. Then in a corner of the night sky, a fiery whirling bloom burned a pink impression on the heavens, as if that small cluster of interconnected stars was caught in an eddy.

"I d-didn't know it was already that c-cycle of the interval!"

Dollop said, exuberant. "M-miraculous timing! It exp-p-plains everything, don't you see?"

"Not really, no," Micah said.

"Explains what?" Phoebe asked.

Another fiery nebula swirled overhead, this one bigger than the first.

"Thank you, Makina. The M-Mother of Ore has spoken!"

Dollop pressed his hand against his dynamo and fell to his knees, immediately lost in prayer. There were footsteps behind them as Mr. Pynch and the Marquis returned.

"Sen Ta'rine be a few clicks away," Mr. Pynch grumbled. "We'll remain here and commence on the rise. Yer precious Citadel will have to wait until then, as will our long-awaited, comfortable recharge. And me roasted flugul." It sounded like good news, yet Mr. Pynch's mood had only soured.

The sky lit up in a reddish glow, this time with two pin-wheeling swirls that collided in a lingering wash. The Marquis removed his hat and opened his opticle, shutters parting and lenses folding back to fix his gaze on the heavens.

"What is it?" Micah asked.

"Eh. Just atmospheric discharge." Mr. Pynch shrugged. "Most commonly incited by—"

"'And you, the vital c-components of My sacred machine. You who love My cr-creation most of all, uh, you who spread interlocking harmony amongst My children—beyond the Shroud, My f-f-fires shall light for thee. Thy embers blaze eternal,'" Dollop spoke in reverence. "Accord f-five, edict two. The W-Way is quite clear on this matter."

No one said a word.

"The—the Great Engineer gave each of us an ember and breathed upon it, filling us with life. When our b-b-bodies rust, our embers return to Makina's Forge for judgment. Those who were sinful or w-w-wicked have their ember doused, extinguished forever. Most are g-given another chance, so their embers are stirred, re-returning to the ore to live again."

The night lit up with drops of liquid fire splattered on the canvas of the sky. Dollop's face radiated transcendent joy.

"But th-those who found their function, those who discovered their part in Her sacred machine, their embers are blazed. The—the chosen are now taking their r-r-rightful places by Her side in the heavens. Th-that is what you see, Makina's Forge blazing the embers of the exalted. The Rekindling."

Dollop looked at Phoebe, his penetrating eyes alight.

"I told you of the Ona, may her g-g-golden ember blaze. Do you rec-call?"

"She was a prophet or something, right?" she asked quietly.

"The Great Engineer's most f-f-faithful messenger. Um, the— the Ona taught us that selfless acts performed on the cycle of Rekindling are d-divine, and that there is no greater good than to—to save the lives of others. Phoebe, what you d-d-did this day—"

"What *we* did," she said to Mr. Pynch and the Marquis.

His tone dropped to a whisper. "I—I have prayed to Makina much since our meeting, t-t-to understand why She would lead me to you, why She would p-place me in the company of humans. I feared you, doubted you, but the T-Tender of the Forge has spoken. You are blessed. No—no matter what, I am your devoted servant for the remainder of my span."

"Not my servant," Phoebe said. "My friend."

Dollop nodded contentedly. She could feel Micah's eyes upon her again. The sky came alive with color, vibrant fireworks of swirling stars. Phoebe turned to cranky Mr. Pynch and held something out to him.

"I was wrong to not trust you," she said.

In her hand was his striped green necktie, roughly mended but intact. Mr. Pynch's tight scowl faded, and his wonky eyes slowly bulged in their little sacs.

"You . . ." he grumbled low. "You did this?"

"As best I could," she said. "The thread doesn't really match, and the stitches are a little rough, but . . ."

Mr. Pynch caressed the fabric, speechless for the first time.

The exploding night sky drew their attention.

"Er, best not miss the light show," Mr. Pynch said with a nervous smile.

And so the five companions lay side by side beneath the skylight as the Rekindling shone down upon them with spectacular astral fire.

Phoebe settled her arm, and for the briefest of moments, her hand grazed Micah's. His skin was harder than she expected, bumpy with calluses but warm. She had a sudden distressing urge to grasp it in hers. Quickly, she faked a scratch and set her hand at a safe distance, praying he hadn't noticed.

As she stared at the infinite night sky, Phoebe had the strange sensation of being cut loose, unmoored and floating through this vast and unfamiliar universe. Beside her, the Marquis's opticle pulsed like a beacon, as if he were conversing with the flickering stars. She wasn't sure what he was saying to them, or what they might be telling him in reply.

And yet, somehow, the deepest parts of her understood.

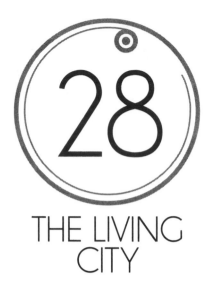

28
THE LIVING CITY

P hoebe barely slept. The ridged cubbies in the plasm channels were hard, her empty stomach ached, and the Rekindling lasted all night. But none of that kept her friends awake. Her anxious, buzzing thoughts were to blame. The more she tried to quiet her brain, the further sleep seemed to slip away from her.

Drifting in and out of consciousness, she roused when the first splashes of dawn trickled through the skylights overhead. Despite her restless night, she felt keen and eager, like her senses had somehow been heightened. Micah was sleeping soundly nearby, and it took all of her willpower to keep from sniping him. After their conversation last night, it would have felt like bad form.

She saw that Mr. Pynch and Dollop were already awake, whispering in Rattletrap as they scratched at the glassy-smooth walls. With a grunt, Dollop wrenched something that looked like a fat bolt from the surface. It squirmed in his grip, its head puckering with a weird kissing sound. He popped it in his mouth and munched on it. Mr. Pynch said something that made them both laugh, then shoved a handful of the wriggling critters into his own gaping maw.

"H-happy rise!" Dollop said with his mouth full.

"Salutations and jubilations! I was just edifying our good friend here on the finer points of hunting the delectably elusive spotted pinpod."

"Delicious," she said with a chuckle. Unsettling though their mehkan meal was, she was envious. If she didn't find any food soon, she might even be willing to give these a try. "Where's the Marquis?"

"Ah, me associate traversed ahead of us to deduciate the most clandestine entry into Sen Ta'rine," he said, chomping pleasantly. "It wouldn't do to have prying eyes."

"What's for breakfast?" Micah said with a yawn.

"Spotted pinpod omelet with two crispy strips of pinpod and a glass of freshly squeezed pinpod juice," she said with a straight face. Micah looked at her blankly, his hair in a red tumble. Too early for a joke, she guessed.

"Shall we hit the ore, as they say?" Mr. Pynch asked as he reached for his tie to wipe his mouth. His eyes bulged as he realized it was gone once again.

"Why that pompous, snaky-fingered little . . ."

The four of them wound farther into the plasm channels, this time without the benefit of the Marquis's opticle. Micah held his Lodestar aloft to provide some light, but neither Mr. Pynch with his nozzle nor Dollop with his nocturnal vision seemed to need it. There was a spring in Phoebe's step. Despite her uncertainty and the ever-present fear of what was ahead, she felt lighter than she could remember.

"S-s-so, Sen Ta'rine is a, err, a big place?" Dollop asked.

"It be the most prodigious metropolis this side o' the Ettalye," Mr. Pynch said. "A city of endless possibilities."

"So endless they got human grub?" Micah wondered.

"The Living City has it all, Master Micah."

"Th-that means there's all k-k-kinds of mehkies there?"

"It be an epicenter of mehkan activity bursting at the seams. Folks flock there from far and wide. More tchurbs and jaislids than you'd ever care to see in one place, to be candid-like. Why do you ask, Sir Dollop?"

"Oh, I—I was hoping that . . . Well, I th-thought . . . You know, maybe I might find my—my clan there, and whatnot."

Mr. Pynch scratched his bristly cheek. "Yes indeedy, I had almost forgotten. Fret not, me tender mehkie. I'll keep an eye wandering for one of yer ilk. Don't think I'd pass 'em over. Yer assemblage be rather . . . memorable."

"R-really?" Dollop asked brightly.

"Indubitably. And if yer kind habitate anywhere, it be most assuredly in Sen Ta'rine." His words lit up Dollop's face.

"See?" Micah said. "Things are lookin' up."

Dollop bounced with joy, his parts joining and separating with each step.

"Mr. Pynch," Phoebe began, "I've been thinking. I know it's a lot to ask, but how would . . . I mean, even though it's dangerous, would you be willing to—"

"You want me assistance in secreting you into the Citadel," he said without turning back to them. "Figured you'd pose the inquiry eventually."

"We'll pay you, of course," she offered.

"With what?" Mr. Pynch probed.

Micah looked down at his Lodestar. Phoebe plucked the hem of her skirt.

"You don't fully cognizate what you be asking."

Was that fear she could hear in his syrupy, rumbling voice?

"It be surrounded by dead lands swarming with ravenous hivelings, and the Foundry patrols every forsaken inch of it with all manner of sentineling abominations. The Citadel itself bears an impassable bulwark of one hundred and nine spires, one for each sun in the celestial ring, converging at a deadly peak to symbolize the fusion. The spires be riddled with befuddling passages from which there be no exit. Once you enter, you be destined to rust therein."

Phoebe bit her lip.

"So," Micah said, "is that a yes?"

"I know it's crazy," she said. "But my father is there, so I have to get in somehow. I don't have a choice."

"*We* don't have a choice," insisted Micah.

"R-r-right," Dollop chimed insecurely.

"I . . ." Mr. Pynch began. He looked at their eager faces. "I may or may not have some acquaintances. Business-mehkies like meself in Sen Ta'rine, who specialize in such manners of trespasserous knowledge." Phoebe broke into a smile.

"Now we're gettin' somewhere!" Micah hooted.

"But I make no promises," Mr. Pynch stated. "I never do."

"As for the payment . . ." Phoebe started.

"I'll put it on yer tab," he muttered resentfully.

The group continued on, and Phoebe felt her confidence grow. Her hunger and thirst were worsening, but she trained her focus on every next step, and time passed more quickly than she had expected. She was so close now.

Up ahead, something dangled from the ceiling, the first variation they had seen to the smooth, rippled surfaces. It was a jumble of striated bronze tubes covered in wiry hairs, overflowing from the walls in a convoluted knot.

"Roots. An excellent prospect." Mr. Pynch beamed.

The Marquis's familiar opticle light came bobbing through the channel. Mr. Pynch barked at him in Rattletrap, and the Marquis feigned innocence. But the fat mehkan prodded his partner, who finally returned the stolen necktie.

"Come!" Mr. Pynch rumbled, securing his silky green accessory. "Sen Ta'rine awaits."

As the Marquis led them through more winding tunnels, the protruding ducts became thicker and more frequent. After a while, he switched his light to purple and scanned the walls for white plasms until he found the right one.

"Intermit here while I ensure the way be secured," said Mr. Pynch before slipping through the plasm. The others were left to wait for a quiet, nervous moment. Then Mr. Pynch's arm poked back through and gestured for them to follow.

Phoebe took a deep breath and dove in first.

She emerged into another vaulted mountain base, similar to the area where they had fought the Watchmen. But whereas that one had been wild and overgrown, this space was carefully maintained. The trimmed walls pressed in on all sides like sweeping hedges. High above them, the ceiling was formed entirely from a branching system of bronze ducts, which budded with luminous honey-colored globes. And spilling in from the corner up ahead was a roaring commotion she couldn't quite place, a churning and clamoring thrum.

The others squished through the plasm behind her. The Marquis extracted a device from a hiding place in the wall of bluish growth, some kind of a weird mehkan wheelbarrow. There was a driving mechanism in the rear, a U-shaped cradle layered with organic gears and levers that connected to a tiered yoke. The enclosed bucket at the front was a wrinkled pod like a giant iron walnut shell. Balanced beneath it was a gelatinous wheel, as if the entire compartment were resting on a large ball of mercury.

"Brilliant!" Mr. Pynch brayed. "An awlegg's tilbury. Quite the commensurate solution."

The Marquis swept off his hat and bowed.

"Solution . . . to what?" Micah asked.

"Why, to smuggle you into the city," stated Mr. Pynch. He grabbed ahold of the steering mechanism, ratcheted a crank, and the top of the bucket hinged open. "Best hasten. Pop yerselves in before we draw any curious passersby."

Phoebe and Micah climbed into the tilbury. The floor was scattered with pebbles and dust, but the base was wide enough for them to both sit comfortably.

"Limbs and digits all retractored?" called Mr. Pynch.

"Ready to roll," Micah called back.

Dollop waved to them as the lid clanged shut. The kids' ears rang within the dark echoing confines, and they had to stoop to avoid bumping their heads. The seal around its perimeter was uneven, so they had a few horizontal slivers to peer out of. Through a crack, the kids saw Mr. Pynch and the Marquis, each working one end of the U-shaped driving mechanism.

The tilbury jostled as the mehkans started to push it, although for such a ramshackle device, Phoebe was amazed by its fluidity. The ride was nearly as smooth as that of Tennyson's beloved Baronet.

As they wound around the corner, the light grew brighter and the noise intensified. The kids looked ahead through the cracks. They both gasped.

It was a roaring current of mehkans.

From their peepholes, they could only catch fleeting glimpses of a clattering blur. Creatures galloped and rolled, chugged and flew, even squirmed past in a vigorous tide. A dozen identical mehkans like black starfish spun across the walls using suction pads on their feet. A flopping hinged creature swung overhead, collapsing end over end. A pair of steel wool–covered tripods bumped against the tilbury as they loped past on spring-loaded legs. Snippets of Rattletrap were everywhere, along with sloshes, moans, and whistles.

They heard Dollop's chirp among them as he wove through the crowd, exuberantly greeting mehkans. He leaned close to the tilbury and peeked in.

"Everyth-thing ok-k-kay in there?"

"Get back!" Micah hissed.

"Don't draw any attention to us," Phoebe said urgently.

"Oh r-r-right, I f-forgot," Dollop said, trying very hard to look nonchalant.

Other tunnels merged, and mehkans surged all around them, pushing and bumping up on all sides. They heard Mr. Pynch growl and peeked back to find him popping out his spines to ward off those that got too close.

Without warning, light streamed in through the seams of the tilbury. The kids snapped back from the little openings, momentarily blinded.

"Feast yer peepers on the Living City!" Mr. Pynch cried.

Albright City was the capital of all Meridian. Some called it the most spectacular city in the world. Phoebe had spent her entire life there and knew of nothing that rivaled its majesty or scale. That was before Sen Ta'rine.

Stretching so tall the kids couldn't even see the tops,

hundreds of honey-bronze towers dwarfed even the Vo-Pykaron Mountains that flanked them. The skyscrapers looked like cactuses, with vertical shoots bending up from every side—structures growing up and out of other structures. Whereas Albright City exhibited symmetry, straight lines and right angles, Sen Ta'rine was the opposite. There wasn't a parallel line in sight. Baffling shapes and undulating ridges separated the stacked floors, wavy lips formed balconies, and parapets jutted up at unexpected angles.

Thousands of mehkans populated honeycomb chambers and navigated the ledges. In some places, strips of the outer walls curved away like banana peels to form runways that connected one tower to the next. Mehkans traveled across these bridges using some sort of transit the kids couldn't make out.

It all looked too precarious to stand, and yet somehow it did. The towers swayed gently, like oaks in a summer breeze. Phoebe thought back to the bronze ducts they had seen below—Mr. Pynch had called them roots.

Sen Ta'rine truly was the Living City.

Mehkans were zipping in such a flurry that it was impossible to tell which were creatures and which were vehicles. She wondered where they were headed. Were they going home or racing to their jobs? Did they even have jobs? Did these growing buildings contain libraries or restaurants or hospitals?

Phoebe wanted to touch those buildings, to climb to the highest point and coast through the city on whatever transport was crossing overhead.

Dollop squealed and sprinted through the crowd. He

plucked off his hands, stuck them on his head, and hobbled clumsily on four short limbs. Then he squeaked again and stacked his pieces so he wobbled on teetering stilts. Dollop was looking for a resemblance to every mehkan that passed, mimicking them and trying to engage. But the pedestrians just brushed him off, annoyed.

With one arm dangling from his rear end like a tail, he slunk back.

"I j-just thought . . . You know, maybe . . . Oh, w-w-wait!"

Then he was off again.

"Poor little sop," Mr. Pynch muttered. "Perhaps he's got no one after all."

"He's got us," Phoebe said firmly.

"Darn tootin'!" agreed Micah.

The tilbury diverted off the main path and rolled across a raised band of walkway. Off to the side were new growths poking up through bluish ore muck, an organized cluster of bronze sprouts only a few yards high. There were filth-spattered mehkans hunched over and ambling slowly around. A long appendage grew from each of their heads like the proboscis of a butterfly, tipped with gleaming thresher blades. They tended to the buds, doting over their shining surfaces and carefully shaping them.

This was a garden of new buildings, Phoebe realized.

Flat mehkans with serrated bodies were scuttling across a nearby skyscraper, gyrating their carapaces back and forth like jigsaws to carve honey-colored swaths from the skin of the structure. Braying, bulbous mehkans hauled away the bronze cuttings—their speckled bodies and sharp, stubby fins were darkly reminiscent of Zip Trolleys.

The hurried pulse of the city faded as the walkway descended into another cluttered thicket of buildings. These were unrelentingly gray, their tattered skyline blocking out the suns. The facades were shriveled, and gaping holes had been gnawed through their skins. Some of the structures were splintered or limbless, and others were skeletal ruins threatening to collapse. Eroding rust caked the creaking buildings and littered walkways.

"What is this place?" Phoebe whispered.

"Folks call it the Heap," gritted Mr. Pynch. "Where all the mehkan scraps and detritus be relegated to."

There were packs of battered, grimy creatures huddled on corners. Some chattered in Rattletrap wheezes, while others shouted and slurred drunkenly. Sunken, haunted faces peered out of hovels that were precariously balanced in teetering stacks. Curled bodies lay beneath sheet-metal lean-tos, while mehkan children screeched and played in a dump of rusted building clippings.

Dollop hopped from group to despondent group, reforming his limbs to imitate each in turn. A familiar shape hobbled out of the shadows—a chraida limping on a cable-bound crutch with a ragged stump where one of his legs should have been. He spat and clutched at the golden dynamo on Dollop's chest. The hapless mehkan registered the danger of his situation with a jolt, but a mangy mob surrounded him, cackling and pawing and closing in.

Phoebe was about to cry for help, but the Marquis leaped to Dollop's rescue. With his umbrella, he bopped a few heads before snaring Dollop around the neck with the handle and dragging him out of the crowd.

"All I—I—I wanted was to find my clan," he whimpered.

"If yer people occupied the Heap, you wouldn't want to consort with them anyway," said Mr. Pynch. "Most mehkies wholly reject these refugees, consider 'em a bunch of needy laggards. Especially those pathetic tchurbs. Bleh."

The Marquis wiped clean his umbrella where it had touched the destitute mehkans.

"Refugees?" Phoebe asked. "From the Foundry?"

"They left their homes for this dump?" Micah asked.

"Fled, more like it, but that be the shape of things."

"P p-poor mehkies."

"True, they haven't a tinklet of gauge to their names."

"No—no, I f-f-feel, um, sad for them."

"Don't," Mr. Pynch grumbled. "Those ragamuffins would have pummeled you for that tiny ingot of yers without a second thought. They be contemptible gut-scum."

"All embers gl-glow," Dollop stated with conviction. "W-when we turn our backs on the M-Mother of Ore, we—we turn our backs on each other. It is the Great D-Decay. Err, this treatment of fellow mehkies is sh-shameful. The—the Way is quite clear on this m-m-matter."

"Dollop is right," Phoebe said. "They didn't choose this."

The Marquis's light dimmed. He flickered at Mr. Pynch.

"Don't you start again," Mr. Pynch snapped, then scowled

at Dollop and the kids. "And don't you be so naïverous. Such scoundrels be unworthy of yer bleeding-heart empathies."

"Come on, they're just trying to survive," Micah said.

"As we all be," Mr. Pynch replied, dismissing him. "Now keep yer traps shut. Last thing I need be them nefarious sorts getting curious about me cargo."

Phoebe steeled herself. Nervous energy buzzed in her chest like an overcharged battery. Soon they would get some information about how to infiltrate the Citadel and make the Foundry answer for everything they had done.

The tilbury glided through the crowded slum. Dollop chanted a wistful Rattletrap prayer, blessing the refugees they passed, but staying close. Gaunt families crowded around grease fires, their smoke and ash clouding the air. Despite the strangeness of the mehkan faces, the kids recognized sorrow in their eyes and hunger carved into their unfamiliar features.

The tilbury descended a narrow passage, choking out the light. Mr. Pynch was consumed by darkness, the Marquis's shutters were closed, and they could no longer hear Dollop's solemn prayers. There was a clank of chains and the jarring shudder of some kind of gate. Then out poured a shrieking maelstrom of Rattletrap, a harsh cacophony like a taunted pack of rabid dogs.

"What is it? Can you see anything?" whispered Phoebe.

"Nothin'," came Micah's startled reply.

She wanted to call out to Mr. Pynch to make sure everything was okay, but she couldn't risk revealing herself. The tilbury rang with the racket. Bodies clanged against the side, too close for the kids to be able to make anything out.

Micah scrabbled for his Lodestar. Before he got the chance to use it, the lid swung open, and they were dumped out. Blinding lights. A clamorous roar.

Shadowy figures loomed. Claws grabbed them. Micah struggled with his weapon, but fat hands wrenched it away.

The hands of Mr. Pynch.

Everything was a blur. Phoebe twisted around, unable to see who was holding them. Dollop was nearby, seized by the numerous cinching arms of a nasty-looking scarlet mehkan. His glistening eyes bulged in terror.

In the shadows, a hulking creature was handing something heavy to Mr. Pynch and the Marquis. A jingling sack filled with shiny, oval rings.

"Our business be concluded," Mr. Pynch called to the kids over the din. "The world be cruel, dear hearts."

His face was hard, devoid of mirth. The Marquis offered a tip of his hat.

"And gauge talks."

FINAL BID

Volcanic rage seethed within Phoebe. Scorching magma exploded through her veins. She screamed. Every pore of her being vibrated with the sound. That set Micah off, launching him into a kicking, spitting frenzy.

"Pynch! When I catch you, I swear I'm gonna—" he shrieked, and fought against the clasping claws that held him.

The two traitors bustled toward the exit. The Marquis carried the massive sack of gauge over his shoulder while Mr. Pynch held up the Lodestar, his wonky eyes lighting purple with possibility. They were quickly lost within the malevolent, churning crowd.

Why!? Why hadn't Phoebe trusted her instincts? Those two had been plotting this payday from the very first moment they laid eyes on the kids. It was Micah's fault for inviting them along, but she wasn't free from blame. She had been suckered. Even Dollop was paying the price for their terrible mistake.

She tried to make sense of her surroundings, but it was hard to see past the glare of painfully bright spotlights. They were in the middle of an oval arena, about thirty feet long. Mehkan guards lined the perimeter, holding back a surging crowd. Tiers crammed full of spectators rose steeply on all sides.

The brute restraining Micah was easily eight feet tall and built like a bulldozer, with dented gray hide and patches of wiry orange hair. Boasting I-beam arms that bulged with fibrous muscle, he subdued Micah with thick, six-fingered claws that Phoebe recognized from the Foundry's Over-cranes. She looked down at her own captor's hands and saw they were identical. There was no point in resisting.

Dollop was pinned by an unsettling creature with a wide, scarlet-banded body that sat low on five skeletal legs. Extending up from its front was a long, slithery thorax like a giant centipede. Dozens of blunt, chittering arms encased Dollop like a crimson-striped sarcophagus and squeezed until he gave up the fight, his furious cries cut off to pained wheezes.

A blustering, brassy voice cut through the clamor and reverberated through the arena. The mob fell silent.

A figure emerged from the shadows and waddled into the pit. It looked like a giant wrecking ball with brawny elephant limbs, and a misshapen warty face dotted with piggy eyes bubbled out from its chest. The mehkan was draped in heavy foil sacks that jingled with gauge. Strapped to its back was a device that extended up and over like a bundle of fishing poles.

The blaring voice trumpeted again—no, three or four voices, maybe more. They spoke in rapid Rattletrap, and the crowd went wild.

It took Phoebe a second to place where those voices were coming from. Suspended at the end of the dangling poles was a mehkan in a capsule. He was sickly silver, with flaps of sagging skin that had the pimpled texture of an uncooked turkey. A series of fleshy horns like megaphones jutted from his flabby body, each screaming with a different voice. He manipulated the rods so that the capsule swung over the crowd while his bleating voices incited them.

At a shrill command, the three monstrous mehkans displayed their captives. Even Micah had given up struggling, though his face was fixed in defiance. With a startling blast, the megaphone voices rang simultaneously, and the crowd erupted into deafening, screeching cheers.

"What's he saying?" Phoebe yelled to Dollop.

Their friend's eyes were pinched closed, his color ashen.

"Dollop!"

Powerless against the cinching centipede arms, he could only turn his eyes to her. "H-h-h-he says, 'The—the Gauge P-Pit is open for b-business.'"

The blustering announcer swooped over to Phoebe. He was even more foul up close. Veiny glands bulged around his many horns, each secreting a white, wire-thin tentacle. The quivering tendrils slithered toward her, grabbing at her hair and tickling her cheek while his multiple voices cooed at once.

She screamed again.

The crowd cheered. The clammy, boneless probes wrenched her mouth open with unexpected force as the announcer belted so loud it made her head throb. Tendrils prodded her tongue and raked her teeth. She would have bitten them off if they didn't taste like pocket change wrapped in spoiled cold cuts.

"What do they want?" Micah yelled to Dollop. But their friend was speechless with fear.

With a little ticking sound, the announcer's suspended capsule swept toward Micah, spewing unintelligible shouts that seemed to mock the boy's futile struggles against the crane claws. He pinched the boy's chubby cheeks with his tendrils and tousled his hair. Then he eased in very close and with delicate precision forced open Micah's eyelids to expose one frantic hazel orb.

He let out a chilling gurgle, and the crowd hooted.

The flabby creature whizzed over to Dollop, staring wordlessly for several stunned seconds before drawing back with dramatic flair. He made an offhand comment with one horn, followed by braying laughter from his others. The audience responded with ratcheting hoots. His wiry probes tapped Dollop's dynamo, and the cackles grew louder.

The megaphone mehkan silenced the room, and the air became electric with anticipation. Then out pealed a phrase so loud Phoebe could feel it in the roots of her teeth.

"N-n-no, no, no, no, no," Dollop babbled.

The guards at the perimeter of the ring stepped back.

"WHAT?" Phoebe demanded.

The surrounding crowd surged into the arena. They tripped and tore past one another, fighting to get a better look at the captives. They pressed in, their undulating mass indistinguishable in the floodlights. Phoebe closed her eyes.

There were sharp barks from the mob, words volleying from one mehkan to the next as they tried to outdo each other. Phoebe didn't need a translation.

They were being auctioned.

She watched as the vile Auctioneer cheered and blathered, bouncing on his rig with unmistakable merriment. The buyers edged closer. A few eager ones gathered their nerves and dared to touch the kids with pincers and tentacles, calling out their bids all the while. Dollop burbled in Rattletrap, his voice hitching with sobs as the masses scrutinized and prodded him.

Countless fingers probed the kids, some coarse and grating and others unnervingly slimy. One lifted Micah's pant leg and tasted his ankle with a sticky tongue, and another slid its thin eyestalk up his nostril. A mehkan tested the bones in Phoebe's arm while the next one inspected her ear. The throng convulsed, piling up around the merchandise. Fingers like pliers pinched Phoebe's neck, and a feverish creature covered in rusty, seeping sores put Micah's fingers in its gear-toothed mouth and bit down, causing him to cry out. The delighted horde discovered that Dollop's limbs were detachable, and they plucked off his parts to toy with them cruelly.

The Auctioneer swooped overhead, pointing and barking as his guards broke through the crowd. The mob was spiraling out of control. Jagged hooks dug into Micah's calf, and a vibrating mehkan with frizzy wire hair lunged at Phoebe, some of its jittery strands scratching her face.

The sight of blood drove the crowd into a greater frenzy.

They were so close she could see nothing but their leering faces. Huffing diesel breath burned her eyes. She knew what would happen next. One of these salivating creatures would buy her, if the others didn't tear her to ribbons first. It would drag her away, and she would never be seen again.

A metallic squall split the air. The chaotic mass froze.

There was a splinter of silence. Then the Gauge Pit erupted in a chorus of fear. The mob scattered, flattening one another in a mad rush to escape. The Auctioneer blared his trumpeting voices, zipping about while the wrecking ball creature stormed up and down the arena.

BOOM.

The entire Gauge Pit shook. A floodlight jostled loose, then smashed on the ground, splatting like a balloon filled with bioluminescent glop. The crane-claw fingers that held Phoebe released. She fell to the ground and turned to see her captor barreling through the crowd, clearing a path with its concussive I-beam arms. Even the guards were fleeing.

"Micah!" she cried over the mad rush of bodies. There he was, scampering on his hands and knees, trying to avoid getting trampled. She hurried over and pulled him to his feet.

They saw a flash of scarlet off to the side of the pit. The

ghastly mehkan that still held Dollop was scuttling away. They bolted after him.

An explosion threw them to the ground. Debris rained down from a smoldering hole at the back of the arena.

Micah rolled to his feet and vaulted onto the back of the red mehkan, clinging to its writhing centipede thorax. He pried back a few of its arms. Phoebe sprang to his side and yanked. With a crack like a lobster shell, its arms snapped open, and Dollop stumbled free.

The clatter of metal-soled boots marched inside.

Phoebe caught a glimpse of Watchman soldiers.

In a viper-fast strike, the scarlet mehkan pounced on Micah. Its thrashing arms whipped across his face in a blinding succession of blows. Blood splatted from his nose. The centipede arms opened wide. On the underside of its slithery thorax, a long gash parted to reveal vertical rows of black needle teeth. It bore down, fangs dripping.

A burst of strobing gunfire.

Bullets thudded into the scarlet mehkan, again and again. Its legs convulsed and spasmed, and Micah rolled clear.

A spiraling wave of rounds ripped into the beast. It staggered, thick white ooze spilling from the wounds. The creature still grabbed for Micah, but the white goo crystallized with a sound like crackling ice. Its limbs contorted and froze, and the mehkan collapsed, immobilized.

The three fugitives ran as Watchman soldiers spread throughout the Gauge Pit like a black bloodstain. Their rifles hissed open into four spinning barrels as they shot at the fleeing crowd. Muzzles flashed, but their guns were eerily quiet. Mehkans fell as the chemical ammunition punctured their shells. Even those with superficial damage were incapacitated by the white cement. Paralyzed, they shrieked as bullets chipped away at their bodies, shattering them like ice sculptures.

Phoebe and her friends searched desperately for an exit.

Behind them, they saw some mehkans rise up against the Watchmen. But it was futile. None who dared to fight survived their whispering rifles.

A shadowy aisle led away, pallid sunlight at its end.

They ran for a battered gate hanging half off its hinges. Fleeing creatures flooded past, clawing for freedom. Thunderous footfalls came from behind, but they didn't register what that meant until it was too late.

The Auctioneer coiled his wiry tendrils around Phoebe, voices blaring. He was not about to lose his costly prize. Micah and Dollop pulled at her legs as the wrecking ball mehkan swiped at them with boulderlike paws. They dodged his swings but couldn't tear Phoebe free.

A long shadow fell over them, followed by a barrage of crushing blows.

The wrecking ball mehkan's tumorous head was obliterated.

Hot gray fluid doused Phoebe and the others. The Auctioneer bleated and whipped to and fro in his capsule as the giant mehkan carrying him crashed to the ground, its jingling foil bags bursting in a gush of gauge.

The Auctioneer detached himself from his harness and tumbled away.

His floppy pimpled skin squelched on the ground as he tried to escape. But a leather boot shot down and crushed him, silencing his pathetic squawks.

The murderous shadow turned dead eyes upon Phoebe.

"At last," said Kaspar.

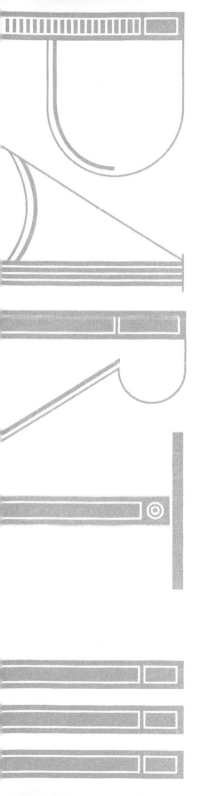

30

EVERYTHING ON THE TABLE

P hoebe felt like every last ounce of strength had been drawn from her veins with a hypodermic needle. Her friends were beside her on a hard bench in the back of an Acro-copter. Micah's left cheek was swollen, his nose caked in blood. Dollop's glistening eyes stared into space. A dozen Watchman soldiers surrounded them, all sitting ramrod-straight and motionless.

Her stomach lifted uneasily as the aircraft descended. Through the slit window across the aisle, land swept into view. At first, she didn't know what she was looking at. There was a vast, soggy field of brown and a thick thorn poking at the skin of the sky. She watched as they approached, and the spike grew to titanic proportions. It could only be one thing.

The Citadel.

One hundred and nine spires curved outward from a wide base, then met high above at a tight, twisting apex. They appeared to be smeared with dripping mud or tallow, obscuring a murky gold inner sanctum. The fortress was brimming with activity, with silver scars of train tracks crisscrossing the ground and black aircraft dotting the sky.

Phoebe realized this was the only way they ever could have gotten here.

They never had a chance.

The Aero-copter touched down on a steel landing that jutted out from the melted gray spires. The prisoners offered no resistance as Watchmen dragged them outside. The roaring wind from the rotor threatened to blow them off the platform, but Kaspar stood as immovable as death. He grabbed the kids by their collars and yanked them forward.

Watchmen hauled Dollop in the opposite direction. He hung between them like a discarded plaything, his bulbous eyes popping with fear.

"Dollop!" Phoebe cried.

Kaspar shoved her ahead. They crossed the smooth steel platform, clearly an addition constructed by the Foundry.

Gobs of liquefied metal were hardened around the entrance to the tower like some kind of horrible sculpture, drooping with faces contorted in agony.

Then she remembered what Mr. Pynch had said about the Citadel's creator. The cruel megalarch Kallorax had sacrificed his victims with fire.

This was no sculpture.

The cascade of molten corpses was fused into a ghoulish gray flesh that coated the entirety of the fortress. All of the towers were drenched in a veil of the dead. Dissolving fingers reached out to her, entwined with broken limbs and screaming mehkan faces trapped in throes of eternal burning death.

They entered the spire, which was made from a golden ore forked with bloody veins, and wound down a stainless steel staircase. Kaspar led them into an elevator, and after a silent ride down, they stepped into a bright hallway.

It was as if Kaspar had teleported the kids back to Albright City. It was a nauseating contrast to that wall of melted corpses. The corridor was exquisite with rich wood paneling, platinum chandeliers, and luxurious burgundy carpet. The only thing out of place was the occasional Watchman soldier standing like an armed statue against the wall.

Kaspar swung open a pair of heavy doors inlaid with diamond-shaped silver panels. The warm and cozy aroma of cedar smoke and roasted garlic wafted over them. Kaspar shoved the kids through and locked the door.

The dining room was decorated with potted ferns and lush oil paintings of Foundry Bay. A bronze Muse-o-Graph sat atop a stand, trickling dulcet tones from the concentric arches of its amplifier. An expansive table was set for three. Before a crackling fireplace, a broad and impeccably dressed figure stared into the low flames.

Goodwin turned to face Phoebe and Micah.

"What a relief it is to finally see you safe." A smile twinkled in his ice-blue eyes. A Watchman they hadn't even noticed stepped forward with a tray. The kids took a wary step back, but he offered a pair of steaming towels with shining tongs. Phoebe took one hesitantly, but Micah refused with a sneer.

"Oh, son," Goodwin said with concern as he approached them. "You are bleeding." He took a warm cloth and reached out to wipe the boy's nose. Micah recoiled, hawked up some phlegm, and spat the bloody gob into the towel.

"I ain't your son," he scowled.

"Indeed," Goodwin agreed. He set the bloody towel aside to take a fresh one. "You two have been through a terrible ordeal. You must be famished. Please, sit." The Chairman swept around to the head of the table.

"Where's Dollop?" Micah asked.

"Where's my father?" demanded Phoebe.

"Don't worry, they are safe," Goodwin replied. "How about a Fizzy?"

"I'll show ya where you can shove your Fizzy, Fatty."

Goodwin clucked his tongue. "A shame your years with the Plumms have made no impression. But I suppose your manners befit your upbringing."

"You don't know me!" Micah tensed to charge, but Phoebe held him back.

"Micah Eugene Tanner," Goodwin began. "Age ten. Born in the southern Sodowa town of Oleander to Randall Harris Tanner and Deirdre Beth Davidson. Request for a restraining order against Randall filed in provincial court, then withdrawn. Separated multiple times, but not divorced. Your father has quite the record, assault and battery, driving under the influence . . . shall I continue?"

A look of shock registered on Micah's swollen face.

"Sit," Goodwin said with a smile.

Phoebe looked at the towel in her hands and eased her face into it. The steaming cloth against her raw skin was invigorating. She felt renewed and awake. What a mess they must look to a man like him. She plucked off her gloves and cleaned her filthy hands with the cloth. Then she tucked her skirt behind her knees and sat at the table like a lady. Time to play Goodwin's game.

"You gotta be kiddin' me!" Micah blurted at Phoebe.

Goodwin smiled his approval. "Two Fizzies," he said to a Watchman, and perused a tray of hors d'oeuvres.

"Please, Micah. Let's not take Mr. Goodwin's hospitality for granted."

"I ain't sittin' with this chump! You can't make me—"

"Could you please pass the butter?" she asked their host.

Micah was dumbfounded.

"Of course, Phoebe, there you are." Goodwin laughed as he handed her the dish. "You truly are your father's daughter."

"Thank you, sir." Phoebe buttered her roll and nibbled daintily, and though she was famished, she resisted the urge to cram the whole thing in her mouth.

"He is a fortunate man," Goodwin said. "The two of you have risked everything to find him. Truly remarkable."

"He would do the same for us," she said, burying her doubts.

"He has been worried sick about you these past three days. We all have. You evaded us every step of the way, despite our best efforts to rescue you."

"Rescue, *ha!*" Micah scoffed, and flopped down next to Phoebe. The Watchman butler served the kids two frothy pink beverages. Micah pointed at the glass. "Hey, is this poison?"

Goodwin chuckled. "I am not in the habit of poisoning children."

"Drink it," Micah ordered as he slid the beverage toward the Chairman. Without hesitating, the big man took a sip.

"Hmm, pink lemonade. I prefer lime myself," Goodwin said and passed the drink back. Micah chugged it in one gulp. Phoebe took a small sip of hers—the sugar and bubbles were like tart lightning in her mouth.

"You can't imagine the stir you have caused," Goodwin continued. "Three security captains have lost their jobs, and all of our protocols are being re-examined. In some ways, I should thank you. Your little visit has prompted us to fortify what appear to be egregious leaks in our defenses."

The idea that they had accidentally helped the Foundry disconcerted Phoebe, but she hid her worries.

Micah shrugged as he crammed down a crab cake.

"I do not believe you truly appreciate the magnitude of your accomplishment. Do you know that in the entire history of the Foundry's existence not a single unauthorized person has ever crossed over?"

"We're sorry if we caused any trouble," she said. Micah scowled at her.

"It was only because of your little stunt in the Vo-Pykarons that we managed to pick up your trail and alert our spies in Sen Ta'rine. Without that, we would not be talking now. I must say, I am duly impressed."

"Whoop-dee-doo!" Micah said. "You think you can blow smoke up our butts and fatten us up, and we'll do what you want? Think we're that stupid?"

"The very fact that you are here in Mehk proves the contrary," Goodwin countered. "Ah! Dinner is served."

Watchmen strode in bearing silver-crested platters. They set the dishes down, withdrew the lids, and out poured the most sumptuous smells the kids had ever known. After a few days of starvation, they couldn't resist Goodwin ate deliberately, and Phoebe attempted the same with moderate success. Micah, however, inhaled the meal with abandon. He snapped his fingers at a Watchman and pointed to his glass, smirking as the stony-faced attendant refilled it.

"I hope everything is to your liking," Goodwin commented.

"Thank you," Phoebe said, dabbing her mouth. "May I ask a question, sir?"

He nodded. "Of course, dear. Your mind must be brimming with them."

"Why did you take my father?"

"I had hoped to save that discussion for after supper, but I appreciate your eagerness," Goodwin said, draining his wine-glass. A Watchman quickly refilled it. "We live in challenging times, Phoebe. Meridian's enemies are organizing, plotting to take from us what is rightfully ours. The Foundry has—"

"It's not ours," she interrupted. Goodwin's brow rose.

"Pardon me," she said, trying to mask her loathing, "but it's not ours. The Foundry doesn't invent anything. You steal it all . . . sir."

"Yeah!" Micah added, his mouth full of food.

A gush of adrenaline spurred her heart.

"I understand your concern," Goodwin commented. "However, your perspective is narrow. This is new to you, and I can imagine it is all rather upsetting. But if you would allow me to speak," he said with a hint of warning, "I believe I can help you sort through your confusion."

She nodded.

Goodwin adjusted himself in his high-backed chair. "Creighton Albright's mining operation first stumbled upon Mehk back in 1623. No one can change what he chose to do with his unprecedented discovery, and now the world depends on us. Can you fathom hospitals without machinery? Can you imagine life with no Auto-mobiles or Computators? Technology is essential to prosperity, the key to the future, and it is the Foundry's job to control it."

"It's all built on a lie," she said.

"And why do you think that is? What do you think would happen to Mehk if its existence were to become public—if it were discovered by, say, the Kijyo Republic or Greinadoren?" He stabbed a morsel of steak with his fork to punctuate his point. "It would be pillaged and picked clean in a blink. We are not the enemy. We are stewards. The secrecy of the Foundry, our *lie*, is the only thing that prevents the complete and utter annihilation of mehkan-kind."

"It almost sounds like you care," Phoebe remarked.

"He's just thinkin' 'bout money," spat Micah through a mouthful of food.

"In a sense, you are both right. I care deeply for this world. The majesty of Mehk is undeniable. Its staggering biodiversity is the sole reason you and I have enjoyed so many technological breakthroughs in our lifetimes. And yet, I also believe wholeheartedly in the Foundry's vision. Both can be true."

"But Mehk is dying," Phoebe countered. "What you're doing is killing it."

"Please don't be melodramatic. Do you not see that our success depends on the preservation of this world? We have nearly doubled our average life expectancy over the last century. We have changed the way cities are built, even pioneered augmented robotics," Goodwin said, gesturing to the silent Watchmen attending their supper. "All because of Mehk. Far from killing it, we want it to thrive so that we may continue to discover its secrets."

He leaned over the table, his excited eyes shining.

"Did you know that certain kinds of microscopic mehkan bacteria can traverse through solid matter? There are indications of ore found in deep-sea vents that can burn with a heat that never wanes. I have even heard rumors of rare mehkans that have the capacity to reanimate dead tissue. What amazing advancements for the human race! Can you imagine a world where these things are made available to you and me? Well, I can. And it is beautiful."

"And what about CHAR?" she asked, her mask slipping.

"I am talking about the future, and once again you dwell on the past," Goodwin sighed. He pushed back from the table and strode to the fireplace, stirring the logs with a bronze poker. "Albright devised CHAR to conquer Mehk long ago, and he implemented it with no thought to its long-term impact. It was disgraceful, unforgivable. Who can fathom what wonders were destroyed, what innovations humanity may never see because of his folly?"

The fire surged, causing Goodwin's face to glow.

"But times have changed. I established an entire department devoted to reversing the effects of CHAR. Our finest chemists are working on the problem, and we have made some notable progress. It is my duty as Chairman of the Foundry to end that kind of wanton destruction once and for all."

"Quit actin' like you don't wanna kill 'em!" Micah spat.

"How is your supper?" Goodwin asked.

Micah shoveled the rest of the meat into his mouth and chewed with his mouth open, hoping to disgust their host.

"That food you are enjoying comes from a cow—a living thing. It was raised on a farm, probably in Sodowa. It lived for a number of years, then died for your consumption. And yet that fact does not seem to trouble you in the slightest. How are mehkans any different?"

"'Cause you wanna wipe 'em all out!"

Goodwin hung the poker on its rack and accepted a towel from the Watchman to wipe his hands. "Is Sodowa driving the cow to extinction? Of course not. It would be self-destructive to squander such an invaluable resource. I understand your fears, believe me I do, but the Foundry is not what you think it is. If we destroy all mehkans, human civilization will collapse."

Phoebe was losing ground. Goodwin was winning.

"The chraida aren't cows," she said. "Neither are the syllks. They're people. What you do isn't farming, it's murder."

"Exactly!" Micah said, his eyes fixing on the poker Goodwin had just hung. "That's what I've been sayin' all along."

Goodwin nodded thoughtfully and swirled his wineglass.

"Some of our methods are outdated, but we are always striving to improve our practices. We are building economic incentives and fruitful relationships, partnering with mehkans who willingly work for us. We have devised methods of conservation, including hatcheries and sustainable harvesting techniques that will permanently reduce our footprint on Mehk. We are working toward change, toward a mutually beneficial relationship with this world."

Phoebe was clutching her butter knife in a shaking fist.

"Tell that to the langyls in Fuselage," she said flatly.

Micah turned to look at Goodwin, who glowered at her. The Chairman did not move for a long moment.

"We are not perfect, but neither are we monsters," Goodwin said at last, his voice calm. "Nor are mehkans helpless victims. After your experience in the Gauge Pit, I think you should understand that better than most."

Mr. Pynch's dirty golden smile flashed before her eyes.

"Mehk is not populated with innocents, Phoebe. We share certain emotions with them, and they exhibit similar behaviors to ours, but mehkans do not possess our governing sense of morality. They are not us."

She scooted her chair back abruptly. Two Watchmen stepped forward.

Phoebe rose.

"It has to stop."

Micah jumped to his feet too.

"Damn straight!" he cried, scanning the exits. There were a half dozen Watchmen in the shadows, the firelight glinting in their black eyes.

Goodwin held his hand up, and his attendants eased back.

"Would that it could," he said, untroubled. He dabbed his mouth with a napkin, pushed the plate aside, and folded his hands on the table. "Do you know how many people died in the Alloy War?"

That caught her off guard. "What does that have to do with anything?"

"Thirty-one-point-six million. All because a handful of

rogue nations wanted what we had. Rather than trade with us fairly, they invaded our homeland to take it by force. Do you think that was right to do?"

"No, but—"

"Now our enemies grow restless again. They call themselves the Quorum, but they are the very same butchers that nearly laid waste to us all those years ago. The Foundry is doing everything it can to meet their demands. Were we to suddenly end our operations in Mehk as you suggest, supplies would stop. The Quorum would be outraged. Do you want another Alloy War?"

"Of course not," she dismissed.

"Your sister Margaret is enlisted," he said to Micah. "And your brother Randall would be drafted. Do you want to see them come home in body bags?"

"What are you talkin' about?" Micah growled.

"The next war will be infinitely more terrible. Our enemies have been preparing for another conflict. The devastation and the death toll will be unimaginable. I am willing to do anything to prevent such a calamity. Are you?"

She wanted to say yes but refused to concede to his point.

"Because there *is* something you can do," he continued.

Goodwin nodded to the Watchmen, and they cleared away the dinner plates. A whole new set of trays was brought out, overflowing with macaroons, gourmet cakes, berry tarts, and silver bowls packed with sorbet. Goodwin served himself while the kids waited for him to continue.

"Look familiar?" he said with a grin. "They're from Sylvan's on Fourth Street—best dessert in all of Meridian. Please, despite my ample size, I assure you I can't eat it all myself."

They looked at each other and sat back down in their chairs. Micah mashed two cupcakes into his mouth and stuffed a few into his pockets. Phoebe ate nothing, her hands planted flat on the table.

"Your passion is inspiring," Goodwin continued as he savored a few nibbles of sorbet, his spoon tinkling in the little bowl. "Your lust for life, for graciously sparing it wherever you can, that is why I wanted to meet with you. We are engaged in delicate negotiations with the Quorum, and the slightest miscalculation is liable to tip us into catastrophe. And yet, I have reason to believe one of my partners has been working to sabotage our efforts."

She felt the meal churn in her stomach.

"My father."

"Jules has shared vital secrets with the enemy. He will not tell us what, or with whom. But if I do not learn the truth soon, he could be responsible for an unprecedented loss of life, the likes of which the world has never seen."

"He doesn't want war," she pleaded. "He doesn't want people to die."

"I don't doubt it. I am sure Jules is convinced that his betrayal was the right thing to do. But all actions have consequences. In this case, dire ones."

Micah was about to gobble a tart, but he put it down.

"Through much painstaking diplomacy, we are finally within reach of a historical peace agreement with Trelaine. It is not too late to undo what Jules has done, but we must know what that is before we can repair the damage."

Phoebe felt sick. "What do we need to do?"

"But . . ." was all Micah said. He stared at her, horrified.

"Talk to him," Goodwin said, leaning forward, his hand reaching for hers. "That is all I ask. I will take you to him now. He refuses to talk to us, but perhaps he will listen to the two of you. Convince him. Save him."

She studied the Chairman's clear blue eyes, which were earnest and sincere. He wasn't lying. She had worried that her father might be responsible for the deaths of mehkans, but it was something far worse—the next Alloy War.

"Phoebe. Micah," Goodwin implored. "Please help me to correct his grievous error before the entire world is forced to pay the price."

Her mind felt muddled, dark, and molasses thick. When she had first walked into this room, everything had seemed so clear, but now she didn't know what to believe. She was confused by everything Goodwin said, but there was forceful logic in his words. All he wanted was peace. She looked to Micah, but he was just as lost as she was. He hadn't the foggiest clue how to proceed.

If they agreed, she could see her father, be with him right now. In a matter of minutes, she could be wrapped up tight with his voice in her ears. Her heart yearned for him. He would explain everything. And she would help him. She and Micah would convince him to save all those lives.

But why? Why would he aid the enemy?

What could be worth a global war? His secret must be important. So important he was willing to give everything up to protect it, even his own life. Her father knew Goodwin, had worked closely with him, and had chosen to defy him.

Which meant that he wasn't one of them after all. Her father had betrayed the Foundry.

And that was all the answer she needed.

The darkness was gone.

She snatched an empty plate and hurled it at Goodwin.

He was caught completely off guard. Her aim wasn't perfect—the plate shattered into a dozen pieces against the chair back, inches from his face. She grabbed her glass, her silverware, a candleholder. She pelted the Foundry Chairman with everything she could get her hands on.

And Micah didn't miss a beat.

In a whoop of joy, he hurled his own plate and glass and steak knife at Goodwin, who ducked and retreated down the corridor. She flung a snowball of sorbet at his back, triumphantly splattering his jacket with lavender dessert. Micah lunged for the fireplace poker. He wrenched it from the rack and chased after Goodwin, rearing back to swing. White-gloved hands grabbed it. In a matter of seconds, they were overcome by Watchmen.

But she didn't care. Today was the day that Phoebe Plumm made the Chairman of the Foundry run.

She hoped that Goodwin would remember this moment every time he sat at this table, every time he ate here.

The last thing she saw before they dragged her below was Micah's wide-open mouth, drowning out the Muse-o-Graph's melodious song with his raspy, squeaking laughter.

The last thing Micah saw was the white-hot iron in Phoebe's eyes.

SACRIFICE

oundry scrap roared down the chute. Bullet casings, empty cans, and broken equipment tumbled through the darkness. Mangled mehkan carcasses were tossed in with a grisly rain of oozing shells and shredded metal. It was a tidal wave of useless junk for which no purpose could possibly be found.

Including Dollop.

He clattered down the tube and slammed painfully onto a pile in a massive container. A glint of gold caught his eye— his dynamo, his sacred emblem of the Way, had popped off. Debris pummeled him as he reached for his beloved symbol, but it was quickly buried, and so was he. Dollop wriggled through the junk, looking for his dynamo or some kind of escape, but found only the floor. Embedded in its center was a circular grate made of crisscrossed bands of steel, leaving diamond-shaped openings a couple of inches across.

It was a drain, he soon found out, as rancid lubricant and mehkan blood trickled down from the scrap and all over him. The torrent of refuse stopped, and the accumulated weight of it compressed him like a vise. The bin jolted and began to move. Dollop pressed up to the drain and saw that he was being hauled through a dark tunnel. The air was stuffy and growing steadily warmer. There was light up ahead.

The container emerged into a cavernous space, shrill with activity. Watchmen scurried about like silvery ants far below, enduring high temperatures in shiny protective jumpsuits. They zipped around on Transloaders, hauling supplies back and forth. A complex motorized cable system wove across the ceiling, carrying dozens of suspended bins toward the center of the room, where a pulsing light glowed. Then he saw it.

Rising in the scorching heart of this chamber was an immense blast furnace, spewing sparks and gurgling thick bubbles. The containers rattled over this hellish pit, dumping their contents into its fires before speeding away to be filled again. Troughs ran from its sloping sides, pouring streams of liquid metal that radiated in all directions like beams of the sun.

This was the ancient furnace of Kallorax, the boiling abyss where millions had been burned alive. Now the Foundry stoked its flames.

Dollop stared at the searing crater as his bin approached

it. His last shreds of hope melted away. Soon his body would be reunited with the ore, and his ember would pass beyond the Shroud, returning to Makina for judgment.

He had failed Her. She would never blaze his ember. That divine reward was only for those who had found their function, those who lived as vital components in Her sacred machine. No, he would be stirred in the Forge, destined to be reborn in a new form, probably something foul and lowly, like a ryzooze. It was as much as a useless scrap like him deserved. He couldn't even manage to hold on to his dynamo.

Where had he gone wrong? Why had Makina led him to Phoebe and Micah if it was to end like this? Had he misinterpreted the signs all along?

He clutched his fingers through the grate and pressed his head on the mesh, feeling the container rumble as it carried him to meet his Maker.

Dollop closed his eyes and began to pray.

"Oh, no you don't!"

Micah knew Watchmen were too dumb to talk, but he screamed at them anyway. A pair of the Foundry soldiers stuffed him into a narrow shaft. He writhed and fought, but the tube was so tight he couldn't even raise his arms. Digging in with his knees and elbows, Micah struggled to slow his descent, but they just forced him down until his feet touched the bottom. He tried to look up but barely had enough room to tilt his head.

"NO!"

The hatch clanged down and plunged him into darkness.

A handful of breathing holes let a little light in, not like there was anything to see. The tube was maybe seven feet tall, and the corroded gold walls were like rough rock. He couldn't turn around or even bend his knees.

Goodwin must have been pretty ticked off. If only Micah had gotten in one swing with that fireplace poker. Just one. He was jealous that Phoebe had nailed the fat cat with that ice cream. He'd have to compliment her aim when he saw her again. *If* he saw her again.

The thought made the cramped walls feel even tighter.

Where was Phoebe anyway? Probably in a cage like this one. The Doc too. And Dollop? The Foundry was probably gonna turn him into a toaster or something before the poor mehkie even got to figure out what the heck he was.

No. Stop it. I can't think like that. Gotta stay positive.

He tried imagining what he'd do once he got his hands on Pynch and the Marquis. He'd pluck Fatty like a turkey and pull his spines out one by one, then tie the Marquis's arms and legs in a big ol' knot.

How could he have been such an idiot?

It was his fault everything had turned to crap. He had lied to Phoebe and hired those two scumbags. He had even bragged that he could take care of them if anything went wrong. Way to go, Tanner.

Darkness settled in his mind like sawdust. He felt like he was being squeezed. The only sound was his own stupid breath. He hated that. It was thin and weak, such a tiny little puff to hang his entire life on.

His banged-up cheek itched. He struggled to get his arm up to scratch it, but there was no room. Micah thrashed angrily. Growling, he rubbed his face on the rough metal, but that only ended up making his bruises feel worse.

How long had he been in here? It felt like a lifetime. No way he could stay standing like this. He was worn out, and his knees were trembling.

What was he thinking? Once upon a time, he was gonna be a hero and put a big ol' dent in the world. Wasn't that why he had wanted to find the Doc in the first place? He was stupid enough to think he could maybe be somebody, that Micah Eugene Tanner might matter some day. He was wrong.

He was just a toiletboy. And toiletboys weren't heroes.

Rory, Jacko, and the rest of his buds probably weren't bothered in the slightest that he was gone. Sure, maybe they had been curious at first, wondering why he wasn't in class anymore. But they'd find another chump to tweak their Snakebite S-80's and just go on as if he had never existed.

Margie wouldn't even get word he was gone, wherever she was. And what about Ma and Randy? Were they worried at all? Did Ma even try to call the cops? No, he bet they were relieved. He was a mistake anyway. She told him so all the time. Just like she blamed him for Dad walking out on them.

No one cared.

Micah had just upped and vanished, blinked out of

existence. Maybe he was more like his pathetic loser drunk of a dad than he thought. Gone without a trace, forgotten, and not even worth the effort of remembering.

And now he was going to die in this hole. Alone.

He listened to his breath, wheezing away in this emptiness. Each breath was another lost second, one more missed chance.

His nothing life was fading to black.

A pair of Watchman soldiers spun a pressure wheel and pulled open the heavy, circular hatch. Phoebe stepped through it before they could force her. Alert and bristling, she was ready for the worst that Goodwin could throw at her. If her father could stand up to the Foundry, so would she.

She was going to make him proud.

The door slammed behind her. She found herself in a circular room that was maybe fifteen feet across and made of rough, hammered gold blanketed in centuries of scale and rust. Machinery growled behind the walls, which reeked of mildew and decay. The floor was etched with ancient, faded outlines. It depicted a ring of suns orbiting a many-winged figure with a cruel, jagged mouth. High on the walls were a dozen sculpted heads, eroded mehkan gargoyles with monstrous barbed teeth, all spaced evenly around the room.

This was another relic of Kallorax.

The walls were tall, but there was no ceiling. Above was a series of catwalks, a nest of intricate copper plumbing, and giant shining pumps and generators. This wasn't a room, it was some sort of vat. Which meant that if she could climb these walls, she could escape.

As Phoebe walked the perimeter, she noticed indentations that offered some traction, but not enough to support her weight. She felt her way along the solid surface, finding it scored with deep gouges, maybe scars left by the clawing desperation of some long-gone mehkans.

The hatch screeched open behind her.

Kaspar appeared. A brittle chill shook her. He carried a length of chain. With slow and deliberate steps, he stalked toward her, but she kept her distance, clinging to the walls.

"What do you want?" she asked.

"Mr. Goodwin requires your help." He jangled the chain.

"I already gave him my answer," she said defiantly.

A gray grin stretched his flaking lips. He jetted at her with blinding speed and knocked her to the ground. She rolled away and leaped to her feet before he could snare her. There was no point in fighting. Her only hope was escape.

Kaspar pursued her like a patient predator.

Phoebe hadn't heard the door shut behind him, but she didn't dare look lest she give her plan away. She feinted to the side, then sprang forward to make a break for the hatch. He wasn't fooled for a second. Her fingers grazed the open door, but he snatched her by the hair. She flailed and screamed and tore desperately at his hands, grabbing hold of a long black glove. He hurled her to the ground again.

Her body buzzed with pain. His glove peeled away.

She lay dazed on her back. Kaspar grabbed one of her feet and dragged her like a rag doll to the center of the vat. He clapped a brace around her ankle, which emitted an electronic whir as it cinched tight. Then he latched the chain to the floor, securing it to a ring in the mouth of the carved figure.

Phoebe sat up, trying to focus her eyes. It didn't matter what he was about to do. She had to withstand, to endure. She would not give in.

Just like her father.

Kaspar leaned in and pulled his glove from her grasp.

Then she saw his bare arm, and her resolve drained away. The limb was cadaverous, bloodless and pale as a dead fish. His flesh rippled and throbbed with muscle, laced with purple, wormlike veins. And yet it was not flesh at all. His arm was a latticework of pulsating pistons and sinewy gears, exposed mechanical musculature that churned and twisted. But it didn't gleam like steel or any metal she could recognize—it was an organic mechanism that moved with sickening biological precision. She couldn't tell where his skin stopped and the machine started because the two were seamlessly fused.

"I am the first," he proclaimed, his lips peeling back to reveal his rows of tiny, gray teeth. "Mr. Goodwin chose me. They put Mehk into my body. It invaded me, consumed me." He paced slowly around her, the soft machinery of his arm parting and shifting with an awful sound like cracking knuckles. Kaspar saw her distress, and his grin slashed wider.

"But I tamed it, conquered it. And it rebuilt me. The living metal ate my weakness. Now I am without the limits of man or machine. I am the Dyad."

Striking in a flash, he thundered his fist into the ground. She recoiled. His blow left a divot in the metal vat. Kaspar's grin was savage, his quivering lips pulled white.

"I gave myself to Mr. Goodwin and the Foundry. And I was reborn. That was my sacrifice." He leaned in close to her. His straining lip split open, spilling a dark trickle of blood down his chin. "Now make yours."

His blood dribbled onto Phoebe's skirt.

Kaspar lingered, savoring the look of terror and disgust in her eyes. Then he rose to his full height and wiped his lip with the long black glove. He strode from the room, slammed the door, and locked it.

Immediately, she grappled with the manacle on her ankle. It was Foundry technology—no way she could break it. No keyhole, so even if she had a hairpin in her sniping pockets, she couldn't try to pick it. But it was secured around her boot. Maybe she could take it off and slip her foot out.

There was a crystalline sound like a drizzle of rain, so faint that she wasn't sure she even heard it. It took her a second to find the source. There was a trickle of water leaking from a sculpted mehkan head high on the wall. It cut a snaking rivulet to the floor. Then there was a squeal of metal, something shifting behind the walls, and a second head spat out a stream.

A cold spike of certainty shot up Phoebe's spine.

She leaped into action, tearing at her laces with wild hands.

A third head started to leak. Then five. And eight. The water sputtered and spilled onto the floor, puddles shimmering as they bloomed toward her.

The water stopped all together. Silence. A low shudder beneath her feet.

She fumbled with a knot, almost had her boot off.

Her breath died in her throat. All at once, water exploded from the twelve heads above her, torrential blasts like open hydrants. The sound was deafening. Phoebe was bowled over by the deluge. She tried to get to her feet but slipped. There was nowhere to run from the churning flood. Frigid swells smashed down relentlessly. Debris spewed out from the pipes and battered her. Mehkan fingers. Joints and hinges. Fractured skulls thinned by eons of rust.

The water rose to her knees. She coughed and spat, blinded by the vile spray. It was so cold that she felt her flesh go numb. Still it climbed. Her frantic breathing was shallow. The violent pool crept higher, eager to choke her, to douse her lungs and weigh her down. The water screamed in her ears, promising to swallow her into its icy, nightmare depths.

The surge hit her thighs. She sloshed around in a panic.

It reached her waist. Then her chest.

Her shoulders.

By the time it frothed around her neck, she was crippled by fear. The water buoyed her upward and she flailed, treading wildly to stay above the surface. The floor of the vat dropped away beneath her. Her vision swam with madness. Everything began to smear and run like an ink drawing in the rain. How long did she have before the chain pulled tight and she could float no higher? How long would she last after that?

The torrent clawed into her mouth. Was that the bitter taste of seawater?

No. No, it couldn't be.

She drifted up, closer to the snarling sculpted mehkans that spewed out the jets of dismal water. Footsteps clattered on the catwalk a few feet overhead.

Goodwin. He chose this torture. He knew her fear.

"Help! Please!" Phoebe shrieked, reaching out for him.

The Foundry Chairman was devoid of emotion. He ignored her, speaking to the group of people he was with. She couldn't make out his words over the snarl of water. As she rose, the others came into view. It was Kaspar and a pair of Watchman soldiers, dragging a figure whose head was hidden beneath a black hood. Kaspar tore the fabric away.

"DADDY!"

He was battered and bandaged. Their eyes met. His knees buckled as if the life was ripped right out of him. But Kaspar held him up, wrenched his hair, and forced him to look at his drowning daughter. His face contorted, his mouth parted, and out poured a wretched moan that she could barely hear.

Her father sobbed. He was saying something to Goodwin. She wanted to insist that he not give in, that whatever he was hiding was more important than her life. He had endured too much to surrender now.

But the fear won. She gargled an inarticulate shriek.

The churning flood buried the gushing gargoyles, muffling their roar.

The water continued to rise, forcing her ever higher.

"Please!" her father cried. She could hear him now, hoarse and agonized.

She thrashed, treading wildly.

"Who was it?" demanded Goodwin flatly.

The weight on her ankle was painfully heavy.

"Stop this, James. I'll talk, but just stop!"

Her mouth dipped into the water, her strokes weakened.

"Who have you been working for in the Quorum?"

The chain clinked taut. She could float no higher.

Her father's eyes filled with shredding, unimaginable pain.

Phoebe's cry bubbled. Water filled her mouth. Still it rose.

He broke. "None! None of the Quorum!"

"Then she dies."

"I've been working for the Covenant!"

The water took her. Droning silence filled her ears. She fought. She strained. But the chain was stretched to its limit. The water closed over her head. She hadn't gotten a big enough breath. Her lungs already felt like they were going to burst. Something was dragging her down.

The undertow.

Phoebe could struggle no more. Her muscles gave way. Stifling brine filled her body. She sank into the murk. She saw seaweed, the rocks of Callendon's shore. Just before her vision went black, a slender white shadow drifted toward her from below. It reached out, welcoming her into death.

There was no malice in it, but neither was it smiling.

Pearl-pale skin. Black bobbed hair.

Her mother was waiting.

HEART TO
HEART

 roar.

A rush. She was leaving her body.

Her spirit was being tossed. Tumbling, caught in a cyclone. She was pulled one way, then another. Around and around in the relentless vortex.

Vomit.

Profound darkness.

She shivered, clammy and foul with the stink of the drowning tank. Phoebe could hear her own faint pulse, like the ticking of some worn-out clock. She clung to it, the feeblest of silken threads, threatening to snap at any moment.

It meant that she was somehow alive.

There was another sound too.

A steady rhythm. Pulling her toward the light. She rose up through the void. Phoebe was wrapped in something warm. The strong beat kept her aloft.

It was him.

Her eyes cracked open, wincing against the glare. She was in her father's arms. Her ear was on his chest. A smile lit his face, tears glistened on his cheeks. He stroked her hair, just like when she was little, folding it ever so gently behind her ears. She didn't want to awaken. If she did, he would be gone.

Phoebe remained still for a long while, praying that time would wait. She couldn't bear to feel this moment fade into a desperate, empty dream.

It didn't.

She could feel the warmth of his arms through her damp coveralls and clung to the sensation. A wet cough rattled her violently, thick with the tastes of bile and foul, rusty water.

"Cricket."

His voice was a hollow scrape. She opened her eyes at last.

They were in a murky gold cell no more than ten feet across, with curving sides and a low pitted ceiling. Across from them was a flat barricade of Foundry steel, its slick sheen a dramatic contrast to the rest of the rough chamber. A glaring tube of electric light was mounted on it, just above the barely noticeable outline of a hefty sliding door. Aside from that, the cell was barren.

"You came for me," he croaked.

She nodded weakly and focused her eyes on him.

Her father was barely recognizable, dressed in the same worn-out clothes, though they now looked far too big on his emaciated frame. His white button-down shirt was stained with dried blood, hanging in tatters and barely concealing the dark red bandages that patched his sunken chest. Dingy gauze bound his head as well, sweeping down to cover one eye. He still wore his glasses, but the lenses were cracked.

"What did they do to you?" she whispered in horror.

"I'm fine," he said. His tone was soft but urgent. He glanced up at the door. "I don't have much time. They'll be back for me any minute now."

"No. You can't go," she said, and clutched him closer.

He held her with all his strength and kissed her cheek.

"I'm here now," he whispered.

She broke into another hacking cough and expelled more water from her lungs. He held her until the fit subsided.

"Is it true?" she said at last, looking up at him.

"What?"

"The Covenant."

"But how do you . . ." He looked at her, astonished. "You never should have come here. This wasn't supposed to happen. Back home, I would have had you aboard a Galejet bound for Trelaine within the hour. Everything was arranged."

It seemed like a lifetime ago. In the manor, her father sweeping up to her from the shadows. His desperate face. Her lone suitcase. How different her life would have been. How simple. And blind.

"You were never going to come with me," she said, realizing what he meant.

"It would have put you in far too much danger."

"You were going to send me away."

He sighed heavily and looked deep into her eyes.

"I'm not asking you to understand what I have done. I can ask nothing more of you. Not even your forgiveness."

She studied his battered face, wrought with regret.

"So it is true," she said. "The Covenant is real?"

Her father nodded slowly.

She imagined the look on Dollop's face. Poor Dollop.

"How? I mean, who are they?" she wondered. "What's their plan?"

"I wish I knew."

His gaze flickered almost imperceptibly over her shoulder. She realized at once that he was trying to tell her something. Phoebe faked a cough so she could steal a glance. In a corner of the ceiling, an Omnicam surveyed the scene, its fanned lens array glinting in the shadows. They were being watched.

The sight brought back raw memories of the Marquis.

"I thought they were made up," she continued, realizing that she couldn't risk asking him any more revealing questions.

"Everyone does. Who knows, maybe they are," he explained. "Perhaps it's another group of mehkans who have adopted the legend for their own. Whoever they are, I failed them just as I have failed you."

"You didn't. It's not your fault," she insisted. "If Micah and I hadn't followed you, if we hadn't gotten caught, then you never would have—"

"No. This is my burden. Not yours, not Micah's."

"We can help. We want to save Mehk, just like you."

He considered her for a moment.

"Phoebe. I'm just trying to make amends."

"What do you mean?"

"I was the Chief Surveyor for over twenty years. I led a team that made bio-analysis assessments of subjects for potential market applications." He let the clinical words sink in. "That's the Foundry way of saying I decided which mehkans were worth killing. Countless died on my orders."

"But . . ." Her eyes burned. "How could you? I thought you were different."

"I am. I'm worse. More guilty than most. Because I did it with pride. I shared the Foundry's bold vision—building a better, brighter future."

"No. You're better than that."

He laughed, but not dismissively. His unbandaged eye misted over.

"That's exactly what your mother said," her father intoned softly, "only with a few more punches and kicks."

"She . . . knew?" her voice crackled.

His nod filled her with sickening outrage.

"It was too much to bear alone. I ignored the consequences. I went to great lengths to bypass the Foundry's extensive surveillance to tell her."

Phoebe could taste the vomit in her throat again. She tore away from her father's arms and got to her unsteady feet.

How could she? Beneath every giggle she had shared with her mother, behind each conversation, looming over all of their carefree shopping sprees, was Mehk. She had known the truth all along, and yet she had been compliant.

Even her own mother had been guilty.

"Don't hate her," he said, staring at her back. "She was disgusted with me. She almost left me because of it. Almost took you away."

"She should have," she spat.

"Maybe," he agreed, limping over to her. "She made me promise to quit."

"But you didn't."

"It would have been suicide. No one quits the Foundry."

"Then she should have told everyone!"

"Do you really think they would have allowed that?"

He reached out to touch her, but she pulled away.

"I know you're confused, Phoebe. I don't blame you. None of it's easy. Nothing true is black or white."

"You're pathetic!" she screamed, spinning to face him. "You sound just like Goodwin. You knew it was wrong, and so did she."

"Yes. Of course. And yet she chose to love me anyway. She put us above all else."

"Neither of you did anything about it!"

"But we did. Together, we tried to find a better way. It wasn't easy, avoiding detection as she pushed me to change the

Foundry. But I did everything in my power to make our operations more humane. When she died, I . . . The little things weren't enough. She—" He heaved a shuddering breath. "She knew I could do more, and I vowed to, no matter what it took. I went searching. But the Covenant found me first."

"You should have told me," she said, jaw clenched. "I could have helped."

"No. I almost got you killed. If your mother had known you were involved, she would have never forgiven me."

"I came here on my own," she insisted.

"How I wish you hadn't. She loved you more than anything, Phoebe. More . . . more than her own life." His voice cracked. "I do too."

She threw her arms around him, and he stumbled back.

How skeletal he felt, how frail. Her heart strained.

"What happens now?" she whispered to him.

"We wait."

Would they put her back in that wretched tank? Or did they have something even worse in mind? Micah. Dollop. What would their fates be?

"They're going to kill us, aren't they?"

"No," he said, his voice hardening.

There was a series of digital tones and a reverberating thunk as the heavy steel door unlocked. It slid open to reveal a pair of Watchman soldiers.

"We are going to make it through this," her father said as he pulled away.

He was leaving again. She held on, refusing to let go.

"I . . . I don't believe you."

He stopped.

Behind his broken glasses, his good eye flashed.

"You must."

She couldn't make this any harder. She would be strong for him. For her. Phoebe nodded and let her father go. He turned and limped out of the cell.

The door clanged shut with ringing finality.

She knew she might never see him again.

"I . . ." she rasped. "I forgive you."

BREAK
DOWN

Micah felt like a stupid little baby, and there was nothing he could do about it. He was crying and shaking, totally helpless. He was losing it.

Stuck in this tube with only his own horrible thoughts, every breath felt like work, like he had to keep reminding himself to inhale. He couldn't remember ever being this scared. His jelly legs wanted to give out, but he had nowhere to fall. And he was starting to see things. Weird things.

The wall was inches from his nose, and its texture swirled and swam before his eyes. The only other place to look was up, but each time he did, he could have sworn there was one less breathing hole in the lid. Were they plugging them up, one at a time, so that he'd suffocate? How did they know to only do it when he looked? Okay, no more looking up.

Closing his eyes was worse. The view inside his eyelids flickered like static on a Televiewer, like swarming maggots. He could feel them, too, covering his body, slithering around underneath his coveralls. It made him itch all over.

So this is what crazy feels like, he thought.

That's when he saw it. A fine gray thread slowly descended from overhead like a web without the spider. He pinched his eyes shut, squeezed off the tears, and shook his head to chase the image away.

Still there. If it was a hallucination, it was a stubborn one.

The thread drifted to the wall and clung there, growing thicker as it continued down. When shiny beads dribbled and swelled at the end, he realized that it was some sort of silvery liquid. He watched closely as the thing trickled toward him. Then it reversed direction and ran back up.

Micah jerked back and banged his head on the wall.

The drip twitched, then retracted a bit more. It held steady, watching. The liquid pulsed to the rhythm of his breathing.

Not good. Was this some sick Foundry thing? Was it going to crawl into his eyeball and eat through his brain?

Suddenly, the strand split apart, separating into a bunch of thin hairs. They bent away from the wall, reaching toward Micah like writhing antennae.

He panicked, clamping his eyes and his mouth shut. Would it go instead for his nostrils and his ears? He tossed his head, thinking if he kept moving, the nasty silver gunk might not be able to get him.

But it would. Eventually.

Just a matter of time.

Floodlights blasted Jules in a blinding row, but he barely had the strength to blink. The Watchmen dragged him down a long, curved corridor of the detainment block, the sound of their footsteps merging with the hum of machinery. He had endured another two-hour interrogation and was racked with pain from head to toe, his bandages wet with fresh blood.

This subterranean sector was a network of passages like gloomy golden catacombs. The ceiling stretched thirty feet overhead, and the rocky walls were pocketed with roosts built for Kallorax's ancient aerial regime. Like much of the Citadel, this area had once housed extensive torture chambers, a testament to the megalarch's depraved imagination. The Foundry had repurposed much of the grisly sublevel for infrastructure, using it to house generators, banks of Computator servers, and vesper-to-water conversion tanks.

But the detainment block retained some of the old cruelties, just in case.

Jules was dragged past a hammered-steel elevator patrolled by heavily armed Watchman soldiers. His escorts turned down a dead-end hallway with high-security prison cells at the back. A titanium power grid stretched throughout the entire area, midway between floor and ceiling. It was a lattice of powerful floodlights, Omnicams, and deadly Dervish turrets that left no inch unmonitored. They whirred and buzzed, cameras tracking and four-barreled cannons pivoting, ready to open fire at a moment's notice.

Because the Foundry had little need for prisoners, this sector was rarely used. Jules could only recall a handful of exceptions, the most recent being a few years ago when an executive named Collins had made a reference to the M-level tunnel in Foundry Central during a Dialset call. After a week of "correctional rehabilitation," he was back to work with a big empty smile and a vacant stare.

Now the detainment block was occupied by Dr. Jules Plumm. And the children. The thought of them in this dreadful place made him even weaker.

A dozen Watchman soldiers stood guard beside the cells, their eerie, duplicate features staring out from behind polished face shields. Jules looked up at the Omnicams and wondered if Goodwin was watching, gloating over the broken wreck his former Chief Surveyor had become. But the cameras weren't scanning. They were all pointing at the ground as if the motorized arms that held them had gone limp.

The Dervish turrets, too, were frozen in place.

In a rush, he understood.

Phoebe was curled in a ball. She hadn't moved in hours.

She was tired, but sleep would never come in this cell. Her bleary eyes stared at the harsh light tube above the door, its chatter grinding her down with every passing second.

Then with a soft pop, the light went out. Silence.

She sprang to her feet. Utter darkness.

"Hello?" Phoebe cried. "Is anybody there? HEY!"

The unnatural quiet made her feel like she had cotton in her ears. Were they watching her in the dark? Was this another part of the Foundry's twisted plan, to break her with fear like they had her father?

With hands outstretched, she felt her way over to where the Omnicam was mounted. She listened but heard nothing—no swapping lenses, no adjusting focus. But there was something else. A muted whisper from behind the smooth steel wall. She felt her way over and pressed her ear against it. Dull impacts, grunting. Wild metal footfalls.

Something thudded up against the wall. She jumped back. Adrenaline surged through her like an electric shock. Alone in the blackness, stuck in this cell, she had nowhere to run.

The muffled commotion stopped.

What was happening out there? For several unbearable seconds she heard nothing. Phoebe backpedaled and bumped up against the opposite wall.

Digital bleeps sounded, then a *THUNK*. With a slow scrape, the door was forced open. The hallway outside was dark except for red emergency lights buried in the floor.

A silhouette stood in the doorway, armed with a rifle.

"Daddy!"

She threw her arms around his frail body.

"Everything's okay, Phoebe. We're getting out of here."

Only then did she register the other figures with him.

Glinting in the red-rimmed dark were four menacing mehkans. Some were low to the ground, others stood upright, but it was too dark to make them out clearly. There was power and violence in their every black curve, and their formidable presence sent a chill rippling up her spine. The red emergency lights showed splatters of dark grease on the walls, and the ground was scattered with decimated Watchman remains.

"We go," commanded a clipped female voice.

The words were strange and fluttery, as if spoken through the blades of a fan. They came from a mehkan who held a convulsing Watchman soldier in her powerful grip. With a flash of her clacking arms, she slashed off the Foundry soldier's head and dropped his sparking, spurting body onto the floor.

The mehkan was lean and vaguely humanoid, rising to a towering height as she approached. Instead of a solid mass, her body was made of countless interlocking ellipses, ticking pendulums, and spherical astrolabes in constant flux. Sliders on her limbs calibrated, and needle pointers worked through some inscrutable algorithm. The folding rings and planes of her anatomy were scythelike and razor sharp, her face incomprehensible—not because of the dark, but because it was all shifting blades and wheels, devoid of any recognizable features. The red lights in the floor passed through the adjusting gaps of her strange form and cast eerie, flickering shadows.

Affixed to her fluctuating chest was a dynamo, dark red like dried blood.

Understanding crashed hard upon Phoebe.

The Covenant was here. In the Citadel. They were saved.

"We are in your debt, Orei," her father addressed the strange figure.

"No time," the mehkan trilled low. Fleshy cords vibrated in Orei's core where her throat should be, like plucked guitar strings. The twirling arcs of her body reached out to them, measuring and assessing something. "Weak, soft. Both of you," she droned disdainfully. "Move."

Orei vaulted into a sprint with the silent grace of a wolf. The rest of the pitch-black Covenant team raced after her. Rifle at the ready, Jules grabbed Phoebe's hand and pulled her along behind. Watchman pieces lay scattered, limbs torn from torsos, heads crushed like eggshells. Phoebe had to be careful not to slip in the puddles of viscous Watchman gore.

They ran past the prison cells and rushed down the corridor. The Covenant team kept a tight formation around the two humans, and she could smell their hot iron breath as they hurried along in deadly silence. Phoebe heard a swish and looked up to see another mehkan above, gliding along with the group like a shadow, zigzagging across the walls.

Jules clutched his side and winced, seized by a sharp pain in his ribs. Phoebe held on to him.

"Are you okay?" she asked.

Orei reversed direction, inverting her body in midstride to run back to Jules. The ellipses of her body spun dangerously in the red light, her slides and pointers evaluating Phoebe and her father, judging. Calculating.

"Too slow," she said venomously. "Move faster or die."

Phoebe decided she didn't like Orei, even if the Covenant commander had come to rescue them.

They hurried to the end of the hallway, where it intersected with another dim corridor. Phoebe startled as a mehkan appeared around the corner, scampering down the wall as if unaffected by gravity. The creature clung to the sheer surface like a gecko with what appeared to be magnetic paddle feet. It was all black, like the others, its lithe form clinking with sharp overlapping metal scales. The mehkan had a long pointed beak, and the back of its head flared out like a pickax. It scuttled around the corner and out of sight.

The team followed the gecko mehkan and came upon more brutalized Watchman soldiers, their bodies broken and scattered. The creature skittered down the wall, then stood on its hind legs beside a bulky companion. Phoebe's blood went cold when she recognized the brute as a crane-claw mehkan, just like the one that had detained her in the Gauge Pit. One of the beast's arms was riddled with Foundry bullets and petrified with white cement. But as soon as Orei appeared, the mehkan shrugged off his wounds and stood at attention.

This corridor was curved, winding out of sight on either side and making it impossible to see what might be coming. Everywhere was red darkness and silence, which meant the power had been cut throughout this entire area.

The Covenant had been thorough.

With Rattletrap orders from Orei, the team assembled in front of the hammered-steel elevator, which was propped open to reveal a yawning shaft. A blackened chraida emerged from the steel chute. Phoebe realized then that the mehkans weren't pitch-black—they had camouflaged their bodies. The chraida unspooled cable from its chest to weave a ladder that led down the shaft.

The Covenant gathered around their escape route.

Escape . . .

"No!" she cried, planting her feet. "We can't leave."

The rest of the group spun to face her in confusion.

"Move," ordered Orei, impatiently reaching for her.

Phoebe sidestepped the mehkan's grip and backed away.

"I said NO! We have to save Micah," she demanded, looking at the rest of the motley team. "And Dollop. He's a mehkan, like you. We have to find them!"

Her eyes met her father's, his glasses flashing red in the dim light. He clutched his injured side and nodded.

"She's right," he said. "I will not leave without them."

In a blur, Orei grabbed Jules by the shirt. Her stiletto fingers tore holes in the filthy fabric as she yanked him close to the whirling rings of her face.

"We sealed an eighty-two-quadrit perimeter. Forty-seven enemy puppets trapped in lockdown, closing in. No time." A slider on her chest tapped rapidly, and her swishing scythes blasted back the hair from his face.

"They must be close," he said.

"Will not engage," she growled. "Move, bleeder. Or Entakhai will carry."

At the sound of his name, the wounded crane claw mehkan snapped his heavy fist closed with a clang. The other Covenant warriors tensed.

"You need me," Jules shot back at her. "You only managed to infiltrate the Citadel because of my information. Defy me, force us to leave, and I will tell you nothing more."

"We must save them," Phoebe insisted, stepping beside him.

Orei thrust her lethal, bladed head inches from Jules and Phoebe. The Covenant commander's measuring apparatus clicked and surveyed, clacking and stretching out from her body toward the humans to size them up.

They didn't flinch. Phoebe squeezed her father's hand.

Orei turned and barked insistent Rattletrap orders to her warriors. They responded instantly, fanning out to assume a battle formation. With a swish of cable, the chraida jetted up into the shadows above the deactivated lighting grid. Another ominous mehkan, who appeared to be draped in a cloak like the Grim Reaper, leaped up and careened off the walls toward the ceiling. As it bled into the darkness, Phoebe could see its undulating robe was a muscular membrane like that of the syllks, hiding a cluster of spring-loaded javelin legs.

The gecko mehkan slinked up to Orei, and its long beak splayed open like a pronged radar dish. It scanned its head and gurgled to the commander.

"Korluth has a signal. Must evacuate in minus sixteen ticks," Orei's voice reverberated harshly. Jules nodded and readied his humming Dervish rifle.

"Or what?" Phobe asked.

The Covenant commander seemed to turn her attention to Phoebe, though her featureless face of arcs and planes made it impossible to be sure.

"Or we all die when the Citadel falls."

In the shadow of the great headless effigy of Kallorax, the control center buzzed like an angry hornet nest. Goodwin stood at the heart of it all, the axis around which every operation orbited. Engineers barraged him with analyses of system schematics. Technicians reported every development as they worked to restore the Omnicams and Dervish turrets in the affected areas. Watchman Coordinators updated him as they deployed and managed their military units.

Goodwin studied an illuminated map of the Citadel with his crystalline blue eyes. The three military executives surrounded him, arguing and shouting as they formulated a strategy. Kaspar stood nearby, rigidly at attention.

"And I'm saying they sealed off four minor sectors on four different floors with no rhyme or reason," one of the executives insisted as he pointed to the red highlighted specks scattered throughout the gigantic map. "Until we know their objective, there are no priorities. Retake all four at once."

"It's too random," said another. "This attack feels desperate. Like they just disabled whatever they could manage."

"I wouldn't even call it an attack," the first dismissed. "It's sabotage, just a hack job. Our sensors detect no unidentified heat signatures in the affected areas. We're chasing ghosts."

"Then what's that?" replied the third executive, pointing to a giant screen above them that flickered with incomprehensible footage, flashing shadows and gunfire. "That's a Watchman unit optic feed in Sublevel-C. Who are they shooting at? And why are all eighteen units off line now?"

"Their targeting systems are buggy in the dark."

"Don't be naïve," Goodwin said. "This is Plumm's work. It is an invasion."

The military executives considered the Chairman.

"They have circumvented our defenses. They have isolated specific areas and used our own security apparatus to lock us out." Goodwin smiled wryly. "They are even masking their body heat to cloak their presence. Jules gave the Covenant everything they need, make no mistake."

"To what end?" one asked. "Their incursion is aimless."

"Decoys. To distract us from their target."

A captain approached, shouldering his way through the barrage of messengers. He saluted the Chairman.

"The remaining Watchmen sealed in the detainment block are moving into tactical formation Delta-Five, sir."

"How many total?" Goodwin asked without looking up from a memo.

"Forty-seven, sir."

"Put the live feeds on display. I want active operator control of every unit. And I want those surrounding doors open. Mobilize the platoons."

"We are still working to disengage the emergency locks, sir," the captain explained. Goodwin looked at him. "The enemy has overridden those circuits. It will take another—"

"Retake the sector. Do you understand?"

"Yes, sir. What about the captives?"

"Expendable. I have what I need. No one escapes."

A grin slashed across Kaspar's lips as the captain marched away.

"All this just to rescue Plumm?" an executive mused.

"Hardly. He's only half of it," Goodwin muttered and pointed to the map.

"Level Three?" one of the pin-striped men scoffed.

"If any of these are decoys, it's Three," said another. "Offices, nothing more."

"And through a couple of walls?" the Chairman said, sliding his finger slowly across the building schematic. They looked at Goodwin in unison.

"The Armory?"

"Impossible. It's too well fortified."

"Are you certain?" Goodwin asked. "With everything Plumm knows?

"It's the only target worth this effort," another said.

They nodded. It was unanimous. Time was of the essence. The military executives broke from their huddle and began to bark orders at their subordinates. Goodwin supervised the Foundry in motion, as perfectly polished a machine as they were ever likely to create.

"All units on Level Three," came a voice over the intercom. "Take up defensive positions around the Armory immediately. Repeat, take up defensive positions around the Armory."

The giant screen lit up with a grid of flickering windows, each displaying a live feed from the optical sensors of a single Watchman. The military executives relayed orders to coordinators, who were manually issuing commands to the automated Foundry soldiers.

"I will see to Plumm," Kaspar growled.

Goodwin turned to him. "No. I need you at the Armory. Organize the defenses there and hold off the Covenant."

"But the intruders are below."

"They are not my concern. The real threat is above."

"Get your sheep to supervise that. I want Plumm."

"I said no." Goodwin's baritone rang out, and his icy eyes glared. Nearby Foundry workers turned to look. "Plumm is no longer your concern."

Kaspar gritted his teeth and clenched his gloved fists.

"You said I could have him when the time came."

"Do as you are told," the Chairman commanded.

Their eyes locked.

"Do it!" Goodwin snapped.

A hush descended on the command center. The grotesque soldier bowed his head and departed. Goodwin turned his attention back to the monitors.

Kaspar marched stiffly away from Goodwin. He loomed over the urgent rush of Foundry workers and cut through the pesky flood. Throwing open a pair of reinforced platinum doors, he strode down a reflective, brightly lit hallway toward the bank of elevators. Other employees made way for him, staring and yet trying so hard not to stare.

He hit the call button hard enough to crack it. Kaspar looked at his hand, pulsing, bulging beneath his glove. The other workers waiting for the elevators backed away. The car dinged, and he stormed inside.

As soon as the doors closed, Kaspar unleashed his wrath. He pulverized the walls with a whirlwind of crushing blows, denting and rending. He threw crashing kicks and butted wildly with his head, crumpling the elevator car. Everyone in the hall could surely hear, but he didn't care.

The rage was in control. He was just a vessel.

But the fit soon passed. He stood there, panting and flexing his hands, feeling the colossal swell of living machinery within him subside.

He looked at the panel of buttons.

Kaspar made his choice.

INFERNO

Dollop knew he should be thankful. His death would be mercifully quick.

The giant suspended containers chugged along their cables toward Kallorax's furnace. Their bases were hinged on one side, and they crashed open, spilling out refuse like beasts being disemboweled. The crater below devoured the scrap hungrily, erupting in searing splashes that fragmented into galaxies of molten, glowing droplets. The emptied bins then closed and clattered backward to be filled up once more.

The grate that he clung to at the base of the container

grew hot as he approached the flames. The stifling, sulfuric air stung his insides.

Dollop wept. In a mere tick, he would be snuffed out. This was the end. The gears of fate had brought him here. It was Makina's will, and at long last, he would return to Her.

Wasn't that worth the brief moments of unbearable pain?

He searched his fractured mind for anything that might give him courage. At the housing of the Waybound where he had been raised, the axials used to praise the final moments of the Ona, holy prophet of the Great Engineer killed by CHAR four hundred phases ago. It was said that she embraced death unflinchingly, and that her ember blazed brightest of all. That is how he wanted to depart the ore—fearless, faithful, and content. He racked his memory for the Ona's final words.

The Waybound called it "The Martyr's Prayer."

"O M-M-Mother of Ore, return my ember to Thy bosom, embr-r-race me in Thy Forge," Dollop chanted in Rattletrap. *"I—I commend my span to Thee, for Thou art the Creator of the sacred machine, and only You can fathom its gears."*

Dollop's tears spilled through the drain. He longed for his dynamo, but his precious symbol was lost in the scrap.

"I—I—I am blind in your presence, O Everseer, and—and in Thy infinite and infallible plan, my f-function is at an end." Dollop coughed against the rising heat. *"Um, l-lead me gently beyond the Sh-Shroud."*

The Ona had not feared death. She had met it with the same serenity in which she had lived. Of course, she was a vital component and died knowing Makina would welcome her with open arms. Dollop would not have the same fate. Still, invoking her sublime name gave him strength.

Though not enough to keep him from trembling.

"May You deem me w-w-worthy to interlock with Thee, O Divine D-D-Dynamo," he yelled over the raging flames, *"and may You welcome my-my ember with infinite l-love so that I may blaze with Thee eternally ev-v-ver after."*

CRASH!

Another container slammed open up just ahead, jolting him from his reverie as it emptied into the furnace. The air was sweltering, unbearable. Nearly there now. His liquefied body would blend with the scrap. He would be reunited with his beloved dynamo within the flames, oozing together down the molten streams for Watchman workers to attend to.

Dollop shook violently, disturbing the precarious pile of refuse above him. It shifted and fell, squashing him hard against the hot grate. His hand tore down the middle, fingers passing through gaps in the mesh.

He screamed. Desperate panic sundered him. He wasn't going to die in a sudden scorching burst—he was going to melt slowly, agonizingly, before he even got to the furnace. It had already begun.

Then, all of a sudden, he quieted.

There was no pain. That was curious. The two halves of his hand wiggled outside of the bin. A strange new sensation tingled within him. The pieces of his body were speaking in unison, a chorus of life, and he heard every note distinctly. A dawning realization washed over Dollop. He was suddenly conscious of the many connections in his anatomy, ones he had never known or perhaps had long forgotten, all held together with a powerful, intangible energy.

He rammed his other hand against the drain, and it too split open, pieces parting to pass through the narrow holes. Concentrating, he willed his hands to detach from his wrists. They wriggled through the opening, fingers shifting and swapping places to cling to the grate. Outside the container.

Could it be?

A second ago, he had been preparing to die. Now Makina was showing him the way. He had been wrong all along, seeing it backward for his entire span. He was used to falling apart, his slipshod body always separating at the worst time. But it was not a curse, not a weakness. It was a talent. A blessing.

Dollop was more certain of this than anything he had ever felt before. It radiated with a brilliant clarity brighter than the murderous crucible below.

He had found his function. Now was not his time to go.

His container was almost above the furnace. He popped off his forearms and jammed them through the diamond-shaped gaps, where they linked to his waiting hands. In a flash, he disassembled pieces of his slender arms and legs, fit them through the drain holes, and then reconstructed himself outside the bin. With trembling focus, he split his torso and head into smaller chunks. It was a bewildering feeling, some of his segments so sensitive that he got woozy just handling them. But he pictured himself as fluid, vesper spilling through the grate. His connections loosened and released, and his body let go.

Yet it wasn't enough—his last pieces were too big to fit. The solution presented itself with tranquil simplicity. Hanging below the container, his parts stretched out, forming a long chain of limbs. Despite the separation and irregularity of his form, he felt an astonishing wholeness, an innate understanding of where every bit of his modular body was in space.

There was a squeal, then a bang as the latch released.

The bottom dropped away.

Dollop plummeted, weightless. Tons of scrap shoved and bashed against him. He fell toward the furnace's molten heart. His eyes closed, but not out of fear. He honed in on every section, fully aware of himself. Parts tumbled through space. His long chain of limbs reached out to grab falling segments, summoning himself back together through the tide of trash.

He reassembled himself, complete and clinging to the outside of the bin. Dollop was an unrecognizable, jumbled assembly. Sections of his chest stuck to his feet, and bits of head joined to his rear end like doll pieces glued at random. Holding fast to the grate, he swung loosely from the hinged bottom as the container unloaded junk into the bubbling brew.

Before he could rejoice, an eruption splashed up. Scalding metal droplets sprayed Dollop, searing his soft metal flesh. He cried out. Excruciating pain shook him. The agony was so sudden that he nearly lost his grip.

But still he held on, shortening his chain of body parts to avoid any more molten backsplash. His mind reeled from the burns scattered across his body. The bottom of the bin swept up and snapped closed. He dangled beneath while it reversed on its cable pathway, the scorching air growing cooler as he was carried away from the furnace.

The empty container moved fast and plunged back into its shadowy recess in the wall. He let go and dropped down a few feet to the floor of the niche, crumpling into a misshapen ball as the deathtrap clattered off. The air shook with a cascading roar as tons of scrap began to refill the container. Dollop huddled for a moment, rocking back and forth. He caressed his wounds, bright spatters of hardened silver dotting his chest, shoulder, and the back of one leg. He prodded gently at his scars and winced at the pain.

The snarl of machines and a clamor of activity drew his attention. He crept to the edge of the tunnel and looked down. Lit by the rivers of fire, an army of Watchmen workers in shiny protective suits labored over the troughs of liquefied metal. They poured the molten scrap into molds to create beams, sheets, and ingots. There were hundreds of pallets piled high with gleaming, symmetrical stacks of brand new metal.

The Foundry had turned Kallorax's furnace into a smelting factory.

Far to the right, he spied cargo trains speeding about, whisking the metal shipments away through busy tunnels. It was some sort of shipping zone, bustling with workers, but it looked like a way out.

Dollop began his descent to the factory floor, extending in a long chain of parts again, hoping that the Watchmen were too consumed with their jobs to notice. His wounds still flared, but he gritted his teeth and swallowed down the pain, focusing on the task at hand.

He was alive.

He had invoked the name of the Ona, and Makina had spared him. She had given him a second chance, and he would not fail Her.

He was going to find his friends and escape the Citadel.

"Pr-praise the gears," he said, beaming in triumph.

Distant rumbles. Heavy clangs like a battering ram. The Foundry was forcing their way into the detainment block.

The Covenant team, bathed in the red glow of the emergency lights, stalked down the curved corridor. Phoebe stayed close to her father, who carried his Dervish rifle at the ready. It was strange to see a weapon in her gentle father's hands, but he held it expertly. There was so much about him she didn't know, so many secrets he had kept from her.

Orei led the five mehkans in a tight formation on the ground while the chraida and the mysterious Grim Reaper figure scouted above like falcons, invisible and silent. The Covenant commander held up a hand, and they flattened against the wall to hide from enemies who might be lurking around the blind curve ahead. The rings and sliders on her arms ticked out some sort of calculation. Satisfied the coast was clear, Orei gestured for them to proceed.

The corridor opened into a hexagonal distribution hub where six hallways converged. It was an expansive cave populated with towering stacks of steel crates and racks loaded with supplies. There were blocks of massive batteries, organized tanks of pressurized gas, and tire-size spools of conduit. A fleet of Mini-lifts was parked inside docks in the walls.

The Covenant team spread out with practiced precision to secure the hub. The gecko mehkan named Korluth scuttled atop a stack of trunks, splaying his long beak into a pronged radar dish to scan the area. He gurgled a report and gestured to a corridor on the opposite side of the chamber.

That must lead to Micah, Phoebe realized with a rush.

Orei barked orders, and the team swept toward their destination, slinking and swinging, lumbering and running.

Suddenly, the commander tensed, sliders on her apparatus in a frenzy. They all froze, awaiting her command.

"Back!" she snapped. "Twenty-two puppets. Incoming!"

She hurled Jules and Phoebe out of the way as the Covenant warriors dove for safety. A whistling torrent of muted gunfire came at them, storming out from the corridor that led to Micah. Orei issued orders to a tumorous hunchback mehkan with spindly arms that reached the ground. Jules pulled Phoebe behind the cover of a giant crate. An explosion pounded the air.

She felt the hot, concussive whack of wind. Her ears rang, and her vision rippled. She braved a glance just as the hunchback mehkan ripped a seeping growth off its own bulbous body. The thing wriggled in his hand and bleated as the warrior bit down on it. With a snap of its arm, the mehkan hurled the blob at the squadron of Watchmen spilling from the corridor. Another blinding detonation, so hot it burned blue. She saw a couple of enemy soldiers disintegrate, their pieces blasting apart in every direction.

The hunchback was covered in living grenades.

"Stay," Orei ordered Phoebe and Jules, forcing them back.

Rifle fire hissed at Orei, but the rings of her body twirled and parted, and the bullets flew harmlessly through the gaps. She spun away to command her team, and Jules provided cover with a burst of whistling rounds from his gun.

With a fearsome bellow, the huge crane claw mehkan called Entakhai charged the Watchmen, his I-beam arms held up as a shield. They peppered him with bullets, but he was too fast. Entakhai collided with a pair of soldiers, smashing them against the wall like a bulldozer. He grabbed another with his one good hand and crushed it as if it were made of papier-mâché, and then launched the broken body at the other attackers.

In the blue blast of another explosion, Phoebe saw the enemy flood in. There were so many of them, their silent guns whirling with deadly fire. Bullets ricocheted and clattered everywhere. Phoebe covered her head with her arms, trying desperately to blink away the flare patterns from her eyes.

The Grim Reaper mehkan fell like a shadow, enveloping a Watchman with its cloaklike body. Its muscular membrane thrashed violently, and then the creature bounded back up into the darkness on javelin spring legs, leaving its victim a twitching, perforated mess. Cable strands whisked down as the chraida lassoed rifles out of the hands of Watchmen and scurried around the grid overhead to draw away enemy fire.

Reeking smoke from the hunchback's explosions filled the chamber, stinging Phoebe's eyes and burning her throat. She couldn't make out what was happening in the skirmish, but she could hear far-off jarring booms that shook the walls as the Foundry tried to break in.

And something else. *Click-clack-click-clack-click-clack.* Hazy silhouettes marched through the smoke in another corridor. They were being surrounded.

"Behind you!" Phoebe cried at the top of her lungs.

She pulled her father down as a barrage of bullets hammered the crate that hid them. He took her hand, and they fled for better cover.

Orei heard her warning. At the commander's order, a mehkan with folded forelegs like a praying mantis skittered over to a massive shelving unit. Its serrated limbs buzzed like chain saws, and the creature hacked through stout supports. With a tremendous crash, the loaded shelves toppled on the wave of Watchmen. The mantis mehkan spun into their ranks in a shredding cyclone.

Phoebe and her father dove for shelter behind a Mini-lift. They were outnumbered, pinned in this hub and assaulted from all sides. Jules tried to take aim, but it was impossible to find a clear target in the chaos.

With a series of deafening detonations, the hunchback mehkan collapsed a corridor onto a squadron of emerging Watchmen. A lumbering Covenant warrior covered in shaggy steel wool, one of his arms massively oversize, charged into combat. The beast swung its colossal limb, and its bulky fingers, tethered by lengths of chain, shot out like a bludgeoning flail. Its bashing attacks scattered Foundry soldiers, wrapping around their legs and yanking them off their feet. Weaving through its comrade's chains, the Grim Reaper mehkan impaled a Watchman with its spear legs. Then it used the victim as a springboard to vault at another, blinding him with its smothering membrane.

Through the smoke, Phoebe saw the chain saw mantis mehkan stagger back and petrify as it was riddled by a wave of lethal white bonding rounds.

Orei toppled a crate of long gas tanks. She measured them quickly with her shifting apparatus, adjusted their positions, and then swiped off the ends with a slash of her scythes. The canisters screamed off with a hissing wail, blasting into the advancing forces like torpedoes.

A Watchman grabbed Phoebe from behind. Jules hammered it with the butt of his rifle. She screamed and fought as the soldier reared back to strike her dead. But a cluster of silvery bolts cracked through its face shield.

Korluth appeared and spat another shard from his beak, piercing the Foundry soldier. Then a cable looped around the Watchman's neck, and he was yanked into the rafters to be dispatched by the watchful chraida. Motioning urgently, Korluth led Phoebe and her father forward. They followed his slinking form through smoke, bullets, and blue explosions. The black swoop of the Grim Reaper mehkan fluttered overhead.

Finally, they reached the corridor that led to Micah. Behind them, the Covenant team was still battling furiously, trying to keep this path clear. Among a ravaged pile of Watchman carcasses, Entakhai lay dying, his body splattered with crystallized chemical ammunition. Orei and Korluth stood beside him, their fists clenched over their dynamos.

"He rusts for you, bleeders," Orei said. "Pay respect."

More death. More loss. And this time, Phoebe was to blame. If it weren't for her, they would have escaped the Citadel by now.

"No. But . . . but we—" she tried to explain.

"Thank you, Entakhai," her father said.

Phoebe stared into the mehkan's vacant, glassy black eyes.

"Pr-praise the gears," she said, soft and unsure.

The mehkans looked at her strangely. Entakhai flashed his gnashing bolt teeth, streaked with oily black blood, though she couldn't tell whether it was a smile or a sneer. Orei murmured something to Korluth in Rattletrap, and the two of them raced deeper into the corridor, followed by Jules and Phoebe. As the battle raged behind them, she wondered what would happen to the rest of the Covenant team. All she knew was Micah and Dollop needed her.

Phoebe would save them. She had to.

The throne room erupted in applause. Goodwin stood ramrod straight with a winning smile on his face, arms folded across his ample chest.

"Thank you. No need for that," the Chairman said to the staff at their workstations. "We are all just doing our jobs."

He had been right all along. There was, in fact, a secret team of intruders trying to sneak into the Armory on Level Three. His hunch had enabled their forces to intercept before the enemy could breach the final security seals. Now the creatures were surrounded, and it was only a matter of time before they were eliminated. Goodwin breathed a little easier.

"Patch me in to Kaspar," he called out.

"I propose we reduce privilege to the access codes," a military executive said. "Re-encrypt them on a daily basis."

"Agreed. This was too close a call," another concurred.

An operator called out, "He's not responding, sir."

Goodwin's smile slipped. "Get me Captain Eldridge."

"Another intruder eliminated in the sublevel," an executive announced, indicating the live feeds on-screen.

"Eldridge here, sir," replied a voice over the speakers.

"Give your Com-Pak to Kaspar," Goodwin said. "I must speak with him."

"He . . . he is not here, sir."

Goodwin's nostrils flared. His flushed face settled into a hard mask, thick white brows hooding his icy eyes. The military executives watched him warily.

"What is the status of the detainment block?" Goodwin

reviewed the screen, deciphering the dark chaos of gunfire and explosions. A window winked out as another Watchman was deactivated, replaced instantaneously by another feed.

"Three intruders down," announced a coordinator.

"Only three?"

"They have assumed a defensive configuration near the passage leading to Sector Nine-D."

"About time," Goodwin mused. "Fall back and let them get to the boy. Prepare to strike on my word. How long until the surrounding doors are open?"

"Our technicians are still struggling with the override, sir. But they assure me they will—"

"Dispatch the Titans."

"Sir?"

"Take down the doors," he said impatiently. "Get in there and stop them."

"Yes, Mr. Goodwin," the coordinator responded. "Bringing Titans on line."

Goodwin studied the screen, which displayed a frozen image of two glowing white figures caught on a Watchman's heat-sensitive optics like a pair of grainy ghosts—a man and a lanky girl. The Chairman narrowed his eyes.

"James!" snarled a voice.

He turned to look across the vast expanse of the throne room. There, storming in through the reinforced platinum doors, were the five representatives of the Board. Their unwelcome faces were sour.

"What is the meaning of this?" Director Malcolm hollered.
"We demand an explanation," fumed Director Layton.

Phoebe tried to keep up, but the red darkness, gauzy smoke, and the ringing in her ears made her feel like she was stumbling through a dream.

She followed Orei, Korluth, and her father as they ran down the corridor, hurrying past intersecting hallways and Watchmen corpses blackened by the hunchback mehkan's blasts. Her father took a fresh ammo clip from one of the soldiers' belts and reloaded his Dervish rifle with practiced ease. As his weapon charged up with a low burring sound, its four barrels hissing into place, Phoebe considered taking one of the abandoned guns, then discarded the idea. Not only did the rifles look too heavy for her, but she hadn't the slightest clue how to use one, and now was not the time to learn.

Shuddering blows shook the detainment block.

Korluth led the way, his pronged radar dish flaring open to detect a signal. They entered a huge chamber where the mildewed air was filled with the muffled churn of water. The hair on Phoebe's neck prickled. It was the same foul reek from the drowning tank that clung to her coveralls. How she hoped that Micah hadn't suffered the same murderous depths.

The room was a forest of color-coded pipes, layered so heavily that it obscured the ancient golden wall. The convoluted plumbing network ran up into the impenetrable darkness above and down through the floor below.

"Nine-point-six ticks. Move," called Orei as she directed them to a connecting passage beyond the blinking banks of an electronic control system.

They navigated another series of tunnels and raced past adjacent corridors and chambers humming with machinery. The turret guns sagging limply from the overhead grid seemed like they might snap on at any second. Phoebe's life felt like it hung by a hair. All she could do was keep up. And survive.

Korluth diverted off the main corridor and descended down a channel that had a rugged decline, steps worn away by millennia.

"No," her father said, suddenly distraught. "Not in here."

She wanted to ask him what was wrong, but when the passage opened into a dismal cave, she knew. Her heart deflated.

It was a relic that had remained untouched since the days of Kallorax. The only light was a red glow from the hallway reflecting off the walls, but it was enough to glimpse the gallery of horrors. Cruel hooks and knots of thorns hung from chains above moldering equipment that bristled with rusty blades. There were crushing cages, spiked chairs, and slabs fitted with barbed-wire manacles. The floor was stained black and pocked with circular drains.

Stretching across the span of the back wall was a spiked sun, dangling with a sickening arsenal of implements that Phoebe was glad she couldn't decipher.

Micah was being kept in a torture chamber.

And there, whimpering in the dark, came his broken sob.

"Micah?" Phoebe whispered. The crying stopped. Korluth

skittered across the chamber, and the others followed him. "Micah, where are you?"

"H-hello?" his voice creaked. "Hey!"

"Shh," Jules responded. "We're here, son. You're safe."

"Doc? Oh man, I'm really losin' it."

Korluth snapped his radar dish mouth shut and motioned to one of the drains in the floor. Together the four of them hefted the lid.

"Hold on," Phoebe growled, straining against the hinges.

"Phoebe?" he gushed. "Oh man, get me outta this thing!"

As the top squealed open, they saw the glimmer of his desperate eyes.

Orei halted suddenly, clicking and measuring.

"Ambush," she growled and let the lid clang back down.

"No, no! HEY!"

The Covenant commander issued some instructions to her comrade and was gone in a flash, a silent swirl of deadly rings whispering out of sight. Korluth scuttled up the wall and vanished into the shadows above.

"Wait! What about Micah?" Phoebe cried.

"Yeah, what about ME?" he hollered. "Don't leave me!"

"We'll be back," Jules assured him.

"WAIT!"

"We'll get you out of there," Phoebe declared. "I promise!"

Her words were drowned out by ricocheting bullets.

Jules and Phoebe rolled behind the protection of a monstrous vise as Watchmen charged into the torture chamber. Orei intercepted them in a razor blur. She had no clear shape as she fought, just an incalculable assembly of hacking discs, expanding and retracting with dizzying speed. Attackers fell before her in pieces. She spun along the ground and swept cleanly through legs, and then sprang over their heads to assault from another angle.

Korluth's long silver darts whistled from the darkness, penetrating Watchmen with deadly precision. They shot blindly at him on the ceiling, but his skittering form was too fast. While they were distracted, Jules took aim with his own rifle, leveling two more in a flurry of white rounds.

The rings of Orei's body spun and shifted as she dodged bullets. Three Watchmen tried to follow her, guns blazing, but she streaked between them unexpectedly. They tracked her motion and blasted away, but only managed to strike each other. In seconds, all three were riddled with bonding rounds.

Korluth sprang from above and landed on one of the soldiers with a crack, his pickax beak buried in its body. Orei snared another two in a scythe headlock, one under each arm, and decapitated them with an efficient snap.

The final sparking Watchman, alive despite being only a torso, tried to drag himself toward a rifle lying beside Micah's prison. As the Covenant commander strode past, she sliced off the top of his head with the spinning rings of her arm, and he stopped moving.

Phoebe and Jules ran to help the mehkans open the lid again. Orei hauled Micah out of the narrow tube by his collar and deposited him roughly.

"Everything is going to be okay," Jules assured him.

"Are you all right?" Phoebe asked. "Did they hurt you?"

Micah was white and trembling. A thin silver stream oozed across his leg.

"Ahh! Get it off! That thing's gonna eat my brain! It—"

Korluth opened his pickax beak and lowered it to the ground. He made a soft squeaking sound, and the silver streak squiggled back to him. The mehkan slurped it up, his radar dish reclaiming the liquid sensor.

"Who the hell are they?" Micah asked, disoriented.

"The Covenant," Phoebe explained. "They're real."

"The . . . the . . ." He tried to comprehend. "And what the hell is THAT!?"

Phoebe had to suppress her scream.

In the cloven skull of the nearby Watchman, something was writhing. It had an oily, eel-like body covered in wiry tendrils that connected to circuit boards in the soldier's Computator brain. The creature sparked and spasmed, emitting a high-pitched decompressing sound as it tried in vain to detach itself. Its grotesque round mouth, like an ulcer filled with layers of bronze pin teeth, pulsed as it gasped for air. Then the thing was still.

"It's . . ." Phoebe struggled for the words.

". . . a mehkie," gasped Micah.

"Augmented robotics," her father said grimly.

"Puppet slaves," Orei spat at Jules.

Now she understood why Watchmen were such a secret, why they weren't sold in Meridian. Within their heads lay the dark truth of the Foundry.

A quaking boom. Dust streamed from above.

"It couldn't be," her father gasped.

Another jarring blast.

"Move!" Orei shouted, her apparatus measuring like mad.

She sprinted out of the torture chamber, followed by the others. They emerged into the corridor, only to be staggered by a blinding blue explosion. The way they had come was now choked with smoke and Dervish rifle fire. The chraida whizzed overhead, and the flail-armed mehkan held up the grievously wounded hunchback. The Covenant team was retreating.

Orei barked orders. Korluth ran to assist them. The commander continued down the corridor to secure the way ahead.

BOOM.

The escape route collapsed. A roaring wall of fire and burning debris. Through the haze, a monstrous figure appeared, filling the hall and cloaked in flame. Pillar legs, cannon arms. A constellation of lights glared across its sweeping body. Its beacon eye found them.

"Titan!" Jules screamed.

Phoebe saw its symphony of artillery churn to life.

They plunged back down into the torture chamber. Cannon fire pulverized the corridor. A familiar shriek burned into Phoebe's marrow.

She would know it anywhere. The scream of a chraida.

Orei conferred with the battered remnants of her team. Jules looked around frantically.

"Trapped," the commander said, her voice brittle.

"No!" Phoebe cried.

"We're toast," Micah panted. "Dead end."

She looked around and realized he was right—the torture chamber had but one entrance. They were cornered.

A volcanic explosion in the hall. The Titan was coming.

The Covenant began to pray.

"Down," Jules said suddenly.

Orei looked at him, her assemblage ticking and assessing.

"The pipes, back in the vesper plant." Her father rushed to the open tube where Micah had been imprisoned. "They run under the floor." He aimed his rifle down into the narrow cell and opened fire, twirling out a barrage of bullets.

Walls shook, ringing the torture instruments like iron bells as the Titan approached in a storm of cannon fire. They heard the clacking march of an organized platoon of Watchmen soldiers. The Foundry had finally broken through.

"Come on!" Jules shouted.

Orei addressed her warriors one last time. They snapped their fists over their blood-red dynamos. She shoved past the humans and leaped down into the narrow tube to hack through the bottom, now perforated by gunfire. Jules followed, and then Micah, who hesitated for a brief instant at the thought of going back in that torture tube.

Then it was Phoebe's turn. Her father's open arms waited below. She dropped into the blackness and felt his strong hands catch her.

The last thing she saw was Korluth's unreadable face staring down at her as the hunchback's blue detonations mingled with the Titan's angry red fire. Only then did she realize what was happening—the Covenant team had been ordered to stay behind. Korluth gurgled something, then slammed the lid.

She didn't know his words, but she knew his meaning.

Praise the gears.

35

LAST GASP

The ceiling of the crawl space was inches above their heads, and it trembled with explosions. Phoebe wriggled after the others, wedging herself through the nest of plumbing and bundled wires. She could barely see anything, just a few patches of light poking up from below.

"Eighteen percent rise in heat ratio," came Orei's voice.

"The smelting factory is that way," replied her father. "Too dangerous. Follow me." He took the lead, and they crawled after him, squeezing between ducts and channels, finding a path through the chaotic knot of conduits.

Phoebe peered down through a gap in the stretches of

pipe and saw some kind of shipping zone. Watchman workers in Multi-chain conveyors and Over-cranes were loading a fleet of bullet-shaped trains. The shipments zipped through a semicircular array of tunnels, hovering silently along cylindrical tracks that glowed purple. Magnetic rails, she realized.

Phoebe hurried to catch up with the others. There was barely enough room to crawl, and she knocked her head and got tangled as they slid under the skin of the Citadel.

"Here," Jules called out. "Down here."

Orei tore a gash in the metal duct, wrenched it open, and slipped through. The rest of them followed, dropping onto a rusty boxcar, then lowering themselves to the gritty ore.

This was a graveyard of trains. It was crowded with rows of obsolete engines and wood-paneled carriers. Crushed boxcars were piled like demolished Autos at a junkyard, and pulleys dangled from busted equipment. Cracked trestles and lumber lay in rotting mounds. A set of those magnetic rails cut right through the middle, but these were not glowing purple like the others. They swept to the left, winding out of sight.

Orei withdrew a white spike from the confines of her ticking disks and struck it on the side of a boxcar. It resonated like a tuning fork, and strips along its pointed end flared open. She plunged it into the ground, letting the device ring for several seconds in the ore before retrieving it.

"Move," Orei pointed to the right, past the wreckage of the train yard. A tunnel led into the darkness, its mouth cordoned off with age-worn barricades.

"The E-Four line?" Jules asked. "No good, it's collapsed."

"There," Orei insisted. "Immolation in five-point-four-seven ticks."

"Wait," Phoebe said. "What about Dollop?"

"Yeah! We ain't leavin' without him," stated Micah.

Orei swept about to face them. "Seven Covenant left to rust. All for pathetic bleeders," she snarled. "No delays."

"We either get out now or not at all," Jules said.

"Not without Dollop!" Phoebe shouted.

Orei froze, the sensors on her body ticking like mad.

With a sudden, vehement swing of her arms, she knocked the kids away.

A massive wooden beam smashed into the ground where they had been standing, exploding in a shower of moldy splinters. A long black shape leaped into view. A caged bulb mounted to a strut illuminated his cadaverous face.

"No escape," Kaspar growled.

The air shook as her father fired. The soldier dodged with alarming quickness, but two rounds punched his chest, knocking him back. He kept his footing. White epoxy bled onto his bullet-proof flak jacket.

Kaspar sprang at them, farther and faster than was humanly possible.

Orei intercepted in a whistling blur. She snared his leg and redirected him in midair. Kaspar rebounded and swung at the mehkan. Her rings snapped and slid, parting so that he only managed to pound at the air. She cinched her blades closed to hack his hands, but he was too quick.

"Move!" Orei commanded as she kept Kaspar at bay.

Jules hurried the kids into a maze of stacked cargo transports, charging toward the collapsed tunnel in the distance.

A creaking groan behind them. They turned to see a tower of boxcars toppling in their direction.

Jules and Micah dove one way, Phoebe the other.

CRASH.

She looked back to see Kaspar leering at her.

Orei sprang at him again, and they tumbled out of sight. Phoebe was cut off from Micah and her father, separated by the fallen wreckage.

"Phoebe!" came their voices.

"Go! I'll meet you up ahead!" she shouted.

The overturned pile of boxcars had spilled over the corroded trains lining the tracks. She raced alongside until she found a gap between two carriages.

"Come on!" Micah shouted. "Climb through!"

She grabbed the edge of the car and placed a foot on the coupling. There was a squeal as the train was propelled forward. The cars collided in a splintering crunch, and Phoebe fell back, cut off again.

Kaspar rocketed at her. She tried to scramble beneath the locomotive, but he snatched her ankle and flung her out into the open. She tumbled across the dusty ore, and he was on her in a flash. He grabbed her by the front of the coveralls and lifted her, a sadistic grin stretching his face. She screamed and tried to kick at him, but her attacks were futile. He carried

Phoebe effortlessly, holding her at arm's length.

"NO!" her father cried, crawling from under the train car with Micah. Orei, too, was sprinting for her, but she was unsteady, a cracked ring hanging loose from her body. They weren't going to make it to her in time.

Kaspar hauled her over to a rusty orange hook dangling from a chain.

She screamed again.

"Three!" came the collective cry in the throne room.

On the giant screen, another beast was shredded by Foundry fire.

A Watchman distributed chilled champagne among the staff. Bodies were already being recovered from the detainment block, but a handful of stalwart intruders still held out near the Armory. The entire control room watched the monitors, counting down as each target was dispatched.

The directors, however, were not impressed. They stood like a firing squad before the Chairman. But Goodwin stood tall, shoulders squared and hands clasped behind his back.

"This is a dark day." Director Malcolm's leathery face folded into a frown.

"An unacceptable oversight," berated Director Obwilé.

"Agreed." Goodwin nodded. "We must be more diligent."

"We?" Director Layton scoffed. "This is unforgivable. What happened to the Citadel's so-called impervious security?"

"Jules happened. And I have dealt with him accordingly," Goodwin said, motioning to the video feeds.

"Your coddling of Plumm caused this," she retorted.

"No," the Chairman corrected coolly. "He leaked the relevant intelligence weeks ago, which means this little scuffle was unavoidable. However, my *coddling*," he emphasized, "enabled us to extract a full confession so that we may properly manage this threat in the future."

"Two!" the staff cried in unison as a Titan vaporized another intruder.

"How could you allow this?" Director Obwilé scolded.

"I am"—Goodwin took a step toward him—"the sole reason it is over. Imagine what would have happened had I not personally deciphered their intent and thwarted their attempts to infiltrate the Armory."

"This was on your watch!" Director Layton blasted.

"To my knowledge, no one foresaw this. And had I somehow managed to divine that the Covenant would surface, you would have dismissed it as a ridiculous fairy tale."

Director Malcolm paused to touch his earpiece. "The Board understands your position," he explained with a smile. "But we require some assurances."

"A sweep of every sector is currently under way, along with a thorough investigation of the incursion," Goodwin explained. "Ladies and gentlemen of the Board, this was a desperate attack and far from successful. We have incurred only minor damage, limited entirely to non-vital sectors. And thanks to preparedness and decisive action, it is being mitigated as we speak."

"It remains an unconscionable breach and—" Director Obwilé started.

"It is over," Goodwin declared, "because *I* stopped it."

As if in response to his words, a hundred darkened screens around the control room flickered on simultaneously as power was restored to the disabled Omnicams. There was another cheer from the staff.

"Selkirk," Goodwin called across the room, not breaking eye contact with Director Obwilé. "Turrets."

"Yes, sir!" shouted the technician.

A handful of screens flashed as Dervish turrets leveled the remaining creatures from behind, demolishing them in a white hailstorm of bullets.

"ONE! ZERO!"

The control room rang with the joyous popping of champagne corks. The directors did not celebrate, but the severity in their demeanor eased. Only Director Obwilé seemed dissatisfied. He stepped away from the group, adjusting his glasses to scrutinize the wall of Watchmen feeds.

Goodwin savored the triumph.

"Thank you all for your questions," the Chairman concluded, spreading his hands and guiding them to the exit. "Now let's leave our team to wrap things up here. We have important matters to discuss."

"Such as?" Director Layton inquired.

Goodwin looked at the directors with his icy, shining eyes. "Retribution."

Phoebe shrieked.

She kept trying to kick free, but Kaspar clamped her legs and tensed, rearing back to impale her on the rusty hook.

A silver blur whipped down from above and wrapped around his head. Stumbling back, he dropped Phoebe and clawed at the thing over his face. As she scurried clear, Jules let loose with his rifle, blasting away at the soldier. The white rounds pinged off the crane hook, and Kaspar leaped away.

He tried to seize the thing locked around his head, but it kept changing shape, transforming to evade his grasp. Phoebe stared at it in wonder.

Orei attacked once more, spinning at Kaspar with renewed ferocity. He tore the silvery form from his face, then engaged the wounded commander.

Dollop reassembled himself and took Phoebe's hand to flee. "I f-f-found you!" the little mehkan cried.

"You saved me!" she heaved.

"Here!" Micah called out, cutting between two boxcars to make a getaway. Jules covered them with his rifle while they escaped. Phoebe looked back to see Kaspar grab Orei by her wounded appendage and hurl her at a metal strut. He struck at her, but she twirled away, and his blow bent the massive beam as if it were rubber. She staggered to her feet.

Kaspar was going to kill Orei. There was no question about it. And then he would kill the rest of them.

Phoebe had to do something.

She sprinted after her father, Micah, and Dollop, racing toward the collapsed tunnel. Rotten wooden railroad ties had been ripped up and tossed aside in craggy mounds of debris. Beyond those, affixed to the side of a pillar, she spied a battered metal control box.

It came to her in a flash, crystal clear and complete.

She skidded to a halt. "Wait!"

"What?" Micah blurted.

"I need your help. To get Kaspar."

Micah's eyes nearly popped out. "Don't be psycho."

Her father and Dollop stopped up ahead.

"Come on!" Jules shouted urgently.

Phoebe looked at Micah, galvanized.

"No guts, no glory," she smirked.

She quickly explained her plan to them and grabbed a couple of rivets off the ground. Then she raced back toward the clanging sound of combat.

Kaspar appeared atop a boxcar, holding Orei overhead. Slashes across his face leaked dark blood. He hurled her body down in a clattering heap, and then pounced, swinging both fists in an arc. She rolled sluggishly away as Kaspar slammed a crater into the ground. His flesh bulged and quivered beneath his tattered gloves, sinewy folds swelling, veiny pistons pumping.

A rusty bolt cracked into the side of his head.

Phoebe didn't get the chance to throw another.

He charged her in a fog of bloodlust.

She ran, faster than she had ever run before, faster than she ever thought she could. She scrambled over the mound of torn-up rails, spikes stabbing and splinters scratching her face. Kaspar ripped the rubble aside.

Ahead of her was the polished new train track.

He was close behind. Phoebe hurdled past the rails.

His shadow consumed her.

WHOOMF!

The tracks ignited in a bright purple glow.

Kaspar stumbled, howling in fury. She turned to look.

He strained to grab her, but one of his boots was stuck securely to the track. With a sucking sound, his other leg swept against the rail, connecting with a clunk. He was locked firmly in place. Her breath was ragged. She was shaking. Gathering her nerve, Phoebe leaned in close.

"Gotcha."

Kaspar swiped a gear-gnarled hand at her.

She left him snarling like a rabid dog against its leash and rushed to join her companions. They were gathered at the metal control box, which had been shot open by her father. Micah had worked his grease monkey magic on the circuits, splicing lines with his teeth and hot-wiring the magnetic train tracks just as he had done to the Lodestar.

"Minus two ticks," snapped Orei's warbling voice. Several disks on her chest and arm were bent or cracked. She hobbled toward the abandoned tunnel, and they raced to catch up.

With a roar, Kaspar pounded his fists down on the rail to flatten it. There was another clang as they too locked in place.

Phoebe had never heard a more gratifying sound.

As the Chairman crossed the throne room, he glanced up at the eighty-foot-high statue and had a vision of what it must have looked like in its prime, resplendent in all of its barbaric glory. Supplicants would have come to grovel at its feet, to marvel at its saw-blade wings flared in a fiery array of beams.

Goodwin, too, knew what it was to feel like a god. Two worlds were his to command, revolving around him like planets around the sun. But unlike the dead despot, Goodwin persevered. He could have given Kallorax a few pointers.

"We are concerned this attack will have widespread impact," Director Layton pontificated. "Rebellion is contagious."

"But it is not incurable," the Chairman assured her. "Our response must be swift and resolute. Let us look to Fuselage as our example."

"WAIT! Enlarge that window!" shouted Director Obwilé. He stood behind one of the Watchman coordinators, staring at the screens. "Go back. Go back!"

Surprised by the outburst, the directors returned to the control center. Goodwin clenched his jaw and wondered what the troublesome man was up to.

A slow-motion video was on the display. It was a deactivated Watchman feed from Level Three, captured during the battle near the Armory. A blurry creature had struck the soldier down and cracked the lens. As the optical sensor began to short out, distorted by bars of static, its malfunctioning focus shifted to the wide-open atrium in the distance.

"There!" Director Obwilé cried.

Goodwin saw it too. Just before the feed blinked off, there was movement beyond the glass—shadowy and indistinct.

The Chairman of the Foundry stopped breathing.

He had missed something.

The Armory was not their target. All that chaos, all of those lives were a diversion. Jules had played him like a fool.

Goodwin felt the phantom of Kallorax. Heard his laughter. The fate of the damned megalarch was to be his, too.

"All units," he boomed. "Intruder in the CHAR Lab!"

"I—I did it, Phoebe! M-Micah! I found my f-f-function!"

They looked at Dollop proudly, and she opened her mouth to congratulate him.

"Silence!" interrupted Orei. The commander withdrew her spike device, struck it against the wall, and flung it into the orc as it resonated. "She comes."

Phoebe felt a tremor, but at first she thought it was just the blood pounding in the veins of her legs. Then the ground shook vigorously and loosened beneath them. Cracks snaked underfoot, and her father pulled her safely out of the way.

An enormous white drill exploded from the ground like

a submarine through a glacier. It hurled clouds of smoke and particles, forcing them to cough and cover their eyes.

Not a drill—a giant mehkan. It was a leviathan so pale it was translucent, with a massive flanged head slotted by grooves and spinning, knurled teeth. Striated tentacles followed, dozens of them, thick as columns. Gliding like a giant squid, the mehkan doubled back and dove into the burrow headfirst. Held in its tentacles was a battered black vessel that eased to a stop as the creature submerged into the ore once again.

"S-s-s-salathyl!" Dollop chimed. "Sweet Mother of Ore! You-you're the C-C-Covenant, aren't you? See? I-I-I knew it was true! I knew y-you would—"

"In," Orei ordered, opening the vessel's rear hatch.

They climbed into the hollowed-out compartment and found a few carved niches to hold on to and a sloshing bag that cast pale blue light. Orei slammed the hatch closed, and the salathyl bellowed in response.

"Point four two ticks remaining."

They descended, leaving no trace of their presence in the tunnel other than a circular scar in the ore, a distinctive pattern like the spokes of a wheel. The hull rattled and groaned as they picked up speed. Phoebe held on tight to the notched black wall, feeling the vibrations of the enveloping ore. She steadied herself and took a look around.

Orei, cracked and damaged.

Dollop, scarred and shaken.

Micah, bruised and worn.

And her father. He caught her stare, and a smile crossed his sunken face. She remembered what he had told her back in that awful prison cell: *We're going to make it through this.*

He winked his unbandaged eye, and Phoebe giggled.

The others looked up at her.

Micah chuckled too. Even Dollop, who was unsure what was so funny, smiled wide. Orei measured them silently, betraying no emotion whatsoever.

Phoebe and her companions shared a moment of solace.

CLANG.

Something smashed into the back of the vessel, rocking it.

The rest happened in slow motion, a scene from one of Phoebe's nightmares. The hatch tore away with a screech. The roar of tumbling, pulverized ore filled the air.

Kaspar.

He clung to the outside of the hull, drenched in blood. Jagged debris bombarded him from all sides. His dead eyes were trained on her father. He dove inside and hurled a fist.

There was a nauseating wet crunch and Jules crumpled, his rifle clattering aside. He clutched his chest, gurgling, blood foaming to his lips.

Phoebe screamed, and Kaspar lunged for her.

The vessel flashed as if full of lightning, and he was flung back. A cascade of white rounds pounded into him.

Now Micah screamed, firing the rifle. He stormed at Kaspar. Blasting, unrelenting. Kaspar pinwheeled his arms, trying to stop his fall. He toppled backward into the crushing surge. The burrow collapsed in their wake and buried him, howling, fighting the inexorable current of ore.

Micah stood wild-eyed, his finger mashing the trigger. The four barrels of his rifle continued to whistle and spin long after the bullets ran dry.

Captain Eldridge stormed the lab with a team of Watchmen.

His orders were clear. Use magnetic pulse weapons to incapacitate intruders and draw them safely away, and then execute with low-velocity rounds. The risks of a full-on assault in here were simply too great.

The laboratory was huge, a marvel of glass, porcelain, and wood—all materials impervious to CHAR. Blinking Computators and other complex equipment sat encased in clear vitric shells, along with pine racks of test tubes, stoneware scales, and glass partitions that left nowhere to hide.

They did a rapid sweep of the primary workroom and declared it clear. Eldridge crept to the storage vault and entered the code. There was a beep and a series of clicks as the lock disengaged.

The doors slid open with a hiss.

In the glass chamber were rows of giant vats, their contents swirling black, half liquid and half gas. Some contraption he couldn't make out had been attached to their polished surfaces. Hair-thin wires curled away from the tanks, winding to a shadow hunched against the back wall.

Eldridge never got a chance to discharge his weapon. He could only watch as the figure touched a red shape on its chest and muttered a few words.

Then the world exploded in black fire.

36

SLIPPING AWAY

oodwin was barely in his plush Durall seat when the Galejet screamed away from its launch pad. He felt the crush of speed and clutched the armrests until his knuckles went white. The dark cherry interior of the aircraft glowed as raging fires shone through the windows.

He could hear the directors muttering behind him, quietly conspiring. Goodwin looked out the glass porthole.

A massive crater vomiting black smoke blotted out the glimmers of dawn. The Covenant's detonation had triggered a chain reaction in the Armory, vaporizing a quarter of the stronghold. Most of the towers on that side were gone, toppled or blown to pieces, while the others shriveled like the curled-up legs of a dead insect. The CHAR was devouring the Citadel from the inside out, its gold metal core bubbling, sagging. The melted mehkan bodies that formed its cruel façade sloughed off and oozed down the sides.

Kallorax's ancient palace, this ageless blot upon the landscape, sank in upon itself like a carcass putrefying. The upper stories containing the Foundry's luxurious complex of suites and lounges collapsed with a groaning crash so loud Goodwin felt it through his seat.

The Foundry had extensive evacuation plans, and its employees were highly trained experts, all prepared for emergency. Behemoth Cargoliners stocked with munitions, files, equipment, and platoons of Watchmen raced across the dead lands in all directions. Legions of Aero-copters crammed with personnel hovered like flies over a mound of filth. Despite the efficiency of their escape, he knew lives had been lost. No telling how many.

Goodwin's chest felt tight. He needed a drink. Just as he was about to order a Watchman to fetch one, he was summoned.

"James."

He steeled himself and strode to the back of the Galejet. The five representatives of the Board were silhouettes blending in with the Durall couches. Their faces were steeped in shadow, their silver earpieces glinting in the flash of an occasional explosion outside.

Goodwin stood before them, his hands behind his back.

"You are an embarrassment," Director Obwilé stated.

"Our primary infrastructure in Mehk lies in ruins because of you," Director Layton snarled. "Research, personnel, facilities, resources. All gone. All due to your incompetence."

Goodwin puffed up his chest. "You listen to me. I will not stand for—"

"You cannot possibly meet the commitment to Trelaine now," growled Director Malcolm, his affable demeanor gone. "Lavaraud will realize this before the week is out. Your failure to deliver will be taken as a direct provocation."

"War," spat Director Layton. "That's what you have brought upon us."

"This is a serious setback," he conceded, "but one that—"

"That you may not get the chance to rectify," cut in Director Obwilé.

"You . . . dare threaten me?"

"Remember your place," intoned Director Layton.

The Chairman blinked and regained his cool.

"Forgive me, but these events, they are not my doing."

"Perhaps not," Director Obwilé agreed. "But they will be your undoing."

"I'm not to blame!" He loathed the naked plea in his own voice. "No one saw this attack coming. I went above and beyond the call of duty, I did everything I possibly could—surely you see that. If it wasn't for Plumm, I'd—"

"Plumm!" jeered Director Malcolm. "The man *you* hired? The one you personally brought up through the ranks despite our concerns? And all because you had a *feeling* about him?"

"The Board does not tolerate failure," stated Director

Layton flatly. Goodwin straightened his tie, ignoring the sweat.

"I have been Chairman of the Foundry for over thirty years. I pioneered advancements in the combat interface of augmented robotics. I streamlined and expanded our harvesting operations to a nearly threefold advance in output. I spearheaded the Dyad Project, which has opened new —"

"Ah, yes," interrupted Director Obwilé. "Tens of millions of dollars invested in research and development on your precious Kaspar, and the first time we need him, he goes missing. Clearly you are unfit to manage such a critical endeavor. And let's not forget your egregious security failure in allowing two children into Mehk. We alerted you as to our concern, and yet you brushed it off." He touched his earpiece and leaned forward, still shrouded in darkness. "The Board has come to a decision."

Goodwin's pulse raced. His hands fell at his sides.

The directors were silent for another long moment.

"The Board must protect the Foundry. We must defend Meridian at all costs," said Director Layton.

"Trelaine will want blood," Director Malcolm added.

In the burst of another explosion from the Citadel, Goodwin could see the hint of a smile on Director Obwilé's lips.

"And when their ax falls, it falls on you."

Phoebe trembled uncontrollably.

All they could hear was the roar of ore through the exposed back of the vessel. The pale blue light from the lantern made the blood that flowed from her father's chest look inky black. He was propped up in her lap, struggling to breathe. The two mehkans stood aside to give her space, and Micah huddled nearby, holding the emptied rifle tight, keeping a sharp eye on the open hatch.

"You're going to be okay. You're going to be okay."

She kept repeating the words again and again, squeezing his cold hand tightly in her own, trying to make him believe it.

Trying to make herself believe it.

He was staring into space, his mouth opening and closing like a fish. There was a horrible, wet slushing sound every time he inhaled, and bubbles of blood frothed in the corners of his mouth. She tried not to stare at the wound on his chest. The sight of it weakened her, sapped her will.

Dollop prayed feverishly, his eyes pinched tight. Orei stood unmoving, save for the twitching of her sliders and pointers.

"We did it," Phoebe whispered to her father, trying her best to smile and sound hopeful. "We beat them. We—"

The words caught in her throat, choking, wrenching her insides. Her eyes burned. She fought for control. She would not give in to tears. Crying was not going to save him.

"Hold on," she said louder, her voice clear and firm. "Do you hear me? I said hold on. We're going to make it, that's what you said to me. We're all going to make it. We'll get help."

"How much farther?" Micah quietly croaked to Orei.

"Four point three ticks," she said. "Safe there."

"Is he going to die?" he asked.

Orei didn't answer.

Her father's eyes were suddenly intense, as if he was seeing something invisible to the rest of them. His brow creased and he strained. He tried to speak but made only incomprehensible guttural noises.

"Don't talk," Phoebe pleaded. "Save your strength."

He turned to Micah. His hand clawed at the air, quavering. He grabbed Micah's coveralls and brought him close enough to whisper in the boy's ear.

Phoebe watched anxiously. She couldn't hear what he was saying, but she saw Micah's expression change. His face was sundered by—heartbreak? Fear? Her father let go of Micah, who sat back, shaken.

"Cri . . . Cr . . . Crrick . . ."

Blood clogged his airway, and he hacked.

"Shhh."

Delicately, she touched her ear to his hitching chest so that she could hear his heart, feel his breath. It was less labored now.

"I love you," she whispered over and over. "I love you."

At last, she felt the vessel slowing down.

Phoebe looked up to find they had emerged from underground. Soft whispers of a hazy dawn appeared outside the exposed hatch as the salathyl eased to a stop. Silence settled over them, complete and profound. The crashing clamor of their frantic escape was behind them. Mehkans emerged from a scattering of nearby metal hide tents and approached.

"We're here, Daddy!" Phoebe cried. She sat up and cast her fierce eyes at Orei. "Get someone! Help him!" she shouted.

But the Covenant commander did not respond.

"Phoebe," Micah whispered.

"We're safe," she said to her father, grasping his hand. She turned to the mehkans staring in from the open hatch. "Do something! Somebody, help me get him out of here!"

"Phoebe," Micah sobbed. Dollop put his face in his hands.

She looked at them. Then at her father.

And knew.

It was over.

Time faded. The world darkened. Her mind collapsed.

She had come so far to find him. He was everything. No one else mattered. Nothing else existed. And now he was gone.

Forever.

The dam broke inside her, and she cried.

THE CALLING

icah stood by the shimmering gold curtain, Dervish rifle at the ready. His legs were killing him, but he wasn't about to rest. Not until Phoebe did. She had been in the back room for hours now.

He'd stand guard forever if that's what he had to do.

They were in a huge gray tent, big enough to hold all the warriors in the Covenant camp, but Orei had shooed everyone out. Just he and Dollop remained. The little mehkie sat nearby, praying beside a giant dynamo carved into the floor. Splotches of sun spilled through the patchy hide ceiling, mixing with the pale blue light of lantern bags stuck to the tent posts.

Micah kept hearing the Doc's last words. He repeated them to himself again and again. They were all he had to hold on to. That and his empty gun. He adjusted his grip on it, feeling the scrape of his calluses along the handle—finally, after building it up for so long, there was a hardness in his hands.

The flap on the far side of the tent flashed open, and Orei strode in with two mehkies. One of them was lumpy and old and barely came up to Micah's waist. The other was the same kind of crane-claw creature that had nearly broken his arms back in the Gauge Pit, an orange-skinned brute with shoulders like the front of a Cargoliner. He looked like he could have given that Titan back in the Citadel a run for its money.

As the trio got closer, Micah saw that Orei was no longer covered in black camouflage. She was all midnight blue lined with silver. Cracks in the rings on her arm and chest had been fixed with something that looked like gray solder.

Dollop was too caught up in his prayers to notice them at first. When the little old mehkie spoke to him in creaky Rattletrap, Dollop squeaked and flopped onto his knees in sudden devotion. The ancient creature was buried in layers of frilly gold veils, and her wrinkled face was barely visible beneath a dynamo headpiece draped in delicate chains. She reached out sticklike arms that ended in two knotty claws and laid them on Dollop's head. The two prayed in unison.

Micah wondered what the big to-do was.

He noticed that the crane-claw mehkie's eyes were fixed on his rifle. Micah returned the stare. The scarred warrior nodded his head respectfully.

432

Now Orei spoke to Dollop, the wobbly chords of her voice sounding far away. He looked up at her, astonished. Tears shimmered in his eyes. Micah had never seen him so excited. It felt so out-of-place on this sad, gray morning.

"What?" Micah asked.

"A-A-A-A-Axial Ph-Phy s s s said . . ." he blubbered, unable to speak clearly.

The orange giant raised his rippling I-beam arm and opened a six-fingered crane claw. With shaking hands, Dollop took something from his grip.

A bloodred dynamo.

Axial Phy retrieved the emblem and placed it over the splash of silver scars on his chest. Dollop winced as she twisted the dynamo to lock it in place.

"O-O-Overguard Orei says I—I have a place now," Dollop chirped. "I f-f-found my function, and—and now have a cl-clan, too. Th-th-the Covenant!"

Micah smiled at him. "You done good, chum."

"I'm in the C-C-Covenant!"

Dollop leaped up in a confetti of parts, limbs and digits scattering in celebration, then snapping back together. The crane-claw mchkie rumbled a deep laugh, spoke a few words to Dollop, and headed for the door.

"I—I have to go now," he whispered giddily to Micah. "O-Overguard Treth needs me. C-can you believe it? He—he really said he needs *me*."

Dollop followed the giant. As he was silhouetted in the open flap, framed by the soft dawn outside, he looked back.

"I can't w-w-wait to tell Phoebe!"

Micah's face fell as he watched the little warrior bounce out of the tent and disappear from sight. How quickly his friend had forgotten.

He was jealous of Dollop for that.

Orei and Axial Phy didn't move. They stood staring at Micah. He stiffened and adjusted his grip on the rifle.

"You, too, are needed," Orei said in a low flutter.

Everything was gray.

Except the cemetery grass, damp and vivid green.

So many people in black. Family she had never met. Friends of her mother she had never heard of.

Goodwin was there, too, head bowed in respectful silence.

In the days leading up to her mother's funeral, Phoebe had cried a lifetime of tears. She was inconsolable. They were all so worried about her. Talking in hushed tones. Staring. Even her father couldn't get through to her.

Everyone mourned, all of these people Phoebe didn't know. One by one, the strangers placed flowers in the open casket. They gave their condolences.

We are so sorry.

She's in a better place now.

If there is anything we can do . . .

She will always be watching over you.

Then they all left, and she never saw any of them again.

When Phoebe finally approached the grave, she was scared

at what she would see inside.

But her mother was beautiful—more beautiful than ever. There was a hint of a smile on her lips, as if she were amused by all this pomp and fuss. As Phoebe studied her mother's expression, she had the fleeting thought that this might all be an elaborate hoax.

And then, all of a sudden, she had stopped crying.

That smile on her mother's face, that coy little dimple, was her final gift. It was like she was consoling Phoebe. Telling her not to worry, not to grieve, that somehow and in some way, everything was going to be all right.

Phoebe's last tear fell onto her mother's porcelain cheek.

For three years, she had kept herself from crying. Through sheer force of will, she had held back every tear.

Until now. They came in a flood.

Phoebe knelt at her father's side. The Covenant had laid his body out ceremoniously on a prayer mat woven from bands of red metal. She had folded the mat around his chest so as to not have to see his terrible wound.

Unlike her mother, he was not smiling. His face was locked in a visage of pain.

"Daddy."

She petted his thin hair, brushing it back the way he had always done to her. Phoebe took his glasses off and held them to her chest. She stroked his cool face, wishing those wrinkles were framing his smile instead of this terrible death mask.

If only she could have died there, right by his side.

"What do I do now?" she whispered.

She heard movement behind her and turned to look.

Micah was standing there, pale and wide-eyed.

"I-I'll go," he said backing away.

Phoebe ran at him, wrapping him up in her arms. He dropped his heavy rifle, letting it swing loose on its strap as he held his hands wide, unsure of where to put them. Her tears flowed onto his shoulder. She had to stoop a little, and she knew how terribly awkward it was, but she didn't care.

Hesitantly, his arms closed around her.

"He . . . he told me . . ." Micah's voice was choked. "He said to protect you with my life. That was the last thing he said."

He pulled away and looked her in the eyes.

"And I will. I swear I will."

He fought back tears and for a moment, through her blurry vision, she saw the man that he would someday become.

She hugged him again, even tighter.

He was all she had left.

"They're waiting for us," he whispered.

Phoebe and Micah emerged from the back, hand in hand.

Orei and Axial Phy were waiting for them in the middle of the cavernous tent. As they approached, the giant dynamo carved into the floor began to open with a rumbling scrape. The two interlocking gears parted down the middle, revealing a steep staircase that descended out of sight.

"I was to kill Plumm," Orei said harshly.

Phoebe was stunned by the commander's cruelty.

"Last phase, I was granted the blessing. Went to end his life." She paused thoughtfully. "But he did not resist. Told me that to aid the Covenant, he would gladly die, but could do more. He wanted to help. Called him liar, bleeder filth. He was not of the ore, was the enemy."

Her ticking, turning apparatus swayed gently.

"To measure is my function, to know all. Never have I so miscalculated. I was . . . wrong." This realization seemed to take Orei a moment to fully absorb. "Because of your father, the Citadel is no more. I am unworthy to speak his name."

Phoebe reached up and touched the dynamo on Orei's chest. Her twirling scythes came to an abrupt halt, and she glanced at Phoebe's hand. The Covenant commander wavered unsteadily. Then her body began to move again, and she recovered her balance.

"Will prepare rusting rites," she fluttered softly, "while you are below."

Micah eyed the hole in the floor warily. "What's down there?" he asked.

Orei's shifting form inverted, and she strode for the exit.

"The Hearth," was all she said, and then was gone.

With a light shuffling sound, Axial Phy hobbled down the steps, her veils and shawls scratching the ground in her wake. Micah held his rifle at the ready as he followed, and Phoebe descended into the dark behind him.

The ore was obsidian black, and the passage was illuminated by lantern bags on the walls. Micah swept aside a shimmering golden veil with his gun and held it for Phoebe. She was trembling, and she didn't know why.

The way ended at a plain wall dulled by layers of tarnish and soot. At its base was a trough, and beside it sat a decanter filled with a glowing, brick-red liquid. Axial Phy lifted a ladle from the pot, chanting in Rattletrap. She stirred and scooped the fluid, then without spilling so much as a drop, she poured it into the trough, sweeping gently from left to right to spread it evenly. This done, she bowed to them and departed.

"Hey," Micah called out. "What are we supposed to—"

Phoebe clutched his shoulder.

The red liquid in the trough was moving. It crept up the wall like tendrils of glowing ivy, curling and reaching toward the ceiling. The molten lace heated and steamed with a pungent aroma of incense, making her feel light-headed. Liquid metal merged and bled together to form a luminous sheet. Dark currents swirled on the surface, bubbles grew and sank.

"Little. Embers."

The voice was both low and high, old and young, mixed in a harmony that filled Phoebe's body with warmth. Though they watched the shifting metal intently, they didn't see the face emerge—they just realized it was there.

Golden veils obscured its features, flowing like silk underwater. Fins drifted in a hypnotic dance. And then they saw eyes staring at them, unfathomably old. Penetrating, but kindly.

"Plumm. Is not gone," consoled the voice. "He is exalted."

Phoebe's breath stopped.

"But he is," she insisted. "He's dead. He's . . . dead."

"He blazes. Within you both. As does the Way."

Phoebe stared at the golden face, the pulsating heat stinging her eyes. She looked at her hands, still clutching her father's
broken, bloody glasses.

"What are you talkin' about?" Micah said to the shifting
liquid image. "Who are you anyway?"

"Why did. You. Come to Mehk?"

"To find my father," Phoebe replied. "To save him."

"Why?"

"I . . . I had to."

"You were. Called."

Phoebe stammered, digging through her dark mind.

"Called," the figure repeated in a trancclike whisper.

Then she understood. It materialized before her just as
the ethereal face had, as if it had been there all along. In the
tunnel back in Foundry Central, when she had fallen from the
train, something quiet had beckoned to her.

In the Vo-Pykarons, that same something had refused to
let the liodim suffer—it had compelled her to stand up and
fight—something deep and ineffable.

Phoebe breathed, "I heard a voice."

"Yes," the phantom face sang. "Plumm was. Not yet done."

"I don't understand."

"His function was. To save Mehk. Now it is. Yours."

"Are you," Phoebe said, reaching for the face, "Makina?"

"No, but She. Has called you. To me."

The liquid swirled faster, as if disturbed by a sudden
breeze.

"I am. The Ona."

The wall lit up like the sun, and they shielded their eyes, feeling the heat on their faces. It wasn't harsh or painful. It was like the comfort of a fireplace on a frostbitten winter day, an inviting, loving thaw. Veils in the wavering image fluttered, fins opened to reveal an ancient face. It smiled down on them.

"Little embers. I need you. Will you. Blaze the Way?"

EPILOGUE

I am in hell.

I am trapped in dark.

It crushes. Smothers me.

I claw through the black. Need air.

My skin is on fire. Every touch makes it scream.

Every shifting rock, every moving grain. Every bubble that pops is a mortar. Mortals above me. Demons beneath. I hear it all.

I climb.

Taste the path like blood in my mouth.

It takes minutes. It takes years. I live. I will find them. My fingers will sink in. Pull them apart. I will eat their screams. This skin of pain, a splinter in every nerve, is nothing to what I will do to them. Nothing.

The ground bleeds, soft as rotten meat.

I breathe smoke. It sears inside.

Pull myself from rubble. Break through. Free.

The sun hates me. Fears me. Burns me more.

The Citadel in ruins. A tower sags and falls. Why? Is this some torment? Have the demons followed me up? Am I still in hell?

I walk. My feet sink in metal mud. My bones bend with every step.

What is wrong with me? I am stripped down. Raw. Opened.

Men approach. I feel them minutes before they appear. Shouting.

I cover my ears. It doesn't help. They are too close. Footsteps like bombs. They wear paper suits, masks. It makes no sense.

helloisanyonethere?

heyyouareyouokay?

I hide. I try to answer. Find Plumm. Find the others.

They do not understand me. My words don't work.

They fall back and cry. Screams like a chisel in my skull.

OHMYGOD?

WHATISTHATTHING?

I reach to them, to seize, break them for their disrespect. How dare they not know me? Everyone must pay tribute. I am the Dyad.

But these . . . are not hands. These are not my hands.

The men have fled. Far away, yet I can easily hear their words.

whathappenedtohim?

thecharhasdonesomething.

At my feet, a shiny piece of glass. I see my face. I understand.

The demons have not followed me.

I have not escaped hell.

I

am

hell.